A SECRET LIFE

Esther Rantzen is one of TV's best-loved personalities, with a career that spans over thirty years. From her first days working in radio, and early fame on *That's Life*, through to *That's Esther*, the show she currently presents, she is one of Britain's most enduringly successful broadcasters. She is also the Founder/Chair of Childline, the pioneering helpline for children. She lives in London and is currently writing her next novel.

A
SECRET LIFE

Esther Rantzen

CENTURY · LONDON

Published by Century in 2003

1 3 5 7 9 10 8 6 4 2

First published in the United Kingdom in 2003 by Century

Random House Group Limited
20 Vauxhall Bridge Road, London SW1V 2SA

Random House Australia (Pty) Limited
20 Alfred Street, Milsons Point, Sydney,
New South Wales 2061, Australia

Random House New Zealand Limited
18 Poland Road, Glenfield
Auckland 10, New Zealand

Random House (Pty) Limited
Endulini, 5a Jubilee Road, Parktown 2193, South Africa

Random House Group Limited Reg. No. 954009

www.randomhouse.co.uk

A CIP catalogue record for this book is available
from the British Library

Papers used by Random House
are natural, recyclable products made from wood grown in
sustainable forests. The manufacturing processes conform to
the environmental regulations of the country of origin

ISBN 1 844 13367 2

Typeset by Palimpsest Book Production Limited,
Polmont, Stirlingshire
Printed and bound in Great Britain by
Clays Ltd, St Ives plc

For Katherine, my mother, with love and admiration

ACKNOWLEDGEMENTS

First and foremost I must thank the television industry which has nurtured, stimulated and exasperated me for more than thirty years, and which inspired this novel. Writing it has been an exciting and intimidating experience – and I owe a great debt of gratitude to the team who made it possible. Luigi Bonomi, my literary agent at Sheil Land, whose unflagging confidence spurred me on; Kate Elton, whose judgement and instinct supported me throughout; and Georgina Hawtrey-Woore, whose meticulousness and encouragement were invaluable. My television agent Jan Kennedy is definitely *not* the model for Suzannah's agent Mandy – Jan is just as tough but far more sensitive and discreet.

My children have employed the stick and carrot method – Emily was particularly helpful with the plot, Rebecca was my literary critic, and Joshua refused to read it on the grounds that he might inadvertently come across a reference to sex. Not that he objects to sex, he just objects to his mother knowing anything about it.

Above all I am grateful for the constant encouragement I received for more than thirty years from my late husband, Desmond Wilcox. He was, and is, a constant inspiration to me.

CHAPTER ONE

'Lucy, Lucy, over here . . .' She obeyed as she had a thousand times before, stretching her face into a wide-eyed unblinking smile so that whichever frame a malevolent picture editor decided to print, they would never catch her squinting at the flashbulbs. She turned slowly, gazing fully into each lens until at last they let her go. Not a tear. Not one flinch.

What did she feel? Alone? Bereft? She dared not ask herself those questions. It was far safer to cling to the anger on the surface.

What a waste. What a mindless, pointless waste. In one moment, late on a rainy night, with one stupid twist of a wheel, her closest friend had been torn from her. Even now, two weeks later, she found it impossible to believe. How could Suzannah, who had been such a life-enhancer, who had rung her every morning with some tantalizing piece of gossip, who had picked her up when she was emotionally in the gutter, and tweaked her vanity when she was overconfident, the star whose picture still appeared on screens and in newspapers all over the country, how could her life have been so instantly and irrevocably blown away?

Life had to go on. Suzannah had taught her that. So when the press had rung Lucy in the middle of the night, one dry-throated sob escaped her before she clamped down on her emotions, and mustered the required quotes. Since then she had done all the right things, made the right phone calls, written sympathetic letters to Suzannah's sorrowing relatives, friends and fans. That had done nothing to dissipate her own rage, and she didn't intend it to. Anger was useful. It cauterized. It meant she stopped bleeding. Bleeding meant you lost your strength, you made a mess. Better to smile at the photographers, and walk briskly away from them into the cool shade of the cathedral.

1

Suzannah would have done it more skilfully. She would have found a gesture, clasping a handkerchief or hugging her daughter, which would have made a front-page picture and touched the hearts of her fans. Not that Suzannah was incapable of real emotion, it was just that she was so practised, the public and the private had become so entangled in her life, that she instinctively turned her best profile to the camera, even when she was screaming inside. But not even Suzannah could attend her own memorial service. For a moment Lucy felt the presence of her friend so real, so solid beside her that she almost turned her head to talk to her. No wonder so many people believe in ghosts. No wonder so many religions paint comforting pictures of an afterlife. When you know and love someone as Lucy had loved Suzannah you can't let them go.

Maybe, Lucy fantasized as she found a place in a pew near the aisle, there would be a pyramid of eager photographers waiting for Suzannah right now outside the Pearly Gates, to catch one final smile before the recording angel pronounced his verdict on her. Which way would it go? She'd had an exotic life, to put it kindly. Even Lucy, who knew most things about her, hadn't known it all. Driven by ferocious ambition, Suzannah had used people and then discarded them – not viciously, but absent-mindedly. Like a jackdaw she had picked the brightest jewels, the sharpest ideas, the most talented youngsters, and then dropped them as she flew onwards and upwards.

As a technique it had worked perfectly. Suzannah rose to become the biggest, richest, most newsworthy television star in the country. Those she left behind described her as arrogant, or vain, but that didn't worry her. You needed arrogance to make the fast, dangerous decisions she took every working day. You needed vanity to dare to expose yourself time after time to unflattering television cameras. The important thing was that the viewers loved her, she had a danger on screen that made her constantly watchable. If you missed one of her programmes, you'd regret it, your friends would all be talking about it the

2

next day. And in spite of her polished good looks and her equally glossy bank balance, her love life was as bruising and dramatic as an assault course. Which, of course, fascinated viewers even more.

Yet for all the success, the ambition, the vanity, there was a generosity about Suzannah that Lucy had recognized from their first meeting. When Suzannah cared about you, she nurtured you, protected you, and fought for you. In an industry where most people were so terrified about losing their own chances of promotion or denting their own images that they would step over your body rather than help you up, Suzannah stood apart. Lucy had been interested to read the hundreds of column inches devoted to her after her death. The obituaries were a rehash of the scandals in her life, all her bad reviews had been lovingly burnished and quoted from, but on the whole the writers forgave her, for her entertainment value if for nothing else. Life would, after all, be far duller without her. In heaven, though, the critics might be colder and more implacable. Lucy hoped that the memorial service might put St Peter into a merciful mood, but it was probably too late to nobble him now.

The deep, sad voice of the organ led the congregation into the first hymn, and Lucy adjusted the lilac silk scarf at her throat, smoothed her elegant black overcoat, and looked about her. She was determined not to break down. Even here, in the heart of the church, there were floodlights and cameras to record the service for the evening news. Lucy's eyes panned across the congregation, without affection. There they were, the brilliant butterflies of the television industry, ranged in rows. There were the three men who all claimed to have discovered Suzannah – two had slept with her, one had slept with Boris, her ex-husband. She had outgrown and surpassed them all. There was her agent, Mandy, a short, dumpy, sharp-eyed woman, heavily made-up, her fingers clashing with diamonds paid for by the commission on Suzannah's huge salary. There was David Jameson, Controller of BriTV, the man who signed her last contract. He was deep

3

in his hymn book. Everyone in the congregation knew the rumour – that he was about to axe her series. Perhaps he had been relieved when it was suddenly axed by the great Controller in the sky.

Boris sat in the front row, his arm round their daughter, Camilla. He and Suzannah had stayed married longer than any of their friends had predicted, then parted amicably. Tall, blue-eyed and loose-lipped, he had an effortless charm, which he used like a harpoon to get whom and what he wanted. Suzannah had fallen for it at first, then resented it, and finally been amused by it. When rumours of his affairs began to infiltrate the gossip columns, she had parted from him, but they had remained friends and business partners. Only Lucy had known the chasm of humiliation Suzannah struggled through to achieve that seem-ingly easy relationship.

She couldn't see whether Boris was in tears now, but she expected he would be. Camilla was more of an enigma. She had inherited her father's height, and her mother's cheekbones, but her mouth tightened in repose and her green eyes were long, narrow and secretive. She could have been very attrac-tive if she smiled, but she rarely did. She was given to moody sullenness, never confronting her mother but instead sliding out of her way with a defiant downward flick of her eyes. Maybe it was lack of confidence. Suzannah had never been obviously proud of her, never attended a school play or prize-giving, they only seemed to meet when a magazine asked for pictures of devoted mother and daughter at home. Lucy could just see Camilla's profile now, pale and thin, defiantly not singing the words of the hymn. There was clearly a great deal of anger in her. Perhaps they'd had a row before the crash, and not had time to make up.

But maybe Camilla was just reacting with understandable nausea to the very public, very tacky service Mandy had put together. Glancing at the hymn sheet as they sat down, Lucy saw that a contralto was about to burst into 'No Regrets', followed

4

by the choir singing 'My Way'. Lord, how Suzannah would have loathed it.

She glanced at the woman sitting next to her in the pew. Janet Lake was a ferocious columnist on a tabloid newspaper. Dyed dark hair, sharp dark eyes, dark red lipstick, she had fought her way up in an industry still dominated by men, proud of the claim that she had the most venomous pen of them all. Had she been invited to the memorial service? Surely not. She had never had a good word to say about Suzannah in her lifetime. Lucy amused herself by visualizing acrid fumes drifting out from the brim of Janet's hat. It was odd, given her own struggle for survival, that a battle-scarred campaigner like Janet had been prepared to bash so many other women who dared to put their heads above the parapet. You present a television programme? Off with your head. Heaven help you if you were a social worker, or a politician in the wrong party, and female. But she had been known to change her mind, and apologize generously when she did. So maybe death would be the healer, perhaps she would do Suzannah justice, now that it was too late.

Lucy looked around for someone, anyone, in the whole distinguished congregation who might be a genuine mourner. Perhaps there were some among the faces she didn't recognize, the friends and family huddled in the back rows. Certainly none of the stars, the producers and directors would have missed a press launch glass of champagne to be here if Mandy hadn't made it an A-list event. The service was being conducted by a television vicar notorious for his chat show about sex and violence. '"And the greatest of these,"' he intoned, '"is charity."' What, thought Lucy, hugging herself for comfort, would you know?

He launched into his sermon, and her mind slipped back through the years to the real Suzannah, the woman she owed so much to, and painfully missed . . .

Their first meeting was nine years ago, when Lucy had joined Suzannah's team as a researcher, on a month's probationary contract. Lucy, at twenty-three, was still chubby with what her tactless uncle called puppy fat. As she stared at herself gloomily in the mirror first thing every morning, she castigated the bulges as loathsome lumps of flesh round her chin, tummy and thighs. Other string-bean researchers on the team (female, of course – all the best people-researchers in television were female, though at that time they never made it through the glass ceiling to become producers) wore tight short skirts and skinny tops, and crossed their legs high. Lucy had long ago decided to retreat behind bagginess, big black sweaters, brown flowing skirts, and self-deprecating jokes.

As the most junior member of the team, and to make up for what she perceived as her own ugliness, she made the rest laugh with her stories of the dismal parties she went to alone, and left alone. She also worked as hard as she could, staying late to make the extra phone calls, asking half a dozen more questions, searching out hidden treasures, a clip of archive film or newspaper cutting that would make the difference between an adequate brief, and a brilliant piece of research. That reputation had landed her the job on Suzannah's team, and now they were to meet for the first time.

The two women could not have been more different. Lucy, twenty-three years old, at the start of her career; Suzannah, thirty-eight, at the peak of hers. Lucy was determined to try to forget her own looks, crushing her feelings of inadequacy with work. Suzannah's photograph was a cliché in listings magazines round the world. Her postbag was crammed with adulation and requests for favourite recipes for charity books. A skinny, honey-streaked blonde, Suzannah had discovered a loyal harem of professionals to preserve her looks. She spent more time with her trimmers, cutters and adorners than with any of her friends or lovers. Every tousled curl on her head was always perfectly coloured and styled – even if it meant hair appointments twice a day. The tips of her fingers and toes were immaculately polished. Her body was caressed with silk and cashmere. Not just out of vanity, but

6

because she was expected always to shine in the spotlight, to charm the lens. Off-days weren't allowed.

She was also a tough, skilled journalist. Unlike the trust-fund heiresses who filled the gossip columns alongside her, and could spend their days relaxing in beauty parlours preparing to dazzle, Suzannah put in long hours in the office, writing scripts, absorbing and learning research, in order to produce the revealing interviews that put her ahead of all her talk-show rivals. She worked a fourteen-hour day – and her team marvelled at the limitless adrenalin that sent her flying out of the television studio to the dinner parties, the premieres, and latterly the beds of a variety of lovers. They admired her, in spite of her exacting moods and confrontational style – but, outside her own tiny world, there were plenty of sharp knives aimed at her back. In an industry fuelled by envy, Suzannah knew she was bad-mouthed, but she no longer cared. As long as she delivered the viewing figures, she would stay poised at the dizzy peak of the television industry. Many rivals aimed swipes at her to knock her off balance. So far, all had failed.

Now, at their first meeting, Lucy would have one chance to impress her, or be lacerated and sharply dumped. Suzannah took no prisoners when researchers let her down. She had called the meeting for nine, and Lucy had worked all through the previous night, filling file after file with careful research on the interviewees of the week. As the first dawn sunlight hit her desk at the back of the production office, she just had time to rush back to her grimy flat in South London, bath, change her underwear, and plunge back into the rush hour. She ran through the corridors to Suzannah's office, and put the files on her desk. Suzannah was already viewing film clips for the programme. Lucy went back to her own desk and waited for Suzannah to read her research. She felt crumpled, and sick with tiredness and suspense. Either Suzannah would be delighted, or Lucy would be out. There was no middle way.

The intercom buzzed on the PA, Sandra's, desk, and she called to Lucy, 'You're on.' Lucy grabbed the nearest pen and her notebook, and went into the office. Suzannah had skip-read the research, and as she watched Lucy walk in, her eyebrows arched with disapproval.

'Lucy Strong,' she said, reading from the label on the file, then looked up. 'Do you want the good news or the bad news?'

'I'll take the bad.' Lucy stayed by the door. 'I'd rather know the worst.'

Suzannah smiled at her. 'That's how I work too. I'd always rather be forearmed.' She inspected Lucy grimly, her eyes taking in her tiredness, her grubbiness, her terrible clothes. 'The bad news is,' Suzannah began, but there was amusement in her eyes that belied the tartness in her tone, 'that if you want to stay on the team, you can't arrive in the office wearing clothes you've obviously slept the night in – and a sweaty, energetic night from the look of them. If we're going to send you out to interview Barbra Streisand at Claridge's, you won't get past the doorman looking dirty and down at heel.'

Barbra Streisand? That didn't sound like the sack. Lucy relaxed a little. Suzannah noticed, and her voice took on a sharpened edge, like a sergeant major sensing mutiny. 'Get yourself a good suit, a good pair of shoes, a briefcase, and a sharp haircut.'

How? Lucy's salary was minimal. BriTV saw no point in being generous to probationary researchers – they were doing them a huge favour employing them at all. So how could Lucy possibly afford to take any of Suzannah's advice?

Suzannah read the rebellion in Lucy's eyes. 'It's important, Lucy. People take you at your own estimation – if you think you're a heap of shit, and look like a heap of shit, they'll treat you that way.'

Anger welling up inside her, Lucy was ready to turn on her heel. 'Is that what you think of my research?'

'Absolutely not. If I did, I wouldn't waste my energy insulting you. Your research is strong, and it's well written. I like the ideas you have for stunts and archive clips. I don't need your

8

ideas for questions, thank you, I'll invent those myself. Sit down.'

Lucy had been so sure she'd be thrown off the team, she was still hovering by the door. Sandra brushed past her carrying a mug of peppermint tea for Suzannah – and not even an offer of a glass of water for Lucy. Her time would come.

But Suzannah had not finished. Quickly she interrogated Lucy about her CV: a good Bristol degree – she was the first in her family to go to university – then a brief job in advertising, and an even briefer spell on a new magazine started by a college friend. Then a leap sideways and downwards to work as a clerk in the BriTV library, 'just to get into television, so I could try for a job in production'. Hearing about a researcher post on Suzannah's show she had applied, and been accepted as a trainee.

'Why did you want to join us so much?' Suzannah asked.

'Because it's a fantastic show. I can learn so much here – how to interview, how to surprise the viewers, how to tell a story, how to stop them switching off. Your show is sold round the world; nobody else can compete. This is the hottest talk show on the air – wouldn't anyone kill to get a job here?'

She kicked herself – of course she should have said something flattering about the star, about Suzannah's personality, quick brain, wonderful sense of style, warmth, humour.

Suzannah drained the dregs of the peppermint tea, the colour and sloppiness of Chinese soup, and grinned at her. 'Good answer,' she said. 'The reason I earn five million a year is because the show works. No presenter can ever be better than their show, and survive. Make the show work, and you'll guarantee your own success. Welcome to the team. Go away, wash, change, and be at Claridge's at eleven.'

Lucy leaped to obey, then turned at the door to thank her, but Suzannah was already deep in a phone conversation.

It was hard to know whether to laugh, rage, or do the practical thing, and swallow the patronizing insults. How dare Suzannah take it upon herself to dictate Lucy's clothes? Had she ever tried to dress herself on Lucy's salary? But as she sat down

9

beside her brimming files, Lucy realized that yes, Suzannah had. She had been a caterpillar once, and had painstakingly created the butterfly she had become. In any case, it was well known on the team that Suzannah only treated you roughly if she thought you were worth the trouble. Otherwise you got a sweet smile and were out on your neck.

Sandra, Suzannah's assistant, dropped a card onto the desk in front of Lucy, the details of the appointment to see Barbra Streisand. It was a rare honour for such a new researcher to be sent to see one of the world's most glittering, volatile A-list celebrities. But if Cinderella was to go to the ball, she had somehow to transform her baggy black sweater and woolly tights into something suitable for Claridge's. What could she possibly find in the time, and how could she ever afford the kind of outfit Suzannah had described?

She thought for a moment – she was no kind of researcher if she couldn't even solve this. Then she rang Lesley, Suzannah's costume designer, and introduced herself, a mere researcher, and the lowliest, newest one at that. The designer rarely deigned to speak to anyone below producer status – researchers were there to be sent on errands, and snapped at – so Lucy decided to risk a humble but businesslike approach.

'Lesley,' she said, 'I need someone generous enough to make an investment in me.' Quickly she summarized her encounter with Suzannah. 'Is there anyone who would lend me, advance me, find me an outfit in two hours? There's no way I can afford it myself right now, but I promise that I will pay for it somehow, some day.'

Silence at the end of the phone, then Lesley said, 'Come round to my house now, and I'll see what I can find.'

The address was a smart mews cottage in Kensington, three of the four little bedrooms had been converted to walk-in wardrobes. There were rail upon rail of dresses and suits, racks of shoes piled neatly toe to toe up to the ceiling, and swathes of velvet scarves, wraps and leather jackets, all arranged in sharp, unusual colours – burnt oranges, rich purples, moss greens. As the two women met at the front door, Lesley breathed in with a gasp of disapproval. Lucy had not confessed that she was an ample size fourteen.

'You think I'm too fat,' she said.

'No. I was just thinking how right Suzannah was. That jacket is terrible. Nobody should wear it with that sweater. Come to think of it, no one should wear that sweater at all.' Clearly Lucy was in for a very honest morning.

It was worth it. Lesley threw some of her gorgeous scarves round Lucy's shoulders, and at once the colours lit her dark hair and eyes. She found silk shirts, and well-cut leather jackets that slimmed and lengthened Lucy without losing any of her curves. By a lucky chance, the two women had the same size feet, and generously Lesley lent her a pair of slender, elegant shoes. When she looked in the mirror, Lucy suddenly saw what Suzannah had meant. She still looked young, but she had style now, and a new sense of status. Much as Lucy resented it, she could see why Suzannah had told her to dress the part.

She flung her arms round Lesley and thanked her. Then she picked up her files in their white plastic bag and went to the door. Lesley gave a horrified shriek, snatched the bag from her, and reached into a cupboard for a briefcase. She transferred Lucy's files into it, and then shoved her baggy sweater and jacket down to the bottom of the plastic bag.

'Give them to someone sleeping rough – at least they can use them as a blanket if there's frost tonight. I'll have the briefcase back when we meet in the studio. You can keep my clothes, just in case you have another sudden interview in Claridge's.'

As the memorial service reached its climax, the cathedral choir rose to sing their anthem, and the congregation sat. Lucy smiled at her memories, glancing down at her expensive shoes, they had cost twice what she had earned each week as a researcher. Over the intervening years she had been promoted from junior

11

to senior researcher, then to reporter, and finally had become the presenter of her own investigative show. As her salary burgeoned, she kept Lesley alongside her, advising and designing for her. That first thrown-together outfit had indeed been an investment for both women.

Still more important was her relationship with Suzannah, which grew into a deep friendship. Lucy proved that she had the one invaluable quality – loyalty – which meant whatever Suzannah confided to her, Lucy would never betray. And that in turn meant she became the recipient of some of Suzannah's most delicate secrets.

Suzannah had been bitterly hurt by the break-up of her marriage to Boris, no matter how well she had concealed it in public. She had sat night after night talking it through with Lucy, twisting like a fish on a hook, trying desperately to avoid the humiliation of a divorce, but aware that Boris's affairs were putting her reputation in danger. Did she still love him? She hardly knew herself.

Suzannah and Boris had first met in the office of a London news programme. 'I was fresh in London from Manchester,' she told Lucy. 'I suppose it was obvious how hungry I was, how keen to be right at the centre of the action. And Boris was a brilliant producer; when he saw my energy, he gave me loads of airtime, reporting and presenting the show.'

Television cameras devour talent, Suzannah supplied it abundantly, and Boris made sure she shone. He gave her the best stories to film, then spent hours cutting them with her so that she learned from her mistakes, and she thrived on the special coaching. The professional partnership extended to dinner, and then they began to spend nights together.

'I realized even then how deliberately he used his charm to get me, like a honey-trap,' she told Lucy during one of their all-night conversations, as the coffee dregs piled higher in the sink, and the level of whisky fell lower in the bottle. 'But although I saw all the hooks under the bait, I swallowed it just the same.'

'Was it lust you felt? Or ambition?' Lucy asked bravely.

Suzannah didn't flinch. 'OK, he was a successful producer. And yes, he turned me on. But the truth is, I fell in love with him, though I knew perfectly well that he was renowned for juggling his lovers without letting any of them drop.' When she discovered she was pregnant (not quite accidentally, she was far too meticulous for that) marriage seemed the sensible option. Soon, though, the couple began to live different lives. Boris was rewarded for the success of his programme by being promoted to management. Suzannah was given her own talk show, and every star worth the autograph queued to take part in it.

As it moved up the ratings, Suzannah became a star herself, invited to the glitziest parties and premieres. Boris flew round the world, buying and selling programmes and signing up new talent. It was lucky that Camilla turned out to be a well-behaved, photogenic baby, because neither of her parents had a career that allowed them to watch her take her first steps, or read her first books to her. Work came first for them both, as it always had, and work also supplied them with company. Boris began to be seen at television festivals, dining with pretty young television executives. Suzannah booked a regular suite in a discreet London hotel, and if she had occasional nightcaps there with the young men who accompanied her to first nights, she was careful, and they were discreet.

Lucy allowed herself to be used by Suzannah as a confidante. If she felt sorry for Camilla over the years, bundled off to boarding school as soon as she could ride a pony, she never revealed it.

Soon after they first met, the two women had a conversation about marriage. Lucy sighed and said, 'I don't believe love lasts. Look at you and Boris: you're still fond of each other, but you need other people, both of you.'

Suzannah winked at her. 'The fact that you usually drink a nice dry white wine doesn't mean you don't try the occasional champagne cocktail. The trick is never to be caught mixing your drinks, or you'll end up sick in the gutter.' Suzannah certainly mixed her drinks – but she was never caught.

Boris was. The ensuing divorce made headlines, but without searing quotes from either of them. They both claimed the parting was amicable, and stuck to that line.

Lucy, watching Suzannah's pain, decided marriage was not for her.

'I'm fine on my own,' she used to tell reporters when they asked, which was often. 'I enjoy my independence. The only person who's unhappy is my mother. She's longing for grand-children.'

As her workload grew heavier, the chances of Lucy meeting someone to provide a grandchild grew more remote. She didn't discuss that with her mother, and she found it more and more difficult to see her family regularly, living as they did in the West Country. When she did, though they tried to watch her pro-grammes, they were far more interested in the latest village feud, or the imminent collapse of the local bakery. Although Lucy refused to admit it even to herself, her visits home were filled with leaden conversations, and long silences. She was richer than they were, and had a glamorous career. Her schoolfriends were all married now, with children. She felt they despised her, or envied her – sometimes it was hard to tell the two emotions apart. She knew why. They were living in a community, while her work was her world. She hardly met anyone outside it.

Then, making a programme about tobacco profiteering, Lucy interviewed Tom Aspern, a solicitor who specialized in medical compensation. She had talked to him over the phone, booked him because she liked his plain speaking, and was greatly relieved to see when he arrived that he didn't look plain at all. His rough dark hair formed a fringe that he kept impatiently pushing off his brow. His dark eyes and white, even teeth gave him the look of a Frenchman, but a Frenchman would have been far more aware of his charm. He wore a muddy-coloured tie and his suit was crumpled. Lesley tutted, and insisted on steaming his jacket to take out the creases.

He took part in the studio discussion, then as usual the

14

researchers herded them all into the hospitality room to wait for their taxis. Tom retreated to the back of the room, and at first Lucy didn't notice him there. He was stooped with tiredness, standing by the wall alone, obviously ill at ease surrounded by television chatter. Out of politeness she went over to him and thanked him for his contribution to the programme. She asked if he thought they'd got it right. The tiredness fell from him, and he began to talk to her about the appalling effects he had seen of the trade in tobacco. He exploded with fury at the way he said huge corporations callously created new young addicts to replace the ones they killed. She listened, interested by the emotion in him. Television programmes came and went, but this man had a real vocation. Their eyes caught, then swerved away, then caught again.

He asked if she would come and watch the trial he was involved in. He was representing a child who had been badly injured in a playground accident. She did, and once again found herself deeply impressed by his commitment to his clients. She was surprised to notice how attracted she was by the urchin's grin that swept the tiredness from his face at the end of a long day.

They met again. Gradually, different as they were, they began to fall in love. She watched him lose sleep over his cases, making long trips to a council estate halfway across the country to grieve with a family, soothe fears and be rewarded with the thrill of victory when a child he was representing won a battle against an insurance company.

After six months they married, quietly, in a register office near his bleak one-bedroom flat. He moved into her house – she was earning twice his salary, but neither of them cared. The long hours they both worked were more destructive. They promised to make time for each other, but each weekend they planned in the countryside, every week's holiday they looked forward to in Italy or Greece was lost as one or other had to go to work instead. Even their conversations petered out in exhaustion. Then

15

they were too tired to make love. After six years Lucy realized they had become strangers again.

She never really knew why, one evening as they sat wearily together in their kitchen, she suddenly decided to make a clean break.

'Tom, are you happy?' she asked. The question sounded deafening in her own ears. He looked at her, then down to the glass in his hand. She blundered on, 'Because I'm not. This isn't why we married. We're wasting each other's time.' He still didn't meet her eyes. For the first time she wondered whether the gulf between them was caused by more than simple tiredness. 'Is there someone else, Tom, someone you'd rather be with?'

He shook his head. 'No, Lucy, I'd rather be with you. But I'm not. This is the first time you've talked to me in months.'

She started to argue, but he carried on. 'No, Lucy, face it. In your mind you're always with your colleagues at work, or the people you interview, or the bosses you work for. You're never really with me. Yes, I think we are wasting time.'

Was this what she had wanted? Even if it wasn't, it was too late to go back. Her pride wouldn't let her. She stood up, finishing the glass of brandy in her hand with one gulp. 'OK, Tom. If you want to go, I won't argue. What's the point? I could blame you, just the way you blame me. Your clients mean far more to you than I do. You say my production team means more to me. If that's what you think, you'd better leave me with them.'

He left that night, packing quickly, driving his car away to his brother's house. That was nearly a year ago, and pride had prevented her ringing him since.

Then Suzannah had died. Late one night, two weeks ago, a few miles west of London, her car had swerved out of control and crashed into a huge oak tree. Newspaper pictures showed that the car had concertinaed under the impact and the engine had been forced back into the driver's seat. Suzannah hadn't a chance. When the police investigated they reported that no other car had been involved, her blood was clear of alcohol, the car itself was exonerated of any mechanical failure. But she had been working very late – her show that night had been lively and argumentative, and she had been under considerable pressure. Her concentration had slipped for a fatal moment, perhaps momentarily she had fallen asleep, and in that instant, she was dead.

At dawn the next morning, Lucy's phone began to ring with reporters looking for quotes. The shock hit her as they told her what they knew, tipped off by the local police, and she responded to their questions on autopilot. The clock radio switched itself on at seven, bringing her the news bulletin. Suzannah's death was the lead headline. The presenter described the accident, then Lucy heard her own voice as they had recorded it on the telephone – steady, and controlled, paying tribute to her friend. She switched it off, and lay, her mind numb, trying to accept the fact of Suzannah's death.

The phone rang again. It was Tom.

'I'm so sorry, Lucy,' he said. 'I can't really take it in. You must be devastated. Is there anything I can do?'

She was silent for a moment. The understanding in his voice brought her tears to the surface once more, and she had to struggle to control them. Then, 'Tom, I don't know how I can cope with this, without Suzannah.' Her voice choked, she stopped.

Then she said, 'Can you come round here for a moment? I need to talk to you. Can we meet?'

Fred turned and stirred in the bed next to her. He was eight years younger than she was, and slept deeply. Usually that amused her. She enjoyed his youth, and his strength, his strong muscular body with biceps he had carefully honed so that he could carry his cameras steadily without a tremor. They had met soon after she and Tom had separated. He had been the cameraman when she'd filmed a tricky interview with a bogus doctor. As she stood unflinching while the conman blustered and threatened her, she saw the admiration in Fred's eyes. When they had a drink together after the interview, she found herself enjoying the relaxation of his body as he leaned backwards on the seat next to her. He was so uncomplicated, so unchallenging. After three months of steady wooing, she secretly allowed him into her bed. Although the press had known about her marriage split, and covered it with their usual appetite, they hadn't discovered Fred yet, and she didn't want them to.

He hadn't woken when the phone rang, or the news came on, so he didn't yet know that part of her world had ended. But in any case, though in his way he could console her, he could never share the depth of her grief. So she got up without waking him and wrapped a towelling robe about her, tying it comfortingly tightly around her waist. She went down to her study, and sat dry-eyed at her desk. On the notice board above it there were snapshots of her with Suzannah laughing together in hospitality rooms, at industry dinners, at end-of-series parties. She saw how like Suzannah she had become over the years, not physically, but in confidence, both of them enjoying facing the camera. She saw Suzannah's hand protectively on her arm, or round her waist. They had depended on each other, trusted each other.

When Tom arrived, she let him in, and walked with him to the kitchen where only ten months earlier they had agreed to part. She switched on the kettle to make them both coffee. Then the tears came. He walked over to her and put his arms around her. She turned towards him, and he took her hand.

'Go and sit down. I'll make the coffee.'

She obeyed him, and he brought her a mug, filled to the brim. Hardly knowing what she was saying, tears falling down her face, she told him stories of Suzannah, how alive she always was, and still seemed to be. How impossible it was to believe she was dead. She couldn't be.

He let her talk. When finally she stopped, drained, he put his hand on her arm. 'Stay home today,' he said. 'Don't try to go

18

to work. The place will be crawling with people wanting to interview you about Suzannah. You don't need that. You need time to yourself.'

'No I don't.' She was indignant suddenly. 'No, Tom, that's just what I don't need. The only way I can cope with this is to keep my normal life going. Otherwise I'll go to pieces.'

'Then maybe that's what you need to do. Maybe if you'd learned to let yourself go when you needed to, instead of trussing yourself up in this superwoman kit, we'd still be together.'

How could he start having that conversation again now, when she was reeling from Suzannah's death?

'Luckily we're not still together,' she reminded him sharply. 'So any cracks in my "superwoman kit" needn't concern you.' She got up. 'Tom, you've got to go now. I must get dressed. There's so much to do.' He got up with her, and held out his arms, but she drew back, memories of Fred's body imprinted on her skin.

'Let me know if you need me,' he said, picked up his briefcase, and quietly let himself out of the front door.

She'd stood in the middle of the empty room, fighting to control her memories. Then she'd gone upstairs to waken Fred.

Now, at last, Suzannah's service ended, not before time. Lucy's anger had protected her from pain, she knew Suzannah herself would have loathed the insincerity, the hypocrisy of it. 'Amen,' said the TV vicar, with a final downward inflection, glancing towards the cameras to make sure they photographed his endearing cleft chin. The organ rippled into 'Jesu, Joy of Man's Desiring' – and Lucy blessed Bach for casting a glow of serenity over the peculiar congregation.

They all rose together, and Lucy joined the queue slowly making their way down the central aisle. Behind her she heard two people discussing the service.

'Not the most tasteful memorial service I've been to,' a man said, his voice a stage whisper loud enough to be heard by half a dozen mourners, 'but Suzannah would have been pleased with the turnout.'

'How many of her old lovers were here? Did you notice?' A woman's voice, tight with curiosity.

'I never pry into my artists' love lives, unless they land on my breakfast table, and then only if they're on the front page.'

Lucy glanced over her shoulder. David Jameson, the controller, was talking to Naomi Leicester, an up-and-coming chat-show host who saw herself as one of Suzannah's competitors. No wonder she was so keen to dish the dirt, even at the memorial service.

'She was supposed to be an almighty bitch,' Naomi went on. 'Most of the people she trampled over on her way up are here today. Not in tears. I wonder they didn't all burst into a chorus of "Oh, What a Beautiful Morning".'

Lucy shivered with disgust. If she turned round and glared at Naomi, would that embarrass her into silence?

But now she heard a familiar voice. Martin Dellaby had joined the other two. He was a local star when Suzannah had joined him as co-presenter on a regional news magazine and had watched her outclass and outgrow him. The whole queue had stopped still while mourners by the door greeted Suzannah's family. There was no escape. Lucy had to listen to Martin ingratiating himself with Jameson.

'What a loss,' Dellaby was saying to him. 'Tough cookie though she was, she was a terrific talent. I count myself very lucky to have worked with her.'

'Yes, Naomi was saying much the same.' Lucy smiled to herself. That put the bitch back in her box.

'What happened, do you know what caused the crash?' Martin asked. 'Was she drunk? I know it happened after a programme. She used to hit the bottle quite a lot in hospitality in my day. She got pissed pretty quickly then. Mind you, she was far younger in those days.'

Terrific. He'd managed to blame Suzannah for her own death,

and point out she wasn't young any more. A complete carve-up. 'Interesting that I don't see any brawny young men among the mourners.' His love of gossip had overcome any pretence of discretion now. 'Suzannah would be disappointed.'

Lucy didn't wait for Jameson's reply. She'd had enough. She couldn't face a confrontation with all three of them. She needed to get away. She escaped back into a pew, and found herself face to face with Janet Lake.

Janet looked at her sharply. There were unshed tears behind Lucy's eyes, and her jaw was tight with tension. Janet's instinct was unerring. Here was someone with a great deal to say. All she needed was a listening ear, preferably with an open note-book ready and a tape recorder running.

'Would you like a drink, Lucy?' she asked. 'I know how close you were to Suzannah, we could both drink to her memory.'

Lucy glanced over Janet's shoulder and saw Tom in the distance, walking away between the pillars. How he would disapprove if she talked to Janet. He would say it was dangerous now when she was at her most vulnerable. Well, damn him for being patronizingly paternal. She could look after herself.

She smiled back at Janet. 'Yes, I could use a drink.'

Janet's dark eyes were calculating. There were other celebrities at the memorial service, international film stars who would be a bigger draw for her readers. But they would be hard to get to, surrounded by their protective entourages, and, in any case, they would simply produce clichés: 'a great loss', 'an irreplaceable talent', 'a lovely, lovely person' . . . Lucy, however, was clearly in the mood to say something far more revealing.

Lucy hesitated. The voice in her head was telling her to beware. It was a risk, but perhaps this would be an opportunity to give Suzannah the obituary she deserved, to put the record straight. This woman was no friend, but her very acerbity might be an antidote to the glutinous ritual they had just endured.

'Thank you, Janet,' she said. 'I don't specially want to go home right now.'

21

As they stepped onto the kerb, a taxi stopped for them, the driver recognizing Lucy.

'The Savoy, please,' Janet said, and the two women slid back onto the leather seat. Odd companions, they would normally have disliked travelling side by side. Suzannah would have warned Lucy against it. But Suzannah had gone for ever.

CHAPTER TWO

The taxi drew up at the Savoy, and Janet negotiated with the driver for a receipt. She had directed the driver every inch of the way, the smoky rasp of her voice cutting easily through the traffic noise. Nothing in Janet's life was left to chance, nothing had come easily. Janet was a fighter, and all her success had been won in bruising contests – to be first with the story, to earn the top salary, to repel all threats. Her heavy make-up and expensive clothes were like a suit of armour, she was determined to prove that she was as good as any man, and could fight as hard as he could. As she leaned forward to pay the fare, Lucy watched her absent-mindedly, wondering whether it had been a huge mistake to agree to an interview. Relieved though she had been to get out of the cathedral, away from the collection of vultures and hangers-on, this was not much better. For the first time she wondered if the sensible thing would have been to go back to her quiet, empty house, and fill it with memories of Suzannah.

The Savoy commissionaire welcomed them as they pushed through the revolving door into the big, highly polished foyer. Lucy felt a moment of incredulity as she looked about her. No matter how often she was bowed into glamorous hotels and fashionable restaurants, at one level she was still the naïve, plump, eager researcher she used to be. Her carefully constructed disguise was eggshell thin. Although she'd learned which fork to use, which wine to drink, not to refold a napkin or pick her teeth, she never felt completely at home beside the other rich customers. She was sure she'd be found out as the clever daughter of parents who had to go without a car or a holiday to keep her at university.

Last Christmas she had given her mother and father a week

at the Savoy, and they'd marvelled at the luxury, and at the cost. 'Don't get too used to this, my love,' her father warned her mother, who laughed and shook her head. It was a treat, and for Lucy's sake they enjoyed it, but she knew they were relieved to go back home to the West Country.

A tall Christmas tree was already in place in the foyer, its dark branches garlanded with silver ribbons and white fairy lights. Janet led Lucy down the stairs to the wide lounge, and found a sofa angled away from passing customers. A waiter bent over them attentively as Janet ordered champagne cocktails for them both, and lit a cigarette. Lucy leaned back in the cushions, and unbuttoned her coat. Suzannah filled her mind. They had sat together on this very sofa, less than a month ago. Lucy could still hear Suzannah's laugh as she described some indiscretion from the night before. Scattered around the lounge they'd noticed other well-known couples deep in negotiation, some clearly business – others, even more clearly, pleasure. It had been fun, watching them pretend not to catch Suzannah's eye.

Today there was a very different woman sitting beside Lucy, watching her intently. She sighed.

Janet took her opportunity. 'You must miss Suzannah very much.'

Lucy's eyes drifted. 'Yes, although I still feel she's close to me. I suppose my mind won't accept her death. She was so alive, she enjoyed every moment, her energy was extraordinary. I can't believe she's gone.'

Janet balanced her cigarette on an ashtray, and pulled a tiny tape recorder from her handbag. 'Do you mind if I use this?'

Lucy shook her head. 'No, that's fine.' Better to be condemned for words she had really used, than for a reporter's invention.

Janet switched on the machine and put it on the sofa between them. 'Describe her to me the Suzannah you knew.'

Where could she begin? 'It's an odd thing, Janet. Everywhere I go people say to me, what was Suzannah *really* like? As if

24

her whole life was a lie. I can only say that from my point of view, she was just the way she seemed on screen. Very warm, very generous, extremely hard-working. That's the Suzannah I knew.'

'But there must have been more to her than that.' Janet was pushing her, not aggressively, but determined to reveal more than a stale clutch of show-business adjectives. 'There are loads of warm generous women in the world,' she persisted. 'There was only one Suzannah Piper. What was unique about her?'

The waiter arrived with their champagne cocktails. Lucy took a quick gulp, and then another. The sharp, hot taste of brandy sweetened with sugar combined with the champagne in her mouth, and coursed down her throat. A celebration drink, to celebrate the years of their friendship. And to inspire an epitaph for Suzannah that was loyal but honest too. 'She was funny. Unsentimental. Unimpressed by all the starry stuff. Perhaps it didn't always show in her work, but she had a way of looking at life – her life, our life – which was quite bleak.'

'Come on, she loved her job.'

'Yes, she loved it, but she saw it for what it was. She was realistic. She was never fooled by the kissy-kissy love-in around her.'

'Meaning?'

'Meaning the celebrity stuff, the parties, the can-we-take-a-picture-in-your-lovely-home stuff. She knew it would fade away the moment they scented failure. High ratings, and you're the centre of the crowd; the moment you start to slip, you're a target.'

'What kind of target?'

Lucy hesitated. Now she had to be careful. Janet had been one of the loudest voices baying for Suzannah's blood, accusing her of becoming stale and predictable. Both women knew it.

'I don't mean criticism,' Lucy said placatingly. 'We all need

25

that. You've been tough on her recently, but she didn't mind that. She didn't like it, but she put up with it. It's the people who should know better, the people who were at her memorial service today. God, they're a vicious bunch, some of them.'

'But she was popular. The cathedral today was packed. Doesn't that prove anything?'

Lucy took another gulp from her glass, and felt the heat of the brandy, the sharp bubbles of champagne. She took a risk, knew it, and plunged on. 'The service was a farce. Suzannah would have loathed it.'

Janet said nothing. Silence was her greatest weapon. More surely than the most acute question, silence at the right moment will tempt a victim into indiscretion, to fill the vacuum. Lucy recognized the trap – she had often used it herself – but this time she chose to fall into it. 'It wasn't just that the music and the readings were tacky and inappropriate. It was the congregation. The pews were packed with Suzannah's enemies, longing for her to fail.'

'But her show was still doing well in the ratings, wasn't it?'

'Yes, but she wasn't popular with the focus groups. They research every show these days, and the groups reported back that men didn't like her, they found her too threatening. Women didn't like her much either, they thought she had become too grand.'

'Then why did they go on watching her show?'

'Some shows are like that: the presenter is the grit in the oyster that makes the pearl. Do you remember Russell Harty? He was mimicked and derided, but his programmes were unique, because they were unpredictable. Suzannah was the same: her shows worked because she made news.'

Janet shifted on her sofa, and stubbed out her cigarette. This was dull. The last thing she wanted was a professional critique of Suzannah's television work. She needed to tempt Lucy out into the open, onto more dangerous ground. 'Who are these enemies you talk about?'

'They were all around her like a pack of wolves. I sometimes think you only have to look for the biggest, brightest smile. "Grandma, what big teeth you have, all the better to eat you with."' A waiter had unobtrusively filled their glasses again. Lucy half drained hers, and put it down firmly in the centre of the little table. She knew she was being reckless but she didn't care. 'David Jameson, the controller of the company, they say, was one. Did you see the way he was hiding in his hymn book? He was just about to axe her series, and we all knew it. He'd been leaking rumours to the papers himself, to make sure nobody would protest. Suzannah suspected it.'

'But she was one of his most valuable presenters. He was paying her a fortune.'

'The advertisers didn't like her, and their money talks. They want the young audience, because kids believe what they see in the commercials. They're obsessed with pleasing the under-twenty-four-year-olds, and they love the men in drag, the women in disguise, who gag their way through an interview and throw four-letter words into every sentence to get a laugh.'

'You don't care for Naomi Leicester then?' Naomi was the leader of the pack, in life an intense young brunette, on screen she put on a huge red wig, a strong Jewish accent, and padded herself to look twenty stone.

'I don't.' Naomi's viciousness at Suzannah's memorial service still rang in Lucy's ears. Why should she hold back? 'She's an insult to fat women, Jewish women and television interviewers. I think she's racist and sexist. I wouldn't care, except that I have a suspicion that David Jameson was going to give her Suzannah's show.'

'That would have been interesting,' Janet said. 'Who else?'
'Martin Dellaby.'
'But wasn't he an old friend?'
'You'd think so, from the way he was sobbing. The truth is that he was crazily jealous of her. He never recovered from the time they worked together.'

Suzannah had talked to her often about Martin. Cuddly and charming on the screen, he relapsed into sullen bad temper when the red light went off. He had been the lead presenter on the news programme until Boris hired Suzannah to sit alongside him. Then, although it was her first job on the screen, it was clear that the cameras loved her. Like a highly bred racehorse, Suzannah even then showed her class: she was very sharp, made good jokes, and her cheekbones were perfect for studio lighting. Martin was solid, good, but easy to ignore. The press began to notice her, but they took him for granted. So Martin snubbed her, and tried to undermine her. When she asked a question, he'd butt in and correct her. But the nastier he became, the more the public loved her. Then she was snapped up for her own show.

Martin's voice echoed in Lucy's memory. How dare he accuse Suzannah of being a drunk? She owed him nothing now. 'He resented every penny Suzannah was paid, every moment she appeared on screen. I'm amazed he didn't try and upstage her in the cathedral.' She knew she was giving Janet irresistible quotes, but why not? At least she was gaining a tiny revenge for Suzannah, after her death.

Janet made a few delicate incisions into Suzannah's private life. 'It was touching to see Boris there. Do you know if Suzannah had found a new man?'

Lucy did her best to evade her. 'Suzannah was attractive, and she liked having fun. Yes, she enjoyed the company of good-looking young men, but nobody replaced Boris.'

Janet had almost enough for her epitaph. 'You've told me you thought the memorial service was a travesty. What would you have said, Lucy, if you'd been writing the sermon?'

If only. All the pent-up anger, the unreleased sorrow suddenly surfaced, and Lucy felt her hands start to shake. 'I would have tried to puncture some of that hypocrisy. It was like incense – the cathedral was so full of it, I almost choked. Now she's dead, people couldn't wait to murder her reputation. I'd

28

have made them all face crucial questions like why did Suzannah die? Was she really so overtired, so mentally and emotionally exhausted that she literally drove herself to death? I don't believe it. It doesn't make any sense. She'd driven that journey a thousand times. There was no reason for her to crash. She wasn't drunk. She wasn't reckless. Let them look into their hearts and answer the question, who really killed Suzannah?'

'I'll ask that question tomorrow,' Janet said, tucking her tape recorder into her handbag and pulling out a mobile phone to ring her office. She had to alert them about the pictures they would need to illustrate her scathing article; shots of David Jameson, the controller of BriTV, of Naomi Leicester, Suzannah's rival, and Martin Dellaby, the colleague she out-classed and outshone. The champagne cocktail had been an excellent investment.

Lucy rose to her feet, and straightened her shoulders. Janet echoed the movement and their cheeks brushed with the obligatory air-kiss. By the glass doors of the Savoy they climbed into separate taxis, bound for their respective offices. Though the winter sky had darkened, there were hours of work still to be done.

At the studios of BriTV, Lucy walked swiftly past reception and into the lift. Somehow she must shake off the unpleasantness of the day, the tacky service and the acrid interview, and concentrate on tomorrow's show. She went to her desk in the busy open-plan office. Shirley Walters, her producer, came over to her and gave her a sympathetic hug. She knew Lucy well enough to be able to read the strain on her face, the taut shoulders, the tiredness in her eyes. Shirley was a quiet woman in her mid-forties, with thoughtful blue eyes, and plain well-cut clothes. Lucy had seen her faced by every possible crisis: threatened with libel writs, with violent interviewees, the show suddenly dragged off the air by a last-minute legal action. Nothing made Shirley panic.

She had come to the memorial service, sitting at the back of the cathedral with her team. She knew how much Lucy would have disliked the toxic mixture of show business sentiment and underlying malice.

'Suzannah deserved better,' she said quietly to Lucy. 'Let's find you a hot drink and a sandwich. We have a heavy show to make tomorrow.'

Files of research were waiting next to Lucy's word processor, but she already knew most of it by heart. She switched on her computer, and started to read her new e-mails. Most of them were memos about the programme ahead, but there were also half a dozen letters of sympathy. One made her stop and catch her breath. It came from the Head of Personnel.

'I'm so sorry I have to burden you with this, but we need to clear Suzannah's office. When you come in, would you mind going through her desk, and taking out anything personal so that we can forward it to her daughter?'

Yes, she would mind. It was such a final step. But it would have to be done, and perhaps better done by her than by a production secretary who might poke and pry into Suzannah's papers. She sent back a reply, agreeing, and rang Suzannah's office. The phone was answered by Sandra, her old friend. She explained the task ahead of her, and Sandra was sympathetic. 'Why not come over now? It's quiet here today. It would be just you and me. If you like we could do it together.'

The office was just as she remembered it. Suzannah was so vivid a presence that Lucy sat down, winded by the impact. This place was truer to Suzannah than any of the cathedral's hymns and eulogies. She looked round the walls. There were photographs taken on the set – Suzannah with Kenneth Branagh, Suzannah with Robin Williams, Suzannah with the whole studio crew. There were awards, strange-looking lumps of distorted bronze and sheets of engraved glass. There were cartoons, and letters from the public pinned on her notice board to make her smile. Janet had been right, it was a happy office.

Suzannah had loved her job. Reluctantly Lucy went round to the back of the desk, sat in her friend's chair and tried to open the drawers. They were locked. On cue, Sandra came in with the keys, a carrier bag, and a cup of peppermint tea. Lucy remembered her first time in that office, no tea for her then. She thanked Sandra.

'If you need me, I'm just doing some paperwork outside. I'd be glad to help,' Sandra told her, and left.

Lucy unlocked the middle drawer. There was a pile of letters in it. Reluctantly, because it felt so intrusive, she started to read one. It looked like a love letter from a besotted fan. 'You make my life worth living, my dearest Suzy.' It was anonymous, of course. Nobody who knew her ever called her Suzy.

Lucy called through the open door to Sandra, 'I'm going to need your shredder.'

'Fine. It's here when you want it.'

At the bottom of the pile was a different kind of letter, a scrap of lined paper written on in biro in capital letters, from a nut, no doubt.

> YOU'RE A BITCH, PIPER, YOU'VE WRECKED TOO MANY LIVES. SOON YOU'LL KNOW WHAT THAT FEELS LIKE, YOU PILE OF SHIT.

What a vile piece of garbage. Why on earth had Suzannah kept it?

There was another one underneath it.

> IT'S COMING TO YOU, BITCH PIPER. YOU WON'T GET AWAY. YOU'LL SUFFER TOO.

And another.

> YOU LOAD OF CRAP, PIPER, YOU'D BETTER TAKE CARE. YOUR TURN WILL COME.

31

Lucy spread all three out on the desk in front of her. She felt her heart pounding. This was evil stuff. Someone had vomited out their rage onto the page. It was violent too. Should she take the notes to the police? Perhaps they knew already. How strange that Suzannah, who told her everything, never mentioned this. But then every presenter receives insane letters from time to time. Television creates a spurious relationship, a technological intimacy that can inspire obsessions in some viewers, but this was more than obsessed. This was deranged. Why had Suzannah kept them? Why hadn't she just torn them up?

On an impulse, Lucy took an envelope from the desk, slipped the three pages into it, and put it into her handbag. She'd think about them later. What about the half-a-dozen love letters? Maybe Camilla should look after them. She put them into the carrier bag, together with the photographs and the awards.

The rest of the drawers contained a few pieces of spare make-up for emergencies, some photographs to sign for fans, a *Who's Who*, and a *Concise Oxford Dictionary*. She packed them all into the bag, and took them out to Sandra. 'I think that's all. Could you send these on to Camilla, with my love?'

Sandra nodded. 'Of course. Thanks for doing that. I didn't feel I could do it – it's so personal.'

'I can understand that.'

And she escaped to her own office. As she walked down the corridor, she passed a huge glossy picture of Suzannah, the jewel in BriTV's crown. There was that familiar wide smile, the startling blue eyes bright with amusement. How could her open face have been concealing such dark secrets? It was an extraordinary thing to discover, a private locked drawer, filled with extremes of love and violent hatred. It was like finding a primed hand grenade. Why had Suzannah kept the letters there, without a word to anyone? Or at least, without a word to her closest friend.

By contrast, the busy activity of her own office swirled around her as Lucy arrived, like a reassuring blast of fresh air, and sanity. Her team of researchers was young and dedicated. But the story they had uncovered had knocked her off balance more than any other she had investigated.

Two months ago she had received a letter from a boy at a small, dingy boarding school, Wantage Grange. She remembered opening the envelope, amused and touched by the young writing, and the fragile spelling. The horror of it struck her as soon as she started reading. The boy had enclosed his school's brochure, decorated with a Latin motto, a grand crest, and offering a 'caring education'. 'We provide individual teaching for children with any special needs,' the prospectus said, and there were cheap rates for the sons of army and navy personnel, whose parents would be out of the country most of the year. What the brochure didn't mention, but the boy's letter painstakingly described, were the repulsive attentions of the owner, Trevor Whitestone, and a few of his teachers.

Of course Lucy knew these things happened. But reading it in the child's own words, as he described his shame and his fear, blaming himself for not being able to prevent it, she shuddered. She took the letter home to Fred and showed it to him.

'This is terrible,' he said, as he read it. 'But do you believe it? Don't children make things like this up, if they don't like a particular teacher?'

Lucy shook her head. 'That's possible, I suppose, and obviously we have to keep an open mind, but look at the way he tells his story. Do you see how little he tells us of the actual physical acts, as if he is trying to protect us, and himself as well? And yet some of the details he tells us no child should know. I'm sure he must have suffered abuse at some time in his life – he knows too much. What we have to prove is that the abuse was by this man he talks about, Trevor Whitestone.'

The research began, and as she learned more, the story began to obsess her. She worked late into the evening, and there were nights when Fred longed to bring her back into his world. But

33

when he put his arms around her he could feel her tension and anxiety making her shiver.

'Don't let these vile men get between us,' he once pleaded with her, and she focused her eyes on him as if she was seeing him for the first time.

'I'm so sorry, Fred. Discovering just how cruel these men can be has been a hideous education. Forgive me,' and she kissed him.

He knew she was struggling, trying to respond to him, so he was tolerant, and took his time. Once the investigation was complete, she would be able to escape from these shadows, or at least he hoped she would.

'Why do these men do it?' Lucy asked the team over and over again. 'How can they be blind to the pain they're inflicting on the children?'

Try as they would, they could not find the answer. They looked into Whitestone's background. He was an old man now, in his seventies. They discovered he was well off and well connected, an ex-public schoolboy who had become a teacher himself. But as they investigated his career, they found that in the past, before the laws were tightened up, he had left school after school without references. Head teachers told them confidentially that there had been complaints against Whitestone, so they guessed he had a long history of abusing little boys and getting away with it.

Lucy came home one evening, and sat late into the night with Fred, sharing with him the rage she felt. 'He must have been attacking children like this for years. He made a career of abusing them.'

Fred was appalled, and incredulous. 'Couldn't the children have told their parents?' he asked. 'Why didn't they put a stop to it?'

'Most of the boys he had in his clutches felt so ashamed and frightened that they didn't dare ask for help. They thought nobody would believe them. They couldn't tell their parents because the truth would cause them so much guilt and distress. It was like a prison of abuse.'

For week after week Fred survived on sandwiches and warmed up soups, while Lucy worked on the story, then crawled at last, dazed at what she had discovered, and emotionally bruised, into his arms in bed at night.

'What a horrible species we must be if we're able to do this to our own young,' she breathed into his shoulder, and he could say nothing to reassure her.

Now at last the investigation was almost complete. She felt drained, battered, exhausted by it all. And there was no Suzannah in her life to take her for a drink, and listen to her, to lift some of the crushing burden of the story off her shoulders for half an hour. Lucy pulled the schoolboy's original letter out of the file again, and looked at his round, childish handwriting for inspiration. What courage it had taken for him to write to her, to ask for help, and to describe his abuse. The letter sent out shock waves of pain.

She remembered showing it to Shirley, almost reluctantly, when it first arrived. 'I believe what this child tells us,' Lucy had said, 'I don't know if we can ever prove his story, but I think we have to try.'

Shirley had read the letter with gathering horror. 'You know, this stuff is going to break the parents' hearts,' she said. 'And no doubt we'll be accused of trial by television. But I agree the kids must come first.'

One child led them to another. The most delicate job had been to try to persuade the boys to talk. In the end, twelve boys had told the researchers appalling stories of abuse by the proprietor and three of his senior teachers. The pictures they described branded themselves on Lucy's mind. The careful grooming, the slow seduction with cigarettes, or money, or pornographic magazines, alternating with anger if the boys protested, or tried to escape. The teachers knew how to use petty punishments and humiliations to make their victims suffer, and they had no scruples. The children told her how they lay in their beds night after night, crying themselves to sleep, hating their bodies, loathing what had been done to them, tormented with flashbacks. At least talking to her researchers about the abuse had helped to diminish their guilt a little. And tomorrow the boys would come to the studio to be interviewed live on air, their faces shadowed and their voices disguised to protect their identity.

The team had tracked down the teachers too and tried to speak to them, but they refused to be interviewed, or to comment. Finally Lucy rang Trevor Whitestone, a multimillionaire who had created the school as his own playground, where he was free to prey on the boys in his power. When she spoke to him, late one night, with the children's statements in front of her, he denied everything, blamed the boys, and accused her of encouraging them to make up their stories.

She kept cool. 'Mr Whitestone, that's your point of view. Can I invite you to come to the studio to tell your side of the story? It's a live show, we won't edit your answers in any way.'

He hesitated, then to her joy his vanity won. 'All right, Miss Strong. But, I assure you, these boys are at the most difficult age. It's just the kind of thing they invent to cover up whatever they're ashamed of. Maybe they've done things together that put these ideas in their heads.'

Her head swam with revulsion at his arrogance. But she didn't argue. She needed him in the show. Critics might call it trial by television, but no other trial would ever take place unless she could broadcast the boys' stories.

So nearly all the pieces were in place now. Lucy worked at her desk as darkness fell, writing the script with the researchers beside her. Shirley sat listening, sometimes interpolating a question of her own, keeping a steady flow of coffee coming, mug by brimming mug, until the last word was written. Then Lucy breathed out a deep sigh, and let herself slump in her chair, leaning her head against her hand.

'What a day,' she said. 'I never want that one back again.'

Shirley pulled out a pack of chocolate biscuits she had hidden in a file for moments just like this. 'Have some energy,' she said. 'You've done well.'

'Don't speak too soon,' Lucy didn't dare to hope for too much. 'It all depends on the boys tomorrow. If their courage holds, and I get what we need from Whitestone, we'll have done our job.' She looked round at the researchers; they were excited now that the show was here at last and their enthusiasm buoyed her up. She needed it.

There was one more hurdle to cross. Shirley rang the company solicitor, and he arrived with a barrister, Robin Campion, in tow. The four of them sat in Shirley's office, and Lucy confronted them with her most difficult legal point.

'Some of the boys have hinted to me that there was more going on in this school than just the teachers abusing them.'

'More what?' Campion looked at her intently.

'I'm not sure. They haven't been precise. Maybe pornography. Maybe something on the Internet.'

'Maybe isn't enough. You know you can't broadcast a vague accusation. This Whitestone is rich. He can afford to take us to the cleaners.'

They sat with the lawyers until midnight, arguing about every detail in the script. Campion, the barrister, was difficult, he was paid to be. 'Show me your evidence,' he demanded over and over again.

Lucy did as she was told. It was difficult, but sometimes the parents could back up their sons' story. One mother remembered her little boy ringing home very late at night, sobbing but refusing to say why. They'd rushed to collect him from school, driving across the country and arriving there at dawn. Whitestone had met them at the door, reassured them, brought the child into his study, and put his arm around the boy's shoulder. They'd left without their son. Lucy shuddered as she visualized the terrified child.

37

The lawyers were far more unemotional. They carefully read the boys' sworn statements, and checked the corroboration. Lucy was impatient, but held tight to her own indignation. Although they had to prune her script, and blur some of the detail, enough was still there to close the school and protect the children from any more abuse. Shirley had to make some tricky decisions too. How far could they describe the abuse? How much could the audience stand? But by midnight the lawyers were satisfied. The script was still intact. Lucy found her car in the company car park and drove home.

Fred was waiting for her in her Notting Hill house. It was opposite a tiny park, the dark branches of the trees were outlined against the midnight sky, a dull orange lit by the city lights. As she put her key in her front door she saw Fred had nailed a Christmas wreath by the letter box, golden baubles hanging from scarlet ribbon threaded through holly. Her heart lifted when she saw him waiting for her at the kitchen table, late as it was, drinking a glass of red wine, a large turkey sandwich on the plate in front of him. He poured her a glass, and took a sandwich out of the fridge for her. She drank deeply, and the pain of the story she'd been working on was soothed a little. Child abuse rubs off like an evil smear on all those whose lives it touches, on the social workers, the doctors, the police, even the journalists.

'Fred, this story is so hideous,' she said. 'I feel almost physically dirty. How can adults have sex with children? Is all sex this ugly?' She looked at him apologetically. How could she share with him the knowledge she had now, the stories she wished she hadn't heard?

Fred took her hand, saying nothing. He had seen her mood darken over the weeks and months of her research into the school. Then she was seared by Suzannah's death. Finally, the memorial service. He had known this would be a terrible day for her. Now that she was safely home, he waited for her to tell him more. But she buried herself in her black coat, like an animal

38

rolling up to keep warm. She didn't dare unwrap her body or her thoughts to him – not until her home and his company had healed her a little. So they sat together in the kitchen, she with her hurt, he with his need to comfort her, but not knowing how. At last she sat up, and began to unbutton her coat. She stretched wearily.

He smiled at her. 'Bad, was it?'

'Worse than I can say.'

'Why?'

'The memorial service was all wrong. Mandy, Suzannah's agent, turned it into the worst kind of show business. And I stupidly agreed to have a drink with Janet Lake afterwards. By that time I just loathed everyone in the congregation, so I bad-mouthed them all. Janet could hardly breathe in case I realized what I was saying, and took it back.'

Fred groaned. The danger of an interview at this moment was obvious, when she was so vulnerable, and so furious. 'How many of the bosses did you blame for her death?'

'Only one – Jameson, the controller. He was going to axe her, so I let him have it. And that horrible Naomi Leicester – everyone says Jameson was going to give her the series instead. And Martin.' She listed them all.

Fred was a cameraman, and he had worked with Naomi and Martin. They were professionals – he had no reason to dislike them – but he knew better than to defend them now. As Lucy recited what she could remember of the interview, his heart sank. This would make her no friends in the industry. With luck they might forgive her, bearing in mind her distress at Suzannah's death, but they would not forget.

'Was it wise to unload all that? It won't make you popular.'

She was not in the mood to hear him although she knew he was right. Instead she started to talk about the next day's pro-gramme. 'Then I had to leave all that, block it, so that I could write the script. I'm dreading the programme,' she said. 'So much is riding on it. It's so important we don't let the boys

39

down, otherwise these vile men will just go back to school, proud as punch, and go on abusing the children, knowing nobody can stop them.'

She described the struggle with the lawyers over the script. 'And I don't expect Jameson will like the programme. In the end it's not going to be a ratings winner. It's going to be so painful to watch. I just hope it's worth it.'

She gave another great sigh, and this time Fred thought it might be safe to take her in his arms. When the stress levels were too high she would hold him away, but now she snuggled into him.

'Take me to bed,' she said.

She lay in his arms, looking into his face, and he saw she had more to tell him. She started, stopped, then began again.

'I found something in Suzannah's desk,' she said.

He waited.

'They asked me to empty her office. She had a locked drawer in her desk, and there were some letters inside.'

'What kind of letters?'

'Some way-over-the-top love letters, obviously from a fan who's been in love with her for years. But there were three others which were quite horrible.'

'Mad, horrible?'

'Yes, mad, but threatening too. I keep wondering if I should take them to the police, or whether that would be stupid.'

'Do you want to show them to me?'

'No. I don't want to show them to anyone. I want to get rid of them.'

'Why not leave it all until tomorrow? You've had a tough day. You need something to take your mind off it all. I know just the thing.'

She smiled up at him. 'Nothing distracts you, Fred.'

'That's why I'm here.'

His hands moved over her, and she allowed herself to relax for the first time that day. He was right. But before his touch blotted out all thought, at the back of her mind the memory of those letters in her handbag burned like a brand. When this programme was over, when she had a moment to herself, she must find out more about them. She owed it to Suzannah.

CHAPTER THREE

She woke early, still curled in Fred's arms. Sex between them was always so good. He was young, energetic, and uncomplicated. She loved the fresh tangy smell of his skin, and as she moved her cheek against his hair, she revelled in the moment. Did Fred love her? Why spoil it with awkward questions? They had fun together. As far as she knew he was faithful to her, or faithful-ish. He was an ambitious, hard-working cameraman, much in demand and therefore often away working on location. When he moved into her home two months ago, it had seemed the most practical thing to do. So far the press had not noticed Fred. She had trained him to use the back door to her house, which opened on to a tiny mews.

'Not,' she impressed upon him, 'because I'm ashamed of you, but because I need a little privacy.'

She liked waking up next to him, it made her smile to remember the pleasure of the previous night. She stroked his face, he moved his lips against her hand, but he was still asleep. So she slid away from him and into the bathroom. She ran the hot water into the bath, and looked critically at herself in the mirror. Face still glowing with the smile Fred had put there. Hair dark, shiny, but ruffled. Eyes big, brown, still tired. Shape unfashionably rounded. She shook her head, and twisted to look critically at her breasts and her backside. Lesley nagged her from time to time, reminding her that the cameras exaggerated every curve, but they both knew she was never going to be a fashion model. And there were moments when she needed the comfort of sweetness on her tongue, the chocolate biscuits Shirley kept in an emergency file for her.

She bathed, dried herself, dressed, and sprayed herself with Chanel. Then she packed her studio suitcase, as she did every week. A change of underclothes and tights, and a stand-by suit in case the one Lesley had picked for her looked wrong. Lesley very rarely made a mistake, but sometimes the colour of the set caused a clash, and Lucy always took something tried and tested with her. Today Lucy picked a dark purple suit, well-cut but subdued. This was not a time to appear frivolous. She put half a dozen oranges into the juicer, brewed some coffee for Fred and herself and filled two bowls with crunchy cereal. She took Fred his breakfast, then gulped hers at the kitchen table while the taxi to take her to the studio waited. She felt a crawl of nervousness in her gut. Best to have breakfast. She knew she would have no appetite for lunch.

The taxi took her to David's, the hairdresser she had used for ten years. They knew her well enough there to understand that she needed to absorb herself in work, rather than engage in conversation. Her hair had been done yesterday for the memorial service, all it needed today was a brush and spray to push it back into shape. Fred's energy in the night had crushed it, but not irreparably.

While the stylist was busy with hairbrush and tongs, Lucy read through the research again. The schoolboys would need gentle handling. The school's owner would deny everything, claim a conspiracy against him, and demand evidence. There were a psychiatrist and a paediatrician to give their views on the boys' statements. Who would the audience believe?

The stylist held a mirror for Lucy to inspect the back of her head, the dark hair sharply back in place. She hardly glanced at it; the concentration she needed for the show ahead had already closed around her.

The taxi took her to the BriTV studio, to the stage door this time, and the driver carried her case into her dressing room. The room was small and functional, bulbs round the big mirror, a hotel-style flower arrangement on a table. In the wardrobe she found a trouser suit Lesley had chosen for the show, a grey pinstripe. Clever Lesley – that would be far more appropriate than the purple she had brought herself. Over the loudspeaker Lucy could hear the clanging and thumping of the studio coming to life, the last touches being made to the set, the cameras being pushed into position. A knock on the door from the floor assistant, and Lucy stood, picking up the file, her face vacant with thought. This was the climax of all those weeks of work. Under her breath she repeated to herself over and over again, 'I mustn't let those children down.'

In the control gallery the director, Michael Black, was marking up his script. Each shot was planned right up to the interviews, but from then on, he and the cameramen would have to improvise. Shirley walked into the gallery, stood beside him and threw down a morning paper, the *Dispatch*, across the script in front of him. The paper was folded open at Janet Lake's interview with Lucy, a huge black headline running across the two central pages: 'WHO REALLY KILLED SUZANNAH PIPER?'

Michael swore softly as he read it. All Lucy's anger had been faithfully captured on the page, complete with pictures. David Jameson had been caught at a most unflattering moment with his finger pointing and his mouth open. The picture had been taken at a press conference for the launch of his autumn programmes, but he looked like a murderer at bay. The caption helped nail the message, 'David Jameson, the axe-man', all in careful quotation marks, to show it was Lucy's description, not the *Dispatch*'s. Next to him, Martin Dellaby smiled his constant, greasy smirk. Once again, Lucy's quote had become the caption, 'Martin would upstage her in the cathedral'. Lucy's verdict on Naomi Leicester was just as brutal, 'Racist, sexist, she's an insult to interviewing'.

The picture they'd chosen of Suzannah was a pensive one, taken by Terry O'Neill, her favourite photographer, and appropriate for the caption, 'Suzannah – driven to her death'. The biggest picture of all was of Lucy, outside the cathedral, smiling bravely, holding her lilac silk scarf tight round her throat, her black coat blowing in the December wind, and here the caption writer had pushed her quotes slightly further than she'd meant: 'Suzannah murdered, claims Lucy'.

In an instant all the staff in the control room had clustered round the newspaper, looking for the names they knew, and giggling as they found them. Rarely had anyone broken cover publicly to attack their own colleagues like this.

Michael reached the end of the piece, and breathed out incredulously. He flicked the switch that turned off the microphone to Lucy's earpiece, so that she wouldn't overhear them. Then he asked, 'Has Lucy seen this? Should we show it to her?'

'No, and no,' Shirley said. 'This will have to wait until we've finished the show. We have enough to worry about.'

She picked up the phone and dialled the BriTV press office. Most of their work consisted of killing and blocking stories, so they would not complain if she told them to try to calm this one down. No doubt other papers would be desperate for more quotes, if not from Lucy, from the big names she had attacked. The story would run and run, but not tonight. Not if Shirley could help it.

'Nobody is to mention this to Lucy, please. She must concentrate on the show. Can we sort the pictures out? Make sure they're in order and ready, and let's get on with rehearsal.'

Michael Black switched Lucy's microphone on again and spoke into her ear. 'Sorry, Lucy, it's chaos in here. We're ready to start, when you are.'

The floor manager showed her the mark for her first position, in front of a giant picture of the school where so many boys had suffered. The studio was as familiar to her as her own home, with its flat painted floor and the lights clustered above her, far smaller than it looked on screen, and less glossy. The back of the scenery flats were rough unpainted wood, scrawled with the title of the show, 'Strong Stories'.

Michael cued her and the Autocue began to roll across the lens of her camera. She read the script as if she was talking quietly in the viewers' sitting room, with the easy naturalness of years of practice.

45

'Good evening. Tonight we reveal a scandal. We show children in danger, the victims of a terrible crime committed against them. All this not in the gutters of a Third World nation, but here, in the heart of Britain.'

When the rehearsals ended, Shirley joined Lucy in her dressing room. They hardly spoke as she changed into the sombre grey suit, then picked up her clipboard and turned to face Shirley. Concentration had been replaced by adrenalin. The preparation was over.

'Here goes,' she said, and Shirley nodded. The show was live, complex, and dangerous. But they had faith in each other, and in the team.

At the studio door she met the children. She smiled at them. 'You OK?' They nodded. 'You'll be fine,' she told them. Trevor Whitestone had arrived, but he had been taken straight to a dressing room on the other side of the building. There must be no risk that he would meet the boys in advance, or attempt to intimidate them.

She took her place in front of the photograph of the school. The red light went on, signalling the live transmission, the titles flickered black and white on monitors slung from the ceiling. She read the introduction, and turned to the children. They talked to her, hesitantly at first, but with gathering confidence. She didn't ask for physical details of their abuse. Lucy knew that paedophiles enjoy listening to children talking about abuse, that they would pass child witness statements around in prison, reading them like pornography. She refused to give them the pleasure. In any case, she and her team were far too professional to offend viewers by telling them more than they needed to know.

Trevor Whitestone was sitting in a leather chair at the side of the set, listening to the boys. She sat down beside him. At first he appeared pathetic, an old man who seemed not to understand her questions. But when she pushed him with more and more evidence, he became hostile.

'You've done this before, to other boys in other schools,' Lucy said.

'They're lying.'

'We've spoken to the head teachers. You abused this boy fifteen years ago when he was in a boarding school in the Midlands.' She showed him the photograph.

He took it, glanced at it, then threw it back at her.

'You've paid the boys to say this. They'll say anything for money.'

'We've paid no one. One of your teachers tried to bribe the boys, to buy their silence.'

'No child has ever complained to me.'

'How could they, when you were abusing them yourself? How do you explain taking teachers with no references, teachers who had complaints against them in their previous schools? Why did you yourself leave school after school without a reference? Are you saying that none of the boys who told us they were abused at your school is telling the truth?' Then, knowing she had the freedom of the live programme, she disobeyed the lawyers. 'Were there others besides your teachers involved in the abuse? Were there links to a paedophile ring outside the school, on the Internet perhaps?'

Whitestone stammered and blustered, and refused to answer the questions she rained down on him. But the boys were their own best advocates. Each one described his feelings – one had sobbed himself to sleep, another had attempted suicide. It made distressing listening, but at least now they had provided enough evidence for the police to take action.

The closing titles rolled, they came off the air, the red studio lights blinked out. Lucy said good night to the children, walked quickly past the old man who had caused them such misery, and into the control room. Shirley and Michael congratulated her, then Shirley held out a piece of paper. 'This is a list of the journalists who want to talk to you. Janet Lake's interview came out this morning. It's strong stuff.'

Lucy flinched. 'You should have shown it to me before,' she said.

'No, I shouldn't. You had enough to think about.'

Lucy picked the newspaper up from the desk. Had she really said all this? In print it looked wildly sensational. Had she been drunker than she realized?

Shirley watched her anxious face, and for once didn't protect her. 'This was not well judged, Lucy. You don't want to say any more to the papers, I hope?'

Lucy shook her head. 'No, I've said enough. I'll go home. Let's see if anything happens tomorrow to the school, and those appalling teachers.'

Except, of course, that Janet's interview would distract from any press interest in the show they'd just painstakingly put together.

She went back to her dressing room. Sue, her dresser, had carefully packed away the clothes she had been wearing. Lucy picked up her case and walked back to reception. Now that the adrenalin was ebbing away, she felt weary. The hospitality room would be full of exultant researchers, and the children and their families. She couldn't face them now. Shirley met her at reception, and Lucy confessed how frail she was feeling.

'Please make my excuses to everyone. Say the boys were brilliant, and very brave. Explain that I'm tired.'

Shirley gave her a quick forgiving hug. 'They'll understand. They know what a tough time you're having.' Everyone by now had read the Janet Lake interview. Lucy followed her driver into the dark, cold night, and bundled herself into the car. Never mind, she'd be home soon.

But as the driver turned into her street, the headlights caught a cluster of people waiting on the pavement outside her small paved garden. Reporters, frustrated not to have spoken to her all day, had ambushed her here.

'What do you want me to do, Miss Strong?' the driver asked. 'I can drive past them and take you to a hotel.'

48

She thought for a moment. 'No, I might as well face them now. I want to spend tonight in my own bed. I know most of them anyway. They're all right really.'

Instinctively she ran her hand across her hair. There would be photographers in the crowd, she might as well look tidy otherwise everyone would say she'd gone to pieces. She got out of the car and smiled at them. Rob, a regular television reporter she knew quite well, called to her.

'Lucy, have you heard that Naomi Leicester says Suzannah Piper was a fossilized has-been, that you are a humourless cow?'

That's a compliment, coming from her, Lucy thought, but she kept her smile strapped across her teeth and said nothing. A reporter she didn't recognize threw the next question at her, 'Come on, Lucy, you must give us some kind of quote. Do you really think she was murdered? Tell us, then we'll leave you alone.'

'Suzannah was my closest friend,' Lucy said carefully. 'I loved her, I miss her. She died far too young. It's no good blaming the weather, or her tiredness for the tragic accident. There are other questions which must be asked.' The memory of the hate-filled letters filled her mind. 'I know there were people who were consumed with hatred of her. I just don't know why. Yet.' The clamour of questions rose again. She shook her head. 'Forgive me, I've just made a programme, it's been a painful time, I need to go home.'

They parted to allow her through, and then scattered with her quotes – bare as they were, at least they had something.

Lucy picked up her case, and turned to open the gate. Car headlights blazed into life at the end of the now deserted street. She looked up, startled to see the car accelerating towards her. For a moment she hesitated. Why should anyone drive so fast down the quiet street at this time of night? It was suddenly frighteningly close. Was the driver drunk?

She fumbled with the clasp of the gate. The car was heading straight at her. She flung her case over the gate, it opened, and

49

she forced herself in between the posts, just as the car reached her and its mirror hit the fence as it passed, exactly where she had been standing. Heavens, that was close. She tried to see the driver, but in the darkness she couldn't even make out whether it was a man or a woman. She was still gathering her nerves together as the car reached the end of the road, and then, with a screech of tyres, turned the corner and was gone.

She stood in the darkness, shattered. Ludicrous as she knew the idea was, it felt as if the driver had aimed the car straight at her. It was almost as if someone had been waiting there in the darkness until the reporters had left her, and then targeted her. She was shaking, although whether with fright or shock she couldn't tell. It took several attempts before she was steady enough to put her key in the lock, and let herself in.

Fred wasn't there yet. Lucy switched on the kettle, and tried to steady herself. It was just a bad driver, maybe a kid with drink or drugs inside him, speeding down the street and mis-judging the distance. She took her suitcase to her room, and sat on her bed. Her memory began running a tape of the programme through her mind – every word, every comma, every shot. She heard the children's voices in her brain, then the proprietor, protesting and stammering. Against the lawyers' advice she had put to him the accusation that he was part of a paedophile ring stretching beyond the school. Of course he had denied every-thing, and in any case it would be impossible to prove. She heard Fred's key in the door, and went down to meet him.

As he turned to put down his bag, she ran into his arms. He responded at once, with surprise. 'What's the problem, Lucy?'

'I know it's crazy, but a car almost knocked me down out-side our door. Some stupid kid, no doubt. But for a moment I thought they were trying to kill me.'

He gently disentangled her, and looked into her face. 'You're in a state, Lucy. You're pushing yourself much too hard. Give yourself a break.'

'How can I?' There was desperation in her voice. 'There's so

50

much on my plate at the moment. Janet Lake's run that inter-view I told you about, and it's pretty bad.'

'You were frightened of that.'

'I know, I know.'

'Personally I can't imagine why you sat down with that woman for a second, given the way she used to write about Suzannah.'

'She caught me at the worst possible time. But I know I was stupid.'

'You might say that.'

She poured them both a cup of tea.

'Don't make me feel worse than I do already,' she pleaded with him. 'I know I've made a lot of enemies today. But at least the show's transmitted, we've done what I promised the brave kid who wrote to me. That school must surely be closed down.'

He smiled at her. 'It was a terrific piece of research. No other show could possibly have taken it on. You may rush in some-times where angels fear to tread, but angels can be very dull. Nobody could ever call you dull.'

She went to her study to check her e-mail, and Fred went upstairs. She called after him. 'I won't be a moment.' Then she turned on the machine and clicked on to her new messages.

The latest one seemed to scream at her from the screen. It was from David Jameson: 'I want to see you tomorrow. I'll call round at nine. David.' Bleak to the point of brusqueness, there was no doubt what he meant. She'd gone too far. He had the power to hire and fire, instantly. She'd made her last show for BriTV.

CHAPTER FOUR

She woke, and her stomach instinctively clenched with anxiety. Why? Her mind caught up slowly, each memory as it surfaced bringing its own bubble of fear. The desperately indiscreet interview, the anger she must have provoked among her bosses, and now the threat that she would be axed from the programme she loved. Fred had rolled away from her in the night, aware that he could do nothing to calm or console her. So she lay straight and tense, staring at the ceiling.

Her memory moved backwards over the evening before, like a slowly rewinding tape. The car that had hurtled towards her out of the darkness. That terrible old man in the studio, brazenly justifying his treatment of the boys at his school. How could he live with himself? If he really was part of a paedophile ring, ruthless men who had felt threatened by her programme, could the car that had so nearly hit her be in some way a warning not to go any further? No. That must be a paranoid fantasy.

And yet her memory reminded her that her own beloved Suzannah had died in a car accident, a death which had been prophesied by the vile letters she had found in Suzannah's desk. She hadn't made those up.

Lucy slipped out of bed, and opened her handbag. There they were, obscene in their violence. Why had Suzannah never told her about them? Had she been so scared or repelled that she had buried them, or was it that she had completely disregarded them? If only she were here to ask. Lucy longed to pick up the phone, as she had countless times, to hear Suzannah's lilt of laughter. How easily Suzannah would have made sense of all this. Without her, it was just a confusing tangle of fear.

What would Suzannah say to her now? Lucy stretched, stared into the darkness and tried to beam into her friend's mind. She

52

would have said, 'Take it step by step, Lucy. One at a time. Take the simplest, most practical step first.'

None of it was simple. But perhaps the most tangible problem was her career. What had possessed her to alienate her own boss? E-mails are often curt and unfriendly, but this one from David was as brusque as an execution. Snick, snack, snick, and her head was in the basket.

She washed and dressed, her mind whirling. Should she approach another broadcasting company? Where else could she go? There was no other investigative programme on the air that invested in such a high-powered research team, and would offer so much scope for her clout and expertise. There had been tentative offers from time to time, but she had always turned them down. At BriTV she had freedom to follow her hunches, and so far they had paid off. She had given the company the prestige and critical acclaim they craved, and they had given her a role that stretched, exhausted and rewarded her. She would be bereft without it. She should have thought of that before she blurted out her bitterness to Janet Lake. What an idiot.

She sat down in front of her mirror, and swore at her own reflection. She tried to conjure Suzannah's face beside her in the mirror. She could almost manage it, she could imagine the eyebrows lifted with exasperation. 'Oh, Lucy, how do we get you out of this one? At least David's going to confront you, face to face, a one-man firing squad. He's got more courage than most of them. It's usually done by back-stabbing, or a lethal injection of pure venom. So put on a brave face, and if he gives you a last request, ask for one more chance.'

Good advice. The brave face lived in a series of brightly coloured wicker baskets – foundations in one, eye colours in another, lip glosses in a third. She put on her make-up with the skill she had learned from watching dozens of professionals at work on her face. She had learned from them how to minimize her faults – blusher on her cheeks drew attention to her eyes, and away from her soft jaw-line. Perhaps if she put herself on a tough diet she would achieve the lean look, the clear profile Suzannah had. But crash diets were so disgusting – cabbage soup and cottage cheese. One day it would be worth the suffering perhaps, but not today.

She went to the wardrobe and chose a black trouser suit, lit with an ivory silk shirt – a memorial service uniform that befitted the death of a career. She sprayed herself with a warm honeysuckle fragrance she had found in the South of France, to cheer herself with memories of springtime in the hills behind Nice. Pearls at her neck and in her ears, to add elegance.

She walked back into the bedroom. Fred was packing his case with his own working uniform: T-shirt, sweater and jeans.

'You look good, formidable, not to be messed with,' he said. 'And you smell even better.' He took her in his arms. 'Good luck. Don't worry. It's only television.'

'When are you back?' she asked.

'I should be back tomorrow, barring accidents. Ring me tonight in the hotel.'

His itinerary was pinned on the kitchen notice board. He was beginning a documentary about sporting children. The sequence of interviews, matches and athletic events would mean he had to spend most of the next month travelling around the country, but that was the deal. Both of them knew their careers were all-devouring. Television is notorious for destroying friendships and marriages. Film crews stick together like small circuses, causing chaos, providing fun for the onlookers, and when love affairs spring up and die as quickly, they tell each other, 'What goes on location, stays on location.' When Fred came home to her after each assignment and greeted her with easy, undemanding affection, Lucy asked no questions.

Now, as she kissed him goodbye and wished him luck, she held him to her. Suddenly she felt lonely and vulnerable. He stayed with her arms around him, then gently pushed her away and picked up his case. He turned back to reassure the concern in her eyes. 'See you soon, darling, don't worry. The show yesterday was brilliant, an award-winner. David Jameson's a fool if he doesn't double your salary.'

She smiled. Then he left, and the house was very empty.

Lucy brewed herself some coffee, and opened a can of grapefruit segments. The sweet tangy fruit slid across her tongue – comfort food, to hell with cottage cheese. She started to make a list for herself. Check the answer-phone and the e-mails for response to last night's programme. Check the ratings, to see what audience they'd had. Look up her CV and bring it up to date. The doorbell rang. It was nine o'clock. Jameson was on time.

He stood on the doorstep, belligerent chin jutting. He was driven by a competitive determination to knock his rivals out of the ratings – a ruthless bully to those who got in his way, but just as tough a supporter to those he valued.

'Morning, Lucy. Not too early, I hope? I know you had a late night. The show went well, I thought.'

Her mind registered the compliment. It was unusual for a boss to praise anything he was about to axe. She smiled, and stepped back to let him pass her.

He strode into her sitting room. Behind him Lucy saw Shirley Walters, her producer, quietly standing. Was it a double assassination or was Shirley's head on the block as well? Or were they going to play good cop, bad cop? Shirley gave her a hug, then winked at her as Jameson continued shouting at her from the centre of the room. 'Nice house you have, Lucy. We must be paying you far too much. How many bedrooms? Two?'

What business was it of his? Lucy avoided an answer. 'I'll get you coffee,' she said, and went into the kitchen. The other two looked round the sitting-room – light river-green walls, pastel silk cushions on pale sofas, everything so ordered and neat it was obvious there could be no children in the house. A big bowl of white cyclamens hovered like butterflies on a low table. Watercolours on the walls added to the space and softness of the room, pictures of orchards in bloom and summer beaches, all antidotes to the intense stressfulness of her working life. It was a lovely house, but there was a sadness in its perfect order. There was nothing battered, nothing out of place. Where was her past? Did she never let down her guard?

Lucy returned with the coffee on a tray. As they took their cups, she wondered whether she should apologize for the insults she had flung at Jameson via the *Dispatch*. Jameson made the decision for her.

'I enjoyed your interview with Janet Lake,' he said. 'It's done me no end of good. The reputation of an axe-man is just what the Board of Management likes. It shows I don't cling on to artists and series beyond their sell-by date.'

No one could accuse him of that, Lucy thought. He seemed in a good mood. The fury she had expected was well controlled, if it was there at all. Her heart had been pounding, but now she felt it slow down and quieten, so she couldn't resist the indiscreet question.

'Was I right, then? Was Suzannah's head on the chopping block?'

'No, you were wrong about that. I wouldn't have axed her. She was a star, and she'll be a huge loss.'

All very well for him to say so now that she was safely dead and buried. All he had done in her lifetime was grumble at her bad reviews, and take her high ratings for granted. Lucy could see Shirley glaring at her, warning her to say nothing more.

Jameson gulped his coffee. 'That's what I want to talk to you about, Lucy. Of course, no one can replace Suzannah, but the show must go on.' He grinned at his own cliché. 'We've put out compilations, as tribute programmes. Now we have to move on. Her production team are all still in place, raring to go. Her audience is out there, waiting to see who we'll replace her with.'

Naomi Leicester, no doubt, thought Lucy cynically.

He read her mind. 'It's a big slot, ten o'clock on Saturday night. Not the place I could put, for instance, Naomi Leicester. Much as I admire her, she divides the audience. That's why I'm here, Lucy. Would you like to see what you could do with that Saturday audience?'

She stared at him, unable to believe he was offering her the biggest talk show on television.

'You worked on it as a researcher,' he said. 'Suzannah trained you herself. You're not afraid of a big story. Everyone knows how close you were to her – no one will say you're dancing on her grave. What do you think?'

She was thinking so many things simultaneously. Suzannah's show was entertainment, dramatic, high ratings. It was a huge leap from a piece of investigative journalism in a quiet place in the schedules, late on a weekday night. If she accepted and failed, it could shatter her reputation, her career. She would not be forgiven by any of the bosses in the television industry. There would be no place to hide.

'Can I think about it, please?' she said warily. 'I never dreamed of this. It was so much Suzannah's show. I don't know if I can do it. Can I have a bit of time to make up my mind?'

He was impatient. He was offering her a tremendous chance, any man would jump at it. 'How long do you need?'

'Just till tomorrow. This is such an extraordinary new idea, and I'm still reeling a bit from last night.'

She sounded feeble, even to herself. Jameson looked at her, and his voice softened a little.

'All right, tell me your answer tomorrow morning, first thing. But please don't tell anyone else I've offered it to you. I don't want the news to leak. That would be bad for everyone.'

She agreed, and looked at Shirley. 'But if I fail the press will tear me to bits. So I won't be much good to you, Shirley.'

Shirley nodded. 'I know. And that's why David wanted me to come with him. Of course it's a risk. But I've thought about it, and I think you can do it. More than that, I think you should do it. I certainly don't want you to turn it down out of loyalty to me, or to our show. For what it's worth, I think you should say yes.'

Lucy showed them both to the door, then walked slowly back and sat down on her sofa. What should she do? In her current programme, in spite of its edgy difficult journalism, she was protected, not expected to entertain a huge mass audience. If she took over Suzannah's show the stakes would be completely different. Against her better judgement she felt her vanity twitch. Instead of *Piper's People*, the show would become *Strong on Saturday*, or something along those lines. Surely it would be pompous and self-important to turn it down.

But how would Suzannah have felt, seeing Lucy step into her shoes? Would she have been pleased that her closest friend, the talent she had discovered and nurtured, had been given such a crucial opportunity? Or furious that Lucy was dancing on her grave? If only Jameson had allowed a year to go by, to let the memory fade a little, the loss become less painful. But he needed to fill the gap in his ratings, and he trusted her not to tarnish Suzannah's reputation. Was he right?

Whatever Jameson said about confidentiality, she desperately needed advice, someone independent to talk it over with. Fred was on the road and out of reach. What about Dan Carlton, Suzannah's producer? Suzannah had liked and depended upon him. He was unshockable, relaxed, steady in a crisis. He knew the pressures on the programme. No doubt he would want it to succeed. His advice would be objective.

She rang Suzannah's old office and asked to speak to Dan. He came at once to the phone. 'Dan, I'm sorry to ring you out of the blue, but would you have lunch with me today?' she asked. 'I'll make you an omelette, here at home. I need your advice.'

He heard the tremor in her voice, he knew how close she and Suzannah had been. Something had happened she wasn't prepared to tell him over the phone. 'Yes, of course. I'd be glad to.'

She drank her coffee, trying to get used to the new world she was living in. No need to brush up her CV. Jameson was offering her the moon and stars. And yet, and yet . . .

She went to her study, and decided to read the e-mails from her production team. That would give her a sense of reality. Last night's programme had stirred things up as she had hoped. The researchers had sent her excited messages. Two MPs were going to table questions about the school. The Secretary of State for Health's office had asked for their evidence. One of the paedophile teachers had moved to another school, and parents there were up in arms.

Shirley wrote, 'Would you believe, they're not attacking him, just criticizing us? A mother left a message on our voice-mail saying, "He is the best teacher my son's ever had. Nobody has ever taught him so well, with such enthusiasm and dedication. Your research must be wrong."'

If only it was, Lucy thought. But that was often the way. Paedophiles were inevitably drawn to careers that brought them into close contact with children, and to avoid being discovered they perfected different methods of entrapment, some through seduction, some by intimidation. This teacher had obviously wormed his way into the parents' confidence. No wonder they had been shattered to see the programme, their shock mixed with guilt at never having suspected him.

Most interesting of all, a young man, who gave his name as 'Max' had left a message on her phone. His voice was hoarse and breathless, as if simply leaving a message was an ordeal for him. 'Your programme only knows the half of it. It's not just the school. There's more, a lot more. I'll talk to Lucy. Nobody else.' 'Max' had left his number, and said she must ring at six thirty that evening. She'd think about it. Sometimes callers who demanded only to speak to her turned out to be persistent nuts, who refused to be shaken off. But sometimes they proved to be vital leads to an explosive story. She took the number down, and stuck the Post-it to her fridge where she could not ignore it.

Meanwhile, there was a big decision to make in her own life. She set the kitchen table for lunch, made a green salad with a sweet vinaigrette, pulled out some creamy blue dolcelatte cheese and a crusty loaf. She liked making omelettes, light and fluffy on the outside, still with a hint of moisture in the centre. She cherished her omelette pan, and kept it shiny and clean with olive oil.

At half-past twelve the doorbell rang again.

Dan arrived, and it was comforting to see him. As he stood on the doorstep, he had none of the tensions, the stress-filled angst of young producers. He had the look of a sailor or an explorer, his eyes blue and drifting to the horizon when he was deep in thought, his smile easy and undemanding, his tanned face looked dried out by the sun and wind. She warmed to the soft Devon burr in his voice. He took her hand and held it sympathetically, Suzannah had been central to both their lives. They kissed the obligatory air-kiss, cheeks brushing, then Lucy led him into the sitting-room and handed him a bottle of red wine and a corkscrew. He filled their glasses, then he looked at her with curiosity.

'How can I help, Lucy? It sounded urgent.'

She turned the glass in her hand, watching the reflections in the red wine tilt and sway. She hated being so indecisive. It made her feel stupid, and childish. She started to explain.

'You know I began in television as a researcher for Suzannah. I went my own way, and ended up doing more investigative stuff. But I always admired her show, the way the team was trained, and the programme was constantly pushing back the barriers. It's as strong as ever with you as producer.'

He smiled, acknowledging the compliment, but waited for her to reach the point.

'David Jameson has just been here to offer me Suzannah's job. I asked him to give me twenty-four hours to make up my mind.'

He sat, frozen. Clearly nobody had talked to him about the possibility.

Embarrassed, she filled the silence. 'You know the show better than anyone, Dan. I've been away from it a long time. My style is so different from hers. I have nothing like her glamour, or her experience. What do you think?'

Still he said nothing.

'I'm sorry to be the one to break it to you, Dan. I thought Jameson would have mentioned it to you.'

Now he showed his irritation. 'Yes, Lucy. I agree. You might well think Jameson would share the idea with me. He hasn't . . .' He paused, and took a breath. 'Not a word of it. Well, that's his prerogative. It's his channel. I don't have to be consulted. But I would have expected the courtesy of a phone call to tell me he was approaching you.'

She tried to soothe him. 'I'm sure it's just that Jameson is paranoid that it will all leak out. He wanted me to make an instant decision there and then. I couldn't, though. Suzannah was such an amazing act to follow. Tell me what you think.'

Dan was still digesting the idea. 'I don't know what to say, Lucy. To be honest, I'm not sure anyone should try to take the show on, the way it was. Suzannah had such a grip on it, she made the programme in her own image. I'm not criticizing her, it was just a fact of life. When I inherited the job the show had been set in stone. I could no more change the format than I could sack the star. So I just tried to keep her and the team happy and working well together.'

His face was rigid, jaw clenched, controlling his emotions. Clearly Suzannah had been a huge part of his life. Losing her must have meant losing a friend, the hub of his career, the most dynamic influence in his life. Lucy tried to comfort him. She knew from the way Suzannah had spoken of him how highly she valued his light touch.

'She always talked about how much she owed you,' Lucy told him. 'It was a successful format, and everyone enjoyed working on it. That showed on the screen. Perhaps I'm mad even to consider taking it on. It would be a poisoned chalice.'

Dan stood up and drained his wine glass. He walked around

her room, lost in thoughts that clearly troubled him. 'I can't advise you, Lucy. I'm too close to it all. I loved Suzannah . . . although not the way you did. And not sexually, of course, but we worked so closely with each other, we depended on each other, respected each other. I couldn't go to her memorial service – I knew it would be ghastly, tacky, and not true to her. And for the same reason it's difficult for me to think of anyone else in her shoes.'

'I know. That's why I asked you. If you think it won't work, it certainly can't. Let's have our food and keep talking. It's the only way I'll ever decide.'

The omelettes were just as she liked them, and Lucy ate hers hungrily while they argued back and forth. Would the public forgive her? Would she get a critical mauling? What kind of show would it become in her hands?

Dan pushed his food around the plate uneaten and refused the bowl of raspberries and blueberries she put beside him. She made him a mug of black coffee and they went together into her sitting room.

She had confided so much to him, against Jameson's wishes. Now she risked an extra indiscretion. 'Dan, I cleared Suzannah's office. Personnel asked me to.'

'I know. Sandra told me.'

'Did you know she had a locked drawer in her desk?'

He glanced sharply at her, startled. 'No.'

'Sandra had the key.'

'She never told me about it.'

'I opened it.'

'What did you find?'

'Just a few letters.'

'Did you read them?'

'Yes.'

'What were they?'

'Some of them were the usual besotted fan stuff. I'm not sure why she kept them. But there were others.'

She went over to her handbag, took them out and gave them to him. 'These really disturbed me, I have to admit. They seem so unbalanced, and so threatening.'

He took them and read them slowly. Then he spread them out on the table in front of them. 'These are horrible,' he said. 'Some people are just sick. I knew Suzannah got crazy letters from time to time, but not threats like these. If I'd known I would certainly have told her to take them to the police.' He stood up and walked to the door. He stopped there, concentrating, evidently working through his memories. Then he said suddenly, 'I do remember now, a couple of letters arrived for her on show days which upset her. I thought they were something personal, maybe about her love life, so I didn't ask her what was in them. She certainly never showed me anything like this. If only she had.'

'She didn't show them to me either – she never mentioned them at all.' Lucy was raking through her own memory now. 'Why didn't she, Dan?' There was guilt in her that she hadn't been able to help Suzannah, or console her.

'Your friend was like that.' He smiled at the thought, and walked back to join Lucy on the sofa. 'So determined to be independent. To be entirely in control. In a way, that was her strength, but in another way it was a weakness. Sometimes we all need a bit of help from our friends.' He put his hand on her arm, and saw that her hands were shaking. 'Can I do anything for you now, Lucy? What do you want to do with these? Take them to the police? Do you want me to take them for you?'

She stared at the scraps of paper on the table, the ugly capital letters: 'BITCH PIPER. . . . YOU PILE OF SHIT . . . YOU'D BETTER TAKE CARE. YOUR TURN WILL COME.' The threats were so brutal, so explicit. What could have provoked such violent hatred? Would the writer turn on her, if she took over the show? They should go to the police. On the other hand it was tempting to destroy them, throw them away, pretend they'd never existed. She hesitated. Then she clasped her hands together, to give herself an illusion of strength she didn't feel. 'Thanks, Dan. It's good of you. Let me think about these a bit.'

She pushed the pieces of paper into a pile in front of her. 'Maybe we're getting worked up about nothing. If Suzannah was alive she might say these are just craziness – some crank who didn't like the colour of her eyes.' Her eyes drifted back to them.

Dan nodded. 'She'd probably call us daft to take them so seriously.' He was trying to cheer her, and she was grateful.

'I must say, it's all we need at the moment, lunatic stuff like this. My life's pretty complicated anyway. I think I may have stirred up a pretty lethal hornets' nest with the programme about Wantage Grange.'

'Has there been much response?'

'Well, yes, parents and politicians up in arms. But those men are still out there, of course, and they may have me in their sights now.'

'Really?' He looked concerned.

'A car nearly hit me last night.' It sounded absurd as she said it, and she wished she'd kept quiet. But he was so calm, so steady, and she needed good advice.

'Tell me what happened.'

She described the huddle of reporters breaking up and going their different ways; the dark, cold night; the flick of headlights at the end of the street. And then the sudden danger as the car hurtled straight at her.

He looked at her, worry in his eyes. 'How do you feel about that, in the cold light of day? Do you still think it was deliberate, that someone was trying to hurt you? If so, you must tell the police.'

It sounded ridiculous, in the mundane reality of her own kitchen.

'No, not really. I think it was some kid with a car too powerful for him.' But much as her head told her that must be the answer, her memory said no. The street was wide enough for

64

that car to have come nowhere near her. It was more than just chance, more than a kid making a misjudgement. Instinctively, she believed she was the target. But if she said so to Dan, he would think she was on the edge of insanity. Nobody would want to employ a woman who jumped at every shadow. She must keep her fears to herself.

He leaned back in the sofa. 'Thank you for talking to me so frankly,' he said at last. 'And please don't think I'm not keen to work with you just because we've wrestled with the idea a bit. The crucial thing is for you to be sure in your own mind that it's worth it for you. After all, you've achieved a hell of a lot in your own show, and that's a great deal to throw away. But if you decide you want to do it, you know you can depend on me, just as Suzannah did. Now I've got used to the idea, I like it, you know. I think you'll bring a different kind of strength to the job, which could refresh the format and bring us some new viewers.'

Is that what she wanted him to say? She still wasn't sure. Had she the talent to carry it off? Dan said she had, but did he mean it? She looked into his eyes to make sure that he wasn't simply saying what he thought she wanted to hear. He looked back without evading her gaze.

'Well, Dan, if you think I can do it, that gives me confidence,' she said. 'You were so close to Suzannah, you understood her so well.' She paused. 'Maybe her spirit will be with us. Thank you for coming. I'm more grateful than I can say.'

He relaxed, and smiled back at her. 'Let me know what you decide, I'd rather not be the last to find out.'

She started to apologize, but he interrupted. 'I know, I know. It wasn't your fault Jameson decided to be so secretive.' He pushed the chair back. 'I'd better get back to the team and make some excuse for being out so long. Christmas shopping, that'll do. It'll be exciting if you do decide to take the job. When the news breaks, our phones will be red hot.'

At the door he turned, and said, 'By the way, I enjoyed your interview in the *Dispatch*. Bless you for setting the record straight. Most people would run scared; they wouldn't dare put the blame where it should be. But I know how the sniping, the lack of support from above, exhausted her. As you said, she must have been under huge stress that night to have driven when she was far too tired.'

Lucy looked back to her peaceful house. There, like scraps of torn flesh, the anonymous letters lay where she had left them. 'You don't think there is some connection with those horrible notes, do you, Dan?'

'How could there be?'

'Well,' as she spoke, she felt foolishly dramatic, 'they do threaten to kill her.'

'But her death was an accident.' He looked genuinely puzzled.

'Yes, I know. The police have crawled all over her car. There was nothing wrong with it, and no other car was involved. I realize all that. But the threats are so vicious, the hatred is so intense, I wondered whether they could have depressed her more than either of us realized. They say a lot of car accidents are really deliberate acts of suicide, disguised to protect families and friends.'

Dan looked appalled at the idea. 'I can't believe she'd do that. No, Suzannah wasn't suicidal. She was a fighter. No matter how tough things got she would always battle on. The police think she was just exhausted after a heavy show, lost control of the car on a greasy road, and there was a tragic accident.'

Lucy nodded, and they exchanged air-kisses again, this time their cheeks edging a little closer to each other. After all, it looked as if their lives might be very closely entwined from now on. Then, after the door closed behind him, she went back to the scraps of paper, and pushed them deep into her handbag again, avoiding reading them. They were unfinished business, still.

The afternoon passed slowly, Lucy not answering the telephone and ignoring the fax. Everything could wait. She replied to her fan mail mechanically, sending out recipes for charity booklets, and signing photographs for autograph hunters. The note on the fridge reminded her of 'Max's' deadline. She knew she had to make the phone call. No journalist could have resisted it.

At six thirty precisely she rang the number. After four rings it was answered, and she could hear traffic in the background.

'Max?' she said.

'Yes.' He recognized her voice. 'Oh . . . hello. I don't know if you can handle this, but I was one of the boys Trevor Whitestone abused. What you said on the show? You were right. There was a ring of them. Once he'd got us, he'd pass us round.'

'Do you mean a ring of teachers in the school?'

'No, that's the point. Not just in the school. There were others outside. Some of them well known. Very well known. Some of them very powerful.'

Could she believe all this?

He heard her hesitate. 'Look, this is dangerous for me,' he said. 'If you don't want to know tell me now, and that's it.'

She couldn't let him go. She thought rapidly. 'What do you want to do next? Can we meet?'

'I'll be at the Fleet service station on the M3 heading west at eight tomorrow night. I'll meet you there. Just park your car in the car park and I'll find you.'

She breathed in to reply, then heard a click and the line went dead. It was bloody inconvenient, but she'd have to go. She had no choice.

She glanced at Fred's filming itinerary pinned on the kitchen notice board. He had finished filming at six. It was twenty to seven now. She rang his room, and he was there, having a shower. It took a moment for him to answer and when he did, he laughed.

'How did you know that would be just the moment I was soaking wet. Are you OK, darling? I'm worried about you.'

'Don't be.' It was a relief to hear his voice, lively and loving. It made everything normal again. 'How was your day?' she asked.

He groaned. 'Just what you'd imagine. As soon as we started filming it began to rain. God, it was freezing. I think we may have given the kid pneumonia. But he was great, running up and down the lanes and over the fields. We've got some fabulous moody shots, on the skyline, against the clouds. How was yours?'

'It was very strange. Jameson arrived with Shirley. I thought they were going to play good cop, bad cop, but it turns out they were offering me Suzannah's show.'

'God. That's amazing. What did they say?'

'Jameson said I had to make up my mind quickly. And I'm not supposed to tell anyone.'

'You could have told me. I'm nobody.'

'Aaaah.' She mocked his affectation of humility. 'Anyway, you were away. I didn't know what to do. I definitely needed some advice. So I asked Dan Carlton over to talk about it.'

'OK.' Fred was still adjusting to the idea. 'And he said what?'

'Well . . . it's hard to know what he really thought. I think he may have been a bit in love with Suzannah.'

'Seriously?' Fred was amused.

'No. Not seriously. And maybe he doesn't realize it himself. But she was obviously very important to him. And I know she liked him. She always said he was good at his job.'

'What did he think of the job offer? What do you think of it, more to the point?'

'Oh, I don't know, Fred.' It really didn't feel as if things were any clearer to her even now. 'Dan refused to make the decision for me, he just said he'd support me if I took it. What do you think I should do?'

Fred's voice was suddenly harsh. 'You don't need this, Lucy.' His reaction dismayed her. She stayed silent to let him carry on, curious to see where he was going. 'Even if it means you get the star treatment, it'll push you right out there where everyone can take a pop at you. Do you really want the intrusion, the gossip columns poking into your private life? Frankly, we don't need that. And your own show's doing fantastically well. Let Naomi take over from Suzannah, for heaven's sake. She'd lap it up. You're a proper journalist. Say no to Jameson.'

She felt her heart sink. She was disappointed by his reaction. Even with the doubts, the dangers, she realized that she had wanted him to tell her to do it, to take on the challenge, to become a bigger, brighter star.

He talked as if it would be simple to turn down the offer, but he had no idea how difficult it would be. Lucy had seen what happened when people rejected the controller's ideas. Gradually they were banished to the edges of the schedule. Their budgets were whittled away. And, in any case, she wasn't sure she wanted to turn down such a big chance, just to protect her private life.

'I'll sleep on it, Fred,' she said at last. And then, so as not to leave him on a sour note, 'Let's talk again in the morning. I miss you.'

'I miss you too, darling. And I'm sorry, I don't want to be selfish. But I've got to tell you what I think.' There was silence between them now, and a new distance. Fred broke it first. 'Let's speak again soon, darling. Sleep well.'

He put the phone down, and went back to the bathroom. He'd better hurry now. Prue, the researcher, was waiting for him at the bar.

All evening Lucy went through what he'd said in her mind. How much machismo was there in it? She was thirty-two, he was only twenty-four. She outranked him in experience, status and income. If she took on the new show, there would be an even greater imbalance between them. If they were outed as a couple, he would be derided by the gossip columnists as her toy-boy, her handbag holder. How much did that knowledge prejudice his response? Jameson thought she should do it. Shirley thought she could. Dan eventually thought she might be able to. Given all their advice, she would be mad to turn it down. But what would she be giving up? What about 'Max'? Could she really continue a complicated investigation while she was fronting the Saturday night show? Tackling a paedophile ring was hardly entertaining material for a glitzy, buzzy show. But if Saturday was a success, maybe Jameson would let her make a special spin-off weekday programme about the paedophile ring. If anything ever came of the story. But these investigations were so tricky, as she knew to her cost. 'Max' could not be the basis for her decision.

She sat up late into the night, staring at the television without pleasure, numbing her brain with the midnight schedule of lurid American talk shows and cheap quizzes.

In his Norfolk hotel, Fred was also awake in bed, watching the soft-porn channels with Prue alongside him, and putting into practice what they learned. He was happily guilt-free. 'What goes on location, stays on location.'

The radio alarm clicked on in Lucy's bedroom at seven. She sat up, her brain instantly clear and her mind made up. She would do it.

She went down to the kitchen, put on the kettle, and wandered through to her study. Suzannah smiled at her from the photographs on her desk. She could hear her voice in her head. 'Go for it, Lucy. I'll be alongside you.' She took her cup of coffee to her computer and put an e-mail together for Jameson. 'Thank you so much for the offer. I'm very flattered, but slightly nervous because I really want to justify your confidence in me. I've decided to accept. I'm happy to make a statement if the Press Office want me to. They can say I was a close friend of Suzannah's and I'll do my best to live up to the example she set, but that she was a very hard act to follow.'

That much was easy. The difficult call was to Fred. She caught him just as he was heading out of the door. 'Fred, darling. I have thought through everything you said. I know in many ways you're right.'

'Am I?' The sarcasm showed he could tell she didn't mean it.

She rushed on, trying to placate him, to make him see that this was an offer she couldn't have refused. 'Purely practically, Fred, I don't see how I could have turned it down. Jameson would never forgive me. Even if he pretended to, it would alienate him for ever.'

'He'd get over it.' She hadn't convinced him.

All right, try another tack. 'Anyway, I'm not sure I could live with myself if I wimped out on a chance like this.' He might not like that, but it was honest.

There was no time to argue, and in any case he could hear from her voice that her mind was made up. 'That's fine, Lucy. It had to be your decision.' His tone was flat, he was obviously disappointed, but he tried his best to disguise it. 'You know I wish you all the luck in the world with it. I was probably being selfish last night, and let's hope I was wrong. As long as you enjoy it, and do it well. And in any case, as we always say, it's only television.'

She laughed, relieved to hear the warmth in his voice again. They really needed to be together, to be able to put their arms around each other.

She shivered. She was leaving the shores she knew, heading out into choppy waters. What would happen if she failed? She would need an iron-clad contract. Perhaps it was time to take on an agent. She'd never needed one before, but it might be a buffer, a protection, a life-belt in these new, uncharted oceans. What about Suzannah's agent, Mandy? She was shrewd, avaricious, a great negotiator, and completely tasteless. But she was streetwise, and Suzannah had managed to curb her worst excesses while she was alive.

Lucy rang Mandy's agency. Cutting through the forest of assistants and deputies, the older woman came straight to the phone.

'Yes, Lucy. How can I help?'

'Mandy, I may need you. I've just been made a very big offer.'

Mandy asked no more questions. Face to face was better. 'The Ivy, lunch today?' she suggested. Lucy was just famous enough to guarantee a table, and there was no better place to celebrate, if the offer was as good as Lucy said.

Lucy agreed, and went to find a suit that would be appropriate for the Ivy, and the paparazzi who took up permanent residence outside the door. Soft red suede looked right. The well-cut trousers flattered her, the soft jacket curved with her, hiding the extra curves she vowed to lose one day. She smiled at herself, and saw how the new challenge had lifted the corners of her mouth and added sparkle to her eyes.

Mentally she pleaded with Suzannah, 'Stay with me, girl. I'm walking in your footsteps now.'

The Ivy was packed, as usual. A mixed crop of television presenters devoured warm duck salad and fish cakes, chattering away together, but constantly swivelling their eyes to check whether someone with commissioning power had come in. A couple of actors, a dozen producers, waved excitedly to each other. Who cared if they had just turned down each other's cherished projects, or sacked the star at the next table. In the Ivy they were all each other's dearest friends.

Mandy was already waiting for her, a glass of champagne at her side. As usual, her hands were clattering with diamonds. She wore a black sequinned cardigan, and had a large Dolce & Gabbana handbag at her side. Nobody could be in any doubt that she and her clients were doing very well indeed. She got up to kiss Lucy, and they sat down together.

'What a remarkable memorial service,' Lucy said. It was true after all, and Mandy took it as a compliment.

'Yes, wasn't it? I loved to see all those bastards who made Suzannah's life such a misery forced to weep into their hankies. Hypocrites. But don't think it's just BriTV – it's the same everywhere. They're all running scared of this brave new world, with so many channels chasing so little money. They're so desperate for ratings, they'd cook their own grandmother in oil live on air to get a bigger audience. Now, tell me about this new big offer.'

Lucy dropped her voice. The envied secret of the Ivy dining room was that although everyone could see and be seen, nobody could overhear what was being said at each table.

'I don't know how to say this, Mandy, or how you'll feel about it, but they want to give me Suzannah's show.'

Mandy's face was expressionless as she absorbed the news. Nobody could have been more protective of Suzannah while she lived, but things move on. The queen of television is dead, long live the new queen.

'That's very interesting. It would be a big challenge for you,' she said quietly. 'But you know, I think they may be right. You're different from her, you'd bring a different style to the show. I think it might well work. I'll be happy to negotiate for you, for my usual fifteen per cent. But it's a career risk for you, so I hope they're talking good money.'

'I haven't asked.'

'Quite right.' She briskly buttered the roll beside her, and took a very large bite out of it. Talk of money always made her hungry. 'Let me sort out the business side, Lucy, so you can stay sweet and above such sordid things. I'll keep you informed. Let me order you some champagne. You deserve it.'

They sorted their way through the menu, ending with the Ivy's legendary frozen berries in white chocolate sauce. The chocolate poured over the raspberries and then hardened on the icy plate. It was a delicious conjuring trick. Lucy hoped she wouldn't get too used to this life style. She'd already grown perilously used to comfort. The glamour of the new job might become addictive, and that would be more dangerous still. Television was littered with the sad relics of yesterday's stars.

They talked together about the heroes and villains of the industry, and then, inevitably, shared their favourite memories of Suzannah.

'The thing is,' Lucy said slowly, 'that she was so vibrantly alive, not a moment of her life was wasted. Obviously she was no saint – she made enemies, mainly because she never minced

73

her words – but I feel bereft without her. I can't believe I'm never going to get one of her midnight phone calls, the last-minute daft arrangements to go to Paris with her for lunch, or a matinée of the latest, newest musical. It's going to be eerie to walk into her office, talk to her team, and know they must be comparing me every second of the day with the way Suzannah would have done it.'

'Don't think about it,' Mandy advised her. 'I know she died far too young. In many ways she was at her peak, still glamorous, though I had suggested to her that a bit of Botox around the eyes might have been sensible.' Lord, what would Lucy be taking on? Mandy carried on scraping her plate to make sure every drop of chocolate sauce had been garnered in.

'But even if Suzannah had lived, things would have changed. She would have had to move on one day, and that team would either have broken up, or found another presenter. It's probably easier for them to know that you were Suzannah's protégée, and that she will be rooting for you in heaven. I miss her too.' She gave her spoon one final lick. 'Every moment. She was a tremendous life-force.'

'Dan Carlton was saying that yesterday. I asked his advice before I accepted the job. I felt I had to. We talked about the way she died, the accident. I asked him if he thought it could possibly have been more than that.' She paused, uncertain whether to go on. 'I suggested suicide.'

Mandy looked aghast. 'What made you think of that?'

Should she mention the vile notes, still tucked deep inside her handbag? Better not. 'I don't know,' Lucy said. 'Suzannah was usually so confident and competent at the wheel. I know she was tired that night, and the road was greasy. But why was she going to the country, anyway? Wouldn't it have been more sensible to spend the night in town? I suddenly wondered whether she had intended to die, and make it look like an accident.'

'Then stop wondering.' Mandy sounded shocked, almost angry. 'I've never met anyone less suicidal than Suzannah.

Whatever obstacles came her way, and there were plenty in her life, she was determined to overcome them. She never let anything get to her. She was constantly optimistic. Even when she split with Boris, with all the public nastiness, she just refused to read what they wrote about her. Specially your friend Janet Lake. And may I just say, as your agent now, be careful of Janet. She's built her reputation on other people's wrecked careers; she has that soft manner which makes you think she's on your side, but she isn't. She's using you, never forget that.'

Lucy's mind went back to the interview with Janet. To be honest, they had been using each other. She remembered the catharsis she had felt, unbottling her rage, knowing it was unwise, but feeling nothing but huge relief.

'Mind you,' said Mandy, following her own train of thought, 'I was surprised Suzannah would take the risk of driving that night. I was at her show that evening. She was exhausted, but she was still the last to leave hospitality. I told her to take a driver, I even offered her a bed in my flat in town, but she said she wanted to go to the cottage. I wish I'd argued with her, but there you are. I didn't, and she died.'

Lucy thought of Suzannah's 'cottage' – not the most accurate description of the twenty-acre estate, the indoor swimming pool, the elegant terraces studded with eighteenth-century fish ponds, the house itself: fifteenth-century with beautiful black wood beams inside and out. It was, to be accurate, more of a manor-house than a cottage. Suzannah had loved it, filled it with light and flowers, and invited colleagues and lovers to stay and revel in the romantic bedrooms, the chintz and four-posters.

Maybe there had been a secret lover waiting for her that night. Perhaps that's why she had driven so fast and hard through the rain. Lucy kept those thoughts to herself.

The meal over, Mandy paid the bill and the waiter fetched her heavy raincoat lined with sable from the cloakroom.

She looked disapprovingly at the plain dark red suit Lucy was so proud of, and her simple black overcoat, and said, 'In future we'll do better than that. I'll be on the phone to Jameson as soon as I get back to the office. We'll make sure you're treated like the star you are, with a generous wardrobe allowance, a chauffeur-driven car on programme day. Anything else you want?'

'A good programme,' Lucy said. 'Nothing else matters. The biggest star in the world can't survive a lousy show.' She took one last look around the restaurant, the conversations rising noisily on fumes of alcohol, and felt a moment of unease. Did she really want the full star treatment that came with Suzannah's programme, in a new and different world, one where Mandy was used to battling? Where your value is always equated with the price someone is prepared to pay for you? Where greed is so endemic that, however big your salary is, someone else is always just that infuriating bit richer?

Maybe jealousy had fuelled the loathing in the notes still concealed in Lucy's handbag. Rain was falling as she stood in the doorway, watching Mandy negotiate for a taxi. She felt stronger with this woman by her side, but as they parted she knew that Mandy couldn't protect her from the worst dangers ahead. She'd just have to save herself.

CHAPTER FIVE

Lucy hated driving at night. Even in high summer, when the sky held on to its pale glow far later, it was an ordeal. In winter, when the world narrowed down to dark streams of traffic scurrying along the motorway, she lost any sense of kinship with the other drivers. Instead their cars closed around them and they became like reptiles, steely carapaces with head-lamp eyes, swerving towards her on every bend in the road, then dashing past and leaving behind them a river of darkness. It was stupid, she knew. The stretch of motorway between Twickenham in West London, and the Fleet service station was suburban and familiar. By day she didn't give it a second thought. At night she concentrated fiercely, and longed for the journey to end.

But tonight distracting thoughts kept attacking her concentration. Flashes of fear made her jump. Alone in the darkness, and against her will, she had to recognize that she was afraid.

She found herself talking aloud. 'Stay calm, Lucy. This isn't like you. You've driven alone before. You can do this.'

But it wasn't the burden of driving by herself through the night that was throwing her mind off balance, there was more, far more. Suzannah's letters kept coming back into her mind, with their cargo of searing, crazy hatred. Then the dread that by taking on Suzannah's show she was putting herself into the frame, and she might become their target.

She reached a roundabout, and as a car moved in front and across her, it brought with it once again the memory of the car that had so nearly hit her. Odd, that: the coincidence that she had survived one car, but another had so recently crushed the life out of Suzannah. Against her will, her mind began to spin a web, twisting strands together to create an assassin's noose.

77

Suppose Suzannah's death had not been an accident. If there was some way of causing her crash that left no trace for the police to find, maybe it was the work of the man who wrote those lurid hate-letters, a lonely maniac perhaps, fixated on women presenters. She thought back to the threat she had read in Suzannah's office, ' YOUR TURN WILL COME . . .' Was it her own turn now?

The car park at Fleet was half full, and she saw the tawdry, cheerful lights with relief, pulled in and prepared to wait. Now at last she could focus on the reason she was here. She had decided she would stay for half an hour. If Max hadn't arrived by then, she'd drive home again. Part of her wanted him not to materialize. Part of her knew that the car that came at her out of the darkness might have been a warning from ruthless men intent on silencing her. Well, if so, it had had the opposite effect.

Lucy checked the tape recorder in her glove compartment, and the notebook in her bag. Fred knew exactly where she was. She'd left a note on their notice board, and her mobile phone was fully charged. If Max's call was a hoax, designed to draw her out into the darkness alone, she had taken care not to leave herself vulnerable. Maybe she was about to confront something vicious or violent. But her instinct was still to believe Max.

Twenty-five minutes went by, cars drove in and out of the car park, weary families walked into the service station, cramped, crumpled and hungry. If the Seven Dwarfs had been drivers, those would have been good names for them. Idly she invented a few more. Sweaty, Dreary, Rumpled, Weary. She looked at her watch. It was almost eight thirty, and she realized she was relieved that Max still had not appeared. She'd grab a cup of coffee and a burger from the service station, then drive home.

She opened her bag to find her purse. At that moment a loud bang on the passenger window made her jump. She turned with an intake of breath, and a young man opened the passenger door and slid in beside her. He was around twenty, with unkempt blond hair, thick with gel, and he wore the uniform of his generation – faded jeans, T-shirt with a torn neck, black haversack. He was smoking, and he looked as nervous as she was.

She steadied herself, smiled at him, and was comforted to hear that her own voice sounded casual and friendly in her ears.

'You're Max, I hope.'

'Yes. I know who you are. I've been watching just to be sure you were alone.'

'I am. But you must understand, Max, although I'm here by myself tonight, it can't stay like this. If we decide to investigate your story, whatever it is, we'll have to put another researcher on it. I can't work with you alone.'

Max shifted in his seat, not meeting her eyes. His voice was gruff. 'In that case, no deal. I'll talk to you, or nobody. This is dangerous stuff. The people I'm talking about have their own friends. They've probably got friends inside your company. If word gets out anywhere they'll try and stop you. And they'll shut me up. They won't mind how they do it.'

It sounded melodramatic, but she couldn't contradict him: that would only frighten him off. Best not to confront him at all. She nodded. 'OK, Max, let's talk about all that at a later stage, when we know what the story is. Do you mind if I take notes?'

He shook his head, and she opened her notebook. She didn't dare suggest the tape recorder. That would certainly silence him.

'Right. You said on your message to me that the school was part of a ring.'

'Yes.' He was hesitant, but he forced himself on, as if exorcizing the memories that haunted him. 'They needed boys. That shit Whitestone got them. He was the head; he did whatever he liked. He made sure we weren't going to talk, then his friends would come down from London and have their fun.'

'How did he know you wouldn't talk?'

'You saw the methods he used. You found it hard enough to get the kids to talk on your programme.' His mouth was twisted with self-disgust. 'He'd make us do things to each other, while he watched, and he'd film us doing it to the younger boys, so we wouldn't dare say anything.'

Lucy shook her head incredulously. No wonder these kids were so deeply scarred.

'He told us if we ever tried to tell, he'd say we'd done it to each other. He said no one would ever believe us anyway. The bigger the names he got involved, the less anyone would believe us.'

Lucy paused in her note-taking. 'Were they big names?'

'The biggest.'

'Show business?'

'Bigger.'

'Politics?'

'Not just politics. The guys who buy the politicians. Millionaires.'

That was bad news. The richer the man, the more legal armoury he could buy. The BriTV lawyers were going to hate this story. Never mind, face that when she came to it.

'Describe what happened to you, Max.'

He did. His father was in the army, so the family were moved to different bases around the country, and sometimes abroad, in Germany and Cyprus. They were delighted when he got into Wantage Grange – it would give his education continuity, and they were impressed by the brochure. They saw him as often as they could, they wrote to him and rang him regularly. But they were out of reach, they never visited the school, and when he wrote letters or spoke to them over the phone he shielded them from the truth.

'I knew it would break my mum up. I couldn't tell them, so I had to deal with it myself. It got to me. I had nightmares every night. I hated what Whitestone was doing to me, and what he made me do to the other boys, but I couldn't think of any way to make him stop. Then he started making me go to his weekend parties. He'd let me smoke and drink.'

'Drugs?'

'Grass. And some of the guys from London were cokeheads. The parties went on all night.'

'How many young people were involved?'

'While I was there? Twenty or thirty.'

'Could you give me their names?'

'I dunno. A few might be safe. They really hated Whitestone. They might talk, and have the sense not to tip him off. But some of them were Whitestone's little pets. They made a lot of money off his friends.'

'Who were his friends?'

'I thought you'd never ask. Paul Wilson, for one.'

Max grinned at her astonishment. Wilson was constantly in the papers. His thick dark eyebrows and slicked-back hair made him instantly recognizable, he was one of the heroes of the news bulletins. He had made huge money manufacturing computers, and bankrolled the opposition party. He knew everyone in the City of London, he was a rough diamond, a bruiser who never lost an argument if he could outshout the other side. He was feared and respected, a married man with three children. This story would be explosive if it was true – and if they could ever transmit it.

'Who else?'

'Plenty of guys who are big in advertising. A couple of police.'

'Senior police?'

'Yes. And Roy Parks.'

This time Lucy couldn't disguise her groan. The ex-Home Secretary, now ennobled as Lord Parks of Shaddleworth. A grey-haired elder statesman, another respectable married man, who stood for law and order, patriotism, and keeping porn off the Internet. He had been stridently vocal during all the cases of child abuse and crimes against children while he was in office.

How could Lucy possibly put together a case against him? It could never stand up on the evidence of a few damaged kids who would be easily minced up in court by a clever defence counsel?

'How will we ever prove it, Max?'

'That's your job. The bad thing is, now you've made the programme about the school, everyone's gone underground. But we're having a reunion tomorrow night in Thritham. One of the boys who left a few years ago lives down there in a b. and b. I've talked to him, he's a mate, and he says you can come down, if you like.'

'OK.' It would be a good start.

He wrote the address down for her, in a small Edwardian seaside resort on the south coast. She asked for his mobile number, but he refused.

'Don't ring me, I'll ring you.'

'OK.' She gave him her mobile number. Then she grasped the nettle, there was no avoiding it. 'I'll certainly come to the party – that's crucial. I need to meet the boys myself – but I've got to bring someone with me, Max. I'm going to have to corroborate what they tell me, and investigate it properly. I really can't do all this on my own.'

'No,' he said flatly. He leaned forward as if to open the car door. 'I told you, that's not on. I trust you. Nobody else.'

Lucy thought through all the members of her investigative team. They were good at their work and they were sensitive enough to handle this – after all, they'd put together the original investigation into Wantage Grange. But she wasn't sure what they would be doing now that she had jumped ship. They might well be moved on to other shows. What about the new show? She didn't know those researchers at all. Who else was there?

'Here's a thought,' she said suddenly. 'What about my ex-husband, Tom? He's a lawyer. He knows the problems with a story like this. He's used to hearing confidential stuff. You needn't worry, he won't tell anyone. He also understands the business

82

I'm in, and he can ask the right questions. And he's worked on a lot of child abuse cases as a lawyer. What do you think?'

Max was silent, working it out in his mind, calculating the risk.

'It's really not negotiable, Max. This is such a big story, we've got to get it right. We mustn't put a foot wrong. Even asking the wrong question at the wrong moment might wreck the whole thing. That's why I think Tom would be the right person.'

Max still looked unsure, his face closed against her.

'You have to see, Max, that I can't possibly handle this alone.'

At last he nodded, slowly. 'I suppose he'll do. But nobody else. The more people we tell, the easier it'll be for them to find out and shut us up.'

'Look, I do understand that,' she said. 'That's why I'm suggesting Tom. I need another brain working on this alongside me. It's going to be extremely tough.'

Max grinned suddenly, triumphant at the effect he'd had on her. 'It's the biggest story you'll ever do.' Then he opened the car door and was gone.

Lucy stayed in the car another five minutes, then she got out and walked to the service station to get herself the hot coffee and burger she had promised herself. As she walked she saw another car in the same row flick its lights on and drive towards her, then swerve away. Her heart leaped. How stupid. Max's paranoia must be infectious, she thought, and then, but just because I'm paranoid doesn't mean they're not out to get me.

She drove home, deep in thought.

Fred had just arrived, and was brewing himself coffee in the kitchen after a long shoot. As he hugged her, she relaxed in his arms, enjoying the sharp smell of sweat still on him from having lugged his cameras around all day. Pheromones, she thought, mocking herself. We're all slaves to our hormones. Another primitive instinct hit her, the need for warmth, and shelter. She looked gratefully around the kitchen, the bright blue and yellow curtains drawn against the night. It was good to be home and safe.

Fred passed her a mug of coffee and asked her about the meeting with Max. She had only told him that she was going to Fleet, and that Max could either be a very important contact, or just a fantasist. 'Which was he?' Fred asked.

'I'm not sure. But he did arrive when he said he would, and he was believable,' she said. 'But even if everything he told me is true, it'll take a hell of a lot of checking to make his story usable.'

Fred didn't ask her for more details. Instead he amused her with stories from his own day, filming on the Norfolk farm where his child star lived. The child's mother was a frustrated athlete.

'She insisted on me filming her vaulting a farmyard gate. She's fifty if she's a day. I was impressed, it was a bit like watching a grasshopper jump: you're amazed how high they get, but they're not very pretty doing it. She made me nervous. You never know with these talented kids whether they push themselves, or the parents push them into it. Whose ambition is it? Who wants to win the most?'

'Both, I suppose,' she said, absent-mindedly.

Should she tell him she had to ring Tom tonight? Best not. Tom might not agree to go with her tomorrow anyway. She went into her study, and left Fred in the kitchen by the open fridge, picking at cheese and miniature pork pies.

Lucy shut her study door, and dialled Tom's mobile number. It was late, but he was never in bed before midnight. At least that had been true when she knew him. It had been so long since they'd shared each other's lives. Maybe he had a new partner, perhaps a woman would answer. How would she feel then? That would be fine, she told herself. There was no point being jealous of a man she didn't want herself any more, and Tom was always very warm and courteous to Fred. Indeed, he seemed unflatteringly pleased that Fred was in her life now.

Tom answered the phone immediately, but his voice was tired. She told him so.

'Sorry, Lucy, I've been reading briefs all night. We're in the middle of a complicated medical negligence case. How can I help?'

'I've got mixed up in a complicated case too,' she said. 'I rang on the off chance that you might be able to help me with it. I know it's a lot to ask, but I can't think of anyone else with your skill and your understanding.' It sounded overingratiating to her own ears, and to his as well.

'Cut the schmaltz,' he said. 'What do you want me to do?'

'I've got a research trip to make tomorrow, to Thritham on the south coast. It's extremely sensitive.'

Tom was exasperated. 'Come on, Lucy. What are you going to do? Measure Julia Roberts' bra size? What could be that sensitive?'

Why was he mocking her?

'No,' she said sharply. 'It's a little more important than that, or I wouldn't be ringing you at midnight.'

'Sorry, I thought from the news you were deep into show business now.'

'What news?'

'That you're taking over Suzannah's show. I heard it on the radio driving home. Mark Lawson was saying what a mistake it was for you to give up a journalistic show for that load of pap, and I must say I agree with him. I suppose the money must be good.'

Here we go again, she thought. Bickering had become a habit for them.

'I don't know what the money is, I haven't asked. I'm doing it because it's a challenge. There's no bigger slot than Saturday night. And because Jameson has faith in me. And because I'd feel a complete wimp if I turned it down without having a go at it.' She paused for breath and forced herself to calm down. 'But anyway, this investigation isn't for the Saturday show. It arose out of the exposé we did of the paedophile school. There may be more to that than we knew.'

85

'Now that was a good show,' he said. 'I saw that. It was worthwhile and well done. Whether it was worth devoting yourself to it night and day I don't know, but then you have got Fred to keep your bed warm. Or I assume you still have Fred.'

His voice was edgy and sarcastic now. What had got into him? She was far too tired for this. 'Tom, if you'd rather I put the phone down now, that's fine. But please stop attacking me. It's late, I've got a long day tomorrow, and I really do need your help.'

'Go on then, you want me to come with you to Thritham. Why? It's miles away.'

'I know, but there's a reunion of some of the boys from the school at a party there. And I've been told they have a big story to tell. I need you to listen to them. It would be so helpful if you came along to ask them questions, and advise me where I should go next.' Heavens, did he want her to grovel? How much more persuasion could she use?

Although he could hear the urgency in her voice, he was determined to keep his distance. 'I'm not your researcher, Lucy. I'm not your producer. Take one of them.'

'I can't. The boys won't talk to them. It's got to be someone completely discreet, who will keep the whole thing confidential. I suggested taking one of the old team, but Max absolutely turned down that idea. The only deal he would accept was if I took you. I said you'd worked on loads of abuse cases, and knew the field. I also said you knew how to keep a secret. Please, Tom. I can't say any more on the phone, but there are reasons why you're the only person I can trust with this.'

She was pleading with him now. It worked. Against his better judgement his voice softened a little. 'What time does all this happen?'

'We have to be there after nine. We could meet at the Majestic earlier, say around six, maybe spend the night there and drive back at the crack of dawn.'

'Two rooms, of course. I've got to protect my virtue. I know about voracious A-list stars like you. A quiet lawyer like me would get eaten up in one bite.'

She breathed deeply with relief. 'Thank you, Tom. I know how awkward I'm being. But I had nowhere else to turn.'

'Think nothing of it,' he said lightly. 'Everything has its price. I'll find a way to make you pay me back. We'll meet at the hotel, you can brief me there. Goodbye, Lucy.'

She clicked off her telephone, and went upstairs to break the news to Fred. He was waiting for her impatiently, a glass of wine on her bedside table and another on his. Obviously he was not feeling sleepy. She slipped out of her clothes and into bed beside him. He put an arm around her, but she struggled free. 'Fred, I've just been talking to Tom.'

'Oh yes?' He wasn't pleased.

'I had to. I need his expertise on this new story. I'm going away with him on a research trip. Tomorrow. Just for the night.'

'What? Why Tom?'

'Because it's too difficult to do alone. And frankly it's a bit dangerous. I will try and pass it on to the researchers as soon as possible, but right now the boys are so suspicious they'll only let me bring Tom. In fact Max wanted me to come alone.'

He wasn't convinced. 'You're telling me you're going away for the night with your ex-husband, and it's just about work. Come on. He's still got the hots for you.'

'He certainly has not. And I haven't for him. It's over, it's been over for ages. We were always wrong for each other.' Why did he still feel this need for reassurance? 'Fred darling, it's no good if you and I don't trust each other.' She smiled. 'And, for some reason, the only man I fancy at the moment is you.'

He looked into her eyes. Liking what he saw there, he kissed her lightly at first, then more deeply. Then he held her face in his hands. 'All right Lucy. Just this once, and for one night only. But I need convincing that you fancy me.'

She proved it to him, with pleasure.

They woke together the next morning, curled around each

other, and lay entwined for another luxurious five minutes before the radio alarm went off. Then, grumbling sleepily, they started the day.

Once again they were going their separate ways. He was back on location. She was to attend the first production meeting of the new show. A momentous morning. The team would be torn between relief that they were still in work, and anger that she would try to replace Suzannah. At least that was how she would have felt in their place. Perhaps, if she was careful and discreet, she might find out a little more about Suzannah's death – at least discover what mood she had been in that night. Maybe someone on the team knew more than Dan had about the hate mail. If Suzannah had received it for years, if they could tell Lucy that it came from a harmless lunatic, that would annihilate the wild conspiracy theories which had crept out of the darkness, like trolls from under a bridge to frighten her, and then disappeared in the cold light of day.

She decided not to dress like a television star, but a working professional. Suzannah had always been the star, never gave up the glitz, but Lucy decided not to try to compete with the memory of her sharp suits and diamond Rolex watch. She pulled on a pair of jeans – Armani maybe but still jeans – and found a plain blue sweater. She tied a darker blue pashmina round her neck, stuffed a change of underwear and a toothbrush into her briefcase and ran out of the door, calling to Fred to remind him that she would be overnighting in Thritham. He waved to her from the window and she joined the convoys of commuter traffic.

Arriving at the studios, she took the lift up to the office, and suddenly slipped into a time warp. There was the scatter of open-plan desks and word processors, where she had once sat as a researcher. She could see herself as she once had been, excited and grateful at the chance of working in television. Was it still as exciting for them? They looked up as Lucy walked past, and smiled at her. She sat on the corner of a desk, and introduced herself. It might be an idea to try to lance the boil immediately.

'This is very strange for me, coming back here as the presenter,' she said. 'You know, I started as a researcher at that desk in the corner.' Annie, the most junior researcher, was sitting there now. She was tall, very young, with pale blonde hair and translucent skin that blushed easily when she was the focus of attention, as she was now. She had the least popular desk, next to the kitchen, where the bin would finish the day full of banana skins and the crumpled foil of old take-away meals. But if Lucy had progressed from her chair to becoming a presenter, there was hope for Annie. Lucy saw the blush, and hurried to make amends.

'I was terrified. Nothing like as competent as you are. I looked like a bag-lady, I carried around all my notes in plastic carrier bags, and I hated ironing, as you could tell from the state of my clothes. God, I was scared that first day. Suzannah frightened me most of all, not that she intended to. I miss her terribly. You must. She's still very alive to me.' She stopped. Suzannah's personality was everywhere in that office.

'She is to us too,' Marion, one of the senior researchers said. 'I had to find the clips for the tribute we made. That was really tough.'

'Because?' Lucy asked.

'Because it's so hard, watching her on the screen, and knowing she'll never come back into the office again. I still can't believe it.' They all murmured agreement.

'You made a terrific show,' Lucy tried to comfort her.

Marion smiled. 'Well, we had great material to work with. But going back through all her interviews, seeing her put questions no one else would dare ask . . . it made you realize just how much she'll be missed.'

'I know,' Lucy sighed. There was no way she could ever be Suzannah, the team mustn't expect that of her. 'She's irreplaceable.

I'm certainly not going to try and replace her.' Not in their minds, and not on the screen.

Through the night various ideas had slipped in and out of her mind, ways she might be able to put her own imprint on the show. But she knew she must talk them over with Dan first. On cue he appeared from a doorway across the room.

'Welcome,' he said. 'Come into my office and let's talk.'

The room was as spare and masculine as a ship's cabin, with one photograph on the wall: a yacht leaning in front of the wind, on a grey English sea. Lucy sat on a leather chair and looked around her with pleasure. She liked the sparseness. There were wooden pencils on the desk, arranged in a silver tankard, some sailing cup Dan had won, she supposed. Beside them were the tools of his trade – a ruler, some highlighters, a laser pointer, some diagrams he was working on. He was a skilled director and often lectured to the company training courses. There was nothing sentimental about the office, no plants, no other photographs.

'How are you feeling?' he asked her.

'Rather nervous. I don't want to let you all down.'

He smiled reassuringly. 'We probably all feel a bit like that. Have you had any ideas about the show?'

'Yes, a couple. I wonder whether it would be possible for me to bring in some investigative stuff. Not to overwhelm the entertainment side, but just to give it a bit of sharpness. Or do you think that would fight the slot?'

'I'm not sure.' He spoke slowly, trying to visualize the mix. 'It might be a bit uneasy on Saturday night. I'm not sure people really want to be made to think too hard.' He saw the disappointment in her face. 'Well, anyway, why don't we go to the conference room for our meeting, and I'll introduce everyone.'

Sandra, Suzannah's loyal PA, stood up as she came out of the office, and took Lucy's hand. 'I remember your first day,' she said. 'You didn't seem that terrified.'

'Didn't I show it? I tried so hard not to.'

90

'Suzannah knew, of course.' She grinned. 'You were right about the way you looked, as if you'd fallen out of bed and into a haystack.'

That was definitely true.

'But you were a good journalist even then.' Sandra felt she might have been a bit hard on young Lucy. 'Suzannah always said you were. She'd be very pleased you're here.'

That was good to hear. At least she was safely over the first hurdle.

The second was harder. Lucy nerved herself to go into Suzannah's office again. This was difficult. She stood in the middle of the room, and shivered. The air vibrated with memories. She put down her briefcase, sat at the desk and looked around her. The drawers were empty now, but Suzannah's awards were still on the wall, framed, designed to impress. So were the covers of the *Radio Times*, and *TV Times* emblazoned with the famous Piper smile. On the bookshelves were biographies, a *Who's Who*, and files of cuttings. Could she cope with this? She'd moved so far away from the elaborate synthetic construct of stars; their managers, their entourage, their demands and vulnerabilities. Or was she now desperately trying to become a star herself? What a frightening thought. Somehow she had to keep her balance surrounded by all this.

Lucy sighed, and whispered noiselessly to her friend, 'Suzannah, stay with me today. I'll need you.' Then she picked a pad and pen from the desktop and followed the team to the conference room.

Dan introduced them round the table, and Lucy asked each one a question or two, about themselves, the programmes they were proudest of, their most difficult moments. They were self-conscious, but she disarmed them with descriptions of her own embarrassments as a researcher.

'My worst moment was our greatest coup, a royal interview with Lily, the Duchess of Hertford, three months after she married. She'd just brought out a book she wanted to plug. It was pretty boring, but what I didn't realize was that the biggest story of all was right there, under my nose: the Duchess was pregnant. I failed. I didn't brief Suzannah to ask her anything about her plans to start a family. I can still see Lily in my nightmares, fluttering her eyelashes, rambling on about her ghastly book, not a word about her super-efficient womb. Then would you believe she went and announced the baby to the press the day after the show. Suzannah roasted me alive. Rightly, I suppose. Shall we make that a standard question to all our female guests – are you now, or do you intend to be in the near future – pregnant?'

They laughed, and agreed.

'So,' said Dan when they had been round the table and she had been introduced to them all, 'are there any questions you want to ask Lucy?'

They looked at each other.

'Yes,' said Alex, a young man with a shock of dark hair. 'There is something we all want to know. How is your show going to be different from Suzannah's?'

'Good question.' She looked at Dan. He was expressionless, waiting to see how the team would react. 'Although I started here, I've moved into a different kind of journalism now, less show-bizzy. I'd like to carry on with some of that, put a bit of an investigative edge into the show. Not just rely on PR hand-outs. Find out what's really going on behind the hype.'

She waited for a response. They looked down at the table, and at each other, not committing themselves. She tried to reassure them. 'I do realize we're a Saturday night show, we've got to be entertaining. But if there is a way of combining the two, maybe we should try.'

Some of the team looked interested, others looked dubious. Dan moved the discussion on to possible guests for the first show. Lawrence Crabtree, a notorious television chef, was about to start a major new series. He cooked with his shirt undone to the navel, gold chains around his wrists, and flaunting the tightest of tight trousers as he bent over his oven. Gone were the old-fashioned traditional chef whites. There was a grubbiness about him that infuriated the health and safety inspectors in the audience. He shook his long blonde hair over his soufflés, talked non-stop about bringing the romance back into cooking, and horrified established cooks by the way he lingeringly licked his fingers and winked to camera as he rinsed them. Critics called him 'the Liberace of the kitchen', and women viewers loved him. His sex life filled the tabloids. He had only to say that peaches were an aphrodisiac for the greengrocers to run out the next day. His new series would be designed to teach viewers the secrets of the best cooks in the world – the French, the Italian, the Chinese.

Annie read aloud the publicity. 'Crabtree excels himself with a feather-light profiterole wedding cake, roasted oysters, and delicately flavoured lemon chicken, designed, he says for the perfect honeymoon feast.'

They groaned, laughed, and made retching noises.

Lucy cut across them. 'He may be a love-god in the kitchen, but I've been tipped off several times in the past that he takes backhanders. Manufacturers pay him to plug their products. Especially the foil he uses for everything, to wrap around ingredients, and line all his tins. They say he does it for the money. We could pull out some clips from his new show, and get in another chef to talk to him about his recipes. Delia, for instance, or Raymond Blanc.'

That looked promising. Marion pulled out the latest list of films opening that week, and books being published. Lucy tried to summon up interest. After all, this had to be the basis of the show. She knew that most chat was based on a back-scratching deal. Even the shyest, most reclusive star was forced by a standard contract to plug his latest film or book. In return, viewers could scrutinize them in close up, without an actor's life-support system of a script or a disguise. The chat show is a peculiar invention at the best of times – the idea that it is intrinsically

93

entertaining to overhear someone else's conversation. The twin dragons, dullness and chemically induced incoherence, always hover threateningly low. On the other hand, the right mixture can create magic, spontaneous, dangerous and revealing. Every week the production team walked a tightrope as they chose their guests. And this time, it was with Lucy, an untried host. They felt the insecurity, but she felt it most of all.

The discussion over, they expected her to pull her notes together and leave. Instead, she relaxed back in her chair, and looked round the faces. 'Listen,' she started, hesitantly, 'I don't want to embarrass you. But I hadn't seen Suzannah for a month or so when she died. It was stupid – we tried to make dates for lunch or dinner, but our work got in the way. Either she was busy or I was. So I'd love to know, how was she? Was she OK?'

Could she be more explicit? Ask about the letters in the drawer? The silence was heavy, tangible. She could feel their anxiety. Her questions had crossed the barrier from professional to personal. She'd asked enough. She'd better wait and see what they said.

They looked at each other, and then Alex took the lead.

'Suzannah seemed fine to me. There were loads of rumours around that Jameson wasn't happy with the show, but she never seemed worried or upset. Even when Janet Lake had a go at her. Do you think?' He looked round the team.

'She never said anything to me,' Marion agreed. 'Not that she would. She seemed great.'

Lucy looked at Sandra. Sandra was drawing on her notebook, a capital S, embellished with curls and spirals. She felt Lucy's gaze and looked up. 'Yes, that's right, she was on terrific form.'

'How were the viewers responding to the show. Nice phone calls and e-mails on the log? Fan letters?'

That was the closest she dared go. They looked at her, obviously confused by the question, and Dan intervened. 'The researchers wouldn't know. I don't pass the log around, and

Suzannah always dealt with her own post. But yes, everything was going very well.'

'Thank you for that. At least I know she was feeling good. I feel so guilty that I hadn't managed to see her, those last few weeks.'

She got up, and with relief they all followed suit, pushing their papers together and noisily closing their notebooks. Dan and Lucy hung back, then followed them down the corridor to the big open-plan office.

'That went well, I think,' Lucy said.

'Very well.'

'I was impressed with them,' she said. It was true. She liked their energy and determination. She felt optimistic for the first time. They needed the show to succeed, after all. And so did she.

Before Lucy left, Annie quickly filled up a preliminary file for her from the Internet, with profiles of Crabtree. He was known for his flamboyant image, his temper, and for the food he served in his restaurant. It was light, subtle, and perfectly presented. Even his harshest critics admitted that he deserved his Michelin star. Crabtree's was always fully booked, crowded with serious gourmets.

Lucy decided to skip lunch herself, and instead drove slowly down to the coast, taking the small roads, enjoying the winter sunshine slanting across furrowed fields. It was a cold, bright day, so she had deliberately left London several hours early to enjoy the country drive, and then the first glimpse of the Channel. She loved it but it made her restless. Every time she saw the sea it created a hunger in her to cross the horizon, find new worlds.

She drove to the front at Thritham, and checked in at the Majestic. Tom had not arrived yet. She left her key at reception and walked across the lawn to the path along the beach. The wind was sharp, whipping through the tussocks of dried grass and summer's old flower heads. The cold air brought tears to her eyes. She wrapped the coat more tightly around her body and walked for half an hour, head down, thinking about the evening ahead.

Would the boys talk to her? What would she do with the information they gave her? How could she test their stories? Abuse was a secret crime. Even if they had witnessed each other being abused, would that be regarded as tainted evidence, cooked up as revenge? Hurry up, Tom. She needed his legal advice.

The light was failing. A grey layer of cloud stretched out across the skyline, and the sun disappeared behind it, leaving shafts of silver. She turned and walked back, listening to the crash of waves on pebbles, the sound of family holidays when she was a child. The salt smell of seaweed on the wind, an up-turned boat on the shingle – she loved it all. But she was cold to her bones now, and ready for a warm scone and a cup of strong tea in the Majestic's lounge, with its battered, comfortable chairs.

She was sitting by the fireside, reading her files, when she heard Tom arrive at reception and check in. She called to him, and he turned and smiled. She ordered him tea, and a few minutes before it arrived he came down the stairs from his room and sank into the chair opposite her.

'How are you?' he asked.

'I'm all right. I walked along the beach. The air is fantastic. I feel much better for it.'

He looked out of the window, but the last rays of sunlight were long gone, and the sky was dark. 'You always did love the sea.'

There was silence between them. They had spent their honeymoon on Mykonos, in a tiny white villa with a bed facing the sea. They woke each morning to that feast of bright blue and white. The picture flooded Lucy's mind. Did he remember it with the same clarity? If so, it didn't show in his face. His jaw was tight, his dark eyes dull with tiredness.

The tea arrived, a girl with wispy long hair and ugly clumpy shoes brought the tray and put it down clumsily in front of them, rattling the china, overawed to see a television celebrity up close and real. For a moment Lucy wished she had reapplied her make-up and combed the salt wind out of her hair, so as not to wreck the illusion. Never mind. She autographed a paper napkin for the waitress.

Tom leaned forward, grabbed a tomato sandwich and wolfed it down. Then he lay back in his chair, his eyes closed.

'Lord, I needed this,' he said. Clearly the case he was working on was not getting any easier. 'Now,' he opened his eyes again and straightened himself in the chair, 'brief me about tonight.'

She told him, very quietly, what Max had said to her. Tom drank the strong tea she had poured for him, and didn't interrupt her. There was nobody else in the lounge, but still she dropped her voice so that he had to lean forward to hear her. As she named names, he looked more and more appalled. At last she came to an end, and he said, 'It almost doesn't matter whether it's true or not, it'll be impossible for you to broadcast all that. They'll sue you for millions.'

She was irritated. 'Of course I know the risks, Tom. I understand that. But if we don't take these boys seriously, we'll be colluding with their abusers. I can't just reject them without listening to them.'

'OK, listen, but be careful. Don't get carried away. Don't turn this into a personal crusade. There's nothing more dangerous.'

He was patronizing her. Her irritation grew and he saw it and changed the subject. 'Tell me how you are, really.'

'I told you, I'm fine. Fred and I are getting along well. It's an uncomplicated relationship.' Not like theirs. She left it unsaid, but Tom understood.

'That's good. And the family?' She told him. Her mother and father contented in their retirement. Her brother working in Australia.

In return Tom told her his news. He was working on the case of a child, damaged at birth, a hospital cover-up, the family extremely hard up, and desperate to know how to help their toddler. As always, Tom was absorbed by the family's need to discover the truth. As he finished describing it, Lucy stared into the fire, watching glow-worms of flame eat along the edges of the charred logs. This was how she respected him the most. She relaxed, her irritation soothed.

They planned the evening. They would have supper in one of the little fish restaurants along the seafront. The fish would be fresh, and if the owner recognized Lucy, he might make sure that the frying oil was fresh too. It would be fun, and they needn't rush the meal. They weren't expected at the party until well after nine.

They went to their separate rooms, and Lucy drew herself a bath. Luckily she had brought her own honeysuckle bath essence. The hotel had supplied a sachet of something green, which smelled of disinfectant. The jeans and sweater would be fine for the evening, so she lay on her bed and watched the satellite news bulletins, repeating each other round and round every fifteen minutes.

Paul Wilson was in the news again, at the head of a giant City merger. The Sky commentator was unimpressed by Wilson's style. 'He's not popular in the City, but there's no doubt he's a big player, and respected on the international stage.' Lucy watched him blustering outside a huge mirrored building in the City. With his high colour, his heavy jaw, and opulent leather jacket, he looked powerful and confident. She tried to visualize him at the parties Max had described, seedy and sordid. She grimaced, and switched the set off.

She took her coat off its hanger; it still smelled of the salt wind that had pierced it. She wrapped it around her, and rang Tom. They agreed to meet at reception.

They walked parallel to the beach, the waves a dim pale line catching the light from the streetlamps. They chose a fish-and-chip shop halfway along the front, and the owner recognized Lucy and was delighted to see her. As she had hoped, the fish was straight out of the sea that day, cooked in hot crisp batter. They ate it with lashings of ketchup, chips heaped on the side of the plate, sprinkled generously with salt and vinegar. With the cold sea air still in their lungs, they were hungry. Lucy watched as the energy and humour came back into Tom's face.

They ate in companionable silence. Then, 'When did we first have fish and chips together?' Lucy asked him, taking a risk. It was important to make a long leap back past the last few months of their marriage, which had been a minefield strewn with explosive rows.

Tom's eyes were reflective. 'Wasn't it in the West of Ireland? Maybe in County Kerry. I remember hot sun, and us sitting on the rocks watching the fishing boats. We'd been mackerel fishing ourselves, and we caught lines full, but you kept taking pity on them and throwing them back, so we had to buy fish and chips instead.'

They'd spent the day exploring tiny villages along the coast, taking shelter from the frequent showers in small bars.

'The time seemed to go at a lovely, slow, human pace then,' she remembered.

'We certainly had time for each other,' he said.

Dangerous ground. Time to move on.

'Tom,' she said. 'I've found something else.'

He knew that tone. There was real concern in her voice. 'Tell me.'

'I found some letters in Suzannah's office. They're nasty.'

'How nasty?'

She reached for her handbag, and got them from the side pocket, then passed them over the table to him. He read them quietly, and looked up at her.

'Who could possibly have hated Suzannah so much?' she asked.

He began to speak, stopped, then started again. 'Lucy, I don't know how to answer that.'

'Why?' She didn't understand. 'Why don't you know?'

'Because . . .' He put his hand across the table and took hers. 'Because, Lucy, you saw a different Suzannah from the rest of the world.'

She moved her hand away. 'How? What do you mean?'

'I mean you were her closest friend. Maybe her only friend. Did you see many others at her memorial service?'

She thought back. Plenty of colleagues, plenty of faces who went there to be noticed, hundreds of acquaintances. But friends?

He saw her remembering, the pain in her eyes at her own disloyalty as she wondered if he could be right. 'Lucy, your friend was a very complicated woman. She showed you her best side. You were very valuable to her, she couldn't afford to lose you. But how did she treat her ex-husband? How did she treat her own daughter?'

'Tom, that's unfair. She worked her backside off, she hadn't time—'

'Who was she working for? For the greater glory of Suzannah. No one else. She was a clever woman, a talented woman, and a deeply self-centred woman. Everyone else existed to prop her up, you included.'

Lucy was angry now. 'Tom, you never understood her. You hate the television industry, I know that. You always hated my work. Now you're transferring that to Suzannah. These letters are mad.' She took them from him and pushed them down deep into her handbag. 'They're crazy. I just wanted you to tell me whether you thought they could be more than crazy, if perhaps someone had tried to kill her the night she died.' She saw the disbelief in his eyes. 'I don't know how they could have done it. I just wondered if you thought it was possible.'

'And I'm telling you that your friend Suzannah had many, many enemies. Nobody who'd want to kill her, but people she'd used and discarded, or despised, and she showed it. I bet there weren't many tears in her team.'

That was grossly unfair. She flushed with anger.

100

Tom carried on. 'Of course these letters look quite mad. I can't tell if they really are, or if someone just wanted to frighten her. Have you thought that she could even have sent them to herself, for some devious reason? You certainly ought to show them to the police.'

But she didn't want to, not yet, anyhow. It still felt as if she had been prying, as if she had delved into a very private part of her friend's life without permission. She certainly didn't want strangers to go there, to revel in the loathing Suzannah had somehow evoked. Tom had thrown up a great steel barrier between himself and Lucy. His hostility to Suzannah hurt her badly, and hardened her against him. She still needed him, but the friendship and the intimacy of the last hour was shattered. He had never understood her relationship with Suzannah, and obviously underrated her on every level. Lucy resolved never to bring the subject up again.

Meanwhile, there was work to be done. They had to find the boys' reunion party. The café owner told her where the street was, a backstreet only walking distance away which ran at right angles to the beach. It was filled with tall Edwardian houses, once-smart little hotels, now far less immaculate bed-and-breakfast accommodation for the homeless and needy. Their white distemper was grimy. The bright paint on their windows and doorframes was grazed and flaking. They were like old ladies still wearing make-up, but failing to disguise their wrinkles. Gallant, but life had clearly passed them by.

Tom and Lucy easily found the house they wanted. Windows on every floor were lit up, and young people were walking up and down the crumbling steps to the front door. Obviously the party was in full swing. Lucy rang the doorbell, and when she heard someone answer, she identified herself. 'Lucy Strong, I'm here with Tom.'

She pushed the front door open and found herself in a narrow hallway, decorated with plastic holly and paper streamers. There were night-lights balanced on each windowsill, tiny flames flickering convivially. The boys had gone to some trouble to make their reunion a real celebration. Lucy and Tom had bought two bottles of Californian wine from the off-licence next to the fish-and-chip shop, and they thought it might be safer to stay with their own drink, so Tom found a corkscrew and filled plastic cups for them both. Max came running down the stairs from the first floor to meet them. Lucy shook hands with him, and introduced Tom.

'Better come into this bedroom,' Max said, leading them into a room on the ground floor, off the hall. 'It's getting packed upstairs. I'll bring people to you.'

He disappeared again and Tom and Lucy sat down, Tom on a bed, Lucy on an old sofa by the window. The springs were bursting out of it, the seat was almost on the floor. She perched cautiously on the edge, and got out her notebook.

The stairs outside were full of young people laughing and drinking, shouting to others on the landing. Lucy went to the door and looked up the stairwell. There were five or six storeys, every landing crammed with people.

Max reappeared with three young men. He introduced them by their first names – Sean, Ben and Nick. They could have been brothers, thin, pale boys, with eyes that never stayed still. Lucy offered them some wine but they refused, they had full plastic cups in their hands. She started to talk to them, while Tom listened quietly.

'You've probably heard that we exposed Wantage Grange on our programme,' she began. 'We had plenty of evidence about Whitestone, and Pincher, and Robinson.' They were the teachers she had named on the report. The boys met each other's eyes and giggled uneasily. They had memories of their own of those men.

'Max met me after the show,' she went on. 'He said there was much more to the story.' The boys laughed again. Lucy had never heard a more bitter, unhappy sound.

'I need you to talk to me,' she urged. As she looked into

102

their faces, their eyes swerved down to the ground. None of them could meet her gaze. She put a little more urgency into her tone. 'Look, you can trust me. I won't pass anything you say on to anyone else without your permission. Tom and I have come here to listen to your story. We believe children should be protected. If there are dangerous abusers in the community going unpunished, we need to try and protect other children from them.'

Still they said nothing, but sat, staring at the floor.

What was she looking at? Fear? Shame? Guilt? Doubtless a mixture of all three. Was there any way she could allay any of it for them? She had to try.

'You do know that none of this is your fault, don't you?' she said. 'Whatever happened to you, the adults were to blame. I've met many young people who've been through this sort of thing. I'm unshockable. Tom's a lawyer. He's represented young people who have been abused. He knows how it works.'

At last Sean looked up. 'What will happen if we talk to you?'

She had to be honest. 'I promise that I won't pass on anything you tell me, without your consent. You must trust me on that. But eventually I want to make a programme to expose them. Obviously it will be extremely difficult. These men will do everything they can to protect themselves. There may be risks for you, but all I can say is we will protect you, give you false names, and disguise your faces and your voices. So far you've survived, knowing what you know, and if we can find enough evidence so that they end up in gaol, you'll be even safer.'

'Some haven't survived.' Sean's voice was truculent; it was all very well for her. 'Do you know how many suicides there've been? In the last two years there have been three. And yet nobody asks why.'

Boys driven to their death by what they'd seen and suffered? Was that what he meant?

'Well, you can understand why that happened,' she said. 'After all, you've been through some horrible experiences, if what Max told me is even halfway true. Abuse can create nightmares which last all your life. Maybe some of the boys just couldn't stand it any more.'

Sean shook his head. 'Yes, but why would someone who was just about to get married throw himself under a car? Unless someone else thought he was a danger, because he might just tell his girlfriend something.'

So he thought they'd been hunted down, and eliminated. Maybe now she was a target too.

'Sean, listen to me,' she said. 'I understand your fears. I share them myself.' She was talking to herself, as much as to them. 'But I believe in my heart and soul that if we stay silent, that's what these men want. It sets them free to carry on doing terrible things to children. In fact it gives them more and more confidence. But it has to be up to you whether you talk to me or not. It's your decision.'

Now she knew she had struck a chord. For once, the boys had been given the power to make their own choice, power over their own lives. That knowledge seemed to give them strength. They exchanged glances.

'OK,' Sean said. He looked round the other three. 'I'm in. It's time these bastards got what's coming to them. As long as you tell me exactly what you're going to put on your programme. I don't want to wake up tomorrow and see myself all over *TV Times*.'

Lucy nodded. 'It's a deal. Don't worry. There are loads of steps we'll have to take before we can get anywhere near making a programme.'

Swiftly she ran through the process. First they would have to talk to her and Tom. Then to the company lawyers. The boys would have to sign a sworn affidavit that everything they had told her was true. And if it ever became a criminal case, and the abusers were charged, they might have to give evidence in court. As she described each stage she wondered if they would shy away, literally run away out of the room and join their friends. But they stayed with her, while the music outside got louder, and the laughter and shouts more raucous. The party was clearly going well.

'We'll have to talk to you one by one,' Lucy explained. 'Tom's a lawyer. He's going to try and assess how much of your story would stand up in court. There are rules about evidence, hearsay and so on. Luckily they don't apply to journalism, so I'm going to ask you not just about what happened to you, but what happened to other boys at the school, and how the ring operated, and who else was involved. OK?'

They nodded. Lucy beckoned Max to sit next to her. At the other end of the shabby room, Tom started talking to Sean. Ben and Nick said they would wait in the kitchen, and escaped towards the drink and the music. Lucy shut the door behind them.

Max stared at the carpet as he answered her questions. The story as it unfolded disgusted her, and she didn't disguise her anger. These men had used every method to trap their prey: seduction, bribery, threats, intimidation. She didn't ask for details of the sexual acts they committed on the boys, although the police would need that. Any physical damage would act as corroboration. But Lucy concentrated on the abusers, who they were, and where the abuse took place. She needed to find factual evidence to support Max's story, if she could.

'Did your parents ever suspect anything?' she asked.

'One night,' he said. There were shadows in his eyes; the memory obviously haunted him and she hated having to make him relive it. She took his hand and he held on to her, gazing unfocused into the mid-distance. 'After one of their rougher games I was bleeding, and scared. I thought I might be dying. So I rang my mum and told her I was ill. She was so worried she wanted to come and see me, to take me to hospital. But they were up north in Catterick. It would have meant her driving all night, so in the end I calmed down and told her I'd see how

105

I was in the morning. By then it had almost stopped bleeding, so she never came. But she might remember that night.'

Lucy wrote down the date, as near as he could remember it. He knew it was the spring term, and that he was fourteen at the time. He started to describe the men who had abused him. 'There were always these two. This Wilson, he was quite violent. He hit me more than once, but always where the marks wouldn't show. He was really kinky. The other one, Parks, liked us hitting him. He was in the papers a lot – we used to tear out the pictures and use them for bog paper.' His face blenched with disgust as he remembered the men.

'You say there were police involved?' she asked.

'I dunno if they were really police, but the others said they were. Not from round here. There were a couple, one from London, one from Wales, he sounded like. And a couple of coke-heads they called Doug and John who had masses of money to throw around. They used to give us cash, buy us music decks, stuff like that. They were in something like advertising. They used to film us doing stuff. They were filming one kid who nearly died. That frightened them. Frightened us too.'

'Tell me about the young people who were involved. I know about Ben and Nick, of course, but were there many others? Do you think they would talk to us?'

Max thought for a moment. 'Yes, there were others. Some of them have died since – I told you about them. You might have trouble getting them to talk.' If it was a joke, there was no laughter in it. 'Some of the other guys are here, but they didn't want to meet you. I think a lot of them just want to forget about the whole thing. The pervs told us they'd find us if we ever told anyone. And they'd kill us.'

'Do you think they meant it?'

'Why wouldn't they? These guys played really rough. It was scary stuff they did to us. And some of the Internet stuff they liked to watch was very bad.'

Lucy tried not to imagine what he meant. She glanced towards

Tom. He was deep in conversation, and making occasional notes.

Then suddenly there was a noise outside, an explosive crash at the front door, and a sound like a deafening blast of wind. Lucy ran to the bedroom door. She opened it a crack, then shut it instantly, and turned to the others, her face white.

'It's fire. We've got to get out.'

She ran to the window, but Tom was ahead of her, pulling back the curtains. Outside the house there were screams. Panic rose in her, and paralysed her. She could hear shouts, cries of panic, footsteps running through the hallway. It must be thick with black choking smoke by now, as lethal as the flames. Tom and the two boys picked up a chair and crashed it against the big sash window. At the second attempt the glass broke into fragments. There was a drop to the basement level, but wasn't too far. The boys scrambled out, and Tom turned to help Lucy. He dragged her up onto the sill. He jumped first, then she fell into his arms.

They looked back to the building. It was ablaze. How could the fire have caught hold so fast? As they climbed up the basement steps and onto the pavement they could hear fire engines approaching, but the fire had already engulfed the stairwell. They could see it flickering all the way up to the roof. Lucy watched in horror as young people crowded out onto the high balconies, leaning out, desperately trying to escape the smoke and the heat. Some jumped, although surely they couldn't survive the drop. She sobbed for them, and hid her eyes. Tom seized her shoulder.

'There's nothing we can do, Lucy. The fire engine's on its way.'

She looked at him wildly. 'But there are people dying in that house. There must be something we can do.' She turned away again and pressed her face into his chest. It was unbearable to stand there, witnessing so much pain, but not to be able to save the boys. Tom held her as the fire engine arrived and firefighters ran past them, unravelling hoses. A vast ladder unfolded up the side of the house. But where were the fire escapes? How many kids had been trapped? The house had gone up in an immense ball of gas, smoke and flames. The rafters of the roof were alight. And now a news crew arrived. She had to avoid them.

Max and Sean were watching, transfixed, next to Lucy on the pavement. Lucy touched Max's arm. 'Ring me,' she said. 'This must have been deliberate. Someone out there knew about your reunion, and decided to shut you all up permanently. Ring me, please, tomorrow.' Her voice shook, but she fought to control it. 'We can't let them get away with it.' He said nothing, his face blank with horror as he looked up at the house.

Tom took her hand, and they walked quickly away from the crowd that had collected. She was recognized by one or two, but they were too absorbed by the spectacle of the tragedy to be distracted.

Lucy and Tom walked together back to the hotel, hand in hand, in silence. Lucy was icy cold now, and trembling with shock. Tom said nothing. They collected their keys from a sleepy porter, who looked curiously at their grimy faces, and the lift took them back to their bedroom floor. Lucy put her key in the lock, then turned to Tom.

'Oh God, Tom, how many kids died there?' He put her arms round her. She shut her eyes, but in her mind she still saw the flames, the silhouettes at the windows, heard the screams.

'Do you want me to stay with you tonight?' Tom asked her.

'No, Tom.' She shook her head. It was not a rejection, just a statement of fact. 'I've got to be by myself. I just don't know what to think, what to say. I think you saved my life, Tom, breaking that window. But so many kids were trapped.'

He felt her pain, but her eyes were dry. She never had been able to share the worst moments with him. It had been one of the insuperable barriers between them. There was no point arguing.

He wrote his room number on the pad by her bed. 'Ring me if you need me. We'll talk tomorrow.' He put his arms around her, and felt her body, cold and rigid. He left her.

108

Lucy walked into her bedroom and sat on the bed, her arms crossed defensively across her chest. Then one deep moan escaped from her, the agony she had just witnessed tore at her, and tears streamed down her face.

CHAPTER SIX

The night was filled with flashbacks. Lurid flames, acrid choking smoke. She had showered, scrubbing her body and her scalp over and over again to get rid of the smell and taste of ashes, to no avail. It was there in her nostrils and in her memory. She put the lights on, paced around the anonymous hotel room, ate a plum without tasting it from the bowl of complimentary fruit left for her by the manager, drank water from the minibar, but nothing could blank out the interminable pictures careering one after the other through her mind.

She looked out of her window at the black sky, black sea. If only she could turn the clock back and somehow warn the kids of the danger ahead of them, persuade them to cancel the party, or lead them out like a pied piper to dance on the beach. Her heart pounded again as their faces appeared in her mind. Sean and Max had escaped with her, thank God, but what had happened to the other two, Ben and Nick? They had said they would wait in the kitchen – was there a way out through a back door to safety? Or had they been tempted up onto one of the high landings, and been imprisoned by the smoke?

From sheer exhaustion she fell asleep at six, very heavily, so that the alarm at seven dragged her painfully back again to consciousness. The little waitress knocked at her door with the breakfast she had ordered before she'd left for the party, a lifetime ago. She drank a cup of tea, left the rest untouched, and walked into her bathroom. Her face was grey with tiredness. Her eyes were puffy and reddened by tears shed and unshed. She must find out the fate of the boys she had met. How many other young people had died, or been injured?

She sat on the bed, and switched on the television. The local news programme had just begun, the headlines completely

110

preoccupied with the tragedy. Nothing has more dramatic impact on the screen than a spectacular fire, and here was one on their doorstep. The heavy middle-aged presenter, Gordon Flambard, was earning his money. He had long been the pin-up of the local ladies, who loved his dimples and his self-deprecating laugh when, as often happened, he forgot the name of his interviewee. Now he was serious and absorbed by the breaking story.

'We go over to Janice Brown, who is at the scene of the fire in Thritham.'

A nervous young reporter was standing in the darkness in front of the house, lit by floodlights as the firefighters worked on. Another crew was sending back pictures from a helicopter circling over the house, looking down at the towering ladders propped against it, and the powerful hoses still playing on the blackened rafters. It had been completely destroyed.

'Have they any idea how the fire started, Janice?' Gordon asked the reporter.

She took a deep breath and launched into the statement she had memorized, the briefing the senior fireman had given her. 'All we know at this stage, Gordon, is that a party was going on in the house last night, and dozens of young people attended it. I've spoken to some of the survivors, and they told me there were night-lights everywhere, on the stairs and in every room. There were Christmas decorations, holly and paper chains, which the firefighters say would have added to the blaze. But even so I've been told the fire could not have spread so fast without help. The police are treating this fire as suspicious. They would like anyone with any information to contact them. And, of course, they are desperately trying to find out who the guests at this party were, and how many are now missing.'

Gordon Flambard took over from her again, his voice sonorous. 'This is by far the worst tragedy to hit the small sea-side town. So far sixteen bodies have been found in the wreckage, and other seriously injured casualties have been taken to local hospitals. No doubt there will have to be an inquiry, not least

111

because the house seems not to have been fitted with the required fire escapes, and so there was no way out once the stairs had filled with fire and smoke. This is what one of the survivors told us last night.'

The picture changed to a boy wrapped in a blanket, standing in the street, his face lit by the flickering light of the burning house. As he answered the reporter's questions, shock was still imprinted on his face. Yes, the house had been full of friends he had met at Wantage Grange School. The stairs had been blocked by the fire; he'd been drinking with friends in the kitchen and escaped through the back door; he'd seen some boys jumping from the windows in despair, but it was such a steep drop that they were badly hurt.

Lucy, sitting on the bed in her hotel room, listened as Gordon ended his report by linking the fire to her own investigation into Wantage Grange School.

'The police are already looking into the allegations of sexual abuse by three of the teachers at the school, which were made recently on a television programme,' he said. He worked for a different company, so he was not going to plug Lucy or her show by name. 'Now they'll be investigating whether there was any connection between those allegations and this terrible event.'

If he had made that connection, so would others. She and Tom had been seen as they stood, transfixed, watching the fire. They would have been seen walking away, maybe followed back to the hotel. Perhaps the cameras were already on the doorstep of her hotel, ready to interrogate her as she left. She stood wearily and went into the bathroom. Somehow she had to get herself into good shape to face them, but all she had with her were the clothes she had worn yesterday. Her jeans were not at all suitable for a sombre interview, but at least her coat was dark blue, and would cover her. The softness of the cashmere sweater comforted her. She wrapped her pashmina tightly under her chin, and brushed her eyelids lightly with pearl grey, to counteract the red rims.

The phone rang, and she picked it up nervously. It was Tom.

'Hi,' he said. 'How are you?'

'Pretty rough. How are you?'

'The same. Have you been watching the news?'

'Yes.'

'They'll be after you for a comment.'

'I know. I don't know what to say.'

'Stay there. I'll come over.'

She walked round the room, automatically packing her brief-case, checking that nothing had been left behind, brushing her hair, spraying herself with perfume, all on automatic pilot, her mind going over and over the tragedy of last night. Would she ever see Max or Sean again, or would they be so terrified they would never dare contact her? She had no means of getting in touch with them. She felt completely helpless.

There was a knock on her bedroom door, Tom was standing there, with the newspapers in his arms. Pictures of the blazing house filled every front page, with headlines, 'The Furnace of Death' and 'The Hell Fire'. On the inside pages were interviews with neighbours and a few survivors.

She shook her head as she flipped over the pages, hardly looking at the pictures, they brought too much pain with them. Her voice was husky with lack of sleep. 'It's such a tragedy, Tom. Those kids had suffered so much already, and now this. It must have been deliberate. Someone knew about the party and wanted them dead.'

Tom nodded. 'If you're right, if it was arson and murder, there'll be forensic evidence. Though whether the police will be able to pin it to anyone is anyone's guess. Whoever planned it will have covered their tracks.'

The phone by the bed rang again. Lucy walked over and answered it. It was the hotel manager with the news she had been dreading.

'Miss Strong, we have a group of reporters here asking to speak to you. What do you want me to say?'

She didn't know. 'I'll ring you back,' she said, then slumped on the bed. 'Tom, I can't do this.'

'I don't think you have any alternative, sweetheart. They'll stay here until you leave. Why not just tell them the minimum. Say you were at the party because you'd been invited by a couple of the boys. You'd become friendly with them after your report on the school.'

'I don't want to put the boys into any more danger.'

'You won't. If the press ask for names, just tell them that at the moment nobody knows who is missing, whether they've been badly hurt, or even killed, so you must respect the feelings of all the families. What they'll want is an emotional response from you. Frankly, sweetheart, you look as if you haven't slept for a week, so I should keep the whole thing as brief as you can.'

She agreed. In fact she wasn't sure she could answer any questions at all, she felt so close to tears. Tom saw that.

'I could go down and talk to them on your behalf, say you're too upset to say anything at the moment.'

She shook her head, and for a moment a half-smile lit her face. 'They'll put two and two together and make fifty. They'll assume we came down here for a love-tryst, or that we're together again. Don't worry, Tom, I can cope. I'm sure the manager will help me.'

The reporters were clustered together in the lounge, turning eagerly towards her as she approached. She walked towards them, pulling her coat tightly around her, and the photographers got the picture they needed of her tired, unsmiling face. Then the reporters clamoured for a statement. She explained that she'd been invited to the party as a result of her investigation of the school.

'Obviously the fire was deliberate. Who do you think did it?' one of the reporters asked, shorthand notebook open in his hand.

'I don't want to make allegations, or start guessing,' she said wearily. 'I've had a sleepless night just thinking about those young lives lost, and the families, and the tragedy of it all. So much suffering has been caused by this fire. If it was deliberate, whoever did this is a murderer, and I'm sure the police will find him. Or them.'

'Do you think it could have been linked to your investigation? Could it be connected to the abusers you named?'

'Could it be some sort of revenge?'

'Do you regret having made the programme?'

She tried to think logically, under the barrage of questions. With conscious effort, she summoned her adrenalin, and pulled her strength together. 'As I've told you, I really don't want to speculate. That would be quite wrong. I just want to express my deepest sympathy to all the families, and the young people who have been injured in this terrible blaze. I saw how quickly it spread. I know I was lucky to escape myself.'

'There were no fire escapes on the house – have you any comment to make about that?'

'No, I don't have the facts, and I don't want to comment, except to say that I'm sure the police will look into every aspect of this crime very thoroughly.'

'What about you, Lucy, will you feature it on your new show?'

'No, I haven't got any plans to investigate this fire. I'm just planning to go home. If you don't mind, let's end it there. I must leave now. Thank you.'

They thanked her and let her go. They were professionals, she'd given them the quotes they needed, and had stood still for the picture she knew they wanted, that was enough. She went upstairs again and found Tom waiting for her in her bedroom.

As she picked up her briefcase, he looked at her intently. 'Are you OK to drive home? It's been a grim twenty-four hours. I don't want you to make it worse by having a crash.'

She shook her head. 'Don't worry about me. I'm fine.' But was she? Was this the way Suzannah had died, not recognizing her own exhaustion?

115

She settled her bill by phone from her room, they would send the account to her office. The sympathetic manager told her how to take the side lifts down to the car park, in case the reporters were still waiting. She needed time to herself. Then she stood, her arms crossed across her chest, her shoulders high with tension, and looked at Tom.

'I'll ring you,' she said. 'I can't thank you enough for being here with me. I just don't know how I would have coped on my own.' She stopped, overcome for a moment by the memory. 'I keep on hearing those screams, seeing those kids at the windows, on the balconies. I'll never forget them.'

'Nor will I,' he said.

She walked away from him to the window, where the grey morning sky hung low over the sea and the shingle beach, the scene that had given her so much pleasure yesterday. Now she just wanted to leave Thritham, to get back to London as fast as possible. Deep inside her, anger was flaring.

'Tom, if I can prove it was those vile men, I'll name the lot of them.' She shuddered at the thought of them. 'They can't be allowed to get away with this. They've got away with so much already.'

He followed her to the window, and put his arm around her. No longer lovers, at least they were friends, battling alongside each other, thrown together in the same fight.

'Be careful, Lucy. This may well be murder, multiple murder. Better to leave it to the police. They have the forensic experts. I doubt your lawyers would let you say anything on the air, anyway.'

She broke away from him, furiously impatient with his caution. 'I understand that, Tom. I told the press that I wouldn't speculate. But nobody else knows about the paedophile ring. If I can get the evidence to put what we know on the air, it'll strengthen the police's hand. And protect other children.'

He didn't want to argue with her. He was tired too. While she had been sleepless, thinking of the boys in that furnace of a house, his head had been filled with the terror of how nearly Lucy had died, and he with her. That reality had not yet occurred to her. When it did, perhaps shock would set in. If that happened while she was driving back to London, the effect might be catastrophic. But she was determined, so he kissed her and let her go.

She walked past him to the door. Then she looked back at him with her first real smile of the day. Only then did she take in the pain in his face. 'I'm so sorry I got you involved in all this, Tom, although for my own sake I'm relieved that you're here with me. Thank you for coming and being so supportive. Love you.' She went through the door, her own words echoing in her head. Love you? Did she still? Well, yes, certainly, as a friend.

Can you be friends with your ex-husband? She played with that idea. They'd hurt each other so badly when the marriage split. It would be good to believe that the passion they'd once shared could turn into a loving friendship. She stopped that thought in its tracks – like hell that could ever happen. Tom was as unpredictable as ever, one minute scathing and unsympathetic, the next sweet and supportive. If he was around on the edges of her life, it would all be intolerably complicated. Still, nobody else could literally have saved her life, as he had.

The drive back passed in a daze, her brain still deeply involved with the tragedy of the last night. But the sheer mechanics of picking her way through the motorways back to London calmed her. Arriving at the studios, she parked her car and took the lift up to her office. As she walked through the labyrinth of open-plan computers and desks she saw that every researcher was devouring the descriptions of last night's fire in the newspapers and each monitor was tuned to the rolling news station.

Dan came to the door of his office as she approached, and beckoned her to join him there. His voice was warm with relief at seeing her. 'Lucy, thank God you're OK. We all saw you on the news. We realized you were safe and unhurt, but you looked desperately tired and shocked. Understandably. It must have been ghastly.'

She walked towards him, and as he hugged her, she relaxed in his arms. He was kind, he cared about her, and there was no history between them to muddle things.

'I heard them screaming, Dan, the ones who were trapped.' Tears welled up, and she wiped them away, still intent on the story. 'They should have been able to escape – if there had been proper fire escapes they would have. I think somebody knew the house was lethal, and deliberately set the fire to silence them.'

He steadied her, and held her away from him, studying her face.

'Who? Those teachers you exposed?'

'Or friends of theirs. There's a lot more to that story that hasn't come out yet.'

'Will it ever come out, d'you think?'

'Tom thinks not. I hope it will. I'll do my best to make it stand up.'

'Not for our show.' The idea clearly appalled him.

'No, of course not. Maybe for a special show. I'll see how much more I can find out.'

'Let me know if there's any way I can help. In the meantime, I hate to force you to think about Saturday, but we do have a show to fill. How soon can we have a meeting?'

She pulled off her coat, unwound the pashmina, and went into Suzannah's office. She glanced at the drawer that had held such secrets, then up to her friend's face on the wall. She needed Suzannah now, longed to hear Suzannah's reassurance that the letters in the drawer meant nothing, that she had kept them just as a whim. She needed to draw on Suzannah's strength to survive the memories of last night.

She stared at the photographs, the bright open smile that charmed the cameras. Suddenly Lucy shivered as she remembered Tom's cruel assessment of her dearest friend. He'd implied that Suzannah had enemies everywhere, even here in her own production team. That had to be untrue. Suzannah had been loyal, generous, and an inspiration to Lucy from the moment they met. She couldn't think differently of her now. That would be a betrayal. It would destroy so many memories and pull down the scaffolding that supported her working life. No, it was rubbish. Lucy pulled her shoulders straight, and stood tall. She must and could survive all this. She had to carry on.

She hung her scarf and coat on a hanger, and called through the door, 'Any time, Dan. I'm ready when you are.'

The team preceded her down the corridor to the conference room, their normal chatter silenced by the tragedy she'd lived through. They sat quietly at the table, and waited for her to speak. She looked round their faces. Some were as young as the boys who had died in the fire. Unexpectedly her eyes filled with tears. That was no good. She remembered all the production meetings she herself had attended as a researcher. She tightened her hands into fists, and summoned up Suzannah's spirit to help her.

'Sorry,' she said. 'I'm afraid I haven't slept much. Last night was more terrible than you can imagine.'

None of them could meet her eyes. They didn't want to see her so raw, so vulnerable. She cleared her throat.

'Perhaps I should explain why I went to Thritham. I was due to meet a couple of the boys from the school we investigated. They were nice kids. Then the fire happened. I was very lucky to get out. They say the police have already found sixteen bodies, and I suppose there may be even more deaths – some of the kids in hospital are very seriously injured. So forgive me if I'm a bit shaken up this morning. I'll try and put it out of my mind. Tell me about the show on Saturday.'

Gradually the mood shifted. The remorselessness of the television conveyor belt took over. No matter how earth-shattering last night had been, her life had to move on. The researchers who had been working to book and investigate the chef Lawrence Crabtree took over the meeting. Subdued at first, soon they were falling over each other with enthusiasm.

'He's booked, he's gagging to appear.'

'Not just to plug the new series – he wants to sell his latest book as well.'

'You can tell he's already planning the new Lexus he'll buy on the proceeds, not to mention the smart hotel he's planning to buy in the Cotswolds.'

'So are we just going to play his game?' Lucy asked.

'Not exactly,' Julie reassured her. 'I've been contacted by one of his ex-sous-chefs. He's got some secret film of Crabtree in the kitchen. You should see it. Lawrence the love-god it is not. In real life he's a foul-mouthed bully.'

'Kitchens are like that.'

'Yes, that's not news, I know. But guess what makes him lose his temper.'

Lucy's interest was caught, at last. 'Tell me.'

'One of his chefs isn't using Gourmet foil when he's making a soufflé, and Crabtree goes mad. The guy defends himself by saying it's unnecessary because he's using greaseproof paper. And Crabtree says it may not be effing necessary to the soufflé, but it's effing necessary to him.'

'Is that verbatim, exactly what he says?'

'Well no, he goes much further than effing. We'll have to bleep him all the way through. His language is fruitier than his soufflé.'

'Does he make it clear that he has a special reason of his own to use the foil?'

'Absolutely. And we've checked with Delia, and Raymond Blanc, and neither of them would use it. Not for a passion fruit soufflé.'

'What do the lawyers say about the film?'

'They say it's fine to use it. And we've had an environmental health officer look at it. Specially the bit where Crabtree sticks his finger in the coulis, licks it, and sticks it back in the dish.'

'Lovely.' She grimaced. Sometimes it was safer not to know what went on in restaurant kitchens.

'Quite.' The researcher smiled triumphantly.

'What's all this going to do to Crabtree's dream of his new Lexus?' Lucy asked.

'It's not going to be all that helpful, I imagine,' Dan answered.

'And how much of this do we have to warn him about in advance?'

'Obviously if we tell him about the film, he'll never turn up,' Dan told her. 'We've argued the toss with the lawyers, and they say as it's clearly in the public interest we don't have to warn him at all.'

Lucy felt a pang of sympathy for Crabtree. Just a small pang. He wasn't a child abuser, after all, just a greedy man who was about to be caught with his snout in the trough. A foil-wrapped snout.

'OK, that'll be the first half of the show. How do we follow him?'

The team glanced at each other, then at Dan.

'We wondered,' he said slowly, 'how you would feel about interviewing Suzannah's ex, Boris.'

Lucy looked at him blankly. 'Explain.'

'OK. No pressure. There are other options. A couple of Hollywood A-list stars are over to plug the new action movie *Mountain High*. But some of us felt it would be wrong to make your first show without any mention of Suzannah, and I thought maybe you'd like to talk to her ex-husband. Just to lay the ghost, as it were.'

Lucy glanced at her friend in the photos on the conference-room walls, laughing and vibrantly alive. How could anyone think of Suzannah as a ghost? 'Have you talked to Boris?'

Marion, one of the senior researchers, nodded. She was slightly older than the rest of the team, a comfortable-looking brunette with dark eyes, and tanned skin. She wore elaborate knitted skirts and shawls that flowed around her in a tangle of olive greens and russets. Marion was a married woman with two children, and had recently lost her own father. Lucy trusted her instinct.

'Yes, I talked to him,' Marion told her. 'He said he'd be glad to come on and pay tribute to Suzannah. He wanted to make the point you made in your interview, that in a way she was killed by her work. Death by television, he called it.'

Terrific. That would sabotage any chance she had of living down the Janet Lake interview. If Jameson had forgiven her when it was printed, he would surely sack her if yet more accusations were flung around the studio.

Marion read Lucy's expression. 'Perhaps Boris won't put it quite as forcefully as you did. He just wants to talk about her life, and how much the job tore into it. He also wants to say Suzannah would be thrilled to see you in her chair. He remembers what she told him about you when you joined the team.'

'Oh yes?'

Dan intervened. 'Sometimes you may find it easier genuinely not to know what's coming, so we'd prefer not to tell you exactly what he wants to say about you. Trust us. It's affectionate, and funny.'

Lucy thought about that. Suzannah had trusted Dan, and it had paid off for her. There were many interviews when the guests had surprised Suzannah on the air, and that had given the show a danger that couldn't be faked. But with Tom's words still sounding in her head, she needed to prepare herself for revelations she might not like. 'Is Boris going to be kind about Suzannah?' she asked.

Marion's face was difficult to read. 'In what way, kind?'

'He's going to have to get behind her public face, otherwise there'd be no point in talking to him. And although they smoothed over it for outsiders, I know their parting was, well, personally hurtful. He might feel wounded now, and bitter.'

'Yes,' Marion nodded, 'although he hasn't expressed that to me – far from it. And I didn't ever hear Suzannah bad-mouth him. As we all know she could, when the mood took her. She didn't hold back when she felt strongly.'

The others laughed. There was an undercurrent of something there. Lucy decided not to push things further.

'Why don't we invite the audience to ask their own questions?' she suggested. 'That would give the show a feeling of freshness, move it on a bit.'

This was a new idea, and they took a moment to digest it. Live shows were risky enough without allowing an audience free rein to take over.

'Couldn't it just encourage exhibitionists – streakers or political nuts who want to cause chaos, and grab a whole lot of publicity for themselves?' Dan said.

Lucy was optimistic. 'Not if we have tight security, and we check everyone's identity at the door to keep out troublemakers. Shouldn't it be manageable?' It would certainly give the show a different flavour, make it Lucy's, rather than an imitation of Suzannah's.

Dan looked at her. 'Only you can decide, Lucy,' he said. 'In the end, it's your neck on the chopping block if things go wrong. Personally, I feel confident you can handle it. And I take your point that it would give an added relevance to the show. Viewers would feel much more involved.'

'Let's go for it,' Lucy said. She was taking a huge risk anyway, why not go for broke?

The meeting ended with the happy chatter of researchers whose ideas had been accepted. They knew things could still change, but at the moment, the shape of the show looked good. They went back to their desks, leaving Lucy and Dan behind.

Her smile left her. He saw it go.

'Not pleased?' he asked.

'No, it's all fine. I just wish I was working on investigating that fire, finding out more about it. I know this is a different show, and of course I'm looking forward to it. It's only that after last night, I keep getting flashbacks. My mind won't leave it alone.'

He nodded. 'That's inevitable. Maybe it's quite nice to have a new show to take your mind off it.' But it didn't. It couldn't.

When she got back to her desk there was a string of messages on her voice-mail. Lesley wanted to know if she could go shopping with her, for clothes for the new series. The press were lining up, asking for interviews, photographs, special access to her. And there was a message from the Thritham police. Could they please come and talk to her, as soon as possible? She dealt with it all quickly. Sandra directed the press to the corporate press office. Lucy rang the police and made an appointment for them to interview her at home that evening.

Then she phoned Lesley's mobile. 'I don't know if I can face shopping at the moment,' she said.

Lesley was sympathetic. 'Absolutely, I understand that. Have you got anything you can wear already in your wardrobe?'

Lucy thought about the businesslike suits, the leather jackets she'd collected for her old programme. 'Not really. This new show is so much more glitzy and show-bizzy than anything I've done before.'

'Don't worry,' Lesley's reassuring voice was a relief. 'It need only take half an hour or so. Let's meet at Harvey Nichols' personal shopping. I'll have a little browse around for half an hour before we meet, then I'll have some idea what there is. We can have a salad together afterwards.'

Maybe it would be helpful – retail therapy followed by lunch with a friend she knew would tolerate her mood. And perhaps the total distraction of trying on clothes would take her mind away from the memories that haunted her.

She took a taxi to Harvey Nichols. Usually the luxury of the shop, the pretty gilded trinkets in the jewellery department, the exotic creams and lotions on the cosmetic shelves distracted and amused her. Not today. Today it seemed like vanity gone mad. It wasn't helped by the fact that it looked as if all the fashion designers had gone into a Shirley Temple fantasy-land this season. In spite of the fact that expensive clothes are normally bought by women well over twenty-four, both in age and in waist size, they'd all brought out girly frills and peasant blouses, flouncy skirts and bright patterns. All of them would be guaranteed to look saggy, baggy and sad under television lights. By the time Lucy arrived in the personal shopping department, she found Lesley sitting in despair on a beige plush sofa, with one silk jacket on a hanger by her side.

'I've failed completely,' she confessed. 'Unless you want to look like Jane Russell in a haystack, there's nothing here.'

For a moment Lucy was tempted. Mean, moody and magnificent could be the style she was looking for. Then, reluctantly, she put the mental picture away. At least the silk jacket was a lovely intense violet colour. She went with Lesley to a cream-painted changing room, and tried it on. The subtle cut flattered her curves, the colour glowed in the light.

'Tell you what,' Lesley said, 'maybe we can find a simple shift dress to put under it, in a soft rose colour, or lilac, or moss green.' But as ever, shopping with a clear idea of what she needed was a disaster. They tramped together through the departments, designer after designer, clothes temptingly ranged in cupboards and racks, but as they pulled the hangers apart, searching for what they needed, it was clear there was not a simple shift dress in the store. In desperation Lucy tried on some of the flimsy, flouncy dresses and blouses. She looked less like Jane Russell, and more like a village maiden in a tacky pantomime. And with her tired, preoccupied face, she looked like a very exhausted village maiden. After an hour of this, they retired, hurt, to the café on the fifth floor, and ordered a scampi salad.

At the tables around them, stick-thin women with honey-coloured faces, shiny lips and expensive haircuts flicked their eyes appraisingly towards them. Lucy could read their minds as they mentally weighed the fifteen pounds she was overweight by their standards, despising her soft curves, her flushed cheeks.

Lesley looked at her friend with sharply appraising eyes. 'You're tired,' she said.

Lucy sighed. 'I am. Tired to the bone. Not with work. But last night's fire really got to me. I hoped that spending this morning with you trying the clothes on would somehow block the nightmare, at least for a time. But it hasn't. I keep hearing those young people screaming, seeing them silhouetted against the fire. I constantly get flashbacks of two of the boys I met, Ben and Nick, in my mind. Lesley, I think they must be dead.' She took a deep breath. 'And what if there was some way I could have saved them? God, I don't know. Should I try to investigate it, or would that put everyone in even greater danger?' She picked up a glass of white wine, and saw that her hand was shaking.

Lesley noticed it too. 'Lucy, you have enough to cope with at the moment.' Her strictness was maternal. 'You've got this huge new show to present and you can't solve everything, or save everyone. Take it step by step. Why don't we just focus on what we're here to do? These fussy styles are useless for television. I'll quickly get some silk shifts made for you, in rose, and dark emerald, and black. I'll keep looking round the shops for jackets. I know what suits you.'

Lucy shook her head. She couldn't pretend the search for the perfect jacket filled her with excitement.

Lesley took her hand. 'Suzannah's death had shaken you badly, even without this fire. What you need to do right now is concentrate on the new show.'

Lucy picked at her salad. Another time she could have relished its crisp freshness. Today the leaves tasted clammy and cold in her mouth. She looked at Lesley.

'You knew Suzannah as well as anyone, better than most,' she said slowly. 'What do you think happened? Why did she die? You were working with her that night, weren't you?'

Lesley nodded.

'Was she tired? I know she wasn't drunk – they checked that at the autopsy. And she hadn't taken any pills. The obvious theory is that she was so dog-tired after the show, she fell asleep at the wheel for a fatal couple of seconds. But that doesn't fit, does it? Suzannah wouldn't let that happen, would she?'

Lesley's face stilled as she pictured the last night in Suzannah's life. She had relived each minute so often. 'I suppose Suzannah could have been extra tired,' she said slowly. 'But if so, I didn't see it. I thought she was elated, the show had gone well. Mick Adams, that rather boring action star, had told her on the air that he wasn't in love with the girl in his new film, but he fancied the villain, and he'd never come out publicly before, so she'd got a scoop. And she had an extra sparkle in her eye – you know how she looked when there was a new man in her life. I didn't ask any questions, and it's quite possible I was imagining it, but when she was happy she had that glow about her. So I packed her bags after the show and sent her off quite expecting to see some story in the papers over the weekend about a new lover in her life. Instead I was woken up by the terrible news about her car crash.'

Lucy pushed her knife and fork together, and thought through Lesley's story. She could well believe that Suzannah had found a new man. She had a gift of intensely concentrating those deep blue eyes, widening her smile, and teasing her hair which hypnotized the muscular young men she liked to entertain. But no new man had come forward to talk about his last days with Suzannah. If he had, the tabloids would have paid thousands for him to kiss and tell. But then with all the mess and speculation surrounding Suzannah's death, it would be quite natural for the men in her life to take cover.

Lucy was curious. She'd love to believe that Lesley was right, and Suzannah had been heading into the night to meet a new lover. Everyone had assumed she was on her way to her house in the country. Perhaps he had been waiting for her there. Or maybe she was going somewhere else to meet him. Lucy blinked, and forced herself to stop speculating. All this was gossip and guesswork.

But were there other secrets in Suzannah's life, maybe secrets that Lesley knew? Perhaps Lucy herself had been too close to Suzannah to see the clues. Could she try to find out what Lesley knew, or would that sound intrusive? She hesitated. Maybe one way in would be to tell Lesley what she had found in Suzannah's desk. Well, at least some of it.

'You know I loved Suzannah,' she said to Lesley. 'You felt the same, didn't you? But when I was clearing her office I found letters.' Lesley's attention was instantly caught. Lucy went on, 'They were horrible. Threatening and unpleasant. I can't help wondering who could have written them.' She paused, unsure how to frame her next question, and then plunged on. 'Did she have any enemies? Was there anyone she told you about?'

Lesley pushed her fork across her salad. She was looking down at her plate, not meeting Lucy's eyes. Lucy tried again. 'I hope you don't think I'm prying, but the letters scared me, and I just wondered who could have sent them.'

Still Lesley didn't look at her. Her voice was strained when at last she began to answer. 'Everyone was jealous of her, Lucy, you know that. Some people always try and explain success away. But she was fine about that. None of it got to her. She certainly never talked to me about any letters.'

'Was she happy with her team? Did she trust them? Did they like her?'

'They respected her. Suzannah could be pretty tough, you know that. But if they did their job well, that's all she asked.'

'In my day she was tough but very popular. The team liked her. But I haven't worked with her for years. Did her current team get on well with her?'

'I think so.' Lesley's eyes were down on the plate again. 'I don't really know.' She was being very evasive. Lucy was having to drag every word out of her. This wasn't like Lesley. She obviously didn't like Lucy's questions, and Lucy felt she couldn't push her any further. What was Lesley refusing to tell her? Or was Lucy having fantasies now? Was it because her own mind refused to accept the obvious explanations, or was there really some hidden key to Suzannah's death she had to find? A key that was there, under her hand, if she could only recognize it.

Lesley was looking at her curiously now, and with concern.

This was becoming obsessive. She must shake herself out of it. Somehow she had to move on. At least, as Lesley had said, there was the new show to create, and that should take all her concentration.

Their meal finished, the two women parted. Lesley to ring a talented dressmaker who knew Lucy's measurements, and could run up a shift dress in half a day, from silk material she would track down herself. Lucy took a taxi back to her home.

As they drove through the lunch-time traffic, she leaned back on the leather seat, and closed her eyes. For the length of the journey she allowed the tiredness to wrap itself around her. The sleepless tortured night had caught up with her and she longed to stretch out on her sofa and sleep for an hour or so. But envelopes of research lay scattered on the carpet as she pushed the front door open. Files on Crabtree. Files on Boris. The team had sent her a copy of the secret film taken in Crabtree's kitchen, and a tape compiled from Suzannah's obituaries, showing her as a very young reporter, when Boris and she had first met.

Lucy put the tape into her machine, and watched as the scene unrolled in front of her. There was the brief glory of a spring garden captured by the camera. There were shots of Boris and Suzannah, with Camilla, their brand-new baby. They were in sunlight, on the lawn of her country house, petals drifting down on them from the apple tree branches above. It was all very idyllic, and carefully posed.

On an impulse, Lucy stopped the machine, reached across to her address book in her bag and found Camilla's number. Camilla answered, her voice distant when she recognized Lucy's.

'I've just been watching you as a baby, under the apple tree with your parents. It's lovely.'

Camilla was unmoved. 'That must have been my first photo-call. There were millions more. I got to hide in the cellar when the *Hello!* photographer rang the doorbell.'

'I'm ringing you now, Camilla, because I want to be sure you don't mind me presenting the talk show. I thought you might

129

think it's disloyal of me to try and take on your mum's show,' Lucy said hesitantly. 'As the first show is tomorrow, your father's coming on to talk about her, and how irreplaceable she was. I wanted to warn you in advance. I wondered if you'd like to come and sit in the gallery.'

Camilla's voice sharpened. 'There's nothing I'd hate more. I can't stand all that false stuff, all the "Darling, you were wonderful" crap. I'll try not to watch.' The sourness of her tone stopped the conversation. There was a long silence, which Lucy made no attempt to fill.

Then Camilla went on, with a touch of warmth in her voice now, 'I don't suppose I mind you doing it, Lucy. I know Mum would rather you took on the show than anyone else. But it's still difficult for me.'

Lucy understood. 'I know that. It's not easy for any of us. You must be going through such a tough time. If there's anything I can say, or do, please ring me. You know how I felt about your mother. I would like to help if there's any way I can.'

The girl thought for a moment. Then she said, 'Thanks, Lucy. It is tough – tougher than I thought it would be – and it doesn't get any easier with all that stuff in the paper.'

Did she mean her Janet Lake interview? Lucy couldn't be sure, and didn't want to ask.

'Mum's memorial service didn't help either, though actually I think Mum would have found it funny – all those hypocrites who were riddled with spite and jealousy when she was alive, pretending to pray for her immortal soul.'

Lucy agreed. 'You're right. It was so grim it would have made her laugh. Maybe she did, watching from Paradise. But I was talking to Lesley earlier today, and she thought your mum was specially happy those last few days, really had a glow about her. Which is comforting.'

'Maybe,' Camilla said. 'Well, Lesley would know more than I would. I hadn't seen Mum for a couple of months. She could have been suicidal for all I know, and she wouldn't have rung me.'

Lucy heard the bitterness again, and again decided to ignore it. 'You know she loved spending time with you, Camilla, it's just this industry. It devours all of us. We never have time for the important people in our lives.'

Camilla was unimpressed. 'Oh, she could have, if she'd wanted. Mum was as maternal as a turtle. An entertaining turtle, fun to be with, always delighted to see me. But I knew she'd much rather have buried me in a hole in the sand, and wandered off to the sea again. That was my mum, and you know it, Lucy.' Whatever Suzannah had been, they had both loved her. Camilla relaxed a little. 'Thanks for letting me have her things. Weird, those love-letters written in red ink. Who are they from? Do you know?'

'I've got no idea. They were in a drawer in her desk. I imagine they were fan letters and she kept them for fun. I thought you'd like to see them.' As against the hate mail, which was still safely in Lucy's handbag.

'Funny how people who didn't know Mum always idolized her.' The words were sharper than the tone. Maybe Camilla would come to forgive her mother, and the industry that had taken over her body and soul.

They said goodbye, and Lucy put the phone down. As she did, the doorbell rang. The Thritham police, exactly on time. She went to let them in, a man standing at the door next to a woman, neither of them in uniform, both of them holding out their identity cards to her. She looked closely at the cards. Detective Inspector Derek White and Detective Constable Iris Watkins, both young, serious, slightly uncomfortable to be so far from their own patch.

Lucy took them into the kitchen, and brewed them the coffee they evidently needed. The pair sat together, holding mugs of the hot, sharp drink. Lucy felt an edge of irritation like a saw blade in her mind. 'Forgive me if I hurry you, but I've got a

131

show to prepare for tomorrow. Not that it takes precedence – of course not – but I have got a great deal of work to do for it.'

Derek White was jogged into speech. 'No, I quite understand, Miss Strong. We're here because we've been talking to some of the survivors. And from what they've told us, we wondered if you had any idea why the fire might have been started.'

'Only what the boys told me, that there was a paedophile ring extending out from the school, and that someone in the ring might have wanted to silence them for good.'

'That's one possibility, of course.'

'And the other?'

He looked straight into her eyes. 'The other, Miss Strong – and I'm sorry to put this to you – but there's no other way, the other possibility is that they weren't the target. You were.'

CHAPTER SEVEN

The world swung round, then righted itself. Herself the target. Had all those lives been lost, simply because she had gone to the party? It couldn't be true. The young policewoman watched her face bleach to ashen, and put out a hand to steady her. As their fingers touched, Lucy stared at her, not seeing the woman's face, only the boys silhouetted against the flames, screaming, knowing they were trapped.

'That can't be right,' she said, shaking her head as if to ward off a blow. 'How could you possibly think that could be true?'

'I'm sorry, Miss Strong.' The detective inspector, Derek White, spoke in a flat, emotionless voice, pulling her back to reality. 'It's not necessarily what we think, just a possibility we have to investigate. We haven't come to any conclusions. The forensic evidence isn't through yet. Though I can tell you that the evidence so far is that a petrol bomb was thrown through the front door, and there were other places further up the house where inflammable material had been placed. Piles of crumpled paper behind chairs on the landings, that sort of thing. This isn't a theory of ours. It's one we've picked up from the boys.'

'Why?' She ran her hands through her hair. 'Why should they think I was involved?'

'Obviously, Miss Strong, because of your programme. You stirred up a hornets' nest. That can't be a surprise to you. It must have been your intention.' He realized that he sounded more hostile than he had intended, and deliberately softened his tone. 'Look, Miss Strong, nobody for one moment blames you for what happened. If it is the work of a member of a paedophile ring, he's extremely ruthless, and we must find him quickly. That's why we're interested in the connection with your programme. We need to know from you how much you knew about a ring, who was involved – anything you can tell us, in fact.'

She nodded, still unable to take in what he had told her. She had been so sure the boys themselves were the target. She had focused her mind on trying to protect them. Now suddenly it was as if a searchlight had sought her out, and was pinning her in its glare. As if someone, somewhere had her in their sights, and was determined to obliterate her. She felt paralysed. She didn't know where to run or how to hide, she had no idea where the danger came from. Her heart began to pound. She tried to control it. Come on now, Lucy, she told herself irritably, get a grip on your imagination. Don't let yourself panic.

The policewoman took out a notebook and a tape recorder and the methodical questioning began. How many of the boys were known to her? What arrangements had she made to see them in Thritham? What had they told her?

Lucy answered automatically, question by question, not volunteering more than they asked, but responding as honestly as she could. 'I had only met one of the boys before, the one who called himself Max. He told me there was more to our story about Wantage Grange, that there was a ring of some kind, but he gave me no details about what happened to the boys, or where they were taken when they went out of the school. I was hoping to learn more at the party, maybe from some of his friends. But almost as soon as we arrived the fire started.'

Derek White persevered. 'Who knew you were going to be there, besides Max?'

'I really don't know. He introduced me to three others, but I only know their first names. Sean escaped with us. Then there were Nick and Ben. I don't know what happened to them.'

He consulted his notes. 'I'm afraid we don't either. They're listed as missing. They were in the kitchen in the back of the house, weren't they? And the fire was between them and the front door. Some of the boys escaped out of the back door, but

134

not all. It's difficult for us because there doesn't seem to have been a guest list of any kind. But it looks as if they may not have got out. I'm sorry.'

She held on to her mug of coffee tightly. He saw the deep frown of pain on her face, and softened a little further. He had no particular love for conceited investigative journalists who thought they were so much cleverer than the police, but she was blaming herself now, unnecessarily, and he tried to reassure her.

'There was really nothing you could have done, Miss Strong. That fire took hold so quickly, the whole house went up like a tinderbox. We're going to find out who was behind it. That's why we're anxious to discover a motive, and it is possible that you could be central to it. Did you tell many people you were going to be at the party?'

'Only Max – and Tom, my ex-husband. I don't know how many people Max told. Not many, I think. He knew the risks. He said to me that there were some very highly placed people in the ring. He said they were extremely dangerous.'

'Did he name names to you?'

She thought for a moment. As a journalist her reflex was to keep the names to herself. But not now. This was a murder investigation, sixteen young lives lost. But she had no hard, cor-roborated facts to give them.

'You do realize that I've got no evidence at all linking these men,' she started. 'I haven't even started to research them. I only know what Max told me. But one name was Paul Wilson.' White nodded, not showing any emotion. 'And Roy Parks, Lord Parks, the ex-Home Secretary.'

'That would be a good story for your show, if you could prove it.'

She looked at him closely. What did he mean? Was he on her side, asking her to carry on with her investigation? Or against her, thinking that she was only trying to implicate these men for tabloid reasons, because she wanted the glory and the sen-sational ratings? She couldn't tell.

'We're aware that you went to the party with your ex-husband, Miss Strong,' he went on.

'Yes, Tom Aspern. He's a lawyer. He does a lot of child abuse cases. He came to be a kind of expert witness for me. I knew he could assess the strength of any stories I was told. I didn't know what I'd find when I got there. Obviously I didn't expect what happened, but I didn't want to go all that way at night, alone, with nobody to support me.' Would that sound stupid? She tried to read the policeman's face, but his dark straight brows and expressionless mouth told her nothing.

'Did anyone else know?'

'The friend I live with here, Fred Miller. I told him I was going with Tom, and that I was staying at the Majestic. I didn't tell him the address of the party.'

Was it dangerous for her to admit to the policeman that she lived with Fred? It was common knowledge that the police leaked like a cracked teapot. Some of them doubled their incomes with the payoffs from journalists for a hot story like this. But she had to tell him. The woman officer made another careful note.

Derek White scrutinized Lucy's face. He was obviously preparing to ask her another difficult question, but didn't want her emotions to overwhelm her this time, blur her memory, close down her objectivity. 'Miss Strong,' he began, 'I understand this has been a very painful time for you. I'm trying not to make it any worse, but I must ask you. I can see what a shock this is for you – the idea that you might have been the real target of the attack – but can I ask you now to examine your memories? Do you think you could have been the target? Do you have enemies?'

She almost laughed. 'Yes, I'm sure I have. People I've criticized over the years. Like the paedophiles I exposed on our last programme. I won't be their favourite TV presenter.'

'Have you been contacted by any of them since the progamme? Have you ever actually felt you were at risk?'

She had been dreading the question, blocking the memory in her mind, but she had to face it now. 'I haven't really talked

136

about this to anyone, because I didn't want to be hysterical.' She hesitated for a moment. She had to risk seeming foolish. 'But when I came home after our programme, there were reporters waiting for me. After they left, a car came down the road. I thought maybe the driver was drunk, or stoned, or that it was some kid who couldn't control the car. Anyway it came very fast, straight at me. I only just got out of the way.'

'Did you see the driver?' He was clearly concerned.

'No. It was dark, and I was a bit shaken up. I've tried to remember more clearly, but I can't. I don't even know if it was a man or a woman.'

'And the make of car?'

She shook her head, maddened by her own uncertainty. 'It was a dark colour. A saloon. Quite big and powerful. But I've no idea what make it was. And I didn't see the numberplate.'

All this time the young woman had been taking notes. Now she looked up, sensing there was more. 'What else, Miss Strong?' she asked.

Lucy smiled at her intuition. 'Well, I'm probably getting paranoid, but when I met Max after our meeting at the Fleet service station, again it was very dark, but as I left I thought I saw another car put on its lights and leave.'

'The same car?'

'It could have been. A similar car, at any rate.'

Derek White asked more questions about the make and the colour, hoping to jog her memory, but there was nothing in her mind to describe, though she could instantly conjure up the panic she had felt the moment she had jumped out of the car's way. Somewhere in the computer of her brain there must be a clearer image. Why couldn't she find it, intensify it, tell them what they needed to know?

'Don't worry, Miss Strong, sometimes something unexpectedly jogs the memory, and brings back a detail. If that happens, please get in touch with us.' He'd put their cards down next to the empty mugs of coffee.

At that moment she heard Fred's key turn in the lock, and he came through the back door of the mews into the kitchen. When he saw the two police officers, he stayed by the door, uncertain whether he was interrupting a crucial conversation.

Lucy went over quickly to him, and he kissed her. She introduced them. 'This is Detective Inspector Derek White and his colleague Detective Constable Iris Watkins from the Thritham police. They've been talking to me about the fire.'

Fred looked at them with interest. 'Do you know how it happened yet?' he asked.

'No,' Derek White answered him. 'We're just beginning our investigation.'

'But they think I might have been the target,' Lucy said, trying to keep her voice light.

Fred's eyes widened with shock. 'What? I thought it was an accident, or someone was trying to frighten the boys. Lucy, if you were the target of some maniac who wanted to kill you, they'll try again.'

She tried to calm him. 'It's only one theory, Fred. They have loads of others. The police aren't worried about me, are you?' She turned to Derek White for help.

He shook his head. 'No, not at the moment. Although I would ask you to stay watchful. Be aware of anything different. If you think you're being observed, or followed, let us know. It sounds dramatic, but there's no harm being careful. And of course we'll let you know if we have any more information.'

'You must tell Jameson what the police have said.' Fred was still angry on her behalf. 'You must make him look after you.'

This time Derek White intervened before Lucy could answer. 'We'd much rather as few people as possible are told at the moment, Miss Strong. As I say, at this stage we have no evidence, no concrete reason to be concerned for your safety.'

'Quite. So you're going to wait until something worse happens.' Fred's anger was growing by the second. 'So you want to use her as a decoy, to bring this murderer, whoever he is, out into the open. Well, I'm sorry, but I think that's quite wrong. It's irresponsible. You can't put Lucy at risk like that.'

Derek White stood up. Iris Watkins gathered her notebook and tape recorder together.

'Let me say again, as of this moment we have no evidence that she is at risk,' the inspector said. 'Even if she was the target of this fire, and as Miss Strong has said, that's only one possible theory, it's extremely unlikely that anything else will happen. She's very high profile, people notice her wherever she goes. I really wouldn't worry.' He reached for his coat. 'We'll leave you now. It's late, you're tired, and Miss Strong has a big show to make tomorrow.'

There was irony in his voice. The 'big show' wasn't high in his priorities. But he was right: she was tired, it was late, so she left the gauntlet where he'd dropped it. She showed them both out, and went back into the kitchen, where Fred was staring into the fridge.

'Come on, sweetie,' he said. 'You're exhausted. I bet you haven't eaten properly, and this place is stacked with dirty cups, and piles of work everywhere. Let me grill you a steak, we'll have a nice big glass of red wine, and you can tell me what's been going on.'

To her own surprise, Lucy ate hungrily. Then they sat together, and Fred said, 'How about some good news – are you in the mood?' She nodded. 'Well, I hope this will please you. Colin, your technical manager, rang and asked if I'd do your show tomorrow. I said yes. We aren't filming on location again until next week. What do you think?'

Lucy leaned closer to him, against his shoulder. It would be comforting to have him in the studio, to be able to go home together. She told him so.

'You are good to me, Fred. It sounds stupid, but I am a bit scared about tomorrow. Maybe the police have put the wind up me.' She sighed. 'But it's not only that. It's going to be so different from the kind of show I'm used to.'

He had no doubts. 'You'll handle it fine, no problem.'

In bed later, Fred put his arms comfortingly around her, and out of sheer exhaustion she fell deeply asleep.

When Lucy awoke at seven the next morning, she felt fear fluttering in her chest before she could identify the cause. The fire. The police. And overlaid on top of that, today she had to take over Suzannah's show.

She corrected the thought instantly. It was her programme now. *Piper's People* had become *Strong Stories*. Her set, with her name emblazoned on it, would have been built in the studio overnight. Right now the lights were being swung and prodded into position. The floor was being painted. By the time the crew and the production team came in at ten, the studio would have been completely transformed, made hers. She tensed in the darkness, and Fred tightened his arms around her, sensing her anxiety, and slowly waking. She smiled at his protectiveness. Not that she usually needed protection, but today she was vulnerable. Then she strengthened her resolve and rolled out of his arms to start the day.

Careful not to wake him, she tiptoed into the bathroom. She laid out her make-up methodically, and packed her perfume into her case. She took a much-loved black Catherine Walker shift dress out of her wardrobe. When she first bought it she had winced at the price – it had cost her a month's salary – but she had worn it so often since, it had turned out to be an investment.

As she turned to the mirror, she saw Fred walk into the bathroom behind her, and he took her in his arms again. They were both naked, and the ease of the embrace comforted her.

'It's going to be fun today, don't worry,' he said, and his confidence made her face brighten.

She dressed, picked up her case, and looked for her handbag. As she opened it she saw, pushed to the bottom of the bag, Suzannah's hate mail. Perhaps now she was a target too. Could it possibly be the same madman? Would he be watching her tonight, planning to send her vicious, threatening letters like these? Or maybe plotting something even worse? She took the letters out of her bag, and put them in the drawer of her dressing table. She wouldn't take them with her today. She refused to allow them to take control of her mind, and sap her confidence. Dan had said some of the letters had been sent to Suzannah on the day of her show, and even with her confidence and experience they must have damaged her capacity to smile, face the cameras and enjoy the moment. Lucy summoned her own strength, and shut her mind to them. From now on the day must be devoted to the show, and only to the show. She owed that to the team, and to herself.

She arrived at the studio to find Alison, the company press officer, waiting for her outside the lobby with a bundle of papers in her hand. On the top was a request from the *Daily News*, who wanted exclusive access to Lucy and the new show. Lucy and Alison sat together on one of the garish blue leather benches in reception and read the e-mail. They asked for one of their top reporters and a photographer to shadow Lucy all afternoon and evening, to watch the rehearsals and then to sit in the audience for the show.

'I'm nervous,' Lucy admitted. 'If things get tense during the day, and there's a row, and it can happen on the first day with everyone a little insecure, the language might get a bit picturesque. I'm not sure I want to see all that in the papers tomorrow.'

Alison didn't hide her disappointment. 'It would be such good publicity for the new series, Lucy. You know how to handle yourself. I'll make sure the reporter stays away from your production meetings. I'll explain they're editorially sensitive.'

'I'm still not sure. But if you're that keen . . .' Reluctantly Lucy allowed herself to be pushed to agree. There were more important battles to win.

When she reached her dressing room she found it crammed with flowers – lilies from Dan, orchids from Mandy, and a very large tied bouquet from David Jameson. There was a sweetly scented bunch of hyacinths from Shirley, her old producer, wishing her well. Lucy put down her case, and went to the production office to meet the team.

They were talking in huddles when she arrived, and turned to greet her, eyes bright with excitement.

'How were the police last night?' Alex asked.

Clearly all the researchers had been speculating. Lucy sat down at the head of the table, next to Dan, and poured herself a glass of water.

'They were quite anxious to find out who could have known I was going to that party in Thritham. They seemed to think the fire might have been designed to frighten me. But I don't believe that. I think someone with a great deal to lose had decided to silence the boys.'

They digested that idea. Dan looked round the table, then at Lucy's tense face. 'I hate to say this,' he told her slowly, 'but I think, for every reason, that you ought to try to forget about the fire for the rest of the day. We've got a new show to put on the air. Let's all concentrate on that.'

The researchers went through the question-lines, the cues and clips of film, all the nuts and bolts of the script. Then they all went together to the studio.

Dan had already walked round the new set. 'It's fun,' he said to Lucy. 'I think you'll like it.'

When they pushed through the heavy sound-proof doors of the studio, it was like walking into a plywood packing case. All they could see was the backs of the flats, ranged in overlapping walls like a maze, rough and unpainted, with *Strong Stories* scrawled in black paint to identify them. Dan led Lucy through a gap towards the front of the stage, picking his way over thick black cables, and suddenly they were in an artificial world of plastic pinnacles and translucent gauzes, with lit stars on the floor, and steep dark ranks of audience seats facing them. It was completely different from the understated black and grey set of her old show.

'What do you think of it?' he asked, turning her to face a flight of steps at the back of the set, each tread rimmed with light.

She tried to smile. Clearly she was going to have to make an entrance, like a star. At the moment she felt she would rather slide in on her stomach.

Dan read her thoughts. 'Try the walk down,' he urged, and took her to the top of the stairs.

At the very top, she turned away from the sheer drop into darkness, and faced the rows of empty audience seats. She took a deep breath and walked down towards the lights, which blazed in her eyes. Maybe it wasn't so bad after all.

Dan grinned at her. 'Every inch the star presenter,' he said.

She shook her head and grimaced. 'I don't think so. The show's the star, the presenter may fall flat on her face.'

A soundman clipped a microphone to her lapel, and handed her an earpiece. Through it she could hear the voice of the director. The script of her introduction rolled up in front of the camera lens. Tina, the Autocue operator, was sitting in the wings, ready to run the script forward when Lucy started speaking. The familiarity of it all was calming.

The camera crew were taking up their positions, dressed in their usual uniform – vintage jeans – balancing polystyrene cups of coffee and packets of crisps on the cameras. They were un-impressed by the grandeur of the new set; they'd seen it all before. Lucy went over to talk to them. She had worked with them often and she knew the speed of the show depended on their fast reflexes. They had to follow the action instinctively: no shot could be predicted in a live debate. She looked for Fred. He arrived last, but barely acknowledged her smile. He was frowning and looked upset. But there were far too many people around for her to ask why.

Waiting for her cue to start rehearsals, she sat in the audience, reading and absorbing her research notes. The lighting director was bathing the empty seats in a rosy glow. The audience would all be clearly visible as they put their questions to the guests tonight, and they would benefit from soft, kind lighting. Then, over all the chatter, the senior electrician barked instructions at everyone to clear the set while a group of lights were lowered to the floor. Lucy took advantage of the moment, and caught Fred's eye.

They met a couple of minutes later in a scene dock which was piled high with spare chairs, crates, and a large cage filled with props and furniture. With practised caution Lucy unplugged the microphone on her lapel, so as not to be overheard.

'Fred, what's wrong?' she asked him.

'Someone's sold us out,' he said. His voice was choked with fury. 'As I came out of the back door I saw a photographer waiting across the mews taking pictures. I have no idea who it was, but he ran off straight away. I didn't have my wits about me, otherwise I would have chased him. It must be one of the tabloids. Why do they bother? Haven't they anything better to do?'

Lucy saw how invaded he felt. She had done her best to keep their life together out of the public eye, but now it seemed she'd failed.

Fred was angry, and sore. He paced around the small, cluttered room. 'Why is it anyone else's business?' he fumed. 'What right have they to tramp all over our lives like this?'

For her own sanity, Lucy tried to stay cool. She could see the studio lights being hauled up to the ceiling again, and the floor manager was calling everyone back into their positions. What could she say? There was no time for rage on his behalf, or even sympathy.

She tried reassurance. 'Let's not get too worried, Fred. It may be nothing. At worst it'll be a paragraph in a diary.' She wanted to hug him, to comfort him, but they were calling her, so she plugged the wire back into her radio mike, and walked back to the centre of the floor. Fred stayed in the dark scenery store, waiting for the moment when rehearsal started and he could return unnoticed to take up his position again behind a camera. The ritual they both knew so well, dissecting the script and practising the camera moves, began in earnest.

When the rehearsal ended, the team scattered to look after their guests. Dan walked up to Lucy from his producer's desk in one corner of the studio floor.

'It's looking good,' he said.

She wasn't sure whether to believe him. Professionally he had to protect her, keep her spirits high and feed her ego. The television camera is like a jackal scenting blood, a nervous and unsure presenter will get savaged. So he might just have been boosting her morale. Even so, she trusted him. All day she had watched him at work, and seen his keen eye for detail. From his desk on the studio floor next to her, he had been adjusting angles and lighting to make her look good, and the set seem bright and impressive. Although the director was in charge in the control room, Dan had a talk-back microphone to him from the producer's desk, and monitors showed him the output from each camera. Lucy was grateful for his meticulous precision. She needed him there, guarding her back.

They rehearsed through the afternoon, then broke for a supper break. At the end of the break Lawrence Crabtree arrived. They had decided Lucy shouldn't meet him in advance. The secret film would be an unpleasant surprise for him, and she would have to deal with that live on the air. She didn't need or want to confront him first in his dressing room, where he was keeping one of the make-up girls fully occupied, blow-drying his luxuriant blond hair. Jim Kelly, his ex-sous-chef, arrived a few moments later, and was hidden in a room in the basement. The research team had strict instructions to keep them apart.

On her way to her own dressing room, she met Alison, the press officer, in the corridor. With her was a thin, dark man with a narrow face and watchful eyes. Lucy recognized Bill Thompson, the television writer from the *Daily News*. He was notorious for the television gossip he uncovered. Some of it was

145

wildly off the mark, but he carried occasional scoops that were the envy of his colleagues, and his sources were uncomfortably well informed, obviously placed at the top of the television industry. The last paragraph Thompson had written about her had been a sarcastic reference in his diary, referring to her as 'fleshy Lucy'. Facing him now, she decided amnesia was the safest symptom to fake. So she smiled at him, and they shook hands.

'How are you feeling, Lucy?' he asked. She was aware that everything she said would be taken down and used as evidence.

'I'm a bit nervous, I suppose,' she said, 'but then I always am. I seem to need that extra surge of adrenalin. And this is a very big show.'

'I know,' he said, 'I've seen the set. Not exactly understated. All those towers and gauzes and staircases. Very Busby Berkeley.'

She smiled. 'All I need is some chorus girls with fruit in their hats, and I'd knock 'em dead,' she said. 'I hope you don't want an in-depth interview right now?'

'No, that's fine,' he said, 'but I'll sit in the audience, if I may, so I can feel the atmosphere.'

'And I've said he can have his photographer in the wings, if that's OK with you, Lucy,' Alison told her. 'They want some backstage pictures.'

'As long as he's not in my eyeline, that's fine,' she said. They wished her luck, and walked past her into the studio.

As she reached the sanctuary of her dressing room, she saw Boris's name on the door next to hers, and knocked on it. He called to her to come in, and they hugged each other. He was as good-looking as ever, tall, wearing a dark denim shirt that showed off his constant golden tan, his blue eyes shining seductively. Lucy knew too much about him to be moved by his charm, but she recognized that the viewers would warm to him.

'Boris, thank you so much for coming in,' she said. 'It's a tough show tonight. I only hope I don't let Suzannah down.'

'You won't,' he told her. 'Wait and see. I predict the viewers will love you.'

146

Lucy unlocked her own dressing room, went in, and sat for a moment staring at herself in the mirror. This was the time for her to withdraw into herself. Deirdre Shaw, her favourite make-up artist, had laid out camel-hair brushes and metal cases and pots in neat rows, and she started to work on Lucy's face quietly, without comment, knowing Lucy was concentrating, arranging facts and questions in her mind. Behind them Lesley let herself into the room, carrying the new dress, a dark rose colour. Deirdre glanced at it, then took out her palette of lipsticks to concoct a colour that matched, and started to paint Lucy's lips. Lucy didn't interrupt them. It was part of the job to look good, but she knew that with all their efforts she would never be beautiful. If she kept her wits about her, and contrived to be sharp and funny, perhaps the viewers would forgive her overexpressive wide mouth, the bump on the end of her nose and her unfashionable curves.

They finished their work, and Lucy stood by the full-length mirror while they inspected her for scuffs on her shoes, or a smudge on her eyelids. The vivid colours of the purple jacket and rose-coloured dress unnerved her.

'Don't I look like a fuchsia?' she asked.

They looked at her critically. 'No,' Lesley said, 'you look like a top television presenter with her own show. Someone who can entertain an audience. Not someone who creeps onto a set in a dingy grey suit or a long, baggy skirt.'

Lucy shrugged. 'Whatever you say, Mum.'

She heard the audience shuffling along the corridor outside the dressing room. The minutes ticked by. The warm-up man would be telling them his well-worn jokes. She breathed in deeply, and tried to control the air as she let it slowly out.

Dan knocked on her door. He came in and gazed at her with affection. 'You look gorgeous,' he said. 'Suzannah would be proud of you.'

She smiled uncertainly, and they walked together into the studio.

As she stood beside Dan behind the set, the warm-up man briefed the audience about their contribution. 'We've got a couple of guests: Lawrence Crabtree, the famous chef, and Boris Crosthwaite, who, as you know, used to be married to Suzannah. So I'm sure you'll have plenty of questions. Just put your hand up, Lucy will call on you, and you can ask what you like. Only please remember this is a live show, don't say anything that might shock my mother.'

The audience laughed politely. Lucy could see them in the soft pink light, and they looked harmless enough. No streakers or football hooligans, as far as she could tell.

Suddenly the floor manager warned them, 'One minute to go, Studio,' then counted down the last ten seconds aloud. A red light flicked on over each door. Lucy went to her position in the dark, at the back of the set. As she passed Fred, their hands touched. A camera shutter moved in the wings behind them, but neither of them noticed. Music filled the studio, Lucy's new signature tune. Then, in a blaze of light, she was cued to walk down the precipitous staircase. She reached her seat, her heart pounding, the music stopped, the audience applause died. There was no way back now.

As she spoke her introduction, Lucy's voice was steady. She'd done this a hundred times before. She could no longer feel her own heartbeat. Professional reflexes had taken over.

'Good evening and welcome to this new show,' she said, reading the script with the professional naturalness that made it sound as if she was improvising. 'It's the first of the series, and we're live tonight, so anything can happen. Especially as our first guest is not known for being dull. You've seen his five series, all of them have been huge hits with the viewers, and millions of you have bought his books. The result? Not only is he on the *Sunday Times* list of the nation's richest men, he has become one of our most popular cookery icons, alongside Delia and Jamie. We've come to know his likes and dislikes: we know he loathes political correctness, for instance, he loves red meat and can't abide haggis. And above all, he has brought sex into the kitchen. Ladies and gentlemen, please welcome Lawrence Crabtree.'

Lawrence appeared at the top of the staircase, and tossed his hair in the spotlight. There were a few screams from middle-aged ladies sitting together at one side of the audience rostrum, invited by his publisher. They were ardent fans, treasuring each crumb that fell from his manicured fingers. He waved to them, and leaped down the stairs towards Lucy, then enveloped her in his arms and kissed her sensually on the lips. She felt instantly nostalgic for the air-kisses she was used to. He settled himself into the grey suede chair opposite her, and flicked his hair back with another toss of his head. He smiled at her with the full force of his dimpled charm. She smiled restrainedly back.

'Welcome, Lawrence,' she said. 'That was some entrance.'

'I've been longing to meet you, Lucy,' he said, pulling his chair theatrically closer to hers. Their legs were practically inter-locking. 'I had to take your stairs two at a time, I couldn't help it.'

Did he practise it all in the mirror at home, she wondered. Although he was physically so close to her, he kept his face turned towards the audience and his close-up camera. This was a bid to take over the show, to prove that he was the star, far more experienced, and more lovable than she was. Lucy let him preen; her moment would come.

She stayed at first in safe territory, talking about his new series, and he became eloquent about his new dishes, created for his fans: chicken with truffles, hazelnut meringues filled with chocolate and cream, and the *pièce de résistance*, his pride and joy, the strawberry and lavender soufflé. They had a piece of film showing him mashing the strawberries and crushing them through his fingers, and as they ran it, to delighted murmurs from his fans, a scene man sneaked another chair in beside Lucy. At the corner of the set, out of Lawrence's sight but directly in her eyeline, Dan nodded to her. It was time to break the news to Crabtree that this was not going to be the happy series of plugs he'd prepared himself for.

'Lawrence, while we're digesting all that, let's meet our second guest,' she said. 'He's someone who knows you well, he worked for you for five years, Jim Kelly.'

Lawrence turned sharply in his chair to see Kelly walking towards him from the wings. Then he turned back to Lucy, his face furious.

'Why wasn't I warned about this?'

'Because Mr Kelly has made a film of you cooking the same soufflé in your restaurant. We want you to see it and tell us what you think of it. Let's have a look at it now.'

The film flickered on a huge screen on the wall of the set. Fred kept his lens fixed on Crabtree's face. Lawrence watched himself working in his restaurant kitchen, swearing ferociously at the young men and women round him, and then concentrating on one chef who had failed to swathe a soufflé in foil. The film ended.

Lucy turned to Crabtree. 'Can you explain why you were so angry?'

He blustered at her. 'Yes, of course. I invented the soufflé. It needs foil to maintain the temperature, otherwise it falls flat.'

'We've checked that with other chefs,' Lucy told him evenly, 'and they don't agree. And, in any case, our viewers will have heard what you said on that piece of film. You said that the foil might not be effing necessary for the soufflé, but it was effing necessary to you. What did you mean?'

Crabtree looked at her, but he didn't reply.

'Can you help us, Jim?'

Kelly could, and did. 'We all knew why. Lawrence has a two-hundred-thousand-pound deal with Gourmet Cooking Foil. We have to use it all the time. The soufflé would be much better with greaseproof paper, but Lawrence won't have it.'

Crabtree found his voice. The dimples had disappeared. The eyes had hardened into sour, shiny blackcurrants. 'So what's

150

wrong with that? Gourmet Foil is an excellent product. Why shouldn't I use it?'

'No reason, as long as you declare an interest,' Lucy told him. 'Then everyone, the broadcasters and the public, can make up their own mind whether you're using it for the sake of the recipe, or your own wallet.'

He tossed his long blond hair one last time. There was silence from the audience where his faithful fans were sitting, stunned. 'I'm not staying here, Lucy Strong, while you try and win awards by libelling me. You can stuff your show.'

'Shame,' said the lone voice of one of the fans, too little and too late.

Crabtree got to his feet, and turned to the audience, bellowing his anger. 'What Lucy Strong wants to do is make a name for herself at my expense. Well, I'm not hanging around to do her dirty work. If you would like my recipe for a delicious light frothy strawberry and lavender soufflé, perfect for an evening of romance, buy my book and watch the series. I'll invent one for you, Lucy Strong, made out of sour grapes.' And he stalked off the set, to applause from the audience, who had greatly enjoyed the exchange. Rightly or wrongly, the show had begun with an enjoyable explosion. They settled back to see what would happen next.

'Goodbye, Mr Crabtree,' Lucy said politely, though he was well out of the studio by now. 'And thank you, Jim Kelly, for showing us your film. I specially liked the moment when Lawrence licked his finger and stuck it back in the sauce. Soufflé au saliva, you could call it. Shall we see it again in slow motion?' They did, and the audience groaned with revulsion.

Lucy moved on. 'As you know, until a month ago this show was presented by a dear friend of mine, Suzannah Piper. I owe Suzannah everything. She trained me to be a television journalist, she won every award going, she became the standard by which every other interviewer is judged, and here's why.'

The film rolled again, and while moments from Suzannah's

151

most famous programmes were running on the screen, Jim Kelly quietly tiptoed from the set.

As the lights went up, Lucy announced the next guest. 'Ladies and gentlemen, please welcome the man who knew Suzannah best, her ex-husband, Boris Crosthwaite.'

He walked slowly down the set, and the audience applauded him. He sat beside her, acknowledging the welcome, as much for his ex-wife as for him. Lucy waited until the applause had died, then she said quietly, 'Of all the questions I'm ever asked, by far the most common one is about Suzannah. So I'm going to put it to you now, Boris. Everyone had their own opinion of her – her face had been on the screen and in our homes for ten years – and yet very few people knew the real woman behind the screen. You did. From your point of view, as her lover, her ex-husband, and her friend, what was Suzannah really like?' This was not the question she had planned, the cue for a slow, entertaining ramble through Suzannah's career, the witty show business anecdotes. On an impulse she had cut through all that. Would it pay off? Would this be more revealing?

Boris was unprepared for her question. He thought for a long moment. 'How do you sum up a complete person, specially a woman as complex as Suzannah, in one sentence, or even in a paragraph?' He paused again. 'First and foremost, I suppose, because for Suzannah her work always came first, she was a consummate professional. The public never saw the effort it took. She worked long hours, she was a perfectionist, she never suffered fools gladly. There was a price for all that fame, and success, and we all had to pay it.'

He was echoing Tom's epitaph on Suzannah now. Lucy pursued the thought. 'What was that price?'

'Well – and I'm still talking about Suzannah in her professional life – towards the end people weren't keen to work with her. She could be sharp, sometimes unforgiving to people who couldn't keep up with her, or who were slipshod or lazy.'

The audience stirred, interested. This wasn't the bland eulogy they'd been expecting.

'Did that cost her friendships?' Lucy asked.

Boris leaned across and touched her hand briefly. 'Not yours, Lucy. You were loyal to her over the years. But others drifted away.'

'And yet you remained a friend too.'

'I did. Not at first, not when our marriage broke. I think anyone who saw the headlines at the time will have thought that our divorce was a modern, civilized arrangement between two people who had grown apart.' The newspaper cuttings appeared on the screen, 'The Piper's Lament' . . . 'Suzannah's Sadness'. Boris glanced up at them, then back to her. 'The truth, as you knew at the time, Lucy, was very different.'

This was fresh, and unexpected. Boris had evidently decided to be bluntly honest. She took him to the wire. 'Yes. As your friend I saw the intense, private bitterness between you,' she said, 'but you managed to keep that to yourselves at the time.'

'We did. At some cost. She drained me financially. And she tore me limb from limb emotionally.'

Unfair. Lucy couldn't leave it unopposed. 'There are two sides to that story, Boris, as you well know. Why are you attacking her now, when she can't answer back?'

'Because it's time the truth was told. And because I think there are lessons to be learned. Camilla and I—'

'Your daughter, Camilla . . .'

A picture of Camilla being hugged by her father, a family snapshot, appeared momentarily on the screen.

'Yes. Camilla and I watched the way Suzannah gave her best to her programmes. The charm, the humour, the insight, she gave all that to her guests in this very studio,' he looked around it with dislike, 'and to the viewers. We got the dregs, what was left over at the end of the day.'

There was real anger in his voice now. Lucy looked into his eyes, the blue pale with fury, the pupils hard. Suzannah's secret

153

letters flashed into Lucy's memory. Could she be looking at the writer now? Was he so embittered, so filled with hate?

'You say you got the dregs, Boris. From where I was sitting you had a fabulous life, materially, all the money you could ever want, lovely houses, great parties and so on. Camilla went to some of the best, most expensive schools—'

'And was so unhappy she was chucked out of all of them.'

'You're blaming Suzannah for that?'

'No. But she had such low self-esteem, and her mother gave her none of her time. I suppose I don't really blame Suzannah. I'm blaming the industry. The all-devouring television industry with its false friendships, and the capacity to drop you like a stone the moment the ratings begin to weaken.'

'But that's the real world, Boris. It's like that in every industry. Nobody is completely secure these days. Are you telling me that ruined your marriage?'

'I'm saying that I believe Suzannah would be alive today, should be alive today, but she was killed by the people she was closest to.'

'Boris, she died in a car crash. Tragically that happens, far too often.'

'Ask a few more questions about that accident, Lucy. Why did it happen, on a straight road, with no other car involved? You're an investigative journalist. God knows what you're doing in a show like this one. You know what Suzannah used to say about you?'

'Tell me.'

'She said she saw herself in you. Or rather, what she could have been. That first day you met, she came home and told me she'd never seen so much native talent in such a bedraggled bundle of old clothes.' On the screen a shot of Lucy as a brand-new researcher appeared. This must have been the surprise the team had secretly prepared for her. She remembered the picture vividly. The BriTV staff newsletter had sent a photographer to capture Suzannah's production team. Lucy had tried to shred every copy in the office. Suzannah must have saved one in her files for her own amusement. Now Lucy looked at the photograph with amused horror. She hadn't seen it for years. She looked as if she hadn't washed her hair in months, it straggled unevenly across her brow. Her favourite baggy skirt and the enormous sweater she thought concealed her extra pounds in fact multiplied them. But still she looked young and eager, and what Lucy didn't recognize herself was that her smile was so appealing and her eyes so eloquent and intelligent, that her talent shone through.

'That was you then,' Boris said. 'I know you wanted to destroy this picture. I can see you still think you looked appalling. But you didn't. You looked like a human being. Look at you now, all burnished and glossy. Don't turn into Suzannah, she wouldn't want that for you. Think how alone she was. Even alone when she died.'

She couldn't let him get away with this. 'Boris, you blame everyone and everything except yourself. How much of the unhappiness you describe, the tragic way Suzannah died, was caused by you leaving her when she needed you desperately?'

He looked at her, startled.

'I don't want to be unfair to you, Boris,' she went on. The audience were silent now, gripped by the conversation. This was real, unfaked, unforced emotion. The two were talking together as if the cameras didn't exist, raking over the ashes of the woman they had both loved. 'But you know you were unfaithful to her. You were polite about it, as discreet as possible, but there were plenty of rumours. Suzannah pretended not to care, but the gossip got to her.'

He shifted in his chair. 'Have you asked yourself why it happened, and who was unfaithful first?'

Oh God, this was turning into a wrangle. 'No, Boris. Is that really important?'

'I think so, Lucy,' he said angrily. 'It was part of the picture. Do you think I wasn't hurt when I was told that although I had

155

been very useful to her at the start of her career, I was old hat now, played out. She needed new, hot young talent to turn her on.'

Lucy felt rage rise within her. This was not the woman she knew at all. 'Boris, I don't recognize the picture you're painting. Yes, Suzannah had other friends, other male friends, but she told me that was because she had felt betrayed by you. Most of all she felt confused and isolated by your bisexuality. It made her feel as if she had never been good enough for you sexually. And as if you had lied to her from the start.'

There was an intake of breath in the audience. He was, after all, newly bereaved. He looked as if the question had winded him, she saw his consternation, and felt a pang of doubt. Had she gone too far? He'd clearly had no idea she would crash through every inhibition with such brutality. Not that he was frightened by the revelation. His friends and colleagues had long known he was bisexual. But he had trusted Lucy to allow him to choose how much of himself to reveal, and instead, she had snatched the control from him. Was it wrong of her? Un-professional? Boris obviously thought so.

'Lucy,' he said, 'you and I have known each other for years. I know that Suzannah confided her secrets to you. I don't think she would have wanted you to ask that question. It goes way beyond a professional interview. You have exploited our friend-ship, and Suzannah's trust.'

The audience grumbled its agreement. Lucy was flustered now. 'I had no intention of hurting you, Boris, but you blamed Suzannah. You said she was unfaithful. I knew, because she told me, how isolated and humiliated she felt.'

At his desk, Dan gestured towards the audience. Lucy under-stood him. She stood and walked down to meet the audience. Now she was really pushing her luck.

'What does our audience think?' she asked. 'Have I gone too far? Was that a question I should never have asked? If so I would be happy to apologize to Boris.'

156

Bill Thompson, the reporter from the *Daily News*, waved his hand towards her. The microphone swooped down and hovered above his head.

'Yes,' she cued him in. 'What do you think?'

'I think, Miss Strong, that in the context it was a good question.' She smiled with relief, too soon. 'Or at least it would have been a good question if you were prepared to be equally frank about your own love life.'

The audience rustled nervously. What was this leading to? Was it planned? Lucy's face was frozen. They could see she was unprepared for it. Bill plunged on, enjoying his moment on live television. 'I know, Miss Strong, that your own lover is here in the studio, working for you, and yet you have gone to great lengths to try and conceal your relationship. What would your bosses say if they knew? Would they think it was proper that Fred Miller, your cameraman here in this studio, is living with you? Is, in fact, your toy-boy?'

Up in the control room, an instant decision had to be made. Should they try to protect Lucy? Dan spat an instruction from the floor, telling them to follow their instincts. A camera zoomed in to Fred's face, as he stood very still, numbly realizing that every eye in the studio, every viewer at home, was staring at him, labelling him Lucy Strong's toy-boy.

There was a long silence. Then Lucy spoke. 'Yes, it is true that Fred is my partner. We are both single, we are harming nobody. And I suppose that if I make my living asking personal questions, it's only right I should have to answer them too. But I know Fred doesn't feel the same way. I know he cares deeply about his privacy. I'm sorry, Fred, that you've been put so publicly on trial.'

Fred turned abruptly away from the camera lenses. Sandra in the control room began counting down to the end of the programme. Lucy's face stayed calm, her hands steady, but her heart was pounding in her chest. She was walking a tightrope over boiling chaos. At any moment she could fall to her professional death. Thank God she was within seconds of the end of the show. She walked back to her seat and faced the camera. She smiled.

'It's been an eventful evening in this studio. I must thank all my guests, especially Boris Crosthwaite, for being with me on my first show. I hope you'll join us next week when the show will be equally unpredictable and perhaps just as revealing. Until then, good night.'

The closing music sounded, a big brazen fanfare. The red lights clicked off. It was over.

CHAPTER EIGHT

Somehow she held on to her smile until the audience had stopped applauding. Every instinct was to run to the wings, to the shelter of the shadows there, but while the lights were on her she had to hold herself together. She looked for Fred. He had cleared his camera to the side of the set, and as she watched he strode away from her down the side of the audience rostrum. At least he had escaped. She glanced across to Dan. He caught her gaze, but his face was pale and closed. He shuffled his script together and gestured to her to meet him in the wings. She nodded. She leaned across to Boris, to shake his hand, but he got up and turned away from her. She had lost a friend.

She rose from her seat, automatically smoothing the rose-pink skirt and tugging the jacket straight. She lifted her chin, and walked briskly from the set as the warm-up man bounded back into position in front of the audience.

'Ladies and gentlemen, the star of the show, Miss Lucy Strong.'

They applauded again, she forced one more wide, bright smile, and at last she had reached the wings, where Dan was waiting for her. Was he angry too?

'Let's go to your dressing room,' he said. 'We need some peace and quiet.' Just before she left, she looked back along the rows of audience seats to see if Bill Thompson was still there, but he had disappeared. Rushing away to write his story, no doubt: 'How I starred in Lucy's show'. The press would howl in delight at her embarrassment.

She followed Dan, head down, to avoid the eyes of any of the team who might cross her path. Her brain was struggling to make sense of what had just happened, like a spade delving down through mud, unearthing disaster after disaster. All the team's hard work researching Lawrence Crabtree's dishonesty would be wasted now. It would be completely lost in a sea of newsprint speculating about Lucy's 'toy-boy Fred'. And where had Fred gone? Was he racing home, trying to get there before the inevitable reporters, barricading himself in, waiting to tear into her for allowing this to happen? Or had he taken off in some other direction, determined that nobody should find him, least of all her? When would she see him again? So much damage had been done in the last forty minutes.

She took off her microphone as she walked and handed it to the sound man who had been quietly following her as she pushed through the heavy studio doors. Dan was silent, walking alongside her. They reached her dressing room, and Lucy unlocked the door. Lesley was there already waiting for her, but she glanced at Lucy's tense face, and instantly took the hint. 'I'll be in hospitality if you want me,' she said, and shut the door behind her.

Lucy sat down in one chair, Dan in the other. The silence hung between them, heavy, angry.

Lucy spoke first. 'I'm sorry, Dan, if I let you down. I know the show went out of control. I don't know what else I could have done.'

Still he was silent. This wouldn't do. She was pleading now: 'Dan, we have to work together. Tonight was a nightmare. We took a lot of risks. But I think the Crabtree interview was all right, wasn't it? Maybe I overstepped the mark with Boris. I went too far. But you know why that happened. I couldn't stand the way he was blaming Suzannah for everything, and accusing her of creating all the problems in her private life.'

Dan stirred. He gripped his hands in his lap, his fingers tightly enlaced, then he looked first at her and then away. His mouth twisted.

'Lucy, if I'm honest it was as much my fault as yours. I suggested Boris as a guest. But I had no idea you would lose your cool like that. I understand how it happened, and what you felt, but even so. You're a professional. You know how important it is to keep your own personal feelings out of it.'

160

This was bad. Worse than she had imagined. Somehow she had to make peace. 'Dan, what can I say to you? That I'm sorry? Of course I am. The programme was a mess. My whole life is a mess. I can't bear to think what Fred is going through now, knowing he's been bad-mouthed, live, in front of millions of people, and there's the press to come. He was desperate to try and hang on to his privacy. I don't know how he'll cope. To be honest, I don't know if I can take much more myself.'

She turned her face away from him, feeling the tears fill her eyes. She looked up and caught her own reflection in the mirror, wet-lashed, lips trembling. What an idiot she had been to agree to the show. Why on earth had she moved away from the programme she was used to, where she could create journalism of some genuine value.

In the stillness, the phone rang. She couldn't trust herself to answer it. She looked pleadingly at Dan, and he reached over and picked up the receiver. 'No, but I'm the Executive Producer of the programme . . . Thank you, yes, I thought there would be . . . How many? . . . Ah. Is BriTV preparing a statement? Jameson himself? Let me know what he says. Thank you for telling me.

'That was Duty Office,' he said. 'The phones are jammed.'

'With complaints?'

'Yes, mainly. But not entirely. There was some praise as well. Some people were definitely on your side. Though most of the complaints were about your "intrusive" questions to Boris.'

Dan stood up and stretched wearily. 'Look, I can't see any point in going over old ground. That show has gone. We'll learn from it. Next week will be better. Let's get a drink.'

She nodded. 'You go down to hospitality, Dan. I need a moment by myself, but I'll come down as soon as I can.'

Left alone, Lucy sat gazing at her own reflection, at the bright clothes, and the highly coloured make-up. Fine to withstand the harsh studio lights, amid all the artifice, but now it looked like a mask which she longed to tear away. Never in a million years would she have wanted to hurt Boris. In real life, sitting in a room together, she would never have asked him those questions. The adrenalin of live television had forced her on. But she also had to admit to herself that maybe a tiny maggot in her id had calculated that a real row would create memorable television, and do no harm to her ratings.

She shook her head, and got up to go, but the phone rang again. This time she had to answer it herself.

Jameson's familiar voice barked down the line at her. 'Is that Lucy Strong, the well-known Rottweiler who makes hard men weep?'

She was not in the mood to respond. 'Oh, David, don't tease me. I was a disaster.'

'Not from where I was watching, you weren't. The atmosphere was electric, absolutely magnetic. Nobody could possibly have switched off. You old professional, don't kid me. You knew exactly what you were doing.'

She started to contradict him, then silenced herself. He wasn't angry or appalled. He was thrilled. She'd better go along with his mood. Maybe the ratings would prove him right; they usually did.

'But I have one thought for you,' he said. 'Just a thought, not something I would impose.' Not much. A boss with his kind of absolute power never needed to use strong-arm methods. The lightest hint was enough to poison the atmosphere against someone who offended him, or create radiant sunshine around the career of someone he developed a fancy for. Lucy waited to see what was coming. 'These insinuations that Suzannah's death was more than an accident – have you any real evidence that could be true?'

The question took her by surprise. 'No, none at all.' This was no time to confide in him about the letters in Suzannah's desk.

'Well then, I should drop them. It's keeping her memory alive in the wrong way, in my humble opinion.' Humble as Versailles, all gold leaf and fountains.

162

Well, if humility was in fashion, she'd better adopt a humble tone too. 'I quite agree, David. I don't know what Boris was getting at when he said that. It's certainly not a theory of mine.'

'Nor mine. She was tired, it was late, she'd done a show, she shouldn't have been driving at all. Actually, Lucy, you must be exhausted after the show you've done. I'll let you go now. Where's Dan?'

'In hospitality, I think.'

'Fine, I'll ring him there. Go home and have a rest, and ignore the press tomorrow, just watch the ratings. You'll be pleased.'

She put the phone down. Once again she caught her own eye in the mirror. She looked relieved but confused. She was still trying to register what Jameson had said to her. He had loved the show. Not a word about intrusion, or chaos. He thought it was magnetic. She stood up, straightened the crumpled silk of her skirt, threw her black dress and the other oddments of washing things and perfume into her case, and went down the escalator to hospitality.

A mass of bodies was crowded around the little bar and the table with its burden of rapidly ageing sandwiches. As she swung the door open, the researchers saw her arrive, and started to applaud her. There was no doubt where their loyalty lay.

Lucy stood in the centre of a semicircle, and waited until she could speak. 'Well, thank you for that. But I should be applauding you,' she said. 'That was an extraordinary show, not at all what we had expected.' One or two of them laughed ruefully. 'But your research stood up brilliantly. The preparation you all did was fabulous. If we stay on the air, I'm sure you'll make the series a great success.'

'If,' said Marion, the researcher who had been responsible for Boris's story. 'And I know it made wonderful television, but I'm not sure how often we can do it. Other guests may not want to appear if we attack them. Boris was genuinely hurt by the questions you asked.' That was greatly daring of Marion, perhaps too daring.

Dan intervened quickly. 'That's something we can talk about tomorrow,' he said.

Marion heard the reproof in his voice. 'Sorry, I only mention it because Boris may go to the press and talk about it. In fact the press may be on to him already.'

'We are friends, though – or at least we were,' Lucy said uncertainly.

Marion persisted 'That was before he was offered a big fee to attack you, Lucy, which I guess may be what's happening right now. He refused to come to hospitality after the show, he just got straight into his cab and on to the phone.'

That did sound ominous, but there was nothing she could do. Lucy looked round the room and saw Jim Kelly, the sous-chef, in a corner of the room, investigating a plate of lugubrious sandwiches which had been filled some hours ago with glutinous flakes of cheese, and waterlogged prawns. From his disgusted expression he was not about to award the show a Michelin star. She walked over to him and shook his hand. At least he would be pleased with the programme. His secret filming had created exactly the effect he'd wanted.

He was exultant. 'That was a great show, Lucy,' he said as she came up to him. 'Crabtree left the studio so fast you couldn't see his broomstick, talking about getting his lawyers on to you.'

'I can't see how his lawyers can argue with your secret film, Jim.' At least here she was confident. 'I'll have to watch myself with his millions of ardent fans, though. I won't be safe in the WI for years. In any case, thank you for your contribution. It was important not to let him get away with it.'

Across the room she could see Dan pouring himself a large whisky. She excused herself, and went over to him. Suddenly exhaustion overwhelmed her. 'I think I'd better go home now,' she said quietly. 'I don't know what I'll find there. Fred was already upset by a photographer hanging around the house this morning, taking pictures of him as he left. Now we know what those pictures were for. It's not going to be much fun tomorrow when the papers come out.'

'If I'd known about you and Fred,' Dan said evenly, 'I would have suggested that he shouldn't work on the programme. It's far too dangerous, specially right now, with all the press interest in you.' He took a gulp of whisky, put down the glass, and looked down at it, not meeting her eyes. 'It's a bit of a problem when a presenter's private life becomes more interesting than the programme. It's not your fault, Lucy, but it may well damage the show. It'll be all the press will notice.'

His tone was level and controlled, but clearly he was still furious with her. There was nothing she could say to defend herself. And, in any case, she was longing to get home now.

Sandra came over to them, purposefully pushing her way through the crowd. 'David Jameson is on the phone. He wants to talk to you, Dan.'

They walked together to the phone in the corner. Dan took the receiver. 'Hi, David . . . Yes, it was quite eventful . . . Yes, I know, masses of calls . . . Ah, do you? . . . Thank you, I'll tell the team. That's good to hear . . . No, no harm at all. Thank you for ringing, I appreciate it . . . Goodbye, David.'

He put the phone down, and stared at Lucy. 'He liked it.' His voice was gloomy, but there was a smile starting in the corners of his mouth.

'I know. He rang me in my dressing room. He said it was magnetic. Nobody could have switched off.'

'So it seems he doesn't care about the complaints, or the press tomorrow. He thinks it'll double our audience. And he wants us to lengthen the run, make twice as many programmes.'

'Ah, did he say that? He didn't say that to me.' That was news indeed.

'Heart-warming, isn't it?' Still his voice was ironic, but there was a sparkle in his eyes. No producer can resist being asked to make more programmes. He gave her a hug. 'We may not agree with Jameson, we may think he's a bit crass, but he is the

165

boss. And if he likes what we've done, who are we to argue?'

He rapped his glass with a pen, and the boisterous chatter in the room died. 'Sorry to interrupt, but we've just had a call from David Jameson. He loved the show.' A whoop of joy from the younger researchers. 'He's put his money where his mouth is, and he's commissioned us to make another thirteen shows.' Another cheer, this time from the whole team. 'I think that is an unprecedented vote of confidence, on the strength of one programme, before he's even seen the ratings. So congratulations, everybody. We'd better get on together now – we've got another six months of living together to look forward to. So start keeping that bloody office tidy.' They laughed. It was a consistent nag from him. They'd better start paying attention now. 'But seriously,' he said over the laugh, 'congratulations, and here's to the next show.'

Everyone raised their glass. They had been wondering, after all the sound and fury in the studio, whether they would be out of work tomorrow. Now it looked as if they had six months' security, a rare luxury in television.

As the noise of happy conversation rose again, Lucy looked wearily at Dan. 'I've got to go home now, Dan. Thanks for your support. Whatever Jameson thought of the show, I'm sorry if you felt that it was a ragbag, and I'm very sorry if you think I should have warned you about Fred. We were trying not to let it affect our professional lives, but I take your point. It was silly to try to work together.'

He took her hand. 'Get a good night's sleep, Lucy. And try not to read the papers tomorrow. We've already had the green light from Jameson. That's what counts.'

Her driver took her back to the quiet mews at the back of the house. There was nobody waiting for her outside. But in the light from the kitchen window cold rain was beginning to fall in thin slanting lines. She hunched her shoulders against it, and ran to the door. She let herself in, put down her case and looked around her.

'Fred,' she called.

There was no answer. But she could see a light in the sitting room. She walked towards it, and saw Fred half-lying on a sofa with a glass of wine and a cup of coffee. He looked at her as she came in, but he said nothing. It was up to her to start. She wanted so much to go to him, hold him, snuggle against him, banish the conflicts of the day. But she stayed by the door.

'I can't think of anything to say to you,' she said hesitantly, 'except that I am terribly sorry, Fred. I wouldn't have let that happen for the world. I never wanted that reporter in the studio. I always thought it would lead to disaster. But, of course, I had no idea what kind of a disaster it would become.'

Fred said nothing.

'And that Boris thing really shook me,' she went on, still standing at the door, trying to justify herself to them both. 'I really didn't want to hurt him. That was the last thing I would do out of choice. I still don't really know how it happened. He kept blaming Suzannah, and I suppose I was overwhelmed by the memory of all the pain he had caused her. I know I went too far. I'd love to start today over again. But I can't.'

His eyebrows lifted ironically, but still he said nothing. She left the room and walked back down the hall, picked up her case, and started to climb the stairs. She couldn't see what else she could say to him. Perhaps silence would heal his hurt feelings a little.

She walked past the full-length mirror outside her bathroom and caught a glimpse of herself, bright make-up beginning to smear and blur now. Beneath it she could see how tired her eyes were. She ran her hands through her hair, loosening the hairspray that held it in place. She still looked like an overblown fuchsia in the pink and purple dress and jacket, but maybe Lesley was right. In the knock-about farce they'd just created, perhaps brash and tawdry was an appropriate look. She stood in the bathroom, and covered her face with cream, wiping away the memory of the night.

167

Fred came in behind her, and his arms slipped round her waist. He met her eyes in their reflection. 'I'm sorry, Lucy. I know you've had a tough time. I don't want to make it worse for you, darling. It's just too much for me, all the publicity. I've watched you go through it, and I know it's part of your world. But it's not mine. I just want to get on with my job, and not be in the spotlight all the time.'

This was better. At least they were talking. She finished wiping away her television face, and doused her skin in cold water. Then she turned round and let him enfold her in his arms.

'Fred, I wouldn't hurt you for the world. Dan said we were mad to work together on the show. He said we should have known it was dangerous. He said if he'd known about us, he would have warned us, and advised you not to take the job. But it's no good trying to unmake all those decisions. We're stuck with them now. I'll talk to Alison, when we're all a bit calmer, and say I really don't think it's safe to give a reporter like Bill Thompson complete access to a new, live show. That's exactly what press officers should protect us from. But what's the use now?'

He let go, and walked away from her, into the bedroom. He was still unhappy. She dried her face and followed him.

'There's good news about the show,' she said. 'Would you believe that Jameson loved it? He's not bothered at all by the chaos. He says it'll just put the ratings up. He's doubled the run. We're all a bit baffled, but he's in charge.'

Fred sat heavily on the bed, shoulders slumped, staring at his feet. Then he met her eyes. 'Lucy, have you ever stopped to work out what matters to you? I've been labelled your toy-boy, as if I have no identity, no dignity of my own. You've labelled your friend's ex-husband a bisexual, which was nobody's business but his own. And yet all you can say to me is that Jameson has doubled your run. I can't believe it.'

Now he was being unfair. He must know her better than that.

'No, it's not what really matters. But it's part of the industry we both work in. Sometimes too many tacky programmes are trying to chase too few viewers. But it's not always like that.' There was gathering passion in her voice. She was defending her integrity, though she saw no reason why she should. He should know her by now. 'Fred, you know I don't want to make voyeuristic programmes. That's not my style. But I think I can really make something of this series. Anyway, I'd be mad not to have a go. I've already apologized to you, and to Boris. I honestly don't know what more I can do.'

He didn't reply. That 'toy-boy' slur had cut deep. The passion, the laughter she was used to in him had completely evaporated. It was as if suddenly they were strangers. She undressed quickly, and slid into bed, hoping that the breach could be healed in the darkness, and that she would feel his arms creep around her. But Fred left a gulf of cold sheet between them. Both were dreading the morning, and when eventually they fell asleep, the row still hovered in the air over them.

She snapped awake at four o'clock, long before dawn, and lay in the darkness. Fred was still deeply asleep, a thousand miles away across the other side of the bed. She must have been dreaming about Boris and Suzannah, because her mind was filled with pictures of them together.

The memory of a weekend she and Tom had spent in Suzannah's country house came vividly back to her. She desperately combed through it, searching for hints of the bitterness Boris had expressed in the studio. Camilla had been a teenager then, a sullen fourteen-year-old, hardly appearing from her bedroom where she played interminable rock music. Boris had flown into Heathrow from wheeling and dealing at a television festival, and arrived late and hungry. Suzannah had been angry with him at first: 'Why does your bloody business always have to come first?' But then the four of them had stood drinking his best champagne in the quarry-tiled kitchen. Boris started teasing Suzannah as she made chicken sandwiches for him.

'Anything more complicated than opening a tin of caviar is a struggle for her,' he said laughing, and she chased him with a bottle of champagne, trying to drench him with a spray of bubbles. Then they had all sat together in the long low-ceilinged sitting room, filled with bowls of late primroses, and gossiped, stretching like cats in the comfortable sofas, making each other laugh with stories of disasters from their own lives.

Tom was agreed the undoubted winner, with his tales of wilful judges and unpredictable witnesses. 'It always amazes me,' he said. 'You'll interview a junkie in the office, he'll be filthy, long-haired, smelling of urine, but then he'll arrive in the witness box so spruce and manicured his own family won't recognize him.'

'It's just the same with my wife,' Boris said. 'Only I know what the real Suzannah looks like, when she takes her teeth out and puts on her torn cardigan. I married a baglady.'

'If my teeth ever do come out, I'll sue that bleeding dentist for millions,' Suzannah said in mock fury. 'What he implanted in my gums cost more than the new roof on this house. They'd better last as long.'

That was the woman Lucy had known, self-mocking and relaxed. Had she really worn such a different face in the office, so tough and uncaring that people had become reluctant to work with her?

The next morning Lucy had wandered into Suzannah's study before breakfast, and found her already there, working on her fan mail. There were piles of requests for photographs and autographs, for recipes and stories from her childhood to include in charity compilations. Lucy had been astonished at the hours Suzannah was prepared to devote to giving each one a personal, handwritten reply. 'They've spent all this time writing to me,' she'd told Lucy. 'This is the least I owe them.'

And yet among those piles of mail, Suzannah must one day have found the poisonous threats, taken them to the office, and carefully preserved them there in a locked drawer. Had she ever tried to trace the writer? Had she dismissed them as harmless

170

garbage? Or been terrified, so terrified that she'd told no one.

The four of them had gone for long walks together that weekend, in woods filled with wild rhododendrons, Tom and Boris deep in conversation about their favourite wines, and where to get them cheaply, Lucy and Suzannah equally absorbed in discussing the politics of television, who was in and going upwards, who was down and out. They'd had drinks in a small local pub, off the main road, obscure enough for Boris and Suzannah to enjoy their drinks without being pestered by tourists with cameras slung around their necks. They'd been well known there by the regulars, and well-liked. Once again, there had been no trace of the bitterness that was to come, nor of the vain, ambitious woman Tom had implied Suzannah became. He'd got on so well with her that weekend – they had all got on so well.

Then Suzannah had died. No more questions about her death, Jameson had instructed Lucy. Easier said than done. Boris was evidently not satisfied with the obvious explanations. Did he perhaps know about the threatening letters? Did he think there was a connection? She must find a way of smoothing his feathers, restoring communication, so that she could ask him about them.

She turned to look at the alarm clock: it was still only just after five. Never mind, she'd make herself a cup of tea and take it back to bed with her. She rolled out of bed as silently as she could.

At the foot of the stairs she paused. There was an envelope by the front door, a hand-delivered letter. She picked it up. Her name was written on the outside, in capital letters, scribbled in biro. She had seen that writing before. Her heart began to thud as she tore open the envelope and pulled out the sheet of paper inside. There were only a couple of lines on it, written in the unformed capitals she recognized too well.

> So you've taken over from Piper.
> Take care. What happened to
> her can happen to you. Leave
> well alone.

No signature of course.

Lucy sat on the bottom stair, feeling her heart race. Someone knew where she lived. Whoever had written this could still be waiting now outside her door for her to come out. Would another car hurtle out of the darkness to knock her out of its path? Should she run to the police? Or should she find the strength to stand her ground and refuse to be intimidated? With the letter in her hand she turned and went upstairs again to wake Fred.

But first she went over to her dressing-table drawer, feeling her way in the darkness, and pulled out the letters to Suzannah she had hidden there. She tiptoed back to the bathroom to compare them with the one she had just opened. As she passed the bed, Fred stirred, sat up and looked at her. He was only just awake.

'What time is it, Lucy?' he asked, ruffling his already vertical hair.

'Quarter past five.'

'What? What on earth are you doing?'

Why must she always feel guilty? 'Sorry, Fred, I went down to make myself a cup of tea, and I found a letter pushed through the door.' She held it out. Barely conscious, he squinted at it with half-closed eyes. 'Show me it tomorrow, Lucy. For God's sake, get back to sleep. This is crazy.'

He fell back on the pillows and in a few seconds had turned over and was breathing deeply and regularly. She knew that sound, Fred the unwakeable.

She took the bundle of letters into the bathroom, and spread them out on the tiled floor. She forced herself to examine them analytically, as if she was investigating a report for her show. Firstly and most obviously, they had all been written by the same hand, in biro, in large unformed capital letters. The writer accused Lucy of taking over from Suzannah. What did that mean? That she should stop presenting the show? Was this the outpouring of a paranoid stalker who loathed all female presenters? Should she check with others to see if they got this kind of hate mail too? How could she find out? Maybe Jameson could help.

172

Fred would say she should go to the police – he would insist on it, would say this was getting far too personally dangerous. The car that had been aimed at her had been parked in the street by her house; now this letter had been pushed through her letter box. Even if it did come from a harmless lunatic, it was alarming to think he was physically so close to her, stalking her out there in the darkness, watching her every move. She'd talk it through with Fred in the morning. In the meantime she carefully folded the letters away and put them back in her dressing-table drawer.

She slid back into bed. Fred had curled his body away from her and left a chilly, unfriendly gap between them but she dared not do anything to appease him for fear of waking him again. She curled up on her side of the bed and fell instantly asleep.

She woke at eight, unrefreshed, and looked for Fred. His side of the bed was cold and empty. She sat up. His clothes had gone. She couldn't hear him in the house. She tied a satin dressing gown tightly round her, and went downstairs. He wasn't in the kitchen either, but on the table was a pile of Sunday newspapers, all turned to the stories she'd been dreading. On top of them was a folded piece of paper with her name on it.

Suddenly the little house, which had always been such a refuge for her, lost its warmth. It was as if the note waiting for her was a splinter of ice in its heart. Her hands were shaking. She knew Fred's careful handwriting as well as she knew her own.

Lucy, darling.

I've tried not to feel hurt and humiliated. I wish I could dismiss these horrible stories about us, but I can't take the pressure. I hate having my private feelings chewed over in public. I've taken my things. I'm away for a couple of weeks on location. Maybe when all this dies down a little we can talk. So sorry.

Love, Fred.

She put the letter down. There was a physical pain inside her now, racking her chest. It was as if her body was in mourning. She sat at the table, looking round the kitchen, not seeing it. Instead she had Fred's face in front of her, Fred's arms around her, the imprint so strong it was tangible. He had buoyed her up, teased her, refused to let her take herself too seriously. She suddenly realized how far she had been depending on his strength to help her deal with the latest threats. How could she cope without him?

She slowly folded up his note and put it in her pocket. Under it were the newspaper stories which had lacerated him. She read the headlines – they were hardly unexpected: Bill Thompson's triumphant 'Lucy Unmasked'; Janet Lake's in the *Sunday Dispatch* a scathing 'Low Life Lucy'.

She flipped open Janet's article first. It spread across two pages: an interview with Boris – Marion was right, he must have rung her after the show – and another with Camilla, which Janet must have obtained well in advance. Lucy tried not to read the words as her eyes scanned quickly over them, but they wormed themselves into her brain. Camilla branded her as the bitch who had ruthlessly stolen her 'friend' Suzannah's show, Boris railed against the invasion of his privacy, particularly now in his bereavement. It was passionate, furious stuff, guaranteed to entertain Janet's readers.

As she closed the paper she saw underneath it Bill Thompson's report, embellished with pictures of Fred leaving the house, and Lucy and Fred touching hands in the studio. This must have turned Fred's stomach. There would be no opportunity now to try to comfort him, or reassure him that the explosion of publicity need not blow their lives apart. She felt alone and vulnerable as never before, sitting at the kitchen table surrounded by the jumble of newsprint, frozen in her unhappiness.

Who could she turn to? Not her family – they would be appalled by the publicity, appalled and hurt. She certainly couldn't mention the hate mail to them. They would be terrified for her, they might even try to persuade her to give up her work entirely. No, with her parents she would have to maintain the fiction that none of it mattered.

Tom then? No, that would be impossible too. It would be trespassing on a dead relationship.

Suzannah? Ah, if only. It was just at moments like this that they would ring each other, knowing they could depend on getting support, but honest support, and good strategic advice. What would Suzannah have said? She might have been quite rough and realistic. 'If Fred can't take this, let him go.' Lucy could hear her voice, see her tossing her blonde hair to emphasize the words. 'You're more famous than Fred, more talented than him, older than him, and he ought to accept that those were all the reasons he went for you in the first place. If he's changed his mind now that the going is tough, if his machismo can't take it and he's wimping out, better that he shows how weak he is now, before you're both any further down the line.'

The trouble with Suzannah alive was that she was often too right to argue with. Lucy realized that was true of Suzannah dead as well. The voice in Lucy's head was telling her the truth, or at least some of it. What it left out was the longing Fred aroused in her, the pleasure he gave her, the physical confidence he instilled in her. She needed him profoundly. She couldn't bear to think that the hyenas who were laughing at her now would cost her Fred's love.

What about the hate mail? What would Suzannah say about that? Maybe she would be less sure how to handle that – after all, Suzannah had received it first. She had simply concealed it in a locked drawer and told nobody.

As she sat longing for her friend, the phone rang. Could it be Fred, contrite at having abandoned her? She answered it eagerly, but she recognized the harsh cockney voice at once.

'What are you doing, darling, reading the papers?'

'Hello, Mandy,' she said. 'Yes, I was.'

'That was a terrific show you did last night, and don't let

175

anyone tell you otherwise. And, for heaven's sake, don't worry about the papers. They'll do you no harm at all. In fact I should renegotiate for you, ask for double the price.'

'They're pretty nasty. Fred hates it all.' She couldn't bring herself to say they had driven him away.

'Yes, but it's something he'll have to get used to, if he's going out with a star.'

A star? She just felt like a target.

Mandy coughed fruitily, on her sixth cigarette of the morning. 'Anyway, love, I just wanted to say well done. Why don't we have lunch together? The ratings will be out by then. I expect they'll be spectacular.'

Mandy's confidence was impressive. She was a tough fighter, she'd been at the centre of this kind of storm many times before. She could advise Lucy what to do, how to handle the hate mail. Maybe other clients had received it too. Lunch would be a good idea. She could postpone the decisions until then. Maybe her own mind would be clearer.

Mandy suggested they should meet in a steak house round the corner from the studio famous for its organic meat, a succulent roast joint on Sundays, served with potatoes roasted with the skins on them. Lucy put the phone down, and gathered up the papers. Then she went back to her bedroom, and gazed at the empty unmade bed. Fred would get over it. This was a temporary glitch. She'd let him stew for a bit, then ring him tonight.

Now, in the light of day, her fears seemed laughable. She'd go into the office, the team would be in quite soon, to pick up the pieces from the night before. At this stage in a new series, Sundays off were a theoretical luxury. And she needed the reassurance of their undemanding company. She dressed, and left the house, looking just a little more carefully than usual to make sure there was nobody crouched behind her neighbours' fences and hedges. Of course not. The sunlight, cold white winter light, had just a touch of warmth on her face. There were vivid pink cyclamens in the window boxes of the pub at the end of the road, her favourite flowers. In their early days together, she and Tom had loved to pick them wild on the autumn hillsides in Corfu. Those had been more delicate, a fragile paler pink, spread in swathes under the olive trees. These were cheerful reminders that Christmas was on the way, and after Christmas came longer days, shorter nights, and spring would soon be here again. Fred would surely be back in her life long before that.

When she arrived in the office, her production team greeted her happily, excited and triumphant. There was no such thing as bad publicity. They read quotes from the newspaper stories aloud to each other, and laughed. There were a couple of favourable references hidden in all the scandal, a few critics comparing Lucy favourably with 'Snoozanah'. Lucy flinched, but she couldn't resist the team; young and insensitive as they were, they were a tonic.

Sandra came out of Dan's office with a list of last night's ratings in her hand. 'Ten million.' The team cheered.

Dan followed her, grinning with pleasure. He came over to Lucy, and whispered to her, 'Those aren't official figures yet. Jameson commissioned a special sample – he must have been pretty worried. But it is good news.'

Sandra was still looking at the print-out. 'We inherited seven, and added three. We won the slot by a mile.' The researchers cheered again as she handed Dan and Lucy copies. This was what Jameson wanted. Their contracts were safe. Lucy looked at Marion, the conscience of the research team.

'Well, what can I say?' Marion responded. 'Boris may not have liked the show, but the viewers clearly did.'

Dan looked round at them all. 'Follow that,' he said. 'Our problem is that we can't possibly make a show like that every week, unless Lucy is prepared to reveal a secret romance with the whole crew, one by one.'

'And be prepared to lose all my friends,' she said. Fun though all this was, she wanted to draw a line under it and start again. Dan heard the bleakness in her voice.

'Now that everyone knows we're on the air, and we've established ourselves with a very loud starter's gun, we've got to create some real Saturday night entertainment for them.'

The researchers went through the list of films and plays about to open, whose stars would be automatically available as part of their promotion circuit.

Lucy's mind drifted. The letters were still in her dressing table at home, burning a hole in her memory. How soon should she ring the police? Then she blinked hard as Alex, one of the senior researchers, brought her back to the discussion as sharply as if he'd shaken her.

'Lord Parks is bringing out his memoirs,' he told the group, looking at a list from one of the biggest publishers. 'He's on offer to us.'

The team looked at Lucy. Would she like the idea, or think that an elderly politician, an ex-Home Secretary, would be ineffably dull? Lucy sat very still, her mind ice cold, while she thought it through. Roy Parks was a regular chat-show participant, but no doubt he had reserved some extra titbits to sell his book, stories of cabinet feuds, and old scores settled, which could make headlines the next day. The real temptation for Lucy was that interviewing him would give her the chance to feel his mind. Was he capable of the horrific crimes Max had described? The systematic abuse of vulnerable boys? Or that final crime, the fire, an utterly ruthless attempt to silence them?

They were waiting for her to answer. She nodded, deep in thought. 'That would be an interesting booking,' she said. 'Roy Parks is never dull. And he'd be so keen to sell his book, I'm sure we could persuade him to spill some exclusive secrets.'

The meeting ended, and Lucy walked back to her desk with Dan. He shut the door behind them. 'Happy?' he asked.

'I'm shattered, to tell you the truth.' She was sitting at Suzannah's old desk, the drawer that had held her dangerous secrets in front of her. Fear welled up in her. Should she confide in him, or would that make him think she was weak and hysterical? She tested the ground. 'The whole show shook me up. It's so different from what I'm used to, and I'm not nearly as sure as everyone else is that it's going to work.'

'We're all on your side, Lucy,' he said, and his voice was sympathetic. 'If you have any problems, you know you can tell me.' No, she wouldn't tell him everything yet, not till she'd talked to Mandy.

'Are you OK with Roy Parks as a guest?' he asked.

'I think so. I think there may be more to him than meets the eye,' she said. 'It may just be gossip. I know most people think he's a loud-mouth self-publicist. I think he's worse than that.'

'Be careful, Lucy.' Dan was clearly alarmed.

'Yes, yes, don't worry, I know.' Had he completely lost his faith in her? She'd better try to restore his confidence. 'I've learned since last night. No personal crusades, I promise you. I just meant that I'm intrigued by the man, and I think he could make a very good guest.'

'Fine.' He was reassured that at least she understood the theory of the Saturday night show they were trying to make. 'We need to sweeten our tone a little. We'll try and put a guest with a bit of glamour next to Parks.'

They worked on until lunch-time. Then the team gratefully took the rest of the day off. By the time Dan left it was nearly one o'clock, so Lucy grabbed her coat, and ran down the corridors. The building was almost deserted. At reception she felt the commissionaires there looking at her appraisingly. Success? Or failure? She was a target for the tabloids, but did that mean she was a star now, as Mandy said, or just notorious, well known for being well known?

Mandy was waiting at a discreet table behind a large palm plant, with an ashtray at her side, and a gin and tonic in front of her. She was wearing an orange wool suit that almost exactly matched the walnut veneer of her fake tan, and she was fettered with enough gold chains to tether the *QEII*.

179

She half got up as Lucy reached her, and they exchanged air-kisses.

Mandy looked at her critically. 'You're worn out, darling. I hope you're not letting all this noise in the press get to you. They'll move on, once they see what a success the show is. I'll talk to Jameson about beefing up his quotes to support you. And all that gossip about Fred and so on will do you no harm at all – warm up your image a bit.'

Oh Lord, she had an image now. Lucy sighed, took her coat off and handed it to a waiter. She was too weary to conceal the truth from Mandy.

'Fred hates it all so much he's disappeared. He left me a note saying he'd gone on location for a couple of weeks, but he's taken all his things with him. It looks as if he's decided to move out.'

Mandy looked at her intently. 'How bad is that for you?'

'Pretty bad. I'm really fond of him. Maybe it wasn't a life-long thing between us, but we were very close, we really care about each other. I feel terrible letting him in for all this. He really doesn't deserve being flayed alive.'

Mandy, who knew a public flaying when she saw one, and this was not one, decided not to argue with her. After all, their relationship was new, and they were still a little mistrustful of each other. 'My advice,' she said, her harsh voice quiet now, 'not that you've asked me, Lucy, and please feel free to ignore me, but my advice is that you just need to wait a little, and the whole thing will die down. They'll soon be on to the next piece of hot gossip. As long as you don't keep feeding them fresh titbits.'

'I'm feeding them nothing,' Lucy told her vehemently. 'I don't know who tipped them off about Fred – someone who's no friend. This is when I need Suzannah. It's amazing how she was able to put things into perspective. I miss her.'

'We all do,' Mandy said.

For a moment it was as if the woman they had both loved

180

and admired was with them again. They could see her laughing, ordering champagne, cheering them up with a wicked joke, or a wild plan. 'She'd be organizing a weekend in a Spanish castle for you and Fred right now,' Mandy said nostalgically, 'so that you could celebrate together. She'd be sending some kind of rude telegram to Jameson. And she'd make a bonfire of all the unpleasant articles, and pin the good ones up on your board. She was a great survivor, our friend.'

But she didn't survive. That was the tragedy. Lucy decided to take a risk. 'I found some letters in Suzannah's office.'

Mandy's small bright eyes in their armour of spiky lashes fixed on her.

'What kind of letters?'

'There were a couple of fan letters – love letters, really besotted stuff. Suzannah must have kept them for fun. But there were others that gave me the shivers. They were horrible, vindictive, threatening. They really worried me. I think they must have worried her, otherwise she wouldn't have hung on to them. They would have gone straight into the bin. Did she ever talk to you about them?'

'No. Not about any letters she took seriously. She used to read me the joke ones, the kind that everyone gets. The ones in green ink, full of exclamation marks and underlining. "You're a disgrace to the nation", that kind of lunacy. Is that what you mean?'

'No. These were much nastier. They called her a bitch, they said she'd wrecked too many lives and soon she'd know what that feels like. It gave me the creeps, they were so focused, as if someone really was out to hurt her. And now . . .' Her voice tailed away.

Mandy leaned forward. 'Now what, Lucy?'

'Now I've had one too, same writing, same threats. Someone pushed it through my letter box last night.'

Mandy was horrified. She twisted the diamonds encircling her knuckles, and there was a new edge of urgency in her voice.

'That's serious, Lucy. I presume you've told the police.'

'Not yet.'

'You must, at once. If someone that crazy knows where you live, you have to tell the police, if only so that they can tell you it doesn't matter. Maybe there's someone around the corner who stalks all the local celebrities. But if those letters are as nasty as you say, you really can't take a chance.'

'But who on earth could have written them, Mandy? Who hated Suzannah so much? I can't think of any lives she wrecked. She didn't make the sort of shows I made, where you can create enemies, sometimes pretty powerful ones. Her show was a bit of harmless froth. What harm could she ever have done?'

For the first time Mandy dropped her gaze. 'Look, Lucy, nobody could have loved the woman more than I did. But she was a tough cookie. She'd learned to be. If she wanted someone or something she went after them. Once or twice I did have to pick up the pieces.'

'Pieces of what?'

'The occasional broken marriage, angry wives blaming her when their husbands strayed into her bed, that sort of thing.'

'You kept it out of the papers.'

'That's my job.'

'Would any of those women be angry enough to write letters like that? And why on earth would they decide to have a go at me?'

'Don't ask me. I know I'm an agent but that doesn't make me an expert on the deranged mind.' She shrugged. 'Or maybe it does, but not this kind of dangerous stuff. You must go to the police, Lucy, you really must.' She took Lucy's hand. With all her comic ostentation, the heavy gold metal at her throat, the diamonds encrusting her fingers, Mandy's blunt sincerity commanded respect. 'Lucy darling, I admire you. I respect your judgement. But please don't be foolishly brave. It's not a favour to anyone – your team, your friends, anyone – to put yourself at risk. Take advice. Ring the police. Let them do their job.'

182

Finally the urgency in her voice convinced Lucy. 'You're right, Mandy. At any rate it won't do any harm. I admit I'm not too happy, now I'm on my own at home. Although I'm sure they'll say I'm making a fuss over nothing.' It was time to lighten the mood. 'What about the passionate love letters I found – did you know about them?'

Mandy buried her face in her glass of gin and tonic. When she emerged she was smiling, but her eyes were still dark with tension. 'What wouldn't I give for a tenth of that woman's sex appeal. She had so many sex-mad fan letters you'd think she did the show topless. I had to open most of them. I used to ban the younger staff from reading them: they'd learn more than was good for them.'

'Do you remember a batch in red ink? Romantic nonsense?'

'If I saw them, they didn't engrave themselves in my memory. I remember the transexual who kept begging to borrow her leather skirt. What have you done with them? Do you want me to answer them?'

'I sent them off to Camilla. I thought they might amuse her. There was nothing explicit about them, just hearts and flowers. They did intrigue me a little. I've heard rumours there might have been a new man in her life. Have you heard that?'

'Is that what the team are saying? What a gossipy bunch they are.'

'No, it didn't come from them,' Lucy said defensively. 'They're all incredibly loyal. But someone else who saw her the night she died mentioned to me that she had a certain glow about her.' She'd better not give Lesley away.

'That's just stupid, pointless gossip.' Mandy's face was thunderous. That door was firmly closed. Lucy admired her discretion. It probably meant she could rely on Mandy not to spread gossip about her, either. Not that there was anything left to spread, the way the papers had amused themselves at her expense.

They enjoyed their meal together. Sharing their fears and

memories had brought them far closer. It was almost four by the time Mandy paid the bill, and Lucy decided to go straight home. She parked her car in the only space, a hundred yards from her house, and walked nervously up the street to her front door. Mandy was right: it would be a relief to have the police on her side now. As she sat down at her study desk, her mobile phone began to shrill. Was it Fred, at last? She answered it.

'Lucy? It's Max.'

Her heart plunged with disappointment. 'Hi, Max. How are things?'

He was not in the mood for pleasantries. 'I saw you all over the news after the fire. Are you still interested? Or has it put you off?'

The urgency in his voice revived her.

'Absolutely. I'm more interested than ever. If I ever had any doubts that we were on the right lines, I've lost them now.'

'Well, some of the boys have had enough. I don't blame them. Loads of our friends died. Those bastards don't care. They think they can't lose.'

Would he stick by the story he had told her? She decided to test him. 'Lord Parks is coming on to our next show.'

Suddenly there was panic in his voice. 'Parks is? Why? Are you going to tell him what I said to you? You'd better not.'

'Of course not.' She tried to sound reassuring. 'I'd just frighten him and his friends off. The company lawyers would never let me, anyway. I only want to establish contact, have a friendly chat about his memoirs, and see what kind of man he is.'

'Why don't you ask him about his holiday snaps?' Max said, a sarcastic edge suddenly in his voice. 'He likes taking pictures. I've seen a few the police would be very interested in.'

'Where are they?'

'With friends.'

'Can I see them?' That would be evidence, explosive evidence.

'We'll see.' Max had talked enough. 'I'll watch the show,' he said. 'I'll be in touch again. I've got to go now.' Then he rang off.

Lucy sat back in her chair, going over the conversation again in her mind. He was scared, but still speaking to her. That probably meant some of his friends were still prepared to talk, or at least listen to her. The boys would be even more scared than ever. She'd have to convince them all over again that she was trustworthy, and determined to bring their abusers to justice. She had a tightrope to walk with Parks in the next show. They would be watching, judging her.

It was dark outside. The occasional passers-by hurried home through the freezing night air, their breath making misty balloons in the glow from the streetlight. She shuddered, partly with the cold, partly with the knowledge that one of them, any of them, could be the adversary who had hunted Suzannah, and now was hunting her. The house felt very empty. She leaned back in her chair, and reached for her address book. She found the Thritham number. This was all too much for her to deal with alone. Mandy was right: she needed the police on her side.

CHAPTER NINE

The detective inspector, Derek White, answered her instantly, and listened without comment to her story. Then, 'I'd like to come and see you as soon as possible, if I may, Miss Strong? Tomorrow morning if you can.' There was no anxiety in his voice, and she tried to make hers match his calmness. She wasn't due in the office until eleven the following morning for a production meeting, so he arranged to come to her home at nine.

That left the night ahead. Somehow she had to get past it. Loneliness was the worst obstacle. The sheer aloneness of having no one alongside her to joke her out of her fears. Perhaps sleep would numb her to them.

She undressed and lay down, but her mind was churning. She looked at the clock by her bed – ten thirty, early enough still to ring someone, but who? Fred was out of bounds. Her pride wouldn't let her pursue him. He hadn't rung her. So if he didn't care enough to understand how isolated she was feeling, he couldn't help her.

Her memory slipped back to Tom. All right, in the end they had hurt each other badly, but there had been good years before that. And their time together in Thritham had proved that a friendship was still there. She'd held back till now. If she rang him, how would he react to her need? He might reject her. If so, she'd have to live with that.

The phone rang for some time, and she had almost given up when it was answered. Tom's voice was so sleepy it was clear she had woken him. She apologized.

'No, that's OK, Lucy. I'd fallen asleep reading some impenetrable medical opinion. You've done me a favour. I might well have slept in my chair all night, and woken up with a mouth like an elephant's armpit. How can I help?'

She hesitated. They were less than lovers now, much less, but he still had a particular place in her heart and mind. She used to be able to confide anything to him, but suddenly she was nervous. 'I just wanted to talk to you, Tom. For a moment or two.'

'Fred's away?' There was a sourness in the question. Had Fred been beside her, she would never have needed to ring him.

'Yes. He's been very bruised by all the fuss. He's gone away, and he's lying low.'

'Ah.' He didn't press her further. 'So, how can I help?'

The emotion she had been holding down suddenly escaped and choked her throat. 'Oh God, Tom, it's all too much for me at the moment.'

He hadn't heard her so vulnerable, so helpless since they'd parted. This was not the self-image she usually clung to – superwoman, able to deal with anything destiny threw at her. The armour was gone.

He roughened his own voice. 'Come on, Lucy, you've faced tougher times than this. Fred'll be back in his own time.'

'It's not really about Fred. Or at least not only about him. But those letters I showed you, the vile ones to Suzannah. I've had one too.'

'When?' His voice was tense with shock.

'Last night. Pushed through my letter box.'

'And you're alone in the house?'

'Yes. I suppose that's why I'm spooked.'

'D'you want me to come over?'

Pretty noble, given the time of night and his own exhaustion. 'No, Tom, I'm fine. The police are coming round to see me tomorrow. I've just got to get through tonight. Do you mind if we talk for a little?'

'No, that's fine.' He flattened a cushion under his head, and put his feet up on the sofa in his study. This might go on for some time. 'Tell me what your letter said.' He kept his voice matter-of-fact. There was no point spooking her further.

187

'Well, it was more of a warning than a threat. It said I should take care, that what happened to Suzannah could happen to me, that sort of thing. It's probably some harmless loony who hates all women on television, and I wouldn't mind, except it was put through my door, so whoever it is knows exactly where I live. And what with the car that nearly hit me, and the police thinking I could have been the target of the Thritham fire, I'm pretty jumpy at the moment.'

'What do you mean, you were the target? How could that be true? Who knew you were going to be there?' He was horrified, but determined not to show it. That would only frighten her still more.

'I don't know, Tom. They say it's only one of the theories. But it shook me a bit.'

'I'm not surprised.'

'Do you think I'm being stupid?'

'No, not at all.' His voice was level. She needed objectivity, not sympathy. 'I think we should try to analyse what's going on. Remember the police only said that was one theory, about the fire. I expect they have plenty of others. I still think you were right, you weren't the target. It was someone trying to silence the boys. So you could take that out of the equation for the moment.'

'OK.' She stretched in bed. It was as if he was there beside her, in the familiar comforting way he used to be, spectacles on the end of his nose, adjusting the bedside lamp so that he could read a brief more easily.

'That leaves us with two threats. Let's take the car that nearly hit you. Now, think back. How deliberate do you think that was? Could it just have been a careless, stupid piece of driving?'

'Truthfully?'

'That's usually more useful. Truthfully.'

'Then I must say I don't think it was accidental. I think someone was waiting for the reporters to go, and then they drove straight at me. But . . .' Her voice tailed away.

'But?' For him too there was an intimacy now, as if they were walking down a difficult, stony path together, occasionally propping up and balancing each other.

'But I'm not sure, Tom, thinking about it, that someone was trying to hit me. They may just have been trying to frighten me.'

'Into what?'

'Well, it was just after the paedophile show. So it could have been one of them, someone in the ring telling me not to go any further with our investigation. Do you think?'

'It's certainly possible. But it doesn't explain the hate mail. Because whoever wrote to you, if you're right, had Suzannah in his sights as well.'

'I know. And she died.'

'But that was accidental.'

'Was it?' This was the central point, the place where her mind kept circling, like a hawk over long grass. Something hidden was forcing her to look, and look again. 'Boris isn't convinced. He told me I ought to ask more questions. Which is funny because David Jameson told me not to.'

'Did he now?' Tom was intrigued.

'Yes, he said I was tarnishing Suzannah's memory.'

'The Blessed Suzannah of sainted memory. Of course, I forgot.'

'Oh, Tom, don't spoil it by having another go at her. She wasn't a saint. Everyone knows that. But she was a generous, kind-hearted woman, and she deserves better, at least from me.'

'All right, all right, let's just agree to differ. You really ought to talk to Camilla, though. She knows more than she's saying. She might have an idea about the letters.'

'Yes, I suppose she might. I was remembering the weekend we spent at the Manor, with the three of them. Good times.'

'So was I, as a matter of fact. Because that's when I had a chance to talk to Camilla. She came out of her bedroom for about ten minutes to forage in the kitchen when I was getting a drink for you. It was very illuminating.'

189

'Because?'

'Because Suzannah used to talk to her far more than we knew. More than she should have, perhaps. Camilla knew a great deal about her parents' love lives, for instance, and she was quite shrewd and funny about them. That's why I'm wondering whether her mum ever talked to her about these letters. But I tell you what.'

'What?' Lucy stifled a yawn and curled round on her pillow, the receiver pressed to her ear. It was almost as though he was there with her, his voice was so clear in her head.

'I don't think you need be too fearful tonight. I think someone is certainly on your case, be they loony or worse, but all they're doing at the moment is warning you not to step out of line. Which you aren't doing, are you?'

Should she tell him about the latest phone call from Max? No, it would spoil the mood. He'd be cross and nannying, and she hadn't the energy for an argument. 'Apart from seeing the police tomorrow, and making the next show, I'm doing nothing.'

'So I wouldn't worry. And I can hear you're practically asleep. Switch the light off, don't dream, and I'll be in touch tomorrow.'

She grunted. He was right. She was almost asleep already.

'Good night, Lucy.'

'Good night, Tom.' She smiled at their formality, put the phone down, obediently switched the light off, and fell instantly asleep.

The next morning, she awoke with Camilla in her mind. Tom was right. If she wanted to solve the riddle of the hate mail, and she urgently did, maybe Camilla might have a clue. She got out of bed quickly, bathed, dressed in a sobre, police-impressing dark red trouser suit, and rang Camilla. It was half-past eight, a fairly civilized time for a phone call, but Camilla did not sound at all pleased when she recognized Lucy's voice.

'I don't want to talk to you, Lucy. You should never have done that interview with my father. That was unforgivable.'

'I know how you feel, Camilla. I read your interview with Janet. I know how cross you are with me. But please believe

190

me, I had no plans to ask Boris those questions. He took the view that your mother treated you both pretty badly. I just felt I should speak for her.'

'What gave you the right?' Camilla's voice was harsh with anger.

'Our friendship.' Lucy tried to soothe her.

To an extent it worked, and Camilla's voice softened slightly. 'Well, as far as I'm concerned you were well out of line. Why did you ring me?'

'Because I found some more letters in your mum's office and I would like to show them to you. I don't specially want to talk about them on the phone.' Describing them might close the conversation down or frighten Camilla away before Lucy could ask the questions she needed to put to her. Besides, it would be helpful to show them to her face to face. There was a chance she might recognize the writing. Maybe some of them had arrived in the heap of mail which was regularly forwarded to the Manor. 'Can I bring them to you?'

Camilla still sounded wary. 'If you like. I'm just sorting Mum's will, and she's mentioned you in it. So it might be a good idea anyway if you came down here. Next weekend, maybe?' They arranged it for next Sunday.

Lucy went into the kitchen and brewed herself some strong coffee. She filled a bowl with cereal, and added some raspberries to it. Monday morning – life went on. Work went on. She opened her briefcase while she ate, and found some newspaper cuttings the team had collected about Lord Parks.

His life made interesting reading. He had had the classic upper-middle-class upbringing, sent away to school from the age of seven. She paused for a moment in her reading, and wondered. Had there been predatory schoolmasters in those far-off times, when child abuse was so taboo it had never been talked about? Had Parks ever been a victim himself? If so, there was no clue in the cuttings. From everything he said, he had a happy, hard-working childhood. At university he had become political,

191

speaking in debates, gradually swerving further and further to the right. There were pictures of him as president of the students' union, his dark hair plastered down across his forehead, thrusting forward his big chin with a broad smile. No problem with confidence there. From university he went into the law, and from law to Parliament. Along the way he collected a charming well-behaved wife, and three children, some of whom had occasional brushes with the press, a drunken moment here, a photograph with a page-three girl there, but nothing significant. Certainly nothing to prevent Parks' appointment to the Home Office, and from there to the House of Lords.

She finished the bowl of cereal, and made herself another cup of strong coffee. She reached a clutch of recent headlines.

Six months ago Parks had taken up the case of a frail old lady who had been beaten and robbed of her pension by a gang of thirteen-year-olds. The old lady's face filled the front pages, with her black eye and bruised jaw. It was a horrible crime. The old lady had suffered a heart attack as a result, and Parks went to town in all the papers. He blamed the parents, the school, but most of all the legal system for allowing teenage thugs to prosper. 'The devil generation', he called them, lambasting the children who, he said, were riddled with original sin. He wrote a think-piece for the *Dispatch*. 'Where is religion when we need it? Where is our morality, when children can turn into brutal little animals, and get away with their crimes unpunished?'

Lucy read the stories with growing fascination. Here was a man who was responsible, if Max was to be believed, for so many crimes against children, and yet with breathtaking hypocrisy, set himself up as a guardian of morality. It might be interesting to test those views of his, to book some young people into the audience to ask him questions. She would put that idea to the team.

The doorbell rang: the police were punctual. She let them in. DI Derek White looked fragile. It had been an early start for them both. DC Watkins seemed to cope with it better. She got out her tapes and her notebook, and smiled as Derek White rubbed his temples and greedily gulped down the black coffee Lucy poured for him. While he drank, she went up to her bedroom and brought down the pile of letters. She went into her study, and photocopied them carefully. No doubt the police would want to take them away, and she needed copies for herself.

When she brought them back and spread them out on the kitchen table, he read them carefully, without touching them. Then he asked, 'When did you find the letters addressed to Miss Piper?'

'The day of her memorial service. They asked me to clear her desk. The letters were in a locked drawer.'

'Was there anything else in the drawer?'

'A few fan letters. That's all.'

'I'd better have a look at those too.'

'I haven't got them here. I didn't keep them.'

He made a note of the half-truth. If he suspected there was more he should know, he didn't pursue it.

'And tell me about the one addressed to you.'

'It arrived sometime during the night. I found it at about five in the morning, yesterday. It had been pushed through the letter box.'

He took her through all the questions she had asked herself over and over again. Did Suzannah have any particular enemies, any obsessive fans who might be reacting to an imagined rejection? Had Lucy noticed anyone else who seemed to be watching her, apart from the two cars she had already told them about?

She longed to be able to answer the questions more competently, but she couldn't. There was nothing, no new detail, no sudden memory. She hugged herself with frustration.

'One thing you should know, Lord Parks is going to be a guest on my next programme.'

That stopped the questions. White thought for a long moment. 'Why's that, Miss Strong?'

'Just because he's brought out an autobiography. His publishers wanted him to do the show.'

'Can I ask what your question-line is likely to be?'

She laughed. 'I'm not sure. But nothing about Thritham, or the boys, I can guarantee that. I suppose it'll be harmless stuff, from your point of view. Just political scandal and intrigue; sex, fear and loathing, that sort of thing.'

'Sounds good television. I'll make sure I watch it.'

He looked round the kitchen. 'Forgive me asking you, Miss Strong, but is Mr Miller still living here?' The policeman must have drawn his own conclusions last night, the anxiety must have shown in her voice.

'Not at the moment. He's on location, filming.' True enough, and her pride wouldn't let her go further.

'So you're alone here right now?'

'Yes.'

That explained her anxiety. He leaned back in his chair. 'Looking at these letters, nasty as they are, I don't get the feeling that they pose a serious threat to your safety, Miss Strong. Although I must take into consideration the other events we've discussed, the fire, and so on. I'll talk to the local team up here and see if they've got any known suspects who send this kind of unpleasant letter to people in your profession. I realize it must be pretty unsettling for you.'

His kindness was unexpected. She'd thought he was dismissive of her world, and herself with it.

'Would it ease your mind,' he asked, 'if we put an officer alongside you for the moment? Would it make you feel safer?'

Would it? Wouldn't that be cowardly? It would certainly mean that Max would be frightened off. She'd never see the pictures he'd talked about so tantalizingly. The police clearly thought she was safe. Tom thought she was safe.

She breathed deeply, then looked into his eyes, keeping her own gaze as level as she could. 'No, Inspector, I'm fine now. I take everything you've said. I realize there's no real danger to me. I don't know why that letter shook me so much. Do you want to take them all with you?'

They did, and when they left, they took the letters carefully folded into a plastic bag.

Lucy fastened a smile onto her face as she walked into the office at eleven o'clock, and the trick worked. The team greeted her cheerfully, and asked her no questions. She sat companionably with them, planning the interviews for the show.

'I wonder if we should get some young people in the audience, quite tough young people, who could give Parks a run for his money?' she asked them. 'Maybe some kids who've had problems with the police, and some God-fearing, law-abiding kids as well. Otherwise we'll end up demonizing children the way Parks does.'

Marion nodded. 'We can find both. Don't worry. We'll interview them first and make sure they're not all total yobs. We don't want a studio filled with junkies and streakers.'

Lucy winced. The audience had been dangerously unpredictable in the last show, difficult for Lucy to control, but obviously that danger was the hook that pulled in the viewers.

'I'm happy to try again,' she said. 'The kids I can handle. In fact, as long as we make sure my own love-life isn't going to feature this week, I enjoy living dangerously.'

Dan had been listening, allowing her to take the lead. 'All right,' he said, smiling, 'but you've got to guarantee that you'll reveal something equally outrageous if the show gets dull.'

'Who else have we got?'

'We've been offered Genevieve,' Alex told her.

This was news. Genevieve was the latest Hollywood beauty, imported from South America. She was mesmerically photogenic: high cheekbones, huge widely spaced green eyes, soft mouth. Her body was the perfect combination of lean and lushness, perhaps with the aid of silicone here and there. But her legs were obviously unaided by cosmetic surgery – long, tanned,

195

always on display in the shortest flimsiest skirts. She had acted very little, just one flashy part as the daughter of a billionaire, kidnapped by revolutionaries who persuaded her to come over to their side. The hero of the film, a stalwart policeman, was played by the hottest male star, Tim Brooks. To no one's surprise the two had become an item, the most photographed couple in Hollywood.

'Well, there's your guarantee the show won't be dull,' Lucy promised Dan. 'Any quiet moments you can pan over her legs.'

'Funny you should mention that,' Alex said, his eyes shining with mischievous delight, as he opened the file on his knee. 'Look what I've found.'

Lucy groaned. There were half a dozen pictures of Genevieve, naked, in a variety of ugly, explicit erotic poses.

'Where on earth have you found those? And are they really genuine?' Lucy asked him. 'They use computers to fake these things. It goes on all the time on the Internet.'

'No, these are real. She had a rather unpleasant boyfriend when she started out, and he had these pictures taken of her.'

'Then why haven't they been published everywhere?'

'When she started making real money, she bought the negatives, or at least she thought she'd bought them. But these have just surfaced, and they're about to feature in an American show. Channel Eight have made it. It's called *The Real Genevieve*, and they found these pictures. I understand they were actually taken by a photographer in her home town, who hung on to half a dozen of the negatives, waiting for a time like this, when she was hot and newsworthy and he could make a good deal. Channel Eight are quite happy for us to use one of them, provided we give their show a plug.'

'Oh Lord.' Lucy slumped back in her chair. She knew it was a scoop. They would have to say yes. It would anger Genevieve. It would thrill Jameson.

Across the table from her, Dan groaned. 'These are so salacious,' he said. 'We'd have to pick a discreet one, specially with children in the audience. But let's stop and think about it. Do we really want something like this on our show?'

The team looked at him, horrified. He couldn't really be suggesting that they forgo the opportunity of scooping the nation's press, providing a story that everyone else would follow.

'There's one more piece of news for you,' Alex said, clearly on a roll. 'Tim Brooks wants to be on the show with Genevieve. How about that?'

That clinched it. The hottest couple in the world, together with a fierily provocative picture. What an extraordinary show, even without Lord Parks.

'Please,' Alex implored the team, 'don't tell anyone about the pictures. I'm still in negotiations with Channel Eight.'

The meeting broke up, and Lucy went back to her desk.

Dan put his head round her door. 'I'm giving a lecture to the training school. I'll be a couple of hours.'

She nodded, deep in the cuttings about Genevieve. Did the woman ever talk about anything other than collagen and the cabbage soup diet? At least the pictures would give them something else to discuss.

Marion came in and sat on the sofa. 'I've been thinking about the kids you want in the studio,' she said. 'There's a black headmaster who's turned around a really tough South London school. He loves the media – he'll bring some of his sixteen-year-olds. And Dan's son Jake is a teacher. I thought of asking him to bring some of his kids along as well. I'm not sure I should do that without Dan's permission, though.'

'Has he brought them before?'

'Yes, and there's been no problem. It's just that Dan likes to be warned in advance.'

'Fine, then I'll warn him. Personally I'd love it if someone in the audience was definitely on my side. It would make such a change.'

She finished reading the cuttings, and packed them away in her briefcase. As she passed Marion's desk she heard her talking on the phone.

'Sure, we'll send transport, Jake, as usual. If you could bring, say, fifteen or twenty kids, that would be perfect.' She mimed goodbye to Lucy, and continued her conversation.

Lucy went down to the conference room on the first floor. It was a big hall which could be used for speeches or concerts, and the red light was on over the entrance to warn her that a session was in progress. She opened the door quietly. The hall was in darkness, but she found the nearest seat at the end of the front row, and slid into it. Dan was standing beside a dais, looking at a photograph of a crying child on the large suspended screen. The child's face was in a huge close-up. There were streaks of tears across her face. Fear was engraved in the lines of pain around her eyes.

'You know she's terrified,' Dan told his audience, 'but you don't know why. As a director, think carefully before you choose a shot like this. It's dramatic, but it's so close it can become intrusive.' He showed with a point of red light where the camera lens was cutting the child's face. 'So let's widen the shot a little.'

The picture changed. Now you could see the child in a barren landscape. 'This time the viewer has more information. The child is frightened, and alone. But still we don't have enough facts to know why. For me, the shot is still cutting too tightly here and here.' The red point of light showed his audience what he meant. 'So let's see the whole picture.' It changed again. Now you could see the child running naked down the road, her clothes burned and stripped from her body, a distant plane in the sky. 'And there's your story,' Dan told them. 'There are those who say the perfect shot is either a tight close-up or a big wide shot. I would say always beware the vague midshot, the picture that you think is safe, but is in fact the most dangerous, because it spells out to your viewers that you don't know what the hell you should be focused on.'

The lights came on. Dan blinked in the sudden glare, and then found Lucy's face in the front row. She watched him with admiration as he dealt with a clamour of questions. She was seeing a new man – not the quiet team manager, but a man in charge, with real leadership.

Finally he drew the discussion to a close. 'Next week we'll do another exercise, this time using the smallest cameras available. And you'd be surprised what excellent pictures you can get from a camera half the size of a penny. Thank you for your attention.' He pulled his papers together, the trainees applauding him enthusiastically.

Then he jumped off the stage and joined Lucy. 'How nice of you to come, Lucy. I didn't realize you were here.'

'I was fascinated.' It was true, she was, as much by the change in Dan as by the subject. 'Marion was a little worried, so I said I'd come and talk to you. She's booking some kids for the show, to take issue with Parks. She's got one school in South London and she wondered whether you'd mind her asking Jake to bring some of his pupils as well. I said I'd like it, if you don't mind.'

'I didn't realize you knew him.'

'I don't. But it would be quite a relief for me to have someone in the audience on my side. In fact she's already asked him. I hope you don't mind.'

His eyes were distant. Perhaps he did mind. That was strange. She looked at him curiously. His eyes fenced with hers, and then looked away.

'No, I don't really mind. In theory I don't think it's a great idea to bring your family to the show, but in practice, given what we went through last week, it might be a good idea. As long as we don't make a regular thing of it.'

So that was all right. She could go home now. But as she visualized the journey, the tail end of rush-hour traffic, the thought was unappealing. The house was empty, and so was the fridge. She and Fred had enjoyed filling it with treats for each other, organic chocolate mousse for her, tiny crusty pork pies for him. Tonight they would have made a trip to the delicatessen together to refill it, finding exotic fruits and strange new packets of spices to experiment with. But he wasn't there.

On an impulse she turned to Dan. 'I'm sorry to sound sad,' she apologized, 'but Fred's on location, and I'm alone this evening. Are you doing anything? Would you like a meal in one of my local restaurants? We have a couple of good Chinese and Italian, or Greek if you prefer. What do you think?'

Dan looked pleased. 'I've got a better idea,' he said. 'I do a great pasta. Why don't I drop by the deli on the way to your place, and do my chef act for you?'

She nodded and hugged him. 'That would be brilliant. I'll see you soon.'

Lucy drove home, looking forward to the evening. This was a new Dan. She would enjoy having some time with him. Her mind shifted to Suzannah. Ending an affair, as she had with Fred, was dreary and saddening. The start of a new one put a secret smile in your heart, revitalizing, even thrilling. Lesley said Suzannah had found somebody new. If she was right, who could he have been? Someone in television? A smart young City kid, dazzled by show business, and with bonuses of millions to cover Suzannnah's opulent tastes? Or maybe an old love renewed, someone from her distant past who could see past the Botox and peroxide to the woman she used to be before all the expensive reinvention?

If Lesley knew who he was and wasn't prepared to tell Lucy, she probably hadn't told anyone else either. No wonder Suzannah had trusted her so completely. Lesley's discretion was rare in an industry fuelled by delicious gossip. Everyone knew who was going out with whom, whose marriage was on the rocks, which pop star insisted on using the washbasin in the make-up room rather than go the extra step to the lavatory. And which actress juggled so many addictions it was a wonder she had a hand free to pick up her heaps of awards. But there had been no hint of a rumour about somebody new in Suzannah's life.

Lucy drove on, playing with the thought. Even if there was nothing in it, it was interesting to explore. Lesley had assumed

Suzannah had been on her way to meet the new man the night she died. Would he have been waiting for her in her manor house, the champagne already chilling? Or, still more romantic, was he standing at the airport with his ticket, ready for a weekend in Venice, or Vienna? When she didn't arrive, did his heart break? If so, why had he never spoken of it? Was he at her memorial service, lost in the crowd of famous faces and the sea of crocodile tears? Had he been as repelled by the vacuous vulgarity as Lucy was?

She found she was smiling with pleasure as she thought of Suzannah at the start of a new affair; she had hated the picture of her friend ending her life tired and drained, falling asleep at the wheel because she had no stamina, no energy left. How much sweeter to believe that Suzannah had been on her way to meet the new lover. Her mind would have been filled with delicious anticipation.

But in that case, why was she overcome with exhaustion? That didn't make sense at all. If Suzannah had been looking forward to a night of love, specially with the tantalizing spice of secrecy, a romance that nobody else in the world knew about, she would be vibrant, tingling, more alive than ever. Surely she would have driven extra carefully, to put nothing in jeopardy. Then why did the car crash, swerving out of control? What had happened that night to Suzannah, alone in her car?

Lucy let herself into her empty house. Dan arrived ten minutes later bearing carrier bags of groceries and Chianti, then started to make himself at home in her kitchen, while she put together a fresh green salad. The pasta was as good as he'd promised. They sprinkled it thickly with newly grated Parmesan cheese and they drank their way through a bottle and a half of the light, delicious red wine. Then Lucy took two porcelain mugs of strong black coffee and a dish of icy mints into the sitting room. Dan sat beside her on the sofa, and looked appreciatively round the pretty room. 'All these quiet colours – this is a very nice place to come home to after a day like ours. Fred's a lucky man.'

Lucy shook her head. 'He doesn't think so,' she said. Why not tell him the truth? 'Fred's gone. I don't know when he's coming back. Or even if. Maybe it's all over. I don't know.'

Dan was startled. 'Why? What happened?'

She sighed. 'Part of me doesn't blame him. But another part of me thinks he's a hell of a wimp to quit now, just because the press got on to him. I suppose it's better to find out where the breaking points are now, than when it's too late, and we're stuck with each other.'

Dan put his glass down and looked at her. 'He's a fool,' he said. 'To leave a woman like you, he doesn't know how lucky he is.'

Lucy laughed. 'Fred wouldn't agree with you.'

'I'm serious. You're too good for him. Don't give him a second thought.'

Lucy's eyes were distant now, remembering Fred. 'That's easier said than done.' Suddenly to her horror she felt tears. 'I know it's stupid, but with Suzannah gone, and now Fred, I do feel a bit alone.'

He put his arms round her comfortingly. She felt safe. But there was more than comfort in his touch – something lit a spark in her. He kissed her neck. She lifted her face with surprise. He kissed her lips. It felt good. Not violent heart-pounding excitement, but easy, and relaxing. He was slow, and gentle, and she liked him, so why not? Who knew what fun Fred might be having on location. They stayed entwined on the sofa, enjoying each other's closeness.

Then Dan held her shoulders and smiled at her. 'Could we go upstairs?' he asked.

She hesitated slightly. She wanted to go with him, but would it be a mistake? Was it simply her body taking revenge on Fred? Or crying out for security, even the false security of one night's lovemaking. Fred had dumped her when she needed him, this man had offered her warmth and reassurance. She stood. Dan followed her upstairs and into the bedroom.

A picture of Fred was tucked into the corner of the mirror, taken in a cottage in Cork, during a stolen week together which was one of their happiest memories. She ignored it, went into the bathroom, took off her clothes, and wrapped her satin dressing gown around her. By the time she came back to the bedroom, Dan was lying under the duvet. Too quickly to let any doubts surface, she lay down beside him. Once again his arms encircled her, and they kissed deeply.

She lost herself as their bodies got closer, his hands moving over her. Then suddenly she woke out of her warm trance as he pulled away from her and sat up. She heard him cursing.

'Dan, what's wrong?'

'I'm sorry,' he said. 'It's no good.' He sat on the edge of the bed with his head bowed, his hands clasped together. All passion had left him.

She realized how deeply embarrassed he was, and rushed to reassure him. 'Don't worry, Dan. You're tired. We've both drunk lots of wine. Neither of us expected anything like this to happen. The room is full of Fred's ghost watching us.'

He cursed again, and got up. He dressed quickly, with his back to her. 'Maybe it's too soon, after Suzannah's death,' he said, mumbling the words with embarrassment. 'It's too complicated anyway, now that I'm producing your show.'

She leaped at the chance to get him off the hook. 'You're right. It's far more sensible just to stay friends and colleagues for the time being. Anything else can wait.'

She slipped her cream dressing gown back on, and as he walked to the door she followed him, still trying to comfort him. 'Don't worry about this, Dan. It'll happen when it's right to happen. We're both under such pressure at the moment, there's no way we can relax and enjoy each other.'

He turned at the door, and she could see he was struggling with his humiliation. 'It would be fatal if the team found out.'

She agreed at once. 'Yes, of course. I'll see you soon, Dan.'

He kissed her once, his lips tight, and walked away from her into the darkness. She turned and went back upstairs to her tousled bed, her head whirling. Had she wanted to sleep with him? Had she been seduced, watching him with his class of trainees? Or was she relieved that his body had failed him? Maybe it was her fault, for being too fat, or too eager, or not sexy enough.

She switched on the television and sat up staring at the screen but seeing nothing, open-eyed but distracted by her own rage. She was furious with herself. How on earth had she allowed this muddle to happen? She'd put far too much at risk. Dan was her boss. She needed a simple, clear relationship with him. Would he hate her now, for causing his humiliation? Time would tell. She just remembered to click off the television before she fell into irritable sleep.

The next morning she woke early, alone, and lay in the dark berating herself. She felt unloved, and ugly. Her hands smoothed her stomach, angry with it for being so unfashionably rounded. Her thighs were too fleshy, her breasts too heavy. Was that why Dan had not been excited by her? It was as if a cold grey boulder was filling her chest, crushing the life out of her.

The alarm shrilled beside her, and the day began.

Walking slowly around the bedroom, she chose her clothes deliberately to cheer herself up. A soft pink sweater, a well-cut Joseph trouser suit in a neutral camel colour. She went to her study and settled down at her desk with the sackload of letters that had arrived after the first show. Suddenly she had joined the A list of celebrities invited to first nights and gala previews. Not that she wanted to go. The strain of buying, begging or borrowing enough glittery evening dresses was beyond her. She signed a standard letter to the viewers who sent her outraged insults, noticing that the more they complained about her rudeness to Boris, the ruder they were themselves.

At lunch-time she made herself sardines on toast, giggling a little at the cosiness of her single life. She must remember to put a pair of carpet slippers by the bed, and hang an apron beside the oven. She tried to tell herself that life without Fred would

204

be tranquil, and enjoyable. But the pang in her heart told a different story, and try as she would, she couldn't ignore it completely. She was instinctively waiting to hear his key in the lock. She missed him. She wanted him back.

The phone rang. She went into the study, but stood by her desk, allowing the answer-machine to take the strain. A voice she didn't at first recognize responded to the recording bleep.

'Lucy, I'd like to interview you about your hopes for the new show. I'm aware that you won't have enjoyed my last article, but I had to let Boris and Camilla have their say. Now the editor thinks it's your turn. Ring me on my direct line and let me know what you think. Janet.'

Lucy's eyes rolled upwards with disbelief. Janet Lake had the effrontery to think that she could offer her the right of reply, when she had already done so much harm. Lucy left the machine on, and took the day's newspapers into the kitchen with her. Fred would never have let her make such a mess of them, marking up some stories, carefully ripping out others for future reference. There were a few advantages to being single.

She didn't hear the answer-machine whirr into life again in the study, and this time Fred's voice filled the quiet room. 'Lucy, darling, I've been thinking about you. Are you all right? Ring me when you get this message.'

Fred would have to wait.

CHAPTER TEN

She drove to work angrily, cursing herself. She dreaded meeting Dan again in the office after their disastrous night together. The clumsy embarrassment of their scene in bed threatened to jeopardize everything. How could she have been so stupid? She should have built a fence around her work. Instead she had endangered her most crucial working relationship. Would he forgive her? Would she forgive herself? It's not as if she had been dying of lust for the man. Looking back, she couldn't understand her own motives. God, she hoped she hadn't been trying to revenge herself on Fred, attempting to prove to herself that she must be sexy and attractive if another man wanted her. But Dan didn't. So it had misfired hopelessly. And maybe shot to pieces the one refuge she had left, her work.

To her relief, Dan carried the moment for her. She had walked into her own office that morning, not putting her head round her door as she usually did, feeling too awkward and unsure. Five minutes later he had appeared in her doorway with a cup of coffee for himself, and herb tea for her. He had settled himself on her sofa, and gossiped comfortably about the latest industry news, which company had merged with which, whose job was up for grabs. She gulped her tea, impressed by his relaxed style. It was quite an achievement, to carry off the conversation without a hint of sourness or hostility. They needed each other, and Lucy was deeply grateful for his cool refusal to allow their relationship to be damaged by the humiliation.

As the week passed, Lucy deliberately filled each minute with chores, piles of correspondence to sift and answer, cuttings and biographies to be digested and long briefings by the researchers. It was easier than trying to sort out her life. She clung to the familiar structure of her working day, and came home exhausted to her empty house. She played Fred's message to herself in the evenings once or twice. It filled her with nostalgic affection. But still she couldn't bring herself to ring him. She would, she promised herself, when she felt strong enough.

Saturday brought its own extra charge of adrenalin. She had woken early, as always these days, her head bursting with pressure. Today above all she must block out all the horrors in her life: Suzannah's death, the hate mail, the Thritham fire, the paedophile ring. The regular appointment with David, her hairdresser, gave her a precious moment to insulate herself. She lay back in a comfortable leather chair, her head doused in warm water, while a patient Estonian shampooist lightly massaged her scalp. A moment of tranquillity to savour, before the clamour and bustle of the day in the studio.

Difficult and dangerous as the new programme was to make, at least the familiar process of putting it together shielded her from reality. The windowless studio, filled with bright artifical light, with its cardboard walls and painted floor, was a tiny world of its own, like a circus tent. It had its own rules and rhythms, its own cast of characters. David Jameson was the ringmaster, cracking his whip. The audience watched as presenters wobbled dangerously. Don't worry, viewers, if they appear to fall from a dizzy height. No real blood is shed in a television show. No real lives are lost.

As the warm water rinsed the bubbles out of her hair, Lucy tried to shut out her real life entirely and concentrate on her show.

Her eyes tightly closed, she visualized the day ahead of her. She was just another circus performer, about to go into the ring again to try to tame a bunch of unpredictable animals. Last time they had almost torn her to pieces. She opened her eyes, and stared up at the ceiling, as the silent Estonian poured conditioning cream onto the roots of her hair. How does a lion-tamer cope, Lucy wondered, when he has to go back into the cage after a mauling? The tent is full, the band is playing, the tickets have all been sold. So he has to make an entrance as bold as ever, moustache twirling, bright red jodhpurs gleaming, brass buttons shining.

But perhaps, when the lion roars, the little man will quaver in his shiny boots, not so much that the lions will know, or spectators will notice, but enough for him to feel. She must make sure that none of her guests tonight, and none of the viewers at home, would suspect that she was quavering. The lion-tamer had advantages. Once bitten, twice shy, he would have an extra gun hidden in his pocket, and someone watching his back when he went back to confront the lions for the second time. Here she was again, about to stick her own head into the lion's mouth. Did she have a gun handy and a friend watching her back? Was she armed well enough this time? Usually she knew she could depend on Dan, but was he still on her side after his humiliation in her bed?

The car took her to the studio. She arrived ten minutes early, and unlocked her dressing room. She hung up her coat, and sipped at the plastic cup of tea she had bought from the tea-bar. The research files lay unopened in her briefcase. She had read and reread them until she was word-perfect. The trick now would be to hold her nerve, and catch the moment. In any new series the second show was always difficult, an anticlimax after the fireworks of the first. The secret was to prevent the audience noticing. You just had to survive second shows, and look forward to the third one.

To her relief she found one problem had already been solved. Lesley had left two new dresses for her to choose from in the wardrobe, both immaculately fitted and finished. There was a black silk dress cut tight and smooth, with transparent lace over the shoulders and arms, to hint at voluptuous flesh without overexposing it. There was another in dark cherry red with long sleeves and a cutaway neck that almost showed her cleavage, but not quite. Lucy held the red dress up against her, and looked miserably at herself in the mirror. Genevieve's body was honed to perfection. Maybe she ought to pledge herself to another new diet, starting tomorrow, when all new diets start.

There was a knock on the door. Lesley let herself in, smiling with pleasure as she saw Lucy holding the red dress. 'That's the one I thought would work tonight,' she said. 'You'll be sitting next to a professional. Genevieve will have an army with her to make sure she looks wonderful, and nobody misses her best features. That dress will make sure she has a run for her money.' She gestured towards the low-cut neckline.

Lucy laughed. 'Come on, Lesley. It's no contest. Genevieve is the eighth wonder of the world. Her legs are lusted after in seven continents.'

'I understand that. Your bust has its fans.'

Lucy stopped arguing. As long as her clothes did nothing to undermine her own confidence, or alienate her audience, she accepted Lesley's advice. The red would do. Much too flash for her to wear in real life, but at least it would show the world that she was in the lion-taming business.

Rehearsals passed smoothly enough. Another cameraman had taken Fred's position, but nobody referred to it. There was nothing especially significant about that, except to Lucy. Cameramen came and went depending upon their own schedules.

While the crew were marking up their camera cards, the director and the vision mixer rehearsed a sequence of photographs of Genevieve, first on the set of her current film, then skipping backwards through her life. They didn't rehearse the most dangerous one of all, of her sprawled provocatively naked. If they put that picture up on their screens there was a chance someone might spot it on the monitors, and word would spread through the building. It was very hot news. A passing technician had only to catch sight of it and phone the press, and their story would be blown. Genevieve and Tim Brooks might well be tipped off in advance, and refuse to turn up for the show. Alex had selected the picture from half a dozen Channel Eight had sent him. It was just the right side of pornography, and they framed it carefully so as not to be too explicit, but all the same Lucy knew it would outrage Genevieve. It would be fascinating to see how she reacted.

Lucy rehearsed her walk-on, entering down the lit stairs to grand brassy music. It still felt extraordinary to her, this bold, starry entrance. Would she ever get used to it? As she reached her seat, Dan joined her, and sat in the chair Genevieve would be using tonight. They exchanged air-kisses, and he sat beside her, gazing out into the dark seats on the audience rostrum. They went through the running order and she told him what she had planned. 'I'll just have to play the Genevieve interview by instinct,' she said. 'I'll keep an eye on you, so that I know how you want me to handle it if she goes wild. But I don't think she'll walk out, she's too savvy. Tim Brooks is the loose cannon. There have been stories of him getting violent with paparazzi in the past.'

Dan put his hands up across his face, in mock terror. 'I'll stay well out of his eye-line, in that case,' he said. 'Do you wonder I always work with female presenters? At least you can protect me if he throws a punch in the studio.'

'The Parks interview is when the studio audience will want to join in.' She pointed to the front of audience rostrum. 'We'll have quite a few kids there in the audience. And feelings will run high. A lot of people will side with Parks about the breakdown in law and order, and blame young people for that. Parks seems convinced that modern youth is possessed by the devil. The kids will be enraged if he starts on that kick.'

Dan walked to the front row. 'We need some of the most articulate kids here, where he can see them clearly and they can respond to him.'

Lucy agreed. 'It'll be best if they can sit together in the front of that middle block. That way they can give each other confidence. The headmaster from Brixton, will be sitting there, and Jake and his bunch will be next to them.'

Dan's face was expressionless with concentration. 'That'll be fine,' he said, and walked back to his production desk.

As the rehearsal finished, Lucy picked up her script and went back to her dressing room. Pinned to her door was a note from Alison, the press officer, wishing her luck. 'We've been contacted by Janet Lake,' she wrote. 'She says she's been in touch with you. I can get rid of her for you if you like. But she left her direct line number if you'd like to speak to her yourself.'

Lucy sat still for a moment in her chair, wondering. Would she like to speak to Janet? Her last article had been so hostile, filled with antagonism, why bother? And yet, crazy as it seemed, when they'd met after Suzannah's memorial service Lucy had felt, if not quite a partnership, at least a duel of equals. She knew nothing about Janet's private life. She didn't really like what she knew of Janet's professional life. And yet there was a calloused toughness in the journalist's mind and outlook that appealed to her. This woman would not be easily fooled. She would see through most bluffs. Now, against her better judgement, Lucy was tempted to ring Janet, just to see what she had to say.

She dialled the direct line and, to her surprise, Janet herself answered. 'It's Lucy Strong,' she said, wondering if she should put the phone down at once.

Janet obviously heard the hesitation in her voice. 'Nice of you to ring, Lucy. I'm quite surprised. I know you must have hated the last article.'

'No, that was fine,' Lucy said dishonestly. 'I suppose I've got used to criticism over the years, and sometimes it's helpful to know my own weak spots.'

'But not always.'

'True. There are times, like when you're putting together a brand-new show, when it can make you wobble a bit.'

'Are you feeling wobbly at the moment?'

Lucy heard the edge of journalistic curiosity in Janet's voice. She could read the headline now: 'Lucy Not So Strong'. She must watch her step. 'No, I'm fine. The show looks terrific tonight. We have Genevieve and Tim Brooks, and Lord Parks. It's a good line-up.'

'I must watch you.' Janet focused on the point of the call. 'Now, when can I have my interview, how about tomorrow? Let's strike while you're hot.'

Strike might be the operative word, like a gauntlet slapped across Lucy's eyes. But she acquiesced, still telling herself she was crazy.

'If that's what you want, why not come round to my home at about eleven?'

Even as she spelled out her address to Janet she was wondering why she'd agreed to see her. The press officer would be delighted, but that wasn't the reason. Tom and Fred would be furious. That wasn't it either. Although their attempts to nanny her irritated her, she wasn't idiot enough to put herself at risk just to annoy them. No, it went deeper than that. At a level of vulnerability she couldn't admit, even to herself, she needed to talk to an objective outsider. Janet had spoken in depth to Camilla and Boris, both of whom had been very hostile, but they were an intimate part of Suzannah's life. Lucy needed to find out what they had actually said, what they had really felt. That might be the first step to making peace with them. Maybe it would bring her closer to Suzannah, help her to discover why she had died.

Lucy put the phone down, and sat quietly in front of the mirror. She must clear her mind for the programme approaching, coming closer minute by minute. Deirdre arrived, and did her discreet best to revive her, her fingers moving softly over Lucy's face as she brushed deep beige shadow into the sockets of the eyes, and brought a touch of rose onto her cheekbones. She tutted quietly to find new dark smudges under Lucy's eyes. The constant anxiety of the last days had left their mark. She covered them with a light-reflective cream, and it worked. When she finished Lucy's face had a fresh glow.

Lesley looked enquiringly at Lucy as she took the protective gown off her shoulders. 'You've decided on the red, then?'

Lucy thought for a moment, then, 'Yes, let's go for it. Why

not?' The audience at home would be expecting more adventure after last week. 'Let's give them something positive.' The black was more elegant, had more of a message of power and control. Next week would have to do for that.

There was a buzz of excitement as the audience came into the studio. Most of them had seen last week's show, and they hoped there would be as much drama in the second programme. The young people took their places in seats at the front, chattering together. What fun, to take part in a live show. Their friends would see them. They would be famous.

Once the warm-up man had introduced her to the audience, Lucy walked over to the group of teenagers and briefed them. 'Enjoy yourselves as much as you like,' she said. 'We want you to make whatever strong points you want and join in the argument, but we'll take the microphone away from you if you swear or shout like lager louts. That would just make the viewers think all kids are mindless idiots.'

She hoped she convinced them. She knew, and they knew, that 'fame' would certainly follow if they threw obscenities at Lord Parks – not just a member of the House of Lords, but a former Home Secretary. And 'fame' had become an overriding ambition, especially for the young. They all seemed to share a fantasy of arriving in a stretch-limo at Oscar ceremonies, the crowds pleading for their autographs. Perhaps, she thought, it's because we all feel so anonymous now, just a number on a credit card or a hieroglyphic e-mail address. Most of us don't even have a familiar place around a family dinner table any more. So perhaps 'fame' is the only way to retrieve our identity. Somehow Lucy needed to convince them that the wrong kind of fame would mean trouble at school, and trouble at home.

She shook hands with the two teachers, Harold Whittaker and Jake Carlton. 'Good luck,' they said to her. She would need it.

The red light flicked on, and Dan, sitting by his desk, smiled encouragingly across to her. She straightened her shoulders. The opening music blared out across the studio, and the audience

213

were whipped into a roar of applause. This was the moment. The lions were waiting for her, tame them or be eaten alive. She walked down the length of the stairs. As she sat down she felt her breathing steady. Thank God for instinct, and experience. She faced the cameras and began her introduction.

'Tonight we have a rare treat for you. One of the most beautiful women in the world, and one of the most talked about, is speaking about her own life for the first time on television. Ladies and gentlemen, please welcome Genevieve.'

Music rang out again, and Genevieve appeared at the top of the stairs. She made the most of her entrance, lingering on each step. The audience were instantly fascinated. She was wearing a tiny wisp of silver material that clung to her body by some technical magic – sticky tape, Lucy assumed – and floated high around her legendary legs. She was sleek and delicate-boned like a cheetah. The cameras were entranced by the planes of her face, her sharply defined cheekbones, her perfect straight nose, and her wide, extraordinary eyes. Lucy wondered what it must feel like, to live inside such beauty. Everywhere she went she must arouse lust and envy, and perhaps contempt. For many men, a lovely face meant an empty head, and a perfect body was a challenge to be exploited, used and then dumped. Is that why so many icons, from Marilyn to Diana, had such miserable lives, and died so tragically young?

As Genevieve reached her chair, Lucy rose and took her hand. 'Welcome.' Better to start cautiously. 'Is this your first time in England?'

'Yes it is. But I love it already.' The standard PR-schooled reply.

'How much have you been able to see?'

'I have seen your Buckingham Palace. With the guards. But I was disappointed. They were wearing uniforms.'

'What were you expecting?'

'I was told they would be in their bare skins.'

The audience groaned at the pun. She laughed delightedly. She had been well coached. Lucy looked down at her notes. If

214

the interview continued as cosily as this, an epidemic of sleepy sickness would engulf the nation. She introduced the obligatory clip from the latest film, in which Genevieve was playing an erotic love scene opposite Tim Brooks.

As it finished, Lucy said, 'He's your co-star, and he's here tonight, your partner in real life, Tim Brooks.' This time the applause needed no whipping up. The audience were delighted. Two of the biggest stars in the world were sitting in front of them, a few feet away, to be inspected, warts and all, diminished to life-size before their eyes.

The stars told a couple of stories from their time on location together, charming and self-deprecating. Then Lucy steadied herself, and her fists clenched involuntarily. Here it came.

'Genevieve, I have some pictures to show you. They come from a documentary which is soon to be broadcast on Channel Eight here. It is an unauthorized biography. And it includes these.'

She ran through the sequence as they had rehearsed it. A moment caught between Tim and Genevieve on the set, kissing, her hand caressing his cheek. They looked at the picture, and laughed with surprise. Tim explained that at the time they had not realized it was being taken, they had thought they were alone. It revealed how soon they had fallen in love with each other on the set, and how many people had known about it, when they had hoped they were keeping their feelings hidden. Then the pictures jumped backwards through Genevieve's life, each one revealing a moment backstage in her most famous films. She capped each one with a little story of her inexperience, or a moment she had learned something of value from a star playing opposite her. Either she was a public relations natural, or the coaching had been very good indeed. Finally they came to the picture Lucy had been leading up to.

'But this picture, Genevieve, was taken we think by your former partner. He took a great many more. This is one of the few we can show. The rest are pornographic, far too explicit for

215

us to broadcast, even as late as this. What can you tell us about this?'

Genevieve glanced at the screen. 'I see. Where did you find that?' Her voice was flat, even, emotionless.

'I think your ex-partner is selling them round the world.'

'So. Silvio was a pimp when I fell in love with him. And he is still a pimp. And you have paid this pimp. Are you proud of that?'

This was interesting. Lucy took her on. 'No, we haven't paid him. As I said, this will be shown as part of a documentary about you, with other pictures which are even more explicit. We want you to have the opportunity of explaining how and why they were taken.'

'How humanitarian of you. How caring.'

Tim Brooks suddenly stood up, towering over Lucy. The camera instantly followed him. Dan stood up too, ready to protect her. She could see Quentin, the floor manager, walking quickly towards her.

'Now listen to me, Miss Strong.' Tim's voice was furious. His height made him intimidating, but he was not physically threatening her. Dan had been right. He had no intention of punching her. 'I know nothing about these photographs,' he said. Genevieve was looking at him, her eyes never leaving his face. 'I don't know this pimp,' he said, and now there was deep contempt in his voice, 'and I never want to. But you, Miss Strong, invited us on to your programme without warning us, and you are using this filth to make your own name and exploit Genevieve. I'm taking no part in this. I'm leaving now.'

He turned. Lucy's mind was in turmoil, on two levels. On the surface, this was a disaster, and once again the papers would have a field day at her expense. But, at a deeper level, she knew the ratings would soar if she could just find the right way to handle him.

'Tim, that's your decision. But I must tell you that I am quite genuinely offering you both the opportunity to put these pictures

216

in context. They are out there in the marketplace. We know they will be used to attack you. But it is clear that Genevieve was quite a young woman in these shots. Let's put the blame where it ought to be. Who took them? Why did you pose for them, Genevieve? What was your life like at the time?'

Tim hesitated. Genevieve looked at him, sighed deeply and then she turned to Lucy. 'You will give me enough time to tell you the story?'

'Of course.'

'Then perhaps it is time to tell the truth. I have never talked about them before. That is because I wanted to forget them. But you can never leave such things behind. And maybe it will give other women strength, to hear my story.'

The tale was beautifully told. She had grown up in a shanty town which had mushroomed on the slopes of a giant rubbish dump, scavenged by the local children. Her family had been poor, and desperate. Her father was out of work, her mother had been extremely ill with dysentery. There were three children. Their very survival was at stake. Their only asset was Genevieve's beauty. She grew from a spindly, gawky teenager to become a lovely woman. Silvio was five years older than she, and he knew how to exploit her. First he befriended her, helped her with money, as a favour, asking nothing in return. Then he began to hint to her that she could help her family, put her younger brother and sister through school, build up her mother's strength, even find a decent house for the family. It took weeks before he told her how. There was no hurry. He used the time to find a customer for her virginity. She was horrified, of course. He didn't insist, or persuade her. He just let the thought lie, while she watched her family suffering at home. He waited until she brought the subject up, and then, seemingly reluctantly, he told her he could arrange things.

'I was raped,' Genevieve said. The audience whispered together, then were utterly silent as she continued. 'But that was only the beginning. There were other men. Many men. And

217

these pictures. Each time, Silvio gave me money. He kept more for himself, of course. I was his cash cow. He needed to keep me coming back for more, and I did. My brother and sister had the money to buy school uniforms now, and that meant they could go to school. We had clean water. My mother began to get well again. And at last my father could start the business he wanted, a little bar. It succeeded. He worked hard. As the money came in, Silvio knew he was losing his hold on me. He tried blackmail. My father agreed to pay him for the negatives of all the pictures he took. But of course Silvio kept some of them. And that is why you have them now.'

Her eyes filled with tears. Unlike a normal human being, instead of getting flushed and swollen-eyed, she simply looked more beautiful. She turned to Tim. 'I suppose, darling, I knew that all this ugliness would have to come out at some time. I'm so sorry I haven't told you before.'

He looked at her, then suddenly swept her into his arms. 'You could have told me. I understand why you didn't, but you should have trusted me, darling. I would never blame you for what you did to save your family. I only blame the men who exploited you.'

Relief shone on Genevieve's face. The audience applauded. Lucy watched them, unable to believe her luck. Another wonderful television event had been created in her studio, and it had been utterly spontaneous. Or had it? Genevieve was so eloquent. Tim had responded perfectly. Was real life like that?

As the applause died, Lucy thanked them both, and then turned back to camera. 'Perhaps, as Genevieve has said, her story will give other women hope. Our third guest tonight was until recently a cabinet minister, and he has very strong views, on morality, on law and order, on how we bring up our children today. Ladies and gentlemen, please welcome the ex-Home Secretary, Lord Parks of Shaddleworth.'

She turned to watch him as he walked down the stairs. His dark hair was white now, the cheeks were rosy with many gallons of port and champagne. He looked as he had in party political broadcasts and news bulletins, like a cherubic Father Christmas. As always, he was neat, the pinstriped suit evidently expensively cut, a Garrick Club tie proclaiming the fact that he was a thoroughly good chap. His smile was carefully judged, broad enough to acknowledge the audience's applause, but not wide enough to be vulgar. He made Lucy's skin creep with revulsion.

Consummate politician that he was, as soon as he had entered and greeted Lucy, raising her hand momentarily to his lips, he turned to Genevieve and Tim and congratulated them.

'I was so moved by your story,' he said to her. 'I had no idea you had such a terrible childhood. It's a tribute to your courage and your talent that you have survived it, and achieved so much.'

The audience applauded again. Only Lucy heard the practised insincerity in his voice. She knew she was not being objective in her reactions to him – how could she be, now she was seeing him through Max's eyes?

But a deal was a deal. She asked him about his autobiography. He was a skilled broadcaster, and he knew what she needed. He paraded the jokes and the anecdotes she wanted. He was indiscreet about another member of the Cabinet, a man who had cut a swathe through all the women MPs in the House. He shook his head with wonder at the man's energy, and at the fact that he remained the darling of his constituency – the more he sinned, the more the old ladies seemed to love him. The audience laughed obediently. They needed a moment to recover from the drama they'd just witnessed. Lucy saw him enjoying their laughter and applause, revelling in the spotlight, and her gut moved again with revulsion. What a hypocrite. She heard Max's voice in her head. On an impulse she obeyed it.

'I do hope, Lord Parks, you'll never have to go through an ordeal like Genevieve's,' she said smoothly. 'I hope that there aren't any pictures in your life that may come back to haunt you.'

He glanced at her sharply. In that moment she glimpsed a

very different man, intent and suspicious. But at once his expression changed again, and he was the good-humoured blustering sensible chap he'd been before, the man you would choose to be your neighbour, or a friend in the pub.

'I hardly think so, Lucy,' he said. 'Kind thought though that is. Unfortunately nobody would make any money at all out of pictures of me in the nude. More likely to put people off their food.'

The moment passed. They started to talk about young people, and his face flushed from pink to crimson with evangelical zeal. He looked straight at the schoolchildren in the audience. 'We have to ensure that you young people are given the right standards. We have to stamp out the evils of drugs, and violent crime. It is a terrible reflection on the young people of today that they can commit a terrible crime, like attacking a defenceless old lady. That's beyond imagination, it's pure wickedness.'

One outspoken black teenage girl answered him from the front row. 'Don't blame all of us,' she shouted. 'It's like if we said if there's one murder, all adults must be murderers. That's not fair.'

'But you must admit that many young people are completely out of control.' Parks was unabashed by her. 'Look at the state of our classrooms. Look at the vandalism and crime on our housing estates. Respectable people are living in fear.'

'So are we,' the girl answered. 'It's just as bad for us. It's adults who go to prostitutes. It's adults who smuggle drugs into the country. Do something about them instead of blaming us for everything.'

Genevieve joined in. 'I believe she's right. In my childhood we knew who was controlling the poverty. We saw how rich they became. You politicians can't shift the blame.'

The audience joined in, most of them on Parks' side, and it became a fiery debate. When the closing music sounded, the time had passed so fast Lucy could hardly believe the show had finished.

In the crowded overheated hospitality room she avoided Parks.

She knew she would have difficulty hiding her disgust. Dan was in deep conversation with Alex in a corner. The teachers and students were standing by the row of tables, picking through the remnants of food, cramming chicken legs and unidentifiable lumps of batter into their mouths. Lucy went over to them.

'Thank you so much, you were all terrific.' They nodded, mouths full of food. They held out pens and their entry tickets to her, and she signed her name two dozen times. They looked critically at her scribble. Maybe they could claim it was somebody else's autograph. Madonna perhaps, or Sting. They were far more thrilled with the autographs Genevieve and Tim had given them, even less decipherable dots and loops, rendered formless from countless repetition.

Lucy turned to the teachers. 'Didn't you think the kids did well?' They nodded. Whittaker was a middle-aged man, smartly dressed in a dark suit and discreet tie. He was beaming with pleasure at his pupils' performance, but his eyes were constantly alert and focused on them, just in case a child disgraced him. Jake Carlton was younger than Whittaker, in his late twenties, and far more informal, dressed in a faded denim jacket and jeans. He was lean and nervy, and for the first time Lucy took in how much he resembled his father, Dan. He had Dan's good looks and blue eyes, but there was a tightness in Jake's face, a strain in his voice as he talked to her. Was it so much of an ordeal, to bring a few children to a television show? She was curious.

'I gather your kids have come to other shows in the past. Do you enjoy them?'

He shook his head. 'No, not much.'

'Because?'

'Not because I'm above it all. I hope I'm not an intellectual snob. That would be pretty hypocritical. But the real world is such a different place. This fame stuff, it feeds into their dreams. In the end they'll have to grapple with reality. This is all so . . .' He gestured to the corner of the room, where his sixth-formers were clustered around Genevieve and Tim again, delightedly persuading the stars to sign their shirts, their hands, their foreheads.

'False?' Lucy suggested.

'Yes, but so seductive.' He blushed at the word, caught her eye, and then looked away. She found herself wondering about him.

'Do you have children yourself?'

'Yes, although they're too young to watch anything except puppets and cartoons at the moment. I'm hoping they'll get addicted to *The Simpsons* soon.'

She smiled. 'So *The Simpsons* has seduced you. Well, it's a start.'

He laughed with her, at himself. 'I know. I'm on the slippery slope. Never mind, I don't claim to be consistent.' He looked over at his class again. 'I'd better get them home.'

She walked with him, and saw that Genevieve and Tim were being wrapped into luscious matching fur coats by a sleek young man she recognized. He turned to Lucy as she approached.

'Hi, Lucy, great to see you again. Will Davidson, from Clarkson's.'

Now she remembered. He worked for the biggest public relations firm in London.

'Terrific show tonight.'

So he was pleased, in spite of the explicit picture of his client, naked. And yet Tim had almost walked out. What was going on?

'Thank you, Will.' Perhaps Dan knew.

Nicky, the youngest runner on the show, sweating with pride and fear, was offering to show Genevieve and Tim the way to reception. Will grabbed his jacket from the back of the chair, and they were gone, followed by their retinue of make-up artists, hairdressers, personal assistants, and three very large men in dark suits who had some important protective role in the stars' lives. Suddenly the hospitality room seemed empty.

Lucy looked around. 'Where's Lord Parks?'

222

'He had to leave,' Marion told her, 'but he said how much he'd enjoyed the show, and asked me to thank you.'

'Fine.'

Dan had finished his conversation with Alex, and walked over to her. 'I need a word with you, Lucy.' They went together to a corner of the room. 'The whole Genevieve row was rigged by Clarkson's,' he told her quietly, his voice tight with anger. 'They used us. They knew about the documentary, and they decided to make a pre-emptive strike, get us to show something comparatively harmless, so that Genevieve could get her story out.'

Hell. She had guessed as much. 'What does Alex say?'

'He realizes now that they were playing him along, that's why Tim wanted to appear with Genevieve. All that shocked surprise, that was utterly fake.'

She looked at the carpet. It was a particularly nasty blue carpet, wall to wall, with the company's insignia picked out in gold. As her eyes drifted over it she realized that she felt irritated, but she couldn't muster up any real fury. She knew she should be enraged. She'd been manipulated. Her integrity had been tarnished. Or had it? Did it really matter, any of it? A couple of actors, protecting their careers, had used her for their own ends. But she had used them too, to provide a little entertainment for bored viewers.

She looked up to see Dan's eyes on her. He was angry, far angrier than she, but then the show had been his baby for far longer. Out of loyalty she should try to share his feelings. 'I'm so sorry, Dan. I should have been tougher with them. But that would have been like clubbing a baby seal. The whole audience was on Genevieve's side. And in a sense they were justified to use us, one TV programme, to undercut another.'

'But I don't like being used like this.' Dan's eyes were hard with anger and resentment. 'I don't like the fact that you and our whole team have been exploited by some smart PR man.'

Lucy tried to soothe him. 'No, I understand that. I know we're vulnerable now. If someone else comes out of the woodwork

223

from Genevieve's past and says she lied to us, we'll look complete idiots. If in fact she was making a fortune out of pornography. If some newspaper discovers that there really wasn't a suffering family back home, then I'll agree with you. But surely it would be too risky for her to lie as blatantly as that. There are too many people back home who would spill the beans if she's fabricated everything. So all we're left with is the fact that she came to the studio knowing exactly what we intended to do, and she and Tim staged their charming scene for our cameras.'

Dan shook his head but said nothing. She tried one last argument.

'Give them their due, Dan. They did it consummately well. If that was acting, it was bloody good acting, and my guess is that the viewers loved it.'

He shrugged, and avoided her eyes. 'It's your name at stake, Lucy, and your face, and your reputation. In your place I'd be angry. But I'm not in your place. And I'm sure you're right, it made great television.'

Sandra called from the phone by the door. 'David Jameson is on the line for you, Lucy.'

She looked apologetically at Dan. Their discussion wasn't over, but she had to take the call. She walked to the phone in the corner of the room.

'What did you think of the show, David?'

Jameson was ebullient. 'Terrific stuff, Lucy. Genevieve and Tim Brooks were A-list guests. I'm sure you'll get loads of press. Congratulate the team.'

'Thank you, that's kind of you.' She wasn't sure she deserved the praise, but she'd pass it on. 'Genevieve and Tim were good bookings.'

'They were indeed. Even Parks produced some fresh stories. Though I'm not sure politicians are right for Saturday night.' Better stick to porn stars then.

As David talked, she looked round the room. The crowd was

224

beginning to dwindle. Dan was talking to his son, Jake. Whittaker was bundling his group into their jackets. They'd foraged through the last of the baby sausage rolls and the curling sandwiches. Only a few crumbs were left on the large tin trays. It was time to go home. She thanked Jameson again, and put the phone down.

'Jameson was delighted,' she told Dan and Jake as she caught up with them at the door. 'He was entirely convinced by Genevieve, and I'm afraid I didn't disillusion him.'

Dan grimaced. 'Why worry then? What does the truth matter?' His voice was tight and sarcastic. He was clearly still feeling bruised. Better to leave any debate until the next day. They left, and she went back to her dressing room to collect her clothes. Lesley was waiting for her there. She was always a good barometer.

'What did you think of the show?' Lucy asked.

'Excellent,' Lesley said. 'You looked great. Even sitting next to Genevieve, you looked great.'

That was reassuring, as far as it went. But how fake was the row, how fake did it look?

'Do you think Tim really intended to walk out?' Lucy asked her.

'Probably not. He's a big star. He knew what he was doing. But to be honest, I don't care. They're both so gorgeous. And I felt quite sorry for her. We've all done things we'd rather forget.'

'There's a theory they staged the scene for our benefit.'

'I wouldn't be surprised. Those tears came very easily, and by some miracle they didn't smudge any of her perfect make-up. But that's Hollywood, after all. I'd much rather watch that than some sordid wife-basher dishing the dirt. I need some glamour in my dull life.'

They laughed wearily together, and Lesley helped her carry her case to the waiting car.

When Lucy got home, all the lights were out in her dark, empty house. She shivered, not with cold but loneliness, as she walked around switching on table lamps. The flowers were wilting in their vases – narcissus, bought on impulse by Fred. She threw them in the bin. She would have to buy her own flowers now. She went to the bedroom, hung her clothes up in the wardrobe, and pulled her curtains cosily together to protect her from the night sky, then turned down her sheets welcomingly. If there was nobody else to pamper her, she'd pamper herself. What she needed was a hot drink, and a late-night movie in bed. She went down again to her kitchen, and put the kettle on.

Her mobile phone rang.

'Lucy, it's Max.'

'How are you? Did you see the show?'

'Yes. Not bad. I liked that question you put to Lord Parks.' There was sarcasm as he stressed the title. 'I could tell you had him worried. I've got the pictures with me. Do you want to see them?'

'When?'

'Now. I'm in the Hare and Hounds.'

The pub at the end of her road. That was risky for him. She checked her watch. It was ten past eleven. She'd better meet him straight away.

'OK, Max. I'll be with you in five minutes.'

She let herself out of the kitchen door, and ran through the quiet mews at the back of the house to the end of the road. The pub was full of Saturday night drinkers, too happy in each other's company to pay much attention to her. As she arrived, she saw Max standing at the other end of the bar. He caught her eye, and slipped out of the door opposite. She walked back out into the street, and they met in a dark shop doorway.

'Here. Take these. But I need to know what you're going to do with them before you show them to anyone else.' He reached into his pocket, and handed her three Polaroid pictures.

She screwed up her eyes to see them in the darkness. One was of Parks, smiling at the camera, bare-chested, holding up a glass.

The others were of boys, very young boys, naked, caught in the obscenity of abuse.

'Horrible,' she said.

'Look more closely.'

He pointed at the picture. A man's hand was holding down one of the children. He was wearing a ring, a gold signet ring with a crest. In the other picture, Parks' hand, holding the glass, was wearing the same signet ring.

'Nice ring that,' Max said. 'It must be a favourite. He was wearing it tonight.'

Lucy struggled to remember. Then suddenly there was an explosive bang, deep and resonant, like a plane crashing through the sound barrier, and shouts came from the pavement opposite them. Lucy, still holding the pictures in her hand, looked back down the road towards her house. In the distance there was a glow of light in the night sky, like a huge bonfire, orange, flickering, illuminating a column of smoke. Dark shapes of people ran towards it.

She turned back to Max. His face was pale. The same thoughts were in his head. Surely it couldn't be happening again.

'Who the fuck are they trying to get, you or me?' he shouted, his voice hoarse with panic.

She couldn't answer. He turned away from her, and ran into the darkness, leaving her holding the pictures. She pushed them deep into her coat pocket and began to run towards the noise. A fire engine passed her, siren blaring agonizingly, tearing at her eardrums. She slowed as she reached her house. A crowd had gathered. Now she could see bright flames flickering behind the windows. A fireman held the crowd back. Then she saw that he recognized her.

'It's my house,' she told him.

His face changed to sudden sympathy. The crowd turned away from the fire to look at her. Choking smoke and soot filled the air. She couldn't speak now. Her throat had closed with horror. She swayed and nearly fell, and the fireman saw and steadied

227

her. Everything she owned was being burned to cinders while she watched.

A police car's siren approached, then slowed as it pulled up at the back of the crowd. The fireman took her arm, and guided her to it. He opened the door.

'Sit here for a moment, miss,' he said. A man sitting in the back moved across the seat to make room for her. There was nothing else she could do, nowhere she could go. She slumped in the back of the car.

'What happened?' she asked.

'We don't know yet,' the policeman told her. 'Over the radio they said there was an explosion. We thought you might be inside.'

'I was. I mean, I would have been.'

'Can I ask where you were, Miss Strong?'

'I went to the pub for a drink.'

'You were lucky. It looks like a petrol bomb through your front window.'

She was shaking now the shock had hit her. She was icy cold. She tried to explain. 'I heard the noise, the explosion. I was on my way back. Then I saw the fire.' She felt completely helpless.

The policeman took over. 'I'll take you to the station.' She started to protest, but he overrode her. 'There's no point you staying here, Miss Strong. You won't be able to get into the house. It's too dangerous. The firemen will keep the crowd back, and they'll make it all as safe as they can. We'll look after you at the station.'

At the police station they made her a cup of tea, and she sat in a bare interview room, huddled in her coat. The lights were glaringly bright, she closed her eyes against them. She pulled her collar high and tight round her throat. The only clothes she had left were on her back. Who could hate her so much they wanted to kill her? The letter-writer was the obvious choice, the shadowy hostile figure who had already pushed his venomous notes through her door. Now this through her window, a lethal jar of petrol with a burning rag in it.

A chill ran through her, and her heart began to pound again.

He must have watched her car arrive after the show, and seen her bedroom light go on. He must have thought she was safely in bed, ready to be trapped there by the fireball and the smoke. He wouldn't have seen her slip out of the back door, and run to the pub.

Who was this man? Why did he hate her? And why had he hated Suzannah even more? If he could try to murder her so easily, he could have found a way to kill Suzannah.

She tried to calm the thoughts that whirled like a hurricane around her brain. There were other possibilities. This was almost exactly the way the house in Thritham had been incinerated. Could this too be linked with Wantage Grange School? Maybe prompted by her interview with Parks. The researchers had said he was happy with the show, but if what she'd heard from Max and the others was true, he must have become adept at subterfuge and disguise. Perhaps her question about the pictures had flicked him on the raw, and driven him to this. Or maybe the paedophile ring spread wider, and someone else had been watching her implacably, realizing that she was dangerously close to the truth, and must be stopped.

Where could she hide now to be safe?

The detective joined her again. 'Are you feeling any better, Miss Strong? I'm afraid I'm going to have to ask you some questions now, but I'll try to keep it brief. First of all, where are you going to spend tonight?'

'I don't know.' In the whirling fog of her brain she suddenly saw a safe place she could run to. 'May I make a phone call?' she asked. He pushed the telephone towards her, and she hesitated until he had left the room. Then she tapped in the number, her hands still trembling.

Tom answered quickly, his voice slurred with sleep.

'It's Lucy. I'm so sorry, Tom, but I need your help again. I have no one else.'

He heard the terror and desperation in her voice. 'Of course, darling. What is it? Are you OK?'

'There's been another bomb. My house this time.'

'God, no. Are you hurt?'

'No. I wasn't there. But someone must have thought I was. The house is still on fire. I have nowhere to stay.'

'Where are you?'

'Camden Hill police station.'

'OK. Get them to bring you here.' He gave her the address. She knew the street in north-west London. He waited until she had noted it down, then he asked, 'Has your house been totally wrecked?'

'I think so. It was petrol again.'

He was careful not to let her hear how aghast he was. 'The crucial thing is you're not hurt. Come round as soon as you can.'

She was hurt, though. Not physically, perhaps, although the shock had left her cold and shaking, but by the deep fear that churned round and round in her brain so that she could hardly think.

The policeman started to ask her more questions. Did she know anyone who could have done this? She did, of course – Parks and his friends – but how could she start to tackle that complex story? She tried.

'I was at the house fire at Thritham. The police there know all about it. That was a petrol bomb as well.'

The Thritham police knew about the hate mail too. If this detective contacted them, that would save her sitting here for hours, trying to piece it all together for him. He made a note.

Who else? A row of faces slid past her memory. Camilla, Boris – they were angry with her, but their anger didn't run to this. Janet knew where she lived, but that was absurd. Lucy shook her head.

The policeman saw her exhaustion, physical and mental, and relented. 'Tomorrow will do. Would you like to have some security tonight wherever you're going, one of our men with you? We might be able to help you feel a bit safer. This must have shaken you up.'

230

It had. But having the police constantly at her side would make it impossible for her to uncover the story behind Max's pictures. 'I think I can cope,' she said. 'I've arranged to go to a friend tonight, somewhere I think I'll be OK.'

'Are you quite sure that's what you want?' Was she? He clearly thought she was suffering from a stupid professional machismo, trying to prove that she was as tough as any man, and just as determined to see her investigation through. Maybe he was right. She clasped her hands to still the shaking. 'Yes, thank you. I'm sure.'

'We'll need a contact number for you, Miss Strong, in case we find out anything more. And we will need to talk to you again tomorrow. But for now we'll drive you wherever you want to go. Just don't give the address to anyone who doesn't need to know.' He leaned across the table, looking into her eyes. 'I don't want to make things even worse for you, but I want to be sure you realize that this was a very clear attempt on your life, by someone who wanted to kill you and almost succeeded. Go carefully, and if you see anything that worries you, if you need any more help of any kind, don't hesitate to ring us.' He gave her his card.

She pushed it deep into her pocket, and as she did so felt the Polaroids next to it. Should she show them to this man? Max had made her promise not to. If she did, that would provoke Furies she might never be able to escape. She needed time to think.

The police driver drove to Tom's home in Kentish Town. When they'd first met he'd lived in a sparse bachelor flat in Clapham. This was definitely a step up. The street was narrow, filled with Victorian houses neatly gentrified. Every hallway shone with the obligatory honey-coloured wood floors, the walls were shelved and stacked with Mozart, the Beatles, Jane Austen and Salman Rushdie. It was intellectual suburbia – not so academic as to intimidate, not low-brow enough for chocolate-box prints or net curtains.

231

She rang the bell, and almost fell from fatigue as the door opened. Tom caught her in his arms and held her.

Behind her the policeman explained apologetically, 'We'll have to contact Miss Strong again in the morning, when we've examined her house and have a few more facts to go on.'

Tom nodded, and the policeman retreated down the path.

Lucy found her feet again. 'Sorry, Tom,' she said. 'It's been quite a day.'

He said nothing, but led her through to his study, where a sofa-bed had been made up. He handed her a new toothbrush and a towel, and gestured towards the bathroom at the top of the stairs. 'I'm brewing up a jug of cocoa for you,' he said. 'I know your dentist wouldn't approve, but you need to sleep right now.'

She washed wearily, feeling six years old, but allowing herself the luxury of giving in, and being nannied. As she slipped naked into bed, she stretched against the fresh, clean sheets. Tom returned with a tray, two mugs and a big earthenware jug. She positioned the sheets primly across her chest. He poured her hot chocolate, and as she cupped it in her hands, he looked at her severely.

'We must think, now,' he said. 'The papers will be full of this tomorrow.'

'So who should I ring tonight?'

'Your parents, first of all. You'd better tell them you're safe.'

'And Jameson,' she said, feeling her brain coming to life again as reality hit her. 'He can tell the team.'

She rang her parents in their home in Cornwall, while Tom talked to the duty officer at the studio, who promised to pass the message on to Jameson. Tom came back while she was still reassuring her mother.

'Mum, I can't give up this job at the moment, but I will be careful. The police will be watching. Don't worry about me. I'll come and see you as soon as I can.'

He took the empty mug from her, and watched her eyes closing as sleep overtook her.

'Good night,' he said. 'There's nothing left now that we can't deal with tomorrow. Try to sleep.'

As he switched off the light and closed the door, she saw her coat hanging by the door, the obscene photographs still hidden in the pocket, another bomb waiting to explode.

CHAPTER ELEVEN

She woke just after eight to find Tom sitting on the bed, his hand on her arm. 'Sorry to wake you, sweetheart,' he said, 'but I think you should see what they're saying about you.' He switched on the little television on the bookshelf.

The presenter of the Sunday news programme, a pert blonde with religious earnestness and the obligatory pastel jacket was in mid-flow. '. . . who has just begun presenting a new series of Saturday night programmes is believed to have escaped without being injured. Jane Haversham is at the scene of the fire in West London now.' The picture changed to a dark sky, and outlined against it, the exterior of Lucy's house, lit by powerful lamps. A group of firefighters was working in the front garden and one last hose was playing on the roof. The house must have been gutted, there were black smoke stains on the bricks outside every window.

Lucy had to force herself to look at the screen as the camera roamed over the destruction of her home. The horror of it hit her hard. Everything must have been consumed by the ferocious blaze, or ruined by the water as the firefighters battled to control it. Her school reports, her treasured scrapbooks, the bridesmaid's dress she had worn when she was ten, everything. But she was alive.

The reporter's voice echoed her own thoughts. 'If Lucy Strong had been inside the house last night, she could not have survived. Eyewitnesses say the explosion sent flames up through every floor in seconds.' A neighbour appeared in close-up, Daphne Harris, an old lady who lived next door. They used to greet each other fondly whenever they met in the street. Daphne was an avid watcher of all her programmes, and Lucy was careful to be complimentary about Daphne's Persian cat. Last night the old lady had clearly been terrified, but she was delighted now to describe the disaster to the hungry cameras.

'I was asleep in my bed,' she told them, 'but I heard a crash, and then a bang like a bomb going off. I remember bombs round here during the war. They used to tell you not to look out of the window then, in case the glass blew in, but I did, and the house went up like Guy Fawkes night. I'm so glad Lucy wasn't at home. She's a lovely girl. Who could possibly have done a thing like this?'

The reporter, Jane Haversham, took over the story. 'And that's the question everyone is asking. It seems clear this was a petrol bomb, but why? Who was responsible? A spokesman for BriTV tells us that Lucy herself is well, and unhurt. Viewers will remember that Lucy was present at another recent bomb out-rage, when a house in Thritham was destroyed with the loss of sixteen lives. Only luck seems to have prevented a second tragedy here. Jane Haversham, BBC Television, in West London.'

Lucy's eyes were blank with horror as she watched. Tom glanced at her, switched off the set, and got up. 'It's only things, darling. Things are replaceable. People aren't.'

She nodded, numbly. She wanted to curl up in his study, like a hibernating animal. She was safe here, snug and warm here. Nobody could find her here. Tom read her mind.

'I'd love to leave you here for the rest of the day. You need to sleep, let it all settle in your mind.' She pulled the sheet gratefully up around her ears, but he wouldn't let her rest. 'But there is one decision I'm afraid you will have to make. You are somebody's least favourite person, and whoever they are, they know now that you are alive and unhurt. So you're going to have to lie very low for a day or two. I'm sure the police will track this maniac down very quickly – they seem to have been very fast on the scene last night – but where are you going to spend the next week, say?'

Where indeed? She stared up at him. 'I'd better go to a hotel. Heaven knows which one. Maybe BriTV will find something for me.'

'Of course they will,' he said. 'You must make them put you up somewhere quiet and very comfortable, off the beaten track. Eventually. But is that a good idea right now? You've had a very tough couple of weeks. Do you really want to be on your own?'

It did sound miserable. She shook her head. She was confessing a weakness she despised in herself, but she was too devastated to care. 'No, I don't really.'

'Then stay here.'

She realized that was what she had been longing to hear. But it would be impossible. 'I can't do that. It's not fair to you.'

He got up from the bed. 'You can go to a hotel in a day or two. Stay here just until the dust settles. I've only been here a couple of months myself, hardly anyone knows my address, and if they do know it, they'll hardly imagine you'd find shelter with your estranged ex-husband. Cup of tea?'

She snuggled down under the duvet, glad to leave the decisions to him. Her mind filled with the pictures of the gutted house, interlocked with the memories of the fear, the smoke, the screams that haunted her from Thritham. Someone had killed the boys there. Someone had just tried to kill her. Though they had failed this time, they would surely try again. Even if Tom was right to be optimistic, and the police found the murderer instantly, she would have to rebuild her life now. Everything she used to own had been destroyed, taking with it so much of her past.

Another thought struck her. Fred. How could she have forgotten him so completely? With a rush of guilt she remembered that some of his things had been left in the house – half a dozen CDs, that photograph of them both in County Cork. She reached for her handbag, fumbled through it and turned on her mobile phone. He answered almost at once.

'Lucy, thank God. I've been watching the news. I've been out of my mind with worry.'

'I'm so sorry, Fred. I should have rung you last night, but after the police had finished with me it was so late, I fell asleep straight away.'

236

'But couldn't you have rung me? Where are you?' His voice rasped with urgency.

'The police have asked me not to tell anyone, even you. I'm in a hotel.' A lie. Why couldn't she trust him with the truth? Was it because she dreaded his jealousy if he thought she had gone straight to Tom? He accepted her story without question, his voice heavy with guilt.

'I can't tell you how much I miss you, Lucy. I can't believe how stupid I was to walk out. Everything just got on top of me, the press and everything.'

She examined her heart. To her weary surprise, she realized she didn't care any more. Last night's flames had cauterized that wound, there was no blood left in it. But she owed him more than a callous rejection.

'Freddy, don't blame yourself. I know how you felt. The trouble is, everything's so complicated now. The police say I have to stay in hiding while this maniac's on the loose. It sounds melodramatic, I know, but I'll ring you as soon as I can so we can get together.'

If he heard a new distance in her voice, he chose not to react to it. 'OK, darling. As long as you're sure you're all right. But ring me soon. I love you.'

'I love you too,' she said automatically, but as she spoke she didn't see Tom walk in behind her with a cup of tea. He flinched, put the tea down beside her and walked briskly out of the study, leaving her to gulp it down alone.

She showered, thinking longingly of the bath in her own home. She borrowed Tom's masculine deodorant spray, pungent with musky pheromones, and dressed again in last night's cherry-red silk dress. She was insured, so Lesley would have a great time helping her to replace her wardrobe, although the insurance policy and all her financial documents, her contracts, her passport, were cinders now. She blinked, dismissing tomorrow's problems. Sufficient unto the day . . .

When she came back to Tom's study, he was sitting at his

237

desk, hunched over piles of paper. He smiled briefly at her, and continued poring over a lengthy legal opinion. She used her mobile to ring Dan's direct line in the office, and heard him gasp with relief when he recognized her voice.

'Lord, Lucy, I don't know where to begin. How are you, first and foremost?'

'I'm fine.' And she realized she sounded it, calm and assured, whatever the maelstrom raging in her life.

'Where are you?' he asked, but once again she felt the impulse to protect herself. 'I'm staying with a girl-friend at the moment,' she said. 'But I'm going to have to find a hotel. Do you think BriTV will cover the cost?'

'Certainly. Jameson's already been on the phone saying so. The ratings for the show are through the roof, so you're his golden girl. Genevieve and Tim are the front page of the first editions, you and your fire are in the later editions, so the Sunday press are all devoted to you, one way or another, and he's thrilled.'

What good news. She must arrange to have her house go up in flames every week. 'Does he realize it was sheer fluke that I wasn't at home when it went up?'

'Yes, and to do him credit, that was his first concern. What happened? How did you escape?'

'As luck would have it, I was out of wine, so I went to the pub on the corner to get a bottle of red. Thank heavens.' She was getting worryingly fluent in these lies. 'Did you mention to Jameson that we suspected we might have been set up by Genevieve's PR machine?'

'No, the right moment never quite came along.'

'More sensible not to worry him.'

'Exactly. The Press Office are desperate to talk to you as soon as possible. They want a statement, of course. And Janet Lake has been ringing them every ten minutes. She says she has a date with you at eleven. Is that true? Do you want us to cancel it?'

'Oh God.' Something else she'd forgotten. 'No, better not.

238

She's such a dragon I'd better not let her down. I'll come in straight away and sort things out.' Could she cope with a heavy interview? Only time would tell.

'Are you sure that's what you want to do? We can send a car for you, if you're sure.'

'No. I'll pick up a taxi.' The less people knew where she was staying, the better.

'Well, take your time. We all care about you, Lucy. You've been through more than enough in the last few weeks. There's no hurry.'

She was grateful for his kindness.

Mandy next, at home. Tom had rung her last night, so she had got over the first shock. She just had to reassure herself that Lucy was not in trauma.

Then she said, 'Come and stay with me, Lucy, if that would help. Whoever this murderous bastard is, I'd love him to try and wipe me out.'

The bravado in her tone made Lucy laugh. 'That's really kind of you, Mandy, but I think I'll probably find a hotel. Thank you for the thought.'

'Here's my take on it, darling. You've obviously trodden hard on someone's toes. If you ask me it's one of those effing paedophiles. Are you sure you want to carry on with that investigation? Your Saturday show is such a triumph, it seems to me that's where your future is.'

Lucy was grateful, but not sure she agreed. Now was not the time to argue. 'I hear what you're saying, Mandy. I'll go carefully. The police are watching over me. They don't seem too worried.'

'Well, I'm happy for them. Just don't give them cause.'

She made a check call to the police station, and they had good news. Her car, which had been parked a few hundred yards down the street in a residents' parking bay, had been untouched by the bomb. The police had moved it to their car pound, and gone over it for any trace of evidence, but there was none. She

239

could collect it whenever she wanted. The bad news was that the fire, smoke and water had wrecked her home. She could come and check everything in a day or so, when they had finished examining the shell of the house for evidence. They would need her to make a full statement, but not instantly. She arranged to spend Monday morning with them.

'And in the meantime, Miss Strong, could you please go through everything in your mind for anything out of the ordinary, it doesn't matter how small, that might be relevant. Don't worry if nothing occurs to you at the moment. We'll take it quite slowly, and you'll find you remember more than you know.'

But there was a trail of stuff, so much that she hadn't told them yet. What should she do?

She caught a taxi to the office. The DIY shops and garden centres were thronged, the supermarket car parks packed, but the back streets were empty – dozing avenues, occasionally brought to life by Sunday bells. The office was subdued. It had the usual Sunday gloom, only a few teams working, lights off in many of the corridors. She felt ridiculous, walking past reception still wearing the bright silk dress from Saturday night.

The researchers were diffident, too shy to greet her. As she arrived they were talking quietly together at their desks, obviously frightened by the violence of the attack. When she reached her own office, she found it piled high with bunches of flowers and cards from them all.

There was a white orchid from Lesley, with a card, 'Stay Strong, darling.' Did she feel strong? No, but there was a hard block of solid determination building in her. She had been involved in battles before. She enjoyed pitting herself against an adversary worth conquering. Whoever this was, paedophile or lunatic, the bomber was too dangerous to be allowed to continue.

She read all the cards, affectionate from the team, a generous one from Dan: 'we need your strength, Lucy, not just professionally, but personally too.'

240

Then she came across a long, white, official-looking envelope. It must have arrived in the office on Saturday, from a city solicitor.

'We have been asked to contact you in relation to Ms Suzannah Piper's estate. Ms Piper specified in her will that she wanted you to have a piece of jewellery, emerald and diamond, made by Cartier. She said, 'I bought it when I made my first big show, it has always brought me luck. I would love my dear friend Lucy to wear it when she feels happy, or needs a little extra luck, in the knowledge that wherever I am, I will be thinking of her.'

Lucy's eyes filled with tears. It was so unexpected, and so appropriate, today. She read on.

'Suzannah's daughter, Camilla Crosthwaite, is one of the executors of the will, and she has suggested to us that you might also like some further mementoes of Ms Piper. She would be pleased to discuss this with you.'

It was an olive branch, and Lucy smiled with relief. Now she was the target of some unnamed, unidentified enemy, she longed to be able to find someone to trust. She was seeing her later that evening, but on an impulse she dialled the number she knew as well as her own, Suzannah's home in Whitbury. When it was answered, she recognized Camilla's voice.

'Camilla, I've just read the lawyer's letter about your mother's will. She was too generous. You should keep that brooch.'

Camilla was indignant, not with Lucy, but at the suggestion. 'I absolutely could not. She wanted you to have it, and so do I. Specially now. I'll give it to you when you come to Whitbury.'

Lucy thought about the fifteenth-century house outside Oxford, with its serene winter gardens, the tracery of branches, the still cool ponds. She longed for its calmness filled with memories of past happiness, a haven from the smouldering wreckage

241

of the rest of her life. She had promised Camilla that she would be bringing the letters she had found in Suzannah's desk. That wouldn't be possible now.

'My house was gutted,' she said. 'I haven't been able to sort through anything, so I just don't know what happened to the letters I found in your mum's desk. I can't bring them with me. Are you sure you still want me to come? I admit I'd love to get out of London at the moment.'

'That's fine,' Camilla said. 'I'm here going through all Mum's things. We can have supper together, and I'll give you the brooch.'

Neither of them touched the edges of the row buried between them – Camilla's iciness on the phone, and her bitter interview with Janet Lake. Would all that rage surface if they were alone together, or would Suzannah's memory act as a peace-keeper? Lucy couldn't face the thought of a furious quarrel. But even so, the visit was worth the risk. They agreed that Lucy would drive to Whitbury in time for dinner.

Sandra came to her office door, apologizing for interrupting her. 'We've had hundreds of e-mails offering you support. The whole world seems to be worrying about you, Lucy. And Janet Lake is desperate to speak to you.'

Lucy rang the press office. This part was comparatively easy. 'Could you put out a statement for me please? Say how grateful I am for all the sympathy and support from the viewers, and that I'm fine. I'm thankful to be alive, and I have every confidence in the police. That sort of thing.'

She knew it was bland and unquotable, but it was the best she could do at the moment. She sat quietly at her desk, nerving herself to make the call to Janet Lake. Janet's voice when she answered almost made Lucy giggle, her tone was so gentle and comforting.

'How are you coping, Lucy?' she cooed, sweet as a dove on a sunny dovecote.

'A bit shocked, as you would expect,' Lucy said, deciding to encourage this new, unfamiliar Janet. 'It's hard to come to terms with being on somebody's death-list, when everything you own has gone up in smoke.'

'Terrible,' Janet said. 'And I suppose the last thing you want now is to be interviewed by me.'

Lucy thought about it. Odd though it seemed, there might be some advantages. Janet could get some useful messages across for Lucy – for instance, make it clear that the police were determined to protect her. And she could convey the impression that Lucy had gone to earth in a small hotel outside London, and that BriTV were investing a great deal of money in keeping her safe. And – it might be rash, but why not – that she was determined to carry on investigating criminals who hurt children, no matter how highly placed they might be.

'No, I'm happy to meet you, as we arranged. But it had better be somewhere quiet.'

'Why not have lunch with me here at my flat? It's quiet, and we can be comfortable. I'd be happy to make you a sandwich.' That sounded fine.

Suddenly Lucy had had enough. She got up from her desk, leaving the rest of the pile of cards and letters untouched. She put her head round Dan's door. 'I'm going, Dan,' she said. 'I've got a million things I have to do. I can't think about the next show. I'm sorry.'

He shook his head. 'Don't worry about us. There's masses we have to get on with, tidying up after the last show. Do what you have to do, don't think about us.'

She went. She took a car to Marks and Spencer's and sped round the store, picking up a selection of underclothes, sweaters, shirts and trousers, a camel coat trimmed with honey-coloured fake fur, and two pairs of comfortable boots. Then, garlanded with carrier bags hanging from her arms like laundry from a washing line, she hailed a cab and took it to the police pound.

When she found her car, she almost hugged it. In all the chaos

243

of her life, at least this had survived. She filled the boot with her shopping, and drove slowly to Kensington, to the address Janet had given her. Each hoot of a horn behind her made her jump. She recognized how tremblingly on edge she was. She just mustn't cry in front of Janet.

She found a parking meter in a square lined with heavy red-brick mansion flats. A brass-gated lift took her up to the fourth floor.

As the doors opened, Lucy hesitated. She'd been put on the rack by this woman before. Why was she volunteering yet again? Because this time, her instinct told her, Janet might be merciful, and might even join forces to protect her.

She rang the bell, and when Janet opened the door, her sharp eyes took in Lucy's pallor at once. 'You're going to have a glass of champagne,' she said. 'Don't argue, I can tell you need it.'

She opened a bottle, and the froth of foam did look energizing. Lucy sipped her glass, enjoying the sparkle on her tongue, but determined not to let it loosen. This was no time to repeat her indiscretions.

'What have you been doing this morning?' Janet asked her. 'You look exhausted.'

'I am a bit,' Lucy admitted. 'The police say I've lost everything. All I'm left with is my handbag, and my car, which escaped, by some miracle. Thank heavens for the council's jobsworth rules about parking. If they'd allowed me to put my car outside my house, it would have been wrecked too.'

'So your clothes have gone . . .'

'Yes, I imagine they have. The smoke and water will have ruined them. And my scrapbooks, my family photographs, all the souvenirs I've treasured, the little gifts from my parents, my friends, that mean so much to me. They were downstairs in my study. That's where the petrol bomb hit. So they're all gone.'

Her hand shook as she held the glass. Janet saw it. 'Who could possibly hate you so much they wanted to kill you?'

Lucy looked at her, and said nothing for a long moment. Then, 'Could we talk off the record?'

Janet hesitated. She took a cigarette from her bag, lit it and breathed out the smoke, considering the offer. 'All right, Lucy. This will be just between ourselves. Tell me.'

'I had some hate mail pushed through the door. It could be from the paedophiles I've been exposing. But the letter is exactly like some stuff I found in Suzannah's office. She had some horrible threats. Why anyone would have hated her so much, I can't think.'

Janet took another deep breath of smoke. 'I could tell you. But I don't think you'd like it.'

'Why, what do you mean?'

'Suzannah was your friend. Even so, when we talked after her memorial service you listed a dozen people you said either drove her to her death, or danced on her grave. I knew there were more. But I kept my mouth shut at the time. I didn't want to hurt you. You were in a vulnerable state. But I could have told you plenty of people who loathed your friend.'

Lucy didn't want to hear this, but Janet went on, 'Her own daughter, for one.'

'Camilla? Come on, Janet. Suzannah wasn't a perfect mother, but whoever is? Camilla adored her.'

'Camilla is a very complicated young woman. She told me a great deal about Suzannah when I interviewed her last week. I didn't print it. It wasn't relevant. I was doing a story about you and your show.'

A venomous story at that. Lucy decided not to point that out. There would be time later.

'You knew Camilla when she was a lumpy, sulky teenager.'

Lucy nodded. It was an unpleasant description, but accurate enough.

'Did you know why she was so unhappy? Did you know that three years in a row Suzannah forced her to spend the summer in a fat camp in America, one of those places that drill kids and humiliate them into trying to lose weight?'

245

Lucy thought back over the years. 'I know she used to go to the States as a teenager. I thought it sounded fun – a way to escape her mum's fame, for one thing. And a chance to meet other kids, and go camping and canoeing, all that kind of out-door stuff.'

'Camilla told me the memory still gives her nightmares. She tried to persuade her mother not to send her, she begged and pleaded, but Suzannah insisted. Camilla says Suzannah was ashamed of the way she looked.'

Lucy was astonished and showed it. 'I didn't know that. I don't believe Suzannah would have been ashamed. It must have been to help her. Maybe it was on doctor's orders. Maybe they were worried about Camilla's health.'

'No, at least not according to Camilla. Suzannah was only worried about Camilla's weight and her width. She told her so. She said she looked like an elephant. She said she was spoiling her appearance with all that excess flesh, and she didn't want a daughter of hers to let her down in public.'

Lucy felt her face flush. 'Suzannah wouldn't talk like that. I know she wouldn't.'

'The woman you knew wouldn't. But there was another Suzannah. She was also a ferocious woman, a driven woman. Her researchers knew that. So did her daughter. You may be right, she may have convinced herself she was doing it for Camilla's own good, but she didn't convince anyone else. She nagged her at every meal-time. Which, of course, made Camilla binge on chocolates in her own bedroom. And as she put on weight, Suzannah banished her from the obligatory star-relaxing-at-home-with-loved-ones photos. Not that Camilla minded that. But then she sent her away to this notorious place in New England, run like a boot camp by an army of vicious sergeant majors, who got the kids to exercise and diet and punished them if they didn't lose weight.'

'Maybe it was good for Camilla.'

'Maybe, physically. She did lose a bit of weight, though she put it all back on when she got home. And she did get fit with all the exercise. But she was utterly miserable. She started cutting herself. Secretly. She would cut her arms. Really slice into them.'

Lucy was horrified. 'What d'you mean? Cutting her wrists? Trying to commit suicide?'

'I asked her that. She said maybe, subconsciously. But consciously she was trying to punish her body. She loathed herself. She wanted to repay her body for the pain it had caused her. She hated it so much, she began to love the pain. Hurting physically somehow released her from her inner agony. I think she never believed she was good enough for her mother.'

'That's rubbish. Suzannah was very proud of her.'

Lucy couldn't stay seated on the overstuffed striped sofa where Janet had put her. The room was claustrophobic. She got up and walked to the window. Searching for space and air she looked out across the square with its melancholy plane trees, stripped bare by the December cold.

Janet's eyes followed her. She knew how difficult this was for Lucy to accept. But she persevered.

'Was she? Really? Or is that just the Suzannah you want to believe in? I know she was proud of you, Lucy. She often told me how well you were doing. She never in all the years I interviewed her talked to me about Camilla.'

'Then how do you know all this, Janet?'

'Because Camilla told me.'

Lucy turned to face Janet, suffocated by the strain. 'Why did she tell you? She never told me anything like this. I've known her for years. I can't believe all this went on without me knowing.'

'I asked her about her childhood when I interviewed her. She told me, but she made me promise not to print any of it.'

'She never told me.' Lucy was deeply bruised. 'Why didn't she tell me?'

'You were Suzannah's friend.'

Lucy thrashed around in her mind, trying desperately to fight her way out of this vicious picture of the woman she had thought she knew so well. 'Maybe Camilla was lying to you. Maybe she was angry with her mother for dying. You know how complicated these things are. How can you be sure her story's true?'

'She showed me pictures of herself at the fat camp. And she showed me her scars.'

'God.' Memories jumbled in Lucy's mind. The weekend she'd spent at Whitbury, the sullen teenager who spent all day in her room. Was she in despair, hating her body, her mother, her life? Tom said Camilla had talked to him. Did he know all this? She couldn't take this savage new picture of Suzannah. If she had been cruel to her daughter, it must have been inadvertent.

'Janet, I just don't believe Suzannah knew the misery she caused Camilla.'

'Maybe she didn't. For three years Camilla managed to keep most of it secret. She wore long sleeves, winter and summer. She stayed in her room over the weekends, and of course Suzannah was constantly taken up with her own work, so they lived pretty separate lives anyway.'

'So when did Suzannah find out?'

'One day, just before Camilla was due to fly out for another three months at the fat camp, Suzannah caught her cutting her arm, ran at her, took the razor blades away, and saw all the old scars. There was a wild row that went on for hours. Suzannah cancelled the booking and Camilla never had to go again.'

'Camilla's thin now. Almost too thin.'

'Yes. I didn't dare ask how that happened. Whether it just happened as she got older, or whether she helped it along with pills, or by throwing up. I don't know. But I do know that she's still very, very angry with Suzannah. And very jealous of you, Lucy.'

'Why jealous? I'm not thin. I've never been thin. Suzannah never worried about my weight.'

'I know. You were perfect. She never criticized you. Can't you see how that made Camilla burn? You were the perfect daughter she could never be, or at least that's what Camilla thought. No wonder her anger rose higher and higher, bottled up inside her.'

Lucy came back to the sofa, and sat down opposite Janet. 'OK. She was angry with her mother, and furious with me. I accept that. But do you really think she could have written those letters? Surely not.'

'I don't know. I'm only telling you what she told me.'

'Well, to me it just doesn't make sense, not with the Suzannah I knew. None of it makes sense.'

'Perhaps, Lucy, you knew a different Suzannah from the rest of us. What did Tom think of her?'

Lucy thought back. 'He agrees with you, I suppose. He says I saw her differently.'

'And Boris?'

'He's just bitter.'

'Is he? Or did he hate living with the knowledge of what she did to their daughter? Maybe she played the same game with him.'

'No.' Lucy leaned back against the unyielding cushions. That couldn't be true, not after the evenings she had spent with Suzannah, comforting her when Boris had tormented her with his promiscuity. 'No, I know the truth about that. He would go out at night looking for other women. Sometimes other men. Suzannah was very hurt by him.'

'I'm told she started first. She used to bring her dates home, and throw Boris out so that she could entertain them in her bedroom.'

'He'd never stand for that.'

'He didn't. Boris is a proud man. After the first time, he left so she couldn't throw him out again.'

Lucy drained her champagne and put it down on the table between them so hard the glass almost shattered. 'You can't persuade me that he hated Suzannah. I know that's not true. He loved her. He still loves her.'

'I know. Camilla still loves her. We cling on, loving the person who rejects us. And she loved them too, in her way. But that didn't protect them from her. Lucy, she was ruthless. They suffered. Oscar Wilde says each man kills the thing he loves. He could have said that about one woman too. Your friend.' Janet's voice was harsh.

She stubbed out the cigarette burning in a vast blue and gilt ashtray, and got up. 'Come on, Lucy. Let me make you a sandwich. I'm not saying the woman you loved and admired didn't exist. She was proud of you and very fond of you, and looked after you. I'm just saying she could be ferocious to her own family.'

Lucy's heart was pounding, as if she had been taking part in a physical wrestling match. They walked together to the kitchen, furnished with state-of-the-art equipment, and grey granite worktops. Lucy suspected the only dish in constant use was a large marble ashtray.

Janet opened the enormous American refrigerator to reveal it was almost empty – just a loaf of bread, some butter and cheese, and three bottles of champagne. Janet sliced the cheese into heavy chunks, balanced them on the bread, and squashed them together. Not an elegant meal, but Lucy could hardly swallow it anyway. Her world was turned upside down. The friend she had loved and admired had been thrown into negative, the colours reversed. She could think of nothing else. Janet watched her, then said, 'I'll tell you what we could usefully do. Let's talk about the other people who might have you at the top of their hate list. Presumably you told the police about the paedophiles. They're the prime suspects.'

'Absolutely.'

'What about the others? Is there anyone you know, or you've come across, who might have thrown that bomb? You really need to start protecting yourself.'

It was probably good advice. 'OK.' Lucy was reluctant. This was going to be an unpleasant process, like a malicious party game. All the people she was used to regarding as friends, as companions, would have to be put under suspicion. Well then, perhaps they should start with Boris, while they were dissecting Suzannah's family.

'You could say that Boris is very angry with me. He hated my show. He thought I was unfair to him, and dancing on Suzannah's grave. He told you so, didn't he?'

'He did.' The two women paused, trying to visualize easy-going, charming Boris in a violent role.

Janet broke the silence. 'I can't see that, can you? Boris may be weak, but he's not a bad man. He's still very fond of you, that's partly why he was so hurt. And he hasn't got a motive, unless there's something else, something we don't know about. Could he be covering up, trying to prevent you finding out something new?'

'What could it be?'

'Something financial perhaps? Maybe he'd been swindling Suzannah while they were married. Or perhaps there's some dreadful sexual secret he's trying to conceal.'

'Something so terrible he'd kill me to avoid it coming out?' Lucy shook her head. It just didn't fit with the man she knew. 'Anyway, he told me I should investigate Suzannah's death. He told me he thought it was suspicious. Why would he say that if he wanted to keep me out of his life?'

'OK,' Janet conceded. 'Then what about your ex-husband, Tom. Was he very bitter when your marriage broke up? And that cameraman of yours, Fred. I'm sorry to have to put him in the frame, but we have to rule everyone in before we rule them out.'

Lucy leaned her head on her hand. Had it really come to this – putting together a random list of everyone she knew, and everybody she cared about? 'Tom's out of the question. He has been helping me behind the scenes. In fact, he was at that Thritham fire, and he was in as much danger as I was then. And he was miles away in his home when my house was hit. You can cross him off.'

'And Fred? Why wasn't he in your house last night?'

'Because,' Lucy said reluctantly, 'he can't stand the heat from the press. He's moved out.'

'He's dumped you?' Not a sensitive question, but one designed to provoke a reaction from her, and it did.

'Don't, please, Janet. Don't wreck my life by doing one of those "Lucy dumped by toy-boy" stories. That's what's driven him away.'

Lucy got up from the kitchen table, and walked over to the door. She looked down the elaborate corridor, with its ormolu mirror and ornate candlesticks. It was a grand flat, filled with antiques and expensive reproduction furniture, designed to demonstrate status. But it was a lonely place – just what Lucy wanted to avoid herself. Now she too was alone. Would she turn into Janet, toughened by a thousand journalistic battles, her soul calloused by fighting through each day alone, with no one to share her triumphs, and her disasters?

She turned back, and stood with her back to the door, her hands clasping each other. 'I don't know what's going to happen between Fred and me. I know he loathed the publicity after the show. He felt hunted, and he's not used to it. So he's gone off on location now until the heat dies down.'

'Have you spoken to him since the bomb?' Janet was unrelenting.

'Yes, I have. He's very concerned for me.'

'Not concerned enough to come back, though, and look after you.'

Lucy felt anger rising in her. 'Janet, that's not fair.' She heard a pleading note come into her own voice. 'Please don't print that. It will just make things even worse for both of us. Please leave Fred out of this. I promise, if this does become a story, I'll tell you. Right now I'm too shaken up to take another piece about my private life.'

'Come on, Lucy,' Janet was robustly unashamed, 'if not me, someone will write about it, if Fred really has dumped you.

Even without the bomb, you're high profile now. You put yourself right there in the public eye. The show you're doing now isn't a quiet piece of high-quality reportage. It's tabloid, you're going for ratings. And that's fine. You've decided to take on the big boys, and make an entertainment show in peak time on Saturday night, and you're asking some pretty "intrusive" questions of your own. You can hardly object if I ask you one or two of my own. Specially since someone, somewhere, hates you enough to try and kill you.'

'Fred would never do that. Fred and I have a good time together. We have a nice, uncomplicated, happy relationship. Or at least that's what we used to have. If you print anything about him now, that'll kill anything we might have left. Please don't, Janet. You agreed that all this was off the record, otherwise I would never have started.'

Janet gave way a little. She stubbed out another cigarette, walked over to the kettle and switched it on. Then she took the shopping list from beside it, and wrote on the top 'Paedophile ring'. Then 'Camilla? Boris? Fred?' As Lucy began to protest, she said, 'Don't get jumpy, Lucy. None of this is on the record. We're just doing a checklist for your own sake. For the moment let's leave Fred on the list.'

'I'm absolutely sure he shouldn't be there. Neither should Tom. While we're crossing people off, let's lose the production team. And my agent, Mandy. These are people I depend on. I work with them all the time, but our lives are quite unconnected. They don't impinge on me, I don't impinge on them.'

Janet contemplated the list. 'All right then, while we're adding names, what about David Jameson?'

Lucy was taken aback. Why on earth would he take to violent crime? Without question he had the ruthlessness to ruin his enemies, but kill a television presenter? Why would he want to?

'He wouldn't have to,' Lucy said, grimly. She'd seen careers killed on the turn of a coin a dozen times. 'If Jameson wanted to get rid of me, all he'd have to do is pick up the phone to a dozen of his cronies, the people who hire, or fire, or write about television, and he could ruin me tomorrow. That would be a far cheaper way to get me out of the way, far more effective and much less dangerous.'

'That conman chef you did over on your show, Crabtree?'

'No. Far too self-absorbed to waste time on killing anyone.'

'Lord Parks?'

'Why would he? He loved the show. He thought we'd sold thousands of books for him, and that's all he cares about.' Had Janet spotted her tiny hesitation? Lucy thought not. Janet spooned coffee powder into a pair of gold-painted china mugs. 'It's going to turn out to be some insane stalker, somebody who has developed a fixation about Suzannah and then me, somebody I don't even know exists.'

'More than likely,' Janet agreed.

Lucy reflected for a moment. That idea of a motiveless maniac was no more agreeable than trying to fit her friends into the silhouette of a murderer. It meant she was at risk on every street corner.

'I'm seeing Camilla this evening,' Lucy said cautiously, taking a mouthful of black coffee.

'Are you indeed?'

'Yes, though I'm not looking forward to it. She wants me to go to Whitbury to collect a brooch Suzannah left me. I'm going to have supper with her.' An idea struck her. It would be a risk, but then she'd taken so many already. She put her mug down. 'I'm not sure I can face it alone, not now I know how much she hates me. Would you come with me, Janet? Otherwise I'm terrified we'll have a row, and I can't stand that just at the moment. She confided in you, she trusts you. You might keep the peace.'

Janet's curiosity was tweaked. She wanted to stay at the centre of this story. 'Are you sure you'd like me along?' she asked.

'Let's think it through,' Lucy said. Janet had forced her to search through her life for enmities. Now that eviscerating

254

process was over, she could begin to relax and think more cheerfully. 'You being alongside me might allow Camilla and me to talk freely together, without hurting each other. And she might have some more clues about Suzannah's death.'

'But why do you want me, Lucy? You and I aren't close friends. There must be someone else you could take who could give you more support than I can. Or go on your own? You might achieve far more if you just had it out with her, just the two of you.'

What was it about Janet that made Lucy trust her? Had she found another older woman to replace Suzannah in her life? Not nearly as warm, as vital, as charming, but Janet was a role model too, someone with the strength to go for what she wanted, to take chances by herself, with no one else to lean on. Was that it?

Lucy tried to explain. 'You've made me face a Suzannah I never knew, that I never suspected existed. I trust you Janet, for reasons I don't understand myself, maybe because I think you're more objective than I can be at the moment. Anyway, for whatever reason, I do trust you, and I think you might be helpful. Provided you give me your word the whole thing stays off the record.'

Janet nodded silently, and handed her the phone. Lucy rang Camilla and tried the idea out on her. Would she mind if Janet came along for the ride?

Camilla hesitated. 'I've had enough of newspapers,' she said.

'Yes, we both know that,' Lucy said comfortingly. 'Janet's not coming along as a reporter. But I'm feeling a bit shaky, and I'd welcome her company on the drive down.'

'As long as she understands the deal,' Camilla said. 'And as long as you and I have a moment to ourselves.'

Janet put her cigarette out, and got up. 'Right, let's go. You know the way, Lucy. Will you drive?' She disappeared towards the bedroom, and came back wrapped inside a bulky fur coat.

As they walked to Lucy's car, darkness had closed in, and

sleety rain began to fall again. The streetlights were mirrored on the dark road. Christmas decorations in the shop windows shone red, gold and green. Soon they would be out in the blank wilderness of a dark December countryside. The weather made Lucy all the more grateful for Janet's company.

They drove westwards, then north to the A40, and out again beyond the friendly towns and villages. After nearly an hour, Lucy slowed down and shivered.

'Do you know where we are?' she asked.

Janet peered out at the wintry countryside dimly outlined against the black cloud-laden sky and shook her head.

'In a moment we'll be exactly where Suzannah died. It's half a mile from here, on this road.'

'I didn't realize that.'

'I've been thinking about it ever since I agreed to meet Camilla. That's another reason I was dreading the drive. Do you mind if we stop a moment when we get there?'

'Of course not.'

Janet stayed in the car. Lucy got out alone, and walked to the corner. It was eerie, standing there in the darkness, the rain falling silently as it must have fallen that night, at the exact spot where Suzannah's car had swerved out of control, then crashed into a tree. There was a little mound of flowers there, wilting bouquets that must have been there some days, and a couple of fresh ones, each one with a card.

Lucy bent to read them. 'Suzannah, you will never be forgotten', and 'For Suzannah, from a grateful viewer'. They were simple, banal, and touching. Someone, or perhaps a group of fans, had gone to great trouble to buy the flowers, to find the place and leave them there.

Lucy stood up, and visualized the scene, as they must have done, like votive pilgrims. It had been so dark that night, and Suzannah had been travelling at speed. It was the end of a long day, but she had chosen to drive herself. Here, at this corner, something had happened and the car had spun across the road.

Had she simply made a tiny, lethal miscalculation? Lucy talked out loud to her friend. She seemed so close to her here.

'Suzannah, I miss you so much. I'm not sure I can carry on alone. I need to talk to you, to share all this with you.'

A sob rose in her throat. She looked back towards her car, and was suddenly blinded as Janet flicked the headlights on to full beam. Behind the glare she could just see Janet climb out of the passenger seat and walk towards her. The rain slanted through the beams of light. Behind her, trees stood tall and gaunt. One of them had crushed Suzannah into her steering wheel, and pulverized her body. Lucy looked at the thick, grey trunks, gleaming in the rain, the trees deep in their winter sleep. They seemed to her bloodless and cold, with a huge, slow capacity for survival.

She shivered again. Janet reached her, and took her arm. 'Come on, let's go back to the car. Don't put yourself through too much. This is a very sad place. Suzannah's not here any more.' She was right. Lucy got back into the car, and they drove on, not pushing the speed, only too aware now of the danger of a winter road at night.

Soon the wrought-iron gates of Whitbury Manor were beside them. Lucy turned slowly between them and drove up the lime tree drive. There was a welcoming light on over the front door, and the two women pulled their coats warmly around them and ran over the gravel to the porch. Bare twisting branches of wisteria and climbing roses were enlaced together over the door. It was like the frame of a picture. Only the frame was empty now.

Lucy rang the doorbell. They waited in the cold. She could imagine Suzannah so clearly. If only she would fling open the door now, so that they could hug each other. The big square sitting room would be bright with copper bowls of scarlet cyclamen, or azaleas, or masses of poinsettias. There would be a Christmas tree in the hall, covered with gold ribbon and glass ornaments. They would sit together over a drink, and swap gossip, and laugh as only friends can laugh, about nothing.

The door opened. Camilla stood in the hallway, slender and pale in a black dress, her white-blonde hair ruffled. Her eyes had dark rings beneath them, her mouth was pressed shut, like the lid of a box with too much inside it. She must have dreaded this moment too. Lucy felt a pang of pity. This was a heavy burden for Camilla to carry alone. On an impulse she leaned forward to hug her. The girl stood straight and tall, her face rigid, eyes flinching, as though she dreaded the touch. Then as Lucy let her go, she stood back so that they could walk past her.

'It's a long drive in this weather,' she said, as Janet held out her hand to her. 'Mum had some very nice red wine she was saving for a rainy day. I reckon there's enough rain tonight for us to open it.'

Lucy and Janet sat at the kitchen table as Camilla opened a dusty bottle. The wine was from a Bordeaux chateau. It poured richly into the glasses, so dark it was almost purple. As she put the bottle down, her sleeve fell away from her wrist. Lucy saw a puckered scar. So it was true. The child had been self-harming, suicidal perhaps. Camilla saw her sigh, and pulled the sleeve back round her wrist. She flushed awkwardly, but said nothing. Instead she took them into Suzannah's study.

On the desk was a leather Cartier box. She handed it to Lucy, who opened it slowly. Inside was a rectangular brooch, square-cut emeralds and diamonds, big and bold, designed to impress. She recognized it. It would take a lot of living up to. Lucy pinned it on her collar, then stood up to see the effect in a mirror over the fireplace.

'It's wonderful,' she said to Camilla. 'But I'm a bit scared of it.'

For the first time Camilla smiled. 'Don't be,' she said. 'Mum used to shove it on any old jacket. She said good jewellery shouldn't stay in a safe. If you've got it, flaunt it. She always said it was lucky. Emeralds are supposed to bring good fortune, that's why she left it to you.'

Lucy looked again at her reflection, and in that moment she saw Suzannah standing behind her, smiling with approval. 'Thank you,' she said to both reflections, the ghostly and the real, mother and daughter, friend and foe. 'Let's hope they bring us all luck.'

Camilla looked around the room with dislike. Lucy realized why. This had been her mother's work room. Even here, in the heart of the country, there was no escape for her family, no chance to find peace or privacy. How could she not have known Camilla felt that, before Janet had opened her eyes?

'Do you want anything from these shelves?' Camilla said. She looked along the lines of meticulously ordered papers. 'These are all Mum's old scripts and the stuff she used for research. They don't mean anything to me. I'll just get rid of it all.'

The study walls were lined with files and video tapes, and shiny books still in their pristine dust jackets, skip-read once rather than loved and pored over. They were autobiographies of the stars Suzannah had interviewed, cosmetically enhanced by ghost writers. Beside them were other books, dog-eared and annotated, the unauthorized hatchet jobs, filled with envious back-biting. Somewhere between the two the truth lay.

Lucy took down a book, and opened it. It was autographed with a scribbled 'thank you' and an indecipherable famous name, the automatic reflex at the end of a programme.

Janet took one of the files, and opened it. Suzannah had been famously organized. Inside were all her drafts, and the completed scripts, followed by the transcripts of each programme. Many of the interviews, especially in the early days, had been exclusive and revealing. The names on the files were an A list of international stars.

'These might make a book,' Janet said, flicking over the pages, 'if someone edited them.'

Lucy opened another file, and smiled at what she found. It must have been a very early stage of a script. An introduction was written out in Suzannah's flamboyant handwriting, but someone else had gone over it in red ink, underlining a split infinitive, and correcting her spelling. At the end the marker had written, 'Good, but you could do better. Give yourself more time next time.'

She had seen that tiny red biro handwriting before. But where? She sat on the floor, with the file open on her lap, wondering.

Camilla looked exhausted. 'I've been trying to clear up,' she said. 'There's so much stuff here. Upstairs all the wardrobes are crammed with clothes. I've never seen so many shoes, most of them she never wore.'

She sat down with them on the floor. 'I hate this house. I know Mum loved it – it was her dream come true, like Hollywood to her, and she adored the weekends she spent here with her smart friends. I used to be embarrassed to bring my friends here. With all these pretentious lakes and statues, who did she think she was? She never managed to impress the duchesses she invited to dinner here. They laughed at her. Dad never liked the place. I was unhappier here than anywhere.' She caught Janet's eye. 'Anyway, I'm going to sell it and buy somewhere of my own.'

She looked at the desk, at a picture of Suzannah at one of her parties beside the lake. She was laughing in the centre of a group, her head thrown back. She looked exhilarated, and exultant. Camilla's face softened. 'In her will she asked me to have a wake for her here, one last get-together, for her friends to remember her. I suppose it would be an improvement on that Disneyland memorial service Mandy created. I'd only invite a few of Mum's real friends. It would be a way of burying my own ghosts.'

There was silence in the room. Lucy broke it first. 'You know I loved your mum, Camilla. I owed her everything. But I never thought she was the perfect mother.'

Camilla stayed silent. She looked intently at Lucy. Then she smiled, a porcelain, painted smile which never reached her eyes. 'Don't feel you have to ingratiate yourself with me, Lucy. I know

260

you saw a Suzannah who looked after you and thought you were perfect. It's just a shame you weren't her daughter. Mum would have much preferred you.' Her voice was high and bright.

What could Lucy say? She looked pleadingly at Janet. Janet decided that any intervention would only fan the flames, and looked away. Lucy tried the truth.

'Camilla, she never treated me like a daughter. I was her friend, that's all. A very close friend. She told me a lot about her life, but certainly not everything.'

Best to change the subject to something safer. She looked down at the open file in her lap. She held up the script. 'I'm sure I've seen this writing before. Have you?'

The others glanced at it. Janet shook her head. But Camilla looked puzzled.

'Yes, I have seen it. Wait a minute.' She reached over the sofa, and pulled a plastic bag out from behind it. She tipped the contents onto the floor. It was the package Lucy had sent her when she cleared Suzannah's office. Camilla pulled pieces of paper out until she found what she wanted – the fan letters that had so amused Lucy.

'Look,' Camilla said. 'Am I right?' They stared over her shoulder. The tiny tight red writing was identical.

'Now, what does that mean?' Janet asked.

'It must mean that she knew this fan, whoever he was. Otherwise he could never have corrected her script.' Lucy was speaking slowly, working it out aloud. 'I can't think who that could be.'

'Don't look at me, I've no idea,' Camilla said, stretching backwards as she sat, looking at the ceiling. 'I hadn't seen her for months. If you don't know, Lucy, who would?'

Mandy? Lucy wondered to herself. Or Lesley? Whoever wrote these letters was disturbingly besotted with her, 'You make my life worth living, my dearest Suzy.' She'd assumed that nobody could have used that nickname if they'd really known Suzannah. She had always rejected it and objected to it vehemently. But

Lucy must have been wrong. The letter-writer wasn't some sad distant fan after all. This must have been written by someone who had wormed his way into the very centre of Suzannah's life, her work. Who on earth could it have been? Why did none of them know him? If this was the man she had been going to meet the night she died, did he hold the secret of her fatal crash?

Lucy shut the file. 'I think your idea of a final party here is terrific,' she said to Camilla. Maybe he would be there. Maybe someone else at the party would mention something that would give a clue as to his identity. 'Why not make it soon, before you have to start putting the house on the market, while the memories are still warm?'

Camilla's face tightened again. There were no warm memories for her in this place. Every word Lucy spoke seemed to lead to another minefield.

This time Janet dared to intervene before the smouldering row reignited. 'Whoever has the perfect childhood?' she asked. 'I certainly didn't, I had an alcoholic dad who hit us all indiscriminately. They say what doesn't break us makes us strong.' She sucked at her cigarette, inhaling a thick lungful of smoke. 'In any case, Camilla, I bet your life would have been even worse if Suzannah had given up her work and kept you here with her. She might have made you her life's project, and then heaven help you. That would have been like having a flame-thrower in your armpit. You'd have burned to a crisp.'

Camilla shrugged, and offered them both another glass of wine. There was a dingy-looking plate of cold meat laid out in the kitchen, but they realized she wanted them to leave. It was a sad house, and she wanted to be alone in it. They had revived for her the memory of her mother's first and last love, her work. The bitterness in her was unrelieved.

So Lucy took her brooch and her file, and Janet took one of the books, and they drove back to London together, saying very little. It had been a sour meeting, they had no appetite for conversation. Lucy dropped Janet at her flat.

262

As Janet turned to say goodbye, a thought struck her. 'Are you going to the Awards tomorrow night? I'll see you there.'

Lucy sighed. It was the last thing she needed, the dross and drama of the annual People's TV Awards, but she would have to go, the team expected her to. She nodded, mustered a smile, and drove slowly on to Tom's house. She saw as she parked outside it that his study light was still on. She was glad. She needed a bowl of hot soup. Comfort for body and soul. Maybe she would find it with him.

CHAPTER TWELVE

Tom looked exhausted. As he let her in, the light from the hallway showed shadows under his eyes, and he greeted her with relief.

'Let's have a drink. I'm up to here with another medical negligence case. I'm sure the old lady should still be alive, but I just don't know how the hell we prove it.' He took a bottle of brandy from the shelf. 'How about this, with some ginger wine, for a cold night?' She nodded.

He had lit a fire in the small grate, and there were fresh branches of holly in a big bronze vase. In spite of the piles of papers like leaning towers on his desk, it was a welcoming sight. She watched him pour her drink, dressed for comfort in a crumpled pink shirt, and old jeans she remembered from far better days. They sat together on the sofa, and he looked at her with concern. 'How was your day?'

She thought back over it. 'Long,' she said finally. 'And rough.' She held the glass in front of her face, so that she could breathe in the spicy scent. Her shoulders dropped. She relaxed for the first time.

'Lord, Tom, I don't know how much more I can stand,' she sighed. Could she tell him how much she had learned about Suzannah? Or, rather, about the three or four different Suzannahs. It was as if someone had ripped a photograph of her into pieces, and the torn fragments of her familiar smile contradicted each other now. She had been a wonderful friend, but a fearsome mother. She was a beloved icon to the distant masses, but the loathed enemy of the people closest to her. A consummate professional, but a brutal colleague. Passionately loved by someone unknown. But even more deeply hated by someone extremely dangerous, not just to Suzannah but to Lucy

264

as well. She felt as if she was on a roller coaster, every value tumbling upside down.

Maybe none of this would come as a surprise to Tom. In her heart she suspected that he knew a good deal of it already. Camilla talked to him more easily, she had confided in him during their weekend in Whitbury. He had no illusions about Suzannah. He had admired her, but he saw her distinctly, as she really was.

Tom watched Lucy sipping her drink, his eyes mirroring her anxiety. She was carrying so much – the destruction of her home, the knowledge that somewhere someone could be waiting to pounce again. He wanted to put his arms around her, but she seemed remote tonight, lost in her own thoughts. He tried to break through them to join her.

'You're safe here,' he said. 'Why not forget everything else for a moment?'

She heard him, and responded without the indignation he had feared. 'I'm sorry, Tom, if I seem somewhere else. It's just . . . it's what I'm learning about Suzannah. I don't know what to believe.'

'I think that happens when people die. In a way it was inevitable,' he said. His voice was gentle. 'People share memories, but they're different memories. You saw one Suzannah. She wanted you to see her that way, she treasured that in you. She needed you to believe in her. You were crucial to her self-esteem. But there were other Suzannahs.'

'Did you know how Camilla felt about her? How angry?'

'Yes, I knew a bit of that. She told me a little of it. Didn't you suspect it, ever?'

'Oh, I knew Suzannah wasn't a perfect mother. But who is? I had no idea things were that bad between them. Camilla talked to me about Suzannah as if she really hated her. Hated her but loved her too.'

'Why not let go, just for the moment? There's nothing you can do until tomorrow. Shut them all out. I'll do the same.' He walked over to his desk and closed the heavy law books lying open there. 'We never made time for ourselves in the past. We can do better this evening, can't we?'

Could they? Without the old habit-forming rows? She stretched her feet towards the fire, and kicked off her shoes. The turmoil in her mind eased a little. When she glanced at him, he too was watching the flames dancing in the grate. She noticed the upturned corners of his mouth, always a sign of contentment in him. His brow relaxed, already he looked far less strained than when he had opened the door to her.

She turned her hand, and the back of it rested against his. Automatically his hand opened and took hers, but there was silence between them. Only now it was a heavy silence. She could hear each breath he took, and was conscious of every movement she made herself. Why? Her body began to tingle. She drank deeply from the glass. This was no good. She'd lost Fred, made a disastrous mistake with Dan, and now this. She started to speak, but her voice was husky, so she cleared her throat and started again.

'Tom, I think I'd better go to bed. Tomorrow's going to be very tough. I've got to talk to the police. My mind's got to be clear.'

'Isn't it now?' He turned towards her, and their eyes locked. Then he looked towards the sofa-bed by his desk, already made up with fresh sheets. 'There's another bed upstairs, bigger, plenty of room for us both.' But there was a question in his eyes. He was aware how vulnerable she was, and much as he wanted her, he didn't want to take unfair advantage of her.

She shook her head. 'That's your bed. I couldn't go up there.' She cursed herself. She'd turned down the place, but not the invitation. He followed her thoughts, and smiled. It was the grin of a triumphant small boy, and it had always amused her. It was mischievous, but not evil. He pulled her onto her feet, and led her over to the narrow bed. He had got his own way, there would be no contest. He felt her tremble, and knew how much she wanted him too.

They knew each other very well; their bodies had missed each other. He put his hand on the back of her neck, under her hair, and pulled her towards him. Still their eyes were locked together, until she felt his lips on hers, and her eyelids closed as he kissed her.

It was like dancing to slow music. There was no hesitation, no embarrassment, even when she was naked. She knew he understood her body better than she did, and she found herself responding to him without conscious thought. They were so good together, she longed for each moment to stretch to an hour. Cocooned in pleasure, she was protected from the outside world.

Afterwards, as he held her, she stretched her legs against his, and she felt as if their skin had fused, they were so close to each other. She let her mind swing free, in a haze of remembered delight, like a kite flying high in the sunlight, dreading being hauled back down to earth again. His breath steadied, then deepened into sleep, but he still held her close.

She stayed awake longer, watching him, measuring each second. If only it would last. If only she could hold back the dawn. Finally she too slept.

She woke with a smile, saw the light from a streetlamp outside the window slanting through the edge of the curtains, remembered the night, and smiled again. Tom had turned away from her, and they nestled tightly together like spoons, her arms around his chest, as they had always lain when times were good between them. She watched the way his dark hair grew on the back of his head, felt the strength in his arms, and listened to the rhythm of his sleeping breath. They were in such deep harmony without words. Why did they have to scrap and squabble so often when they started talking? He turned in her arms, and without opening his eyes, began to stroke the length of her back. His hands instinctively knew their way. She felt her body wake and, once again, she lost herself happily in their passion.

Again he entranced her with his knowledge of her body. Had they always been so good together? How could she possibly have given this up? At the end, she brushed her lips over his cheek, feeling its roughness, and grateful for the extraordinary happiness they had created for each other. But was this happiness real? Or was it just a bubble of illusion? There was so much danger in her life outside this bed. She longed to be able to stay here, floating like a warm, safe boat on a cold sea. But though she tried to block them out, question after question began to crowd her mind again with layers of doubt and anxiety, and her body straightened with tension.

He felt her move, and murmured into her hair. 'You know I want to help, if there's any way I can.'

She nodded. 'I know. You have.' She stroked his hair back from his forehead. 'Was it always so good?'

'Perhaps not always,' he said. 'Perhaps we've missed each other.'

The fax machine beside the door rang, then clattered into life. The world was too much with them. Her gaze moved to the back of the door, where her coat hung on a hook. Through her sleepy contentment an idea slowly surfaced. There was another way he could help her.

Reluctantly she pulled herself out of his arms, and walked to the door, naked but unembarrassed. His eyes were dark with pleasure as he watched her. She pulled Max's Polaroid pictures out of the pocket, and brought them back to the bed.

Tom switched on the light on a bookshelf. 'What are these?' he asked her. He looked intently at them as she explained. His mouth turned down with revulsion as he realized exactly what the pictures showed.

Lucy pointed to the signet ring on the man's hand holding down the child.

'That's Parks' crest,' she said. 'He was wearing that ring on the show. You can just see it in this other picture. There, where he's holding the glass of beer. Do you think this is evidence that would stand up in court?'

Tom put the pictures down, sat up, and thought for a long

moment. 'It depends how unique that ring is,' he said. 'If the defence can prove that there are hundreds produced in Thailand, for instance, you're on a loser. But if it really is his crest, and you can prove it is, I think you've got him bang to rights. You'll have to give these pictures to the police. See what they can discover.'

'I can't possibly do that.' She was shocked at the thought.

He caught her alarm. 'Why not? You must, Lucy.'

All her professional journalistic instincts were outraged. This was her unique material, her exclusive story, and a big one. Besides, no journalist could reveal a source. Nobody would ever trust her with a story again if she gave Max away. Not only would it destroy her credibility, it would put him in grave peril. How could Tom suggest such a thing?

She kept her anger under control, and answered him levelly. 'I can't put Max in danger. He's my source – he gave the pictures to me. If I tell the police, and they question him, the paedophile ring will move heaven and earth to silence him.'

'You don't know that.' Tom's conflicting instincts were as strong as hers. She had in her hands evidence of a serious crime, far more important than any programme, or any scoop. The police must be allowed to follow it up. What's more, Lucy herself was in serious danger. Her life was under threat. She must be protected.

His voice rose as he tried to convince her. 'It's all very well, Lucy, to try and look after Max, but he's already at risk. They must have believed he was a threat to them. Why else did they burn down that house in Thritham? First they were determined to silence the boys, whatever it took. Now you. It's your safety I'm worried about.' Seeing her stubborn face, he took her hand again and his voice softened. 'I beg you, Lucy, let the police follow this up. You're not doing them justice.'

'What do you mean?'

'You're assuming the police are fools. They're not. They've dealt with paedophiles before. They know what dangerous ground this is.'

She shook away his hand, got out of bed, walked to the door, took her coat, and wrapped it around her naked body. 'Tom, this is way out of their league. Parks is a very big fish indeed, part of the Establishment. They'll never dare go after him. When did you last hear of a paedophile case involving anyone with any clout? Invariably those cases get hushed up. The guy gets sent abroad. There are mysterious suicides, or car accidents.' She was pacing furiously now. The precious moments they had just spent together had joined them body and soul. Now they were being torn apart. Though their bodies were used to lovemaking, their minds were just as accustomed to struggling and separating.

'Lucy, you're being melodramatic.' Tom's voice was loud with emphasis. 'This is Britain. Those things don't happen, except in fantasies.'

She was infuriated. This was no fantasy. Why didn't he understand? Her voice rose to match his. 'They do happen, Tom. Open your eyes. Unless we expose this man on television, nobody else will be able to touch him. The CPS won't let it go to trial. You've seen the boys, you've met them. They're vulnerable, they've been damaged. As witnesses under a tough cross-examination, they'd be destroyed. But if we can put this evidence on our programme, either Parks will sue us for libel, or he won't. If he does, we'll give him a run for his money. If he doesn't, that will be like a confession of guilt.'

He was appalled to hear the passionate edge to her voice. She was on a crusade, and crusaders took no prisoners.

'Lucy, you're in cloud-cuckoo-land. Do you really think your lawyers will let you put this on your show? That's crazy. This is no time for trial by television. Your own life is in danger. Your house has just been wiped out by a petrol bomb. You're bloody lucky to be alive at all. Leave it to the professionals. Give the pictures to the police.'

By now she was so angry she could barely look at him. All memory of the passion they had shared minutes before had been blasted out of her mind.

Tom got out of bed, wrapped a towel around his lean body, and walked quickly to the door. Then he stopped and said to her with cold finality, 'I'm not shouting at you for fun, Lucy. This is desperately important. It's not a choice you can make. Those pictures must go to the police, for everyone's sake.' He left the room.

Lucy dressed in a blaze of anger. How dare he dictate terms to her, like the pompous lawyer he was? Did he not give her any credit for understanding anything? It was not that she despised the police – far from it. An investigative journalist for years, she had often provided the police with evidence for criminal cases – not just with what her team had uncovered. After a programme was broadcast, viewers often were able to contribute even more facts, so the eventual case was even stronger.

She put the pictures in a side-pocket in her handbag, drank a glass of mineral water, and shouted up the stairs, 'I've got to go, Tom.'

When would she see him again? At the moment, she didn't want to. Not when he was in this high-and-mighty mood, like a headmaster ticking off a naughty pupil. Let him cool off for an evening. It would do them both good.

'I may be out late tonight,' she called to him. 'There's an awards do at the Towers in Park Lane.'

There was a jingle of keys on the carpet by her feet, as Tom shouted back, 'Let yourself in then. Good luck with the police. I'll see you later.' The words were supportive. The tone was flat. The gulf between them was as unbridgeable as ever. She climbed into her car with relief, once again answerable only to herself. What on earth gave him the right to patronize her?

Her voice-mail in the office was filled with messages. She spooled through them. The police wanted her to come to the local station at eleven. She rang and confirmed the time. There was a message from Camilla – she was organizing her mother's wake, inviting Suzannah's closest friends for drinks tomorrow evening.

271

It would be a difficult occasion. But Lucy left a message saying that of course she'd be there.

And there was one from Boris. As she recognized his voice, her heart sank. Not another spiky conversation, another squabble. But his voice was warm, and she relaxed as she listened.

'Lucy, let's be friends. I'm horrified at what's been going on. Are you OK? Can we meet? I hear they're going to do something about Suzannah tonight at the Awards. Would you come with me?'

Relief filled her. At least he was back on her side. She realized how much she was dreading the Awards. She'd been to the same event last year. The dinner was an indigestible mixture of show-business back-slapping and gossip columnists relishing every titbit of garbage they could nose out. This year would be even worse, Janet had left her with no illusions about that. The place would be full of Suzannah's enemies, motivated by envy or resentment. But perhaps among them would be one with a deeper, darker reason to hate Lucy too. A motive so strong it lit the bomb that destroyed everything she owned. Would he or she be laughing and applauding with the crowd, but simply waiting for another chance to hurt her?

She would much rather have spent the evening quietly with Boris in a cosy French restaurant near his flat, where she could confess her fears to him, and perhaps he would lift the heaviness in her heart by sharing good memories with her. But instead she would have to climb onto the crazy show business carousel, round and round in front of the cameras, like a battered old horse, painted hair blowing, painted eyes glazed, rising and falling alongside all the others.

It didn't make it easier that her previous series was being considered for one of the few journalism awards. That just meant she would have to prepare her face for the cameras, finding the right expression as the modest winner or, more likely, the gallant loser. If she had been allowed to sit with Shirley and her team, they would have supported her, and shared the moment of triumph or humiliation. But waiting on her desk was a letter from Controller Jameson's personal assistant. Lucy was invited to sit at his table, nearest to the stage. She was going to be on duty all night.

At least if Boris was on form the journey there and back would be entertaining. She rang him, and he answered at once. His voice was as warm as ever, he must have forgiven her.

'Hi, Lucy, how are you? I can't believe the time you've been having. Are you surviving all right?'

'I don't know, Boris. I'm just trying to make sense of things at the moment, and not get panicked.'

'Well, if there's any way I can help, give me a call. If you need somewhere to stay, or just an evening with an old friend, I'm here.'

'I'd love that. I'd much rather have dinner somewhere quietly with you tonight, but I've got to go to this thing. It would be such a help to go with you, Boris, if you don't mind. It would be great to have a friend to hide behind. I can't bear to think what the press will ask me.'

'You'll be fine. Just wear something with your gorgeous chest on show and they'll forget everything else.'

At the moment she felt like going there in nose-to-toe chain mail. But somehow she must muster the energy to find something glitzy, something to prove to the press and the viewers that she hadn't fallen to pieces under the ferocious pressure. As she sat talking to Boris, she felt her heart lifting, and a smile slide over her lips, Tom's imprint on her hormones, damn him. Maybe he'd be sitting at home tonight, missing her and regretting their quarrel. She finished her conversation with Boris, bought a large sugary doughnut, and devoured it in two minutes, just for the hell of it, then drove herself to the police station.

They showed her to a small office, and gave her the cup of tea she asked for. They introduced themselves: DI Johnson, and

Sergeant Ash. Johnson was elderly, with a flushed face and thinning hair. He was so obviously unimpressed at meeting a television presenter that Lucy found herself trusting him. It helped that he had an ordinariness, a fatherly style. In his dark suit he looked portly and ungainly, and there was a trace of cockney in his voice. He began by reassuring her.

'This is just a preliminary interview, Miss Strong. We've been in touch with the Thritham police, so we know the score there.' That was useful: at least she wouldn't have to go over all that old ground. But the next news was not so good.

'We should tell you,' he said slowly, 'that we're not at all convinced that there's any connection between the two fires, whatever the press may say. Obviously it makes a much better story for them if there is some mad arsonist following you around. But we don't agree. Nor does the Thritham team. We think this could be a copy-cat case, designed to make us think the same person was responsible for both.'

So there were two murderers abroad. While she was still thinking about that unpleasant idea, the detective continued his explanation.

'So we need to know in detail all the events of last Saturday, specially the hours leading up to the moment when the bomb went off. This will take a little time, I'm afraid. The best thing is just to take it quite slowly, and tell us everything you can remember about that day, whether it seems relevant or not.'

Lucy did as she was told. They interrupted her very occasionally, to clarify a detail, or ask her to paint a word picture of the people she met, even the members of her own production team. Lucy protested.

'They're a new team I haven't worked with before,' she said, 'and I can't think of any possible motive they might have to blow up my house.'

'That was a big petrol bomb,' Johnson said patiently, 'and it was pushed through your letter box at a time when anyone who knows your movements would expect you to be in bed. If you had been, you would certainly have been trapped by the flames, or suffocated by the smoke. Think for a moment. Who knew where you lived, and when you would arrive there? Nobody knows your life-style on a programme day better than your own colleagues.'

'But most of them have never even been to my home.'

'Miss Strong, they all know where it is. You're on the production database in case anyone wants to send research round to your home, or book a car for you. It's hardly a secret.'

That was true, difficult as it was for Lucy to accept. She went through the team one by one. Lesley, her designer, had greeted her first that day, and left when she did. Deirdre, the make-up artist, had worked with her for years. Alex, Marion, and the team of researchers. Michael, the director. Quentin, the floor manager. Why on earth would any of them have a motive to kill her? Dan, the series producer. She hesitated over his name. They saw, and waited. She'd better tell them the truth.

'It's complicated with Dan,' she said. 'I think he was a bit in love with Suzannah a long time ago. That's what he told me. Although he didn't choose me to take over from her, perhaps I have, in his mind, because he came round one night last week. Maybe he got a bit drunk because he . . .' Her voice died away and she avoided their eyes in embarrassment.

'He made a pass at you?' Johnson finished the sentence for her.

'Yes, sort of, slightly. Nothing much happened.'

'How was he when you saw him again after that?'

'Fine. He didn't refer to it, and nor did I.'

She watched the sergeant make a careful note. They moved on.

'The technicians, the cameramen? Can you tell me about any of them?' Johnson asked. There was a little more underlining in his voice than was necessary. The sergeant looked at her curiously. Clearly they both read the tabloids. She named the crew, and then said, wearily, 'Fred Miller wasn't in the studio. He's away on location. Fred used to live with me. He doesn't any more. He moved out when the press stories started, over a week ago.'

'On what terms did you part, Miss Strong? I'm sorry to have to ask.'

'We parted on good terms. We've spoken to each other since. He's very upset for me. I think he'd like us to get together again.'

They needed convincing. They asked the predictable questions – how long Fred and she had been together, when they expected to see each other again, whether there was anyone else in Fred's life who could have wanted her out of the way, because 'there's nothing more ferocious than a jealous woman'.

'Except a jealous man,' Lucy reminded them. She thought through what she knew of Fred's life. There were always a great many women, probably more than she knew, but none of them could afford to be jealous. Fred never promised exclusivity to any of them. 'You ought to ask him about his private life, not me,' she told them. If there was a compliant girlfriend on location he could use as an alibi for Saturday night, she didn't really want to know. The smile flickered over her lips again. She was in no position to criticize him.

They went methodically on through Saturday. The guests on the show; the two teachers, Harold Whittaker and Jake Carlton; their pupils; the two stars, Genevieve and Tim; Lord Parks.

Lucy stopped there. The policemen waited. She looked at them both, Tom's voice echoing in her head. Should she meekly obey him? Hadn't she got a mind of her own? She picked up her bag. This wasn't play-acting cops and robbers. The threat on her life was real, it had almost worked. She had to be grown up now. The two watched her, still without speaking. She opened her bag.

'This is difficult,' she said. 'As a journalist I must protect my sources, you understand that. But I've been given some evidence I think I should show you. I've been given some photographs.'

There, Tom would be pleased with her. But only half pleased. She was not going to give Max away.

'One of the boys at the party gave me the pictures,' she said hesitantly. 'It was very dark and crowded, and with all that went on I'm not sure I'd know him again. I don't even know if he survived the fire. He said there was a paedophile ring involving some very powerful men who passed round the boys from Wantage Grange between themselves. He claimed that one of them was Lord Parks.'

The policemen exchanged glances, but still said nothing. Lucy took the photographs out and passed them over. 'These are the pictures.' That's what you wanted, Tom. On your head be it. 'As you see, one is of Lord Parks. Of course it could have been taken at a different time from the others. Except if you look closely at the signet ring he's wearing, and the ring on that man's hand, you'll see they are identical. I think that's his crest engraved on it.'

She showed them the photograph with the child. Johnson flinched, and shook his head. He flushed more deeply, and looked at Lucy, ashamed of his own emotional reaction. 'You never get used to it, you know, no matter how often you see it.' With obvious effort, he looked closely at the picture.

'Parks was wearing that signet ring on the show,' Lucy said. 'We have the video. You can take a relevant frame from it.' This time they made copious notes. They wanted to know everything she could remember about Parks' behaviour on the night, especially the time he left the studio.

'Did you mention these pictures to him? Could Parks possibly have realized the damage you could do to him?' Sergeant Ash asked her. 'I watched the show myself, and I don't recall anything.'

'Just one tiny remark,' Lucy remembered. 'I'd been talking to Genevieve, and I made a joke to Parks. I said that I hoped he didn't have any pictures that would come back to haunt him.' As she repeated the words, she realized the police might be appalled by her impetuous indiscretion. 'It was stupid,' she admitted. 'Not that it's any excuse, but I was angry. He sat there

277

in the studio laying down the law about the sins of young people today, and all the time I knew the vile things he did to children. I just couldn't take his hypocrisy any more.'

'I can understand that,' Johnson said, and there was sympathy in his face now. 'When you find out what's going on in the homes of some of the solid citizens who shout the loudest about how the police should do more, and what's the country coming to, it's enough to make your hair fall out. If you had any.' He ran his hand over his scalp, and smiled at her. She recognized the tiredness in his eyes. The man was weary with the secrets he'd had to carry over the years.

'Don't take it too hard, Miss Strong,' he told her. 'Thanks for showing us the pictures. I realize it must have been difficult. It could have been a temptation for you to keep all this to yourself, for your programme. But I'm sure it's better if we know about it. These men have everything to lose. That means they could be very dangerous. When there's this much at stake, I think they might well be prepared to put a bomb through your door. Can you tell me anything more?'

'Paul Wilson was another name I was given, the computer millionaire.' She heard Johnson's sharp intake of breath. 'We could never identify him, though. We have no other evidence against him. And he's made such a huge fortune that he could afford to put his lawyers on to us instantly if we even hinted he was involved in anything like this. I've never met Wilson, or interviewed him, so I have no idea whether he'd be capable of trying to kill me. All I can tell you is that he was mentioned by the boys at Thritham.'

She told them as much as she knew about the other men, although the descriptions were extremely vague. But she fudged and hedged when they asked her which boys had talked to her.

After three hours Johnson gestured to Ash to shut his notebook. 'Let's leave it there,' he suggested. 'We'll have another talk in a couple of days, when we've had a chance to check a few facts, and you've had a rest.' She was near breaking point.

278

He could see it was time to stop. He looked at her kindly. 'Miss Strong, you've had a couple of very nasty near-misses. You look as if you're coping perfectly well, but sometimes these things lie in wait for us. Don't be surprised if you have flashbacks. I've experienced that myself, I know what can happen. Go easy on yourself.' The stocky, middle-aged man with the patient voice, the careful control, but the high flush of a heavy drinker, must have had traumas in his own past. Lucy didn't envy him his job.

She thanked them both, stood, and looked at her watch. Two o'clock, no lunch, and a hard night ahead. She still had a dress to find for this evening. There was no time now for a quick counselling session, even if she'd been in the mood. Perhaps retail therapy would do the trick, distract and refresh her.

What was the choice? She could struggle her way through the traffic to Harvey Nicks or Fenwicks, trying to find something in the racks of clothes stretching from wall to wall. Or she could try Brigid.

Brigid Walbury had a studio in Chelsea. She had tight blonde curls, wide blue eyes and she came originally from Dublin. She had cleverly and carefully retained her Irish accent throughout her apprenticeship in the workroom of Emile Estragon. He was a Viennese designer, little and excitable, who specialized in heavily beaded dresses designed to out-glitz every other diner in the Queen's Grill of the *QEII*.

As Emile grew older and more autocratic, his crow-black hair developed bright white wings, and Brigid was promoted to become a *vendeuse* in his showroom. There she would whisper hints and compliments in the customers' ears: 'Try the pale blue, it's the perfect colour for your eyes' or 'Why not get the dress in black – much more dramatic, but you can carry it off.' She had learned how to cut and sew the most fragile fabric, she had the eye to temper Emile's flamboyance with her own good taste, and gradually the richest customers began to ask for her by name.

When finally Emile retired, he told his backers to appoint Brigid as his successor. To his fury, she only agreed if she could start to design under her own name. He raged and fumed, 'The Estragon name is the finest brand in the business.' But his anger was ineffectual. Behind Brigid's soothing lilt there was a razor-sharp business sense, and the investors trusted her. So did her customers. She used fewer sequins but achieved just as much glamour as Emile. With a well-placed strip of whalebone or a well-hidden bustier she could whittle a waist and lift a bust more effectively than the most sought-after plastic surgeon.

Workman came and removed the shiny brass plaque, 'Estragon', by the front door and replaced it with a more dis-creet 'Brigid Walbury'. The plush red carpet was torn up, and replaced by grey with a specially woven hyacinth motif, Brigid's chosen symbol. She recruited Irish saleswomen, and coached them in her techniques. No dress ever left the showroom with a label larger than size ten, no matter what its real dimensions. No customer was ever sold a yellow dress, 'Yellow makes pale women look sallow,' she declared, 'and dark women look dingy.' No shoe was ever sold for less than two hundred pounds – 'Shoes that cost a lot are treated with respect,' not scuffed or driven in.

With the savings from her first contract as a reporter, Lucy had bought one dress from Brigid. She wore it year after year until it fell to pieces. But the dress she needed now would be filmed and photographed once at the Awards night, everyone would comment upon it, and the next day it would be dead, like a moth that flies for one night only, and the next morning drops to the ground in a heap of dusty wings. Maybe Brigid would be feeling generous enough to lend her a dress? It might be worth the publicity to her.

Lucy rang to say she was on her way, and Brigid sounded amused by the challenge. Usually she took six weeks to make a dress, now she had six hours. 'Lucy, we'll find you something dazzling. Come over straight away.'

When Lucy arrived in the Chelsea showroom, Brigid took a quick look at her and ordered a cup of aromatic tea, 'to revive the spirit'. Lucy would have preferred a less aromatic chocolate bar, but when she mentioned the thought, Brigid frowned and wagged a finger at her. 'Not if you're going to wear one of my dresses tonight. We need you glamorous, not bloated and exhausted. You sit on my sofa and relax. We'll show you the collection and find the perfect one for you.'

As the girls in the showroom lifted light shimmering dresses from the rails, delicate as petals, Lucy's heart dropped. It was impossible. Even if she hadn't been so vulnerable, dresses like these made her feel like a sad old carthorse. They were designed for seventeen-year-olds with no anatomy. But she was made of flesh and blood, plenty of it, with curves that needed disciplining. The girls saw her despondent face and brought out velvet, heavy and opulent, but Lucy knew that would make her feel uncomfortable under bright television lights, and look matronly.

She gathered her bag and her coat, drained her tea and got up to go. 'It's no good, Brigid, I'm just not a dazzling shape.'

Brigid pushed her gently back into her chair. 'Don't despair, Lucy. I have the dress for you in my studio. Wait here a moment.'

She came back a few moments later with a beige linen sack over her arm. She pulled it open and revealed, like a pearl in an oyster, the dress that dreams are made of. It was sequined all over, the palest lilac and blue and pink combining to make a soft mother-of-pearl colour, like a waterfall. It seemed as delicate as gossamer, but Lucy could see that beneath the shimmering surface there was a strong corset to hold the shape.

Her face fell further. She felt completely disheartened. 'I could never wear a dress like that,' she said. 'I'm not brave enough. Lovely as it is, it would frighten me to death. In that corset, for a whole Awards night, sitting in all that heat, I'd faint.'

'Try it on,' Brigid urged her. 'You'll be surprised.'

When she got up obediently from the chair, Lucy realized how exhausted she was. She needed to sleep. Her face in the mirror looked blotchy and depressed, her hair unkempt, her clothes crumpled. Brigid followed her eyes.

'Lucy,' she said, 'you'll be fine. All you need is an hour of pampering in the hairdresser's, and you'll twinkle like the star you are.'

Without much hope, Lucy pulled the dress around her, and a miracle happened. The soft colour dramatized her dark hair, the strapless bodice flattered her skin, the corset sucked in her waist, and pulled her upright, and yet it was as light as a feather. The mother-of-pearl followed the outline of her body, with its soft sheen. Her chest was certainly on show, as Boris had suggested it should be. That at least might distract the reporters from too many questions. Brigid pulled from a drawer two tiny sandals, their heels totteringly high, held to her feet by straps embroidered with pearls.

'There you go, my girl,' Brigid told her. 'You shall go to the ball. I'll lend it to you with pleasure. But remember, you must be home by midnight.'

'Otherwise I'll turn back into a pumpkin.' Lucy grimaced. 'No problem, Brigid. The way I feel now, I'll fall asleep on the way to the ball.'

But Brigid was right, as usual. An hour of being pampered, the nails on her fingers and toes laquered to tone with the dress, ten minutes to fall asleep as they dried her hair, and she felt refreshed again. She changed in the hairdresser's comfortable beauty salon, where they promised to look after her day clothes for her until the next day. It was difficult to see herself full length in their mirrors, but the dress seemed shorter than Lucy remembered it, and she tugged at the hem. Her shoulders were bare; Brigid had recommended her not to wear any opulent jewellery, just to dust her skin with silver, and she had lent her some pearl drops for her ears. Lucy felt as if she was putting on fancy dress. Who on earth had she come as?

She had agreed to meet Boris in the palm court of the

Landmark Hotel. Businessmen were snoozing in wide cushioned sofas, waiting for their next deal to arrive. They woke to watch her as she passed, following her with their eyes as her little high heels clicked away from them on the marble. Boris arrived a minute later, immaculate in his black tie and expensively cut dinner suit. He whistled appreciatively as he saw her.

'That won't keep the draughts out,' he said. 'Do you want me to wrap you in my car rug to keep you warm?'

She shook her head. 'Boris, in my present state I don't care if I catch pneumonia. Nothing worse can happen.'

'In that case a strong drink is prescribed,' he said. He ordered a gin and tonic. It arrived fresh with ice and she gulped it greedily. He watched her with a frown. 'You're pushing yourself too hard,' he told her. 'Take it easy tonight. I've seen all this before. Suzannah and you were always sisters under the skin. She pushed herself to death, none of us could stop her. Don't go the same way, Lucy. Nothing's worth it.'

She saw tears in his eyes, and took his hand. 'Suzannah would have done this so much better than me,' she said. 'She could carry anything off. I just feel like a poodle dressed up for Crufts.'

'Some poodle.' He smiled at her. 'This is going to be tough for both of us, so let's just try and enjoy ourselves. She'd be giggling now at the prospect of all her enemies having to bite back their insults. Have you any idea what they plan to do tonight in her memory?'

She shook her head. 'Don't get your hopes up too high. This isn't like the British Academy or the Royal Television Society. These are at the trashy end of the market. Wet T-shirt television awards.'

'Good. In that case that dress should be a wow.' She glanced in the mirrors as they walked to the door. Was the dress a terrible mistake? Too late now to worry.

When the car pulled up outside the Towers Hotel in Park Lane, she saw crowds massed against the restraining railings. There was a pyramid of photographers, their lenses like the multifacets of a fly's eye, all turning in the same direction. As she climbed out of the car, Boris whispered in her ear, 'Knees.' Quickly she clamped them together, frustrating a pair of photographers who had sprawled across the pavement, hoping for a glimpse of thigh. She swung her legs out of the car, and levered herself up on the tiny shiny spikes that went for shoes. The crowd applauded and shouted her name. The cameras flashed like fireworks.

She slipped her arm through Boris's for protection, but the attention was so intense, he whispered to her, 'Take centre stage, darling,' and stood away from her, as the photographers shouted to her to twirl and pose for them. It seemed to last a lifetime. Then Boris was beside her again, his arm protectively around her as they negotiated the revolving door.

'What did that look like?' Lucy asked him nervously.

'I tell you what,' Boris said. 'It should double your salary. I've never seen you looking so sexy.' Was that the effect of fear, or adrenalin, or was she still lit by a glow from last night? Probably it was just Brigid's wizardry.

At the reception she clung tightly to Boris. They made their way together to the end of the bar, to find Shirley and her old team. If only she had them around her all evening. They were enjoying the occasion, exclaimed about her dress, and chattered excitedly about their chances of winning.

Shirley pulled her closer, and whispered, 'Guess who's presenting the award for journalism?' Lucy shook her head. 'Lord Parks. Isn't that a thrill?'

Startled, Lucy looked around her. He must be somewhere in the crowd. Then she saw him at the other end of the bar, a glass of champagne in his hand, holding forth to a group of advertisers. He caught her eye, and lifted his glass to her. She responded, smiling tautly, longing to be somewhere, anywhere else.

Boris took her to her table, and then they had to part, Boris to sit with some of his business partners, Lucy to find her place between Jameson, and Martin Dellaby. What fun. It was time

284

to play the party game – smile, air-kiss, flatter; smile, air-kiss, flatter – until the toast master rapped with his gavel and they all had to sit down. Martin joined them, walking slowly around the table, looking dourly at the place cards. He didn't brighten to see her. She smiled at him, and offered him both cheeks for the obligatory kiss.

'Hello, Martin,' she said. 'Are you up for an award?'

'No,' he said, with an edge to his voice. 'I'm here to pay tribute to Suzannah.' She clung on to her smile with considerable effort. How typical. The man who had most resented Suzannah's success had been chosen to celebrate her. She hoped he would behave himself.

He read her mind. '*De mortuis . . .*' he said, and he smiled his easy, beguiling smile. Indeed. Did he expect her to believe he would have nothing but good to say about Suzannah? She trusted him as far as she could throw his chunky body across the table. It would be difficult for him, though, to bad-mouth Suzannah in front of the viewers, who missed her deeply, and would dislike him for it. And he was, above all, a great survivor.

'Ah, if only, Lucy,' he said, reading her mind, and unable to resist a morsel of malicious gossip, even though he knew what close friends they had been. He leaned closer. 'I could certainly tell a tale or two about her which would brighten the long, dull evening ahead. So could you, no doubt. Did she ever tell you about the time she bonked a guest in her dressing room with her radio mike still on? The boys were flogging the tapes for a fiver for years.'

That was the oldest scrap of gossip in the industry. Of course it hadn't been Suzannah, it had far predated her. A muscular DIY expert, in the days when programmes were made in sets like houses, and all the guests arrived pressing the doorbell of a fake front door, had been overcome with passion for the fashion expert. His radio mike had transmitted to the control room as he hammered his point energetically home, accompanied by her breathy squeaks of joy. It made a far better story to recast it with Suzannah. Did she have the energy to contradict Martin? And would it prevent him telling the story his way in the future? No, and no. She picked up the menu.

'What are we in for?' she asked. Food was definitely his subject. His round, soft cheeks were his unique selling point to women viewers who liked to mother him in their dreams. 'Will it be salmon? Or chicken?' Both, one after the other, it seemed. He pointed to the salmon already lying sadly on the plate in front of her, dyed bright pink, tasteless and slightly slimy. Some poor farmed fish, which had never known the joy of a river or a waterfall. Beside it was a brick of diced vegetables, glued together with some gelatinous material. Lucy found herself longing for a lightly boiled egg and soldiers. No chance.

Around her the guests were finding their tables, calling excitedly to each other, embarking already on the chatter that made the evening worthwhile for them. Jameson arrived next to her, and kissed her on both cheeks. He gazed appreciatively at her chest. 'You look terrific, Lucy,' he said. 'And the ratings do too. How you'll keep it all up I do not know.' Did he mean the dress, or the audience figures? An elderly television reporter who had just been sacked inched past their table and greeted Jameson, whose face hardly moved in response. When you were in, you were in. When you were out, you were invisible.

A bony young woman in high anxiety and a cheap black evening dress pushed her way through the crowd to Lucy's side. 'Miss Strong, would you present the Top Soap Award for us?'

She could hardly refuse. 'Yes, of course. Let me know when you want me.'

'It's just before your category, the Journalism Award. So you open the envelope, read out the winner, and then go back to your table again.'

'Fine.'

The evening passed as slowly as she had feared. Jameson kept his nose buried in the glossy brochure from the moment the awards began, marking it like a scorecard, one to them, one to us. BriTV did well, unexpectedly winning a panel game award with a recycled Spanish game in which pets competed in a beauty contest alongside their owners. About halfway through, the young woman in black came to fetch Lucy. She was led backstage, where Quentin, the floor manager from her own show, greeted her affectionately, and handed her the golden envelope, and the award she had to present. It was alarmingly heavy, and she struggled to hold it in one hand.

'I know,' said Quentin, watching her juggle. 'They must be made of solid lead. They'd make wonderful doorstops.' That seemed unlikely. The dull-grey trophy bristled with metal spines like a porcupine, each spike intended to represent either the radiance of the winner or the programme beaming out into the ether. Whatever the symbolism, it would certainly impale an ankle if you tried to wedge a door open with it.

On Quentin's cue, she walked up the rickety steps at the back of the set, a fanfare blared, and she heard her introduction. '. . . presented by the lovely Lucy Strong.' A patter of applause. She walked forward, holding the award in front of her with both hands, for safety. But as she moved, she felt her dress begin to slide downwards. She clenched her arms tightly to her body, to stop it slipping further. In the brilliant light, with the cameras trained on her, the lectern looked a hundred miles away. She could hear a murmur of laughter, as the crowd recognized her dilemma. She couldn't put the award down, and tug her bodice upwards. Still the dress slipped, millimetre by millimetre. All she could do was pray, as fervently as she could, 'Dear Lord, please keep me decent.'

He did, just. As she arrived and put the award on the desk, she looked down and saw the outline of her breasts almost entirely exposed, but not – Thank you, dear God – her nipples. Camera bulbs were popping from every corner of the room. Her hands free at last, she pulled the dress back into position, and the crowd groaned in mock disappointment.

'The danger of being overexposed,' she said, and they laughed, more in sympathy than amusement. 'This is the award for the Best Soap,' she continued briskly. The lights faded. The clips played on the giant screen behind her. The lights came up again. 'And the winner is,' she wrestled with the envelope, '*Downshire Hill.*'

A cheer, a blast of music, twenty-five people pushed their way between the tables, and clattered up the stairs, some pushing to the front by the microphone, others standing sheepishly in a line behind them. Lucy passed the award to the leading actor, a tiny man who was so inflated with joy that she expected him to bob up to the ceiling like a helium balloon. Then she retreated to the far corner of the stage.

She was overwhelmed with embarrassment. Why did television oscillate so wildly between farce and tragedy? Any humiliation was so very public, every mistake so hugely exaggerated. She longed to get off the stage and back into decent privacy. The little actor, revelling in his moment, offered his heartfelt thanks, 'to the cast' (who unanimously disliked him), 'to the producer' (who had tried to fire him; no mention, of course, of the writers, who had created him), and finally to 'you the viewers. Without you, we would be nobody.' At last the cast dragged him off the stage for their victorious photographs, the lights dimmed for a commercial break, and Lucy was back in the tiny anteroom, face to face with Lord Parks.

'That was memorable,' he said. 'How did you arrange that? The incredible shrinking dress, ideal to grab all the front pages.'

Heavens, he thought she'd stage-managed it. What did he think she was? A tart? A desperate porn star, on the beach at Cannes? Anger swept over her. 'I've had a long day, Lord Parks,' she said, tight-lipped. 'With the police, as it happens. I've had more to think about than what to wear tonight.'

'Ah, yes.' There was still a sarcastic note in his voice. As he shifted the award he was about to present from hand to hand, she saw the gleam of gold on his finger.

288

'Tell me about that ring, Lord Parks,' she said. 'Is it your family crest?'

'Yes, it is now. I had it engraved when Garter gave me my coat of arms.' He looked at it smugly. 'I always think the cherub has a family resemblance.'

The bastard. How could he be so confident, so complacent? To put a smiling child on his coat of arms.

'It comes out very clearly in photographs.' Her words were out before she could stop them. 'The police thought so, at any rate.'

What had she said? He stared at her, instantly taking in the words she blurted out, then Quentin, the floor manager, came running off the stage and down the steps towards them. 'Lucy, can you get back to your table? Lord Parks, you're on in ten seconds.'

She ran quickly across the darkened stage, and back to her table.

Martin Dellaby grinned at her spitefully as she sat down. 'You got a lot off your chest,' he hissed, eyes flicking down to her now-discreet bodice.

He was right. She had exposed herself rashly and foolishly, though not in the way he meant. Why had she said so much to Parks? He had flicked her on the raw, but she should still have controlled herself. When she mentioned the police and asked him about the ring, he knew exactly what she meant. No doubt he had his own collection of photographs to mull over. She had put herself in still greater danger now.

Sensing her distress, but misunderstanding its cause, Jameson whispered to her, 'Don't worry, love. You looked fantastic. Every man in the room lusted after you, every woman envied you.'

But that was wrong, all wrong, for the job she wanted to do. She wanted to curl up in a corner and hide, but there was Parks, in the limelight he loved, smiling like the insensitive bull he was, striding across the stage with a gold envelope and an award in his hand. He looked down at his amply filled shirt, then pretended

289

to jump with horror. 'Whoops,' he said, and buttoned up his jacket. The crowd laughed, and Lucy tried to laugh with them.

To her relief, the lights darkened while they showed the clips from the nominated shows, her own among them, then brightened as Parks announced the winner. The cameras were on Lucy smiling numbly as the gallant loser, while a programme about brain surgeons from hell took the prize, and the show moved on.

It was interminable. After midnight the final tribute to Suzannah was announced, and Martin Dellaby walked solemnly to the podium wearing his sincerest furrowed brow. 'Suzannah Piper was one of my closest friends, and my most respected colleagues,' he began. 'I feel privileged to be standing here, presenting a tribute from us all, programme-makers and viewers alike. She would want to be judged by her work, and we have a selection of some of her most effective pieces of broadcasting to remind us of her strength, and versatility. But I would just like to make the point that this was Suzannah the woman as well: warm, loyal, inspiring. For the rest, judge for yourself.'

The lights went down, the film flickered on the huge screen, and there was Suzannah, heart-breakingly alive, laughing with a star comedian, egging him on to wonderful crazy heights of comedy. Then the picture changed to an empty landscape, Suzannah on her knees beside a row of coffins, struggling with tears as she reported a famine in Africa. She had the gift of holding and dominating the camera, her vitality lit the screen, but in the darkness of the hushed ballroom Lucy was overcome by loneliness.

Now she felt more sharply than ever before the sharp pain of loss, the realization that every memory of Suzannah must be prized and cherished, because there would be no more moments together. She banished from her mind all the sniping criticisms. This was her friend in action – the friend she missed so desperately. She could barely watch the screen as Suzannah's voice filled the room, strong, confident, happy. The film ended with

Suzannah closing her last show. She said goodbye straight to the camera, and then smiled, her eyes dancing, as if she knew a secret that filled her with pleasure. The final image froze for a moment. Then the credits rolled, the fanfare blared, and the lights in the ballroom went up.

For an instant no one moved. Suzannah had broken through the artifice and reminded them of the real world, where one brutal accident could smash a woman into fragments, no matter how great her fame, her beauty, her love of life. Then the audience stirred again. They began to talk quietly together, their mood sober now.

Lucy stood, and Jameson put his arm round her, and nodded towards the screen. 'At least we have that,' he said. 'Suzannah's work will live on, in archives around the world. She will be remembered, unlike most of us.' Unable to reply, Lucy picked up her brochure, and smoothed her dress. She longed to escape.

Shirley came towards her through the tables, her face a picture of concern. 'You look worn out, Lucy.' And suddenly Boris was beside her, his arm encircling her like a warm wrap. She snuggled into him.

'Come on, princess,' he said. 'You've had an eventful night. Time to go home. Are you staying at the Landmark?'

'Yes.' Still the lies, just in case. 'But don't worry about me, just put me in a taxi, I'll be fine.'

He glanced at her, but clearly wanted to believe her, there was still business to be done, deals to be brokered at the bar. He put her into a taxi. There were no photographers now. Like bats at dawn they had long flown home.

The suburban streets were empty, she shivered in the freezing night air, fumbled her key into Tom's door-lock, and gratefully flung herself down on the sofa-bed. There was no note from him on the pillow. She roused herself to hang the borrowed dress on a hanger, wiped her make-up off with hard strokes, as if she could wipe away the memory of the day, and fell into a deep sleep.

Once again there were flames in her dreams, and the figures of men silhouetted against them, but she couldn't see their faces. All she recognized was the threat, and the target. Their violence, their hatred, were aimed straight at her.

CHAPTER THIRTEEN

Lucy woke in the darkness, adrenalin charging through her body. Something in her mind hurt like hell. What was it? Like a shaft of blinding light the memory hit her. Last night had been grotesque, absurd. The humiliation of her treacherous dress. The stupidity of her conversation with Parks. She groaned and buried her head in the pillow. How could she have given herself away like that, putting herself in such danger, imperilling Max and the other boys? There was no question in her mind, Parks had instantly understood her reference to the photographs. Now he knew for sure that she had seen them, and had shown them to the police, what else would he do to silence her? He was part of the Establishment, and had so many powerful friends. It had been idiotic to take him on impetuously and recklessly. She couldn't bear to think what she had done.

There was no excuse. The police had been blunt with her about the danger she was in. Someone close to her wanted to hurt her, frighten her, kill her. But was it Parks himself? Her heart wanted to believe it must be – either him or one of his friends. She could handle that idea, intellectualize it. They were not part of her life. She could hold them at arm's length. Frightening as the Thritham fire had been, she had only been a guest, a visitor to that drama. The boys were the real target.

But her head reminded her that the bomb in her home had been aimed squarely at her. It was far, far closer, and more destructive. She couldn't shrug it away. It was right there, in the very centre of her life. It was premeditated, mulled over in someone's sick mind. Whoever had written those hideous letters to her, and to Suzannah, had not been bluffing. They had made good their threats. More and more, as her mind circled around Suzannah's death, she knew that it couldn't have been a simple accident. Someone in their lives, their shared lives, had been nurturing a bitterness that was lethal to them both. Maybe someone who'd been there last night, applauding the tribute to Suzannah. She went through the faces in that audience. Who could it possibly be? And why?

Lying in the narrow bed with her arms across her body, bent like a kidney bean, her legs drawn up to her chest, glimpses of the night before jostled each other agonizingly in her mind. She unwound one hand to find the television control on the table by her bed, and clicked it on. The picture shivered into shape, the BBC's breakfast news programme was on, and they were featuring the morning papers.

'And yet another picture of Lucy Strong's chest,' John Worcester, an overtanned young presenter recently promoted from the radio, was saying with smug sarcasm. 'She really put the show into show business last night,' he went on, and Yvonne, the woman presenter next to him, giggled meanly, hugging her bright coral jacket round herself with pleasure.

Lucy's embarrassment acted like a tonic to them both. One by one they put the tabloid front pages in front of the prurient studio cameras. Each newspaper had its own version of Lucy's nightmare moment, when her breasts were lavishly displayed. The headlines were predictable. 'What a Pair of Boobs, Lucy', 'Lucy Goes Bust', 'Loosee Lucy', and on, and on. The two presenters were enjoying themselves.

'Wasn't she once a serious reporter?' Yvonne asked, and although John reproved her with a joking 'miaow', Lucy knew that's what they must have been saying in the newsroom. Editors loathed reporters who became more newsworthy than the stories they were reporting. There was no doubt there would be plenty of criticism when the bosses met to discuss the awards night. She had made herself no friends.

'Blast, bugger and hell.' She switched off the television, and hid her face under the duvet. This was where she would spend the day, in this darkened room, with the curtains drawn. She couldn't face them all in the office. Either they would avoid the subject, as if by ignoring it they could make it go away, or someone brave would make a joke, and she would have to laugh along. She groaned again, and went back into the foetal position. Let them giggle as much as they liked without her, she would stay in bed, for a week if necessary.

And then there was the memory of Suzannah. Over and over again that last image kept flicking into her mind. Suzannah had looked so happy on her final programme – that smile with a secret locked into it. If only she would come back, just for a moment, so that Lucy could ask her what had given her that intriguing glow. It was certainly not an exhausted face, not the face of someone who was about to drive out into the rain, and kill herself at the wheel. She looked as if she was at the top of her form, ready for anything.

The study light went on, and Lucy flung one hand over her eyes and turned away from it, huddled beneath the duvet. Tom stood at the door, already dressed, looking down at her.

'Sorry, Lucy. Time to get up,' he said. 'Time to face the day.'

'I can't, Tom.' Her voice pleaded for mercy. 'Last night was horrible. The papers are full of ghastly pictures. I'm staying here.'

'No, you're not,' he said, and now there was a tough edge to his voice. 'You've faced worse than this. Far worse. Many times. This is just froth, a bit of fun to please the bored readers. It's got nothing to do with real life, or with your real work. Come on, out of bed.'

'But you haven't seen them . . .'

'I certainly have. They're piled up on the kitchen table, if you want to have a look.'

How could he take it so lightly? Her career was ruined. Her reputation as a journalist was lost. He didn't seem to care.

'If you paid for that dress by the yard, you were robbed,' he said. 'But you're in the entertainment industry now, and it's certainly an entertaining dress, no doubt of that.' He smiled down at her.

She heard the amusement in his voice, and slowly crept out to see the expression on his face. His eyes were gleaming with fun. At her expense, but maybe he was right. She managed to smile back at him.

'That's better,' he said. 'Look, the world hasn't come to an end. Go and have a shower, sort yourself out, and I'll put the coffee on. Then you can tell me all about it.'

Meekly, she followed his advice. Not because she wanted to, but because he gave her no choice. She couldn't stay hidden in that snug bed, like a cornered vixen retreating into her earth, much as she wanted to. The hounds would soon find her and drag her out. A hot shower refreshed her, so did her practical new clothes – a white silk shirt, black wool trousers and a black leather jacket were like a uniform, reassuring in their anonymity. She brushed shadow onto her eyelids, and bright colour on her lips. At least she would look more confident than she felt. Then she joined Tom in his minimalist, masculine kitchen.

She guessed that the microwave and the coffee pot were the most used items there. But as she arrived, he pulled a warm baguette out of the oven, and put it alongside a pat of unsalted French butter. He took a jar of cherry jam out of the fridge, and pushed it towards her. She tried to resist, but the fragrance of the new loaf was irresistible. She took a deep gulp from the mug of strong coffee, and watched the butter melt into a chunk of French bread. As she crammed it into her mouth, like a hungry child, she didn't see the warmth in his eyes. His emotion responded to her need, as it always had. But his mind clamped down. He knew that she needed his will to impel her on through the day. When she did look at him, his face was stern again.

'You've got to carry on, and cope with whatever today throws at you, Lucy. There's too much at stake, too much that really matters, not this junk.' And he gestured to the pile of papers on the breakfast bar.

She sneaked a look at the top one. God. There she was, caught by the flashbulbs, her eyes starting out of her head with the effort of clenching her arms by her side, the little shiny dress hardly covering her nipples. She closed her eyes with embarrassment. Tom turned the paper over, and cut another chunk of bread for her, piling it with succulent black cherries in thick syrup. 'What else happened yesterday? Tell me,' he asked.

Lucy thought back over the day. 'Well, you'll be pleased with me because I gave the pictures to the police. And Parks was actually at the Awards do. I asked him if the signet ring is unique, and he said it is. In fact he designed it himself, cherub and all. So with those photos the police should have him bang to rights. Which is one good thing.'

He could tell from her tone that was not the whole story. 'And . . . ?' he prompted her.

'And I more or less told Parks that I had been to the police, and shown them the pictures.'

'Oh.' He digested that slowly, turning it over in his mind. Why on earth hadn't she kept those facts to herself, and allowed the police to put their own case together and confront him in their own time? How fatal was it that Parks knew now? He thought it through. Not desperate, perhaps. After all, he couldn't try to get hold of the pictures and destroy them, now that the police had them. Silently Tom thanked God that she no longer had them in her coat pocket. That would have made her even more dangerously vulnerable.

'It's the boys I worry about,' Lucy said, following her own train of thought. 'They're the witnesses he'll have to silence. If they do give evidence, those pictures would be the strongest corroboration for their story.'

'In theory,' Tom said. 'But in reality everything would depend on the judge. He might not allow them in as evidence. Judges sometimes rule out corroboration because they say it's prejudicial. A judge might take that view about these pictures, if you were unlucky. Unless you were able to trace the actual child in the photographs and persuade him to give evidence.'

That would be an impossibly long shot. That child could be

anywhere in the world. She flicked urgently in her mind through all the faces at the Thritham party, but it was no good, she couldn't conjure up any of them clearly enough to match the pictures. Besides, the boy in the pictures looked far younger than they were.

'Did you tell the police about Max? That he gave you the pictures?' Tom asked her.

She shook her head. 'No, not yet. I have to protect him. He's my source. I couldn't possibly give Max away to the police without his permission.'

Tom looked at her, eyebrows raised questioningly, then changed the subject. He picked his dark blue jacket off the kitchen table and slung it over his arm. 'You'd better get into the office now. Show your face. Give your team the support they need.'

'I can't.' She looked pleadingly up at him. Was he really going to force her to go?

'You can, and you must. Come on, Lucy. Think of Suzannah. She's up there, urging you on. She'd have no sympathy if you let a daft event like last night put you off.'

Which Suzannah? The friend she loved, and thought she knew? Or those other Suzannahs she had never glimpsed before. 'I'm not sure I know what she would have said. So many people seem to have such different pictures of her these days.'

Tom dismissed her doubts. 'They're not so very different, are they? Aren't they just aspects of the same woman? Your picture is as accurate as anyone's. She was strong, and focused, and that's what other people resented, perhaps. But in your life she always encouraged you, and supported you. That's what she'd be doing now. You owe it to her not to weaken.'

She knew he was right. She had to admit it to herself. She climbed off her stool, and picked up her handbag, while Tom went ahead of her to the study, and folded the bed back into a sofa. She zipped her notorious dress into its bag and put it over her arm. Then they went together down the path, and she threw the dress bag onto the back seat. 'That can go straight back to Brigid,' she said, without regret. 'I hope she's happy with all the publicity.'

'She will be,' Tom assured her. 'Good luck, sweetheart, stay in touch,' and he swung away from her, down the street. He would have liked to hold her in his arms for a moment, to stop her flinching at the day ahead, but he didn't want to weaken her.

She watched him striding away, half cursing him for his decisiveness, half grateful for it. Then she drove to the studio.

By the time she reached her office, walking briskly between the desks, it was as if she had caught Tom's courage. The researchers waved to her, and shouted jokes across the office. 'Hope you'll wear that for the next show. We'll double our ratings.' They seemed cheerful enough.

Dan came out of his office to greet her. Lucy shrugged apologetically, and he rolled his eyes to heaven. 'That's what I call grabbing the headlines. Terrific stuff, Lucy.' So he was pleased too. What had she been worrying about?

She looked at the duty log. Middle England was up in arms, spluttering with indignation. But even then there were appreciative calls: 'At last we're seeing more of Lucy,' phrased in a dozen different ways.

She settled down at her desk, and tackled the post waiting for her there. She had to replace all the precious documents lost in the fire, her passport, her insurance policies. She rang the transport department, to arrange for yesterday's day clothes to be collected from the hairdresser, and for Brigid's dress to be returned.

Then Dan came to her doorway. 'There's some breaking news. Have a look, it's about Lord Parks.' She switched on her television, and turned to the rolling news station. Across the bottom of the screen a tape was running, 'Lord Parks found dead.' The shock of it winded her. How could this be true?

The news presenter looked solemn. Behind him was a picture

of Lord Parks as Home Secretary, sitting at his desk with a red box open beside him. '. . . as Home Secretary he brought in measures to support the police, and more recently he has been vocal in a number of campaigns, particularly against youth crime. Our reporter Ben Sussex is outside Lord Parks' home.'

The picture cut to a young man with an unfortunate moustache, obviously too new and inexperienced to have been the subject of any focus group research, which would instantly have shaved his upper lip. He clearly thought it gave him authority.

'The Parks family have not commented, but we understand that Lord Parks died in his car.' The picture changed to Parks' trademark classic Rolls Royce while the reporter continued, 'A hose pipe had been attached to the exhaust. The police say no other person was involved. It's not known whether he left a note of any kind. News of his death has surprised all his friends and colleagues, since only last night he was enjoying a major media event, the People's TV Awards.'

Once again the picture changed, this time to Parks enjoying the applause as he stood on the stage. And then, suddenly, Lucy found she was watching herself, as they showed a clip from her interview with Parks on her last show. He looked happy and confident, talking about his life, telling anecdotes, ending by saying, 'I think if you can look back, as I can, on a life spent with fascinating and distinguished colleagues, working together for the good of the country, you can die happy.'

'Few people,' said Ben, moustache quivering, 'could have guessed that Lord Parks may even then have been contemplating his own unhappy death.'

Certainly Lucy hadn't guessed anything of the kind. She switched off the set, and sat at her desk, her mind in turmoil. Why had he done it? He had seemed so confident last night, so ebullient. Guiltily she recognized a deep sense of relief. At least Max and the boys were a little safer now. Perhaps she too was safer.

As she tried to analyse what she'd heard, Dan came in. They

sat for a moment in silence, immersed in their own thoughts. Then he said, 'Did you have any idea he was this fragile?'

'None at all.' That was true enough. He had seemed completely insensitive, bullish. But had that rough skin really been eggshell thin? Her guilt flared into life. Could it be that her own flippant remark about the photographs had been enough to tip the balance in his mind? Had she killed him? Perhaps he thought he was about to be arrested for child abuse, and he couldn't take that knowledge. If so, should she now be riven with regret? She searched her conscience. No. If what Max had said about him was true, if the photographs were genuine, the world was better off without Parks. But *was* it true?

Her mobile phone rang. She looked apologetically across to Dan as she answered it. He nodded to her and discreetly left the office.

It was Max. His voice was hoarse and urgent.

'Have you seen the news?' he asked.

'Yes, just.'

'Good riddance.'

'Maybe.' She hadn't quite his confidence.

'Why do you reckon he did it?'

'Perhaps it's my fault, in a way. He knew I'd spoken to the police.'

'When? What have you said?' There was panic in his voice.

'Don't worry, Max. I didn't mention you. But I did give them the pictures.'

'What?'

'I said I had no idea where they were taken. Which was true. And that I didn't know the boy who gave them to me at Thritham. Which is less true.'

'Have you told them anything about me? God, Lucy. I knew I should never have talked to you. I told you not to say anything.'

She tried to calm him down. 'I didn't. I just said I had met a group of boys at Thritham. They knew that anyway.' She was

301

desperately trying to win back his trust. But there was more she had to confess to him. 'I did tell the police what you had said about the paedophile ring and I named the two names you gave me.'

'And?'

'And that was all. That was yesterday morning. Then last night I met Parks at the awards. I told him I'd shown those pictures to the police.'

'Jesus. You didn't tell him that.'

She felt guilty and ashamed. There was no point trying to disguise it. 'I'm afraid I did, Max. He was wearing that same ring. He was so confident, so full of himself. But I know it was stupid. I suppose he realized the game was up. Those pictures are completely damning. That might have been enough to tip him over the edge.'

'It might be enough to do for all of us. The guys will go mad when they realize what's happened. They'll blame me for talking to you.' His voice lifted as another thought struck him. 'The pervs will be panicking.' In spite of himself he was enjoying that idea. 'Nobody knows what else Parks has in his house. There were plenty more pictures, you know. They love that kind of stuff. I bet he's got thousands on his computer.'

'Maybe. On the other hand he had enough time to get rid of anything he didn't want people to find after he'd gone.' She took courage from the new tone in his voice. Perhaps this was the moment to put a dangerous idea to him. 'I've been thinking, Max.' When had the idea come to her? Had it been building in her subconscious ever since she heard of Parks' death? 'Dead men can't sue for libel. This means the lawyers might let us transmit the truth about him now. Or at least some of it. We could talk on the show about the things you've told us. What do you think? Would you or any of the others be prepared to be filmed talking about Parks, if we conceal your identity? We can always hide your faces, and disguise your voices.'

He was tempted. 'That's a thought.' Then his voice changed.

'But it would still be fucking dangerous. Parks wasn't the only one. His friends know how to look after themselves, as we know.'

'Is there no way we could do it?' The disappointment rang in her voice.

He tried to comfort her. 'I'll talk to the others and see what they say. But don't hold out too much hope, Lucy. Nobody's going to put themselves in the firing line now. Not after what happened to you. I'll ring you.' And the line went dead.

She went into Dan's office. She looked at the chart of her series pinned up beside his desk, twelve more recording dates, with star names pencilled against one or two of them. He looked round to greet her, turning away from the list of e-mails on his computer. 'I've been wondering about our next show,' she said.

'Good. Right.' He scrolled down, and clicked on one of his e-mails. 'I've got a list of possibles from Marion. A few minor Hollywood celebs. Nothing very special, I'm afraid.'

'What about Parks, then?'

He looked incredulously at her. 'Even you'd have some trouble persuading him to come back now, Lucy.'

'I know that.' She smiled to acknowledge the barb. 'I wish I had that kind of influence. If I had, there are plenty of other people I'd bring back before Parks. But now we're free to say more or less what we want about him on the show.'

'What do you mean? Some kind of post mortem? Wouldn't there be a taste problem? Unless you want to say what a wonderful chap he was, and sell a few extra copies of his book.'

'That's not what I had in mind. Not at all. But I may know why he died. It could be one hell of a scoop.'

He was instantly intrigued. 'Why? What do you know?' She got up, shut the door, and came back to his desk.

'When I went to that party in Thritham, one of the boys there gave me some pictures. They show Parks in the act of abusing a child of about twelve.'

Dan was appalled, his face froze with shock. 'God. Is Parks identifiable?'

'Absolutely.'

'That still sounds incredibly risky, in every way. Taste. Legally. Everything.'

'I know. But I'm sure we've got him bang to rights. I gave the pictures to the police. Then when I met Parks at the awards do, I told him I'd seen the pictures, and I'd passed them to the police.'

'When did you give them to the police?'

'Yesterday.'

He thought about that. 'Could we have used them on the show? How explicit were they?'

'I don't think we could have. I don't think we would have wanted to.'

'Thank God for that.'

It was not going to be easy to sell the idea to him. She tried to reassure him. 'I know it's not normal Saturday night viewing, but we would have such a dramatic story to tell. We'd be showing viewers the monster behind the image. Parks was such a high-profile character, never out of sight, always bellowing on about the rising tide of crime, and the lowering of public standards. I think there would be a huge audience for the real Lord Parks.'

Dan wasn't meeting her eyes. He was still unconvinced.

Lucy plunged on. 'I could describe the pictures, and talk to the boys. They'd have to be disguised in some way, maybe in silhouette. We could explain why Parks decided to kill himself. That he couldn't stand the world knowing the truth about him. And he knew he'd end up ruined and in gaol.'

Dan shook his head. Then he stood up, and looked out of the window. His face was rigid. His hands were clasped behind his back. Still with his back to her he said, 'We'd lose our usual Saturday night audience, I'm pretty sure of that. They don't want such strong meat. They need some glamour, some laughter. Why shouldn't they? And of course we'd have to lawyer the whole thing thoroughly. Would we be in contempt? When will the coroner's inquest be? We've got to be absolutely sure of our facts. I know dead men can't sue, but his family are so recently bereaved, and he had very powerful friends. Let's think about it.'

Lucy had never seen him so unnerved. 'Tell you what,' she said, getting up to join him at the window, looking out at the traffic streaming into the city, 'why don't I ring the police and ask them what they'd like us to do? They may want us to show the photographs. I know they'd be keen to try and find the child in the pictures, firstly to help him, secondly to see what he can tell them. If we put the child's face on the screen, we might get a response from someone who knows him.'

'Well, yes, good idea. Ask the police, why not?' He was still reluctant. These were very deep waters. 'But it's a long shot. You have to remember we are an entertainment show, Lucy, specially now that you're on all the front pages.'

She relaxed. 'I could always interview Brigid Walbury about my bloody dress,' she suggested. 'Ask her why the hell it fell down, that would be entertaining. We'd end up hitting each other over the head.'

'That is tempting,' he said. He walked round the corner of the desk towards her. Now that he had digested the idea, his mood was sunny again. He looked at her with concern. 'Are you OK, Lucy? I realize you've been under a load of stress, and I know I haven't made things any easier for you. I'm so sorry I behaved like that the other night.' He was very close now. There was something endearing, unthreatening about this man, in his unfashionable brown flecked tweed jacket that smelled of pipe smoke. 'You were so vulnerable,' he said softly. 'I suddenly felt so close to you. But I was wrong. I hope I haven't wrecked our relationship.'

What could she say? She was on a razor's edge. Somehow she had to protect his self-esteem, without getting uncomfortably close to him again. She did her best. She held his arms, her own outstretched, at once reassuring him and keeping him at a distance. 'No, Dan, of course you didn't wreck anything. I was

305

flattered. We were both very stressed out that night. I have no problem about working with you. I enjoy it.' She kissed him lightly on his cheek, then let go, and walked to the door. There she turned and said, 'I'll ring the police now. I'll let you know what they say.' She went straight to her desk. She had to capture the moment of his resolve, before he recanted.

Sergeant Ash answered the phone when she rang. She recognized the young man's voice, and he responded politely to hers.

'DI Johnson's out, I'm afraid, Miss Strong,' he told her. 'You'll understand why things have got a bit complicated now, with Lord Parks' death.'

'I'd like to talk to Mr Johnson about that,' she said.

'I thought you might. I'm sure he'd be glad to talk to you. Is there anything you can tell me, to pass on to him?'

She might as well confess again, quickly. She picked up a pen and twisted it unhappily between her fingers. 'I'm afraid I may have been indiscreet last night at the Awards night. I met Lord Parks there. He was wearing that ring, as he always does. So I asked him about it, and he told me it's unique. He had it made when he got his peerage. It's got his crest on it, which he designed himself. I'm afraid I went further. I told Lord Parks I'd given you the pictures. I'm worried now that might have pushed him into suicide.'

The sergeant gave nothing away. His voice stayed calm and noncommittal. 'I'll tell Inspector Johnson as soon as I can reach him. I know he'll want to speak to you directly he gets back.'

There was another loose thread still untied, an even more difficult phone call to make. She had been dreading this. She leaned back in her chair and tried to plan what she ought to say. Then she dialled the mobile phone number she knew better than her own. Fred answered. She warmed to his voice. Why did she feel so nervous?

'Fred, it's Lucy.'

'At last.' His tone was flat. He was very hurt.

She tried to soothe him. 'I'm so sorry I haven't rung.'

'That's not the point.' He was getting angrier. 'I don't even know where you are. What game are you playing?'

'Fred, you left me.' His possessiveness was a bit rich. 'You wanted a break from the heat. You told me so. I understood that. But now everything's even worse. I didn't ring you because there's no way I could get you involved in all this mess.' And she hadn't rung him because she'd spent an extraordinary night with Tom. But that knowledge she could never share with Fred. She pushed the memory down deep to the very back of her mind, where she could still feel it glowing.

'I was wrong, Lucy, to leave you like that.' There was a new humility and self-reproach in Fred's voice, which was out of character. But at least he recognized he was unfair to blame her for neglecting him. 'I wasn't thinking straight,' he said, still humble. 'I was thrown off balance, and I ran. It was stupid and cowardly, and I apologize.'

'I'm not asking for an apology. In a way you were right. Freddy, we've had such a fabulous time together, we always get on so well.' It was beginning to sound like a goodbye. Was that what she meant? 'But we've always known we're quite different kinds of people. We're at different stages in our lives.' Goodbye was on the tip of her tongue now, she just couldn't quite enunciate it. She had to let him down more gently. 'Why not let's give ourselves a bit of time, while everything's in such chaos? Then maybe get together again when things are a little calmer.'

He grasped at that straw. 'Let's meet soon, Lucy. I need to see you again, to make sure you're all right.'

She knew she wouldn't be able to give him what he wanted. There was no room in her mind and body now for the kind of easy, casual loving they had enjoyed so much before. She certainly couldn't commit herself to anything more passionate or demanding with him. That had never been the deal between them.

'Fred,' she said, finding a compromise for him, 'why don't you come to the next show on Saturday? I promise you'll be

307

safe this time. We could have dinner afterwards, and I'll bring you up to date with everything.'

It would have to do. He accepted gracefully. They said goodbye affectionately, Lucy switched off her phone, and looked into the distance.

Poor Fred. She felt unfair. He'd given her a great deal of pleasure in the past. They'd shared their lives, and she owed him something for lifting her morale and making her feel desirable again when Tom left her. Maybe they could get together again once all the noise had died down. But at the back of her mind there was a doubt. He had jumped ship once when there was a hurricane on the horizon. Might he do that again?

Sandra appeared at the door of her office, looking apologetic, an e-mail in her hand. 'This is from the Press Office. They've been inundated with requests for interviews from everyone, all the tabloids, every broadsheet. They want pictures, profiles, the lot.'

Lucy felt an immediate urge to crawl under her desk. Hadn't they had enough of her? She asked Sandra to get hold of the senior press officer, Mike Thomas, the veteran of a thousand skirmishes with journalists. An ex-reporter himself, he knew the rules. He'd learned that there was no point taking on the press. Sometimes the newspapers won a battle, sometimes they lost, but to their credit, nothing discouraged them when they were on the track of a big story. At the moment, Lucy was the biggest story in television, so he cautioned her to try to give them a little of what they wanted. 'We could get them all together, and answer all their questions that way. Is this afternoon any good?' he asked her. 'They only need half an hour to get the quotes they're after.'

Lucy sighed, but she could see the logic of it. 'I'm spending the evening with Camilla at Suzannah's place,' she told him, 'so I'd have to be able to leave town by four.'

'Perfect. I'll arrange it for two. We can hold a press conference in our VIP suite. The photographers like that because there's a plain background. The reporters will like it because we'll give them a drink.'

'Must I?' She could visualize the barrage of questions already.

'No. But why not get it over? At least it may stop you being door-stepped or pursued.' It sounded like a nightmare to Lucy, having to tiptoe through the minefield of a press conference. But she respected his advice. Maybe it would be less painful than constantly avoiding the paparazzi.

She snatched a quick, cold, dank salad in the canteen, a plastic plate filled with limp vegetables. Then she took the lift to the fourth floor, and sorted out her reflection in the sumptuous cloakroom there. There wasn't much she could do. Her hair badly needed professional fingers to control it, but there was no time. She pushed it into shape, refreshed her lipstick, and prepared to face her interrogators, already filing into the press conference.

The VIP lounge had one wall filled with trophy pictures, the stars the company was proud of, the ones who had not yet been disgraced or discarded. In a corner, there was a glass cabinet filled with the awards the company had won over the years. There was a large picture of David Jameson showing the Queen around the largest studio, she smiling dutifully if vaguely at a row of soap stars lined up to greet her. Huge plasma screens hung round the room, displaying the BriTV logo, a golden flaming sun. Mike had put a table in front of one of the screens, to brand her with the company image. She would probably look like Medusa, with the twisting rays shooting out of her head. If only she had Medusa's power to turn spiteful questioners to stone.

Lucy sat waiting, she looking at them, and they looking back at her. It was a peculiar event. There was so much suspicion on both sides. They suspected the company of trapping them into a public relations exercise. She suspected them of planning a hatchet job, to slice her into ribbons. It was not conducive to a happy conversation. Her heart lifted as she saw Janet Lake marching in, wearing her largest, bulkiest fur coat. Janet sat four-square in a chair on the back row, and lit a cigarette, oblivious to the no-smoking signs beside the door. Mike contemplated confronting her, then thought better of it.

He stood next to Lucy behind the table, and welcomed them all. 'Good afternoon, ladies and gentlemen. Thank you for coming at such short notice. I wanted you to have the chance to put your questions directly to Lucy Strong, and for her to answer them now, so that she can get on with preparing her show. She is hosting the most talked-about show on television, there's another in the series on Saturday, so I hope you'll forgive her if she only stays about half an hour.' The cameras were already whirring or flashing in front of her, so as not to miss a single grimace. She controlled her face carefully, and waited for the first question.

'Can we have your reactions to Lord Parks' death, Miss Strong? You must have been among the last to see him alive.'

She clung on to her expression of serious concern. 'I know nothing about the circumstances. His death must have been a sudden impulse. When we last met, Lord Parks was optimistic and entertaining, as you probably saw if you watched our programme.' Should she take a risk? Why not. She'd taken enough in the last week. 'We are looking at perhaps revealing a little more about his life in our next show, on Saturday.' There was a murmur of interest.

'Can you give us some idea of what you intend to reveal?' a reporter in the front row asked.

Draw back quickly, she mustn't give too much away. 'I have no details at the moment, I'm afraid. But Lord Parks had a very complex life, and not all of it was in the public eye. We may have facts to reveal which will surprise, and maybe even shock our viewers.'

'What sort of facts?'

'I'm sorry, Pat, you'll have to watch our next show.'

A young woman put up her hand. She had shaggy blonde

310

hair and eyes outlined with thick, black pencil. 'Lucy, looking at the pictures from last night, do you regret that dress?'

'Not at all. It was a gorgeous Brigid Walbury dress. I don't think I broke any laws, did I? I was still legal, tasteful and decent.' A reporter at the back muttered, 'Just,' and there was a laugh. Lucy responded with a smile. 'OK, just. But it gave your headline writers a field day for all their bust and chest jokes.' Her good humour appeased them. She decided to push her luck a little. 'For me,' she said, 'the high point of the evening was the tribute to my friend, Suzannah Piper. I thought Martin Dellaby spoke that beautifully.' The irony would not be wasted on him. Every word he had said in praise of Suzannah must have burned his tongue like acid. 'But I feel her loss every day, every minute of every day. It is acutely difficult for me, because now I'm presenting the show she created. How can I live up to her example?'

She glanced at Suzannah's picture on the wall. That radiant smile had been polished by years of practice, but all the same, she looked so vital, so happy. Lucy came to a decision; it was always dangerous to take on the boss. Jameson had forbidden her to cast doubt on Suzannah's death so he would be furious with her now, but the publicity might provoke someone to break cover. She owed this to her friend.

'I've been thinking about her so much in the last few days,' Lucy said, almost to herself, so that the reporters craned forward in their seats to hear her, and catch any glisten of tears in her eyes, 'and I can't believe that she killed herself by accident in that car. She wasn't exhausted. She was tired, she'd made a programme, but she had driven herself home a hundred times after a show, and driven very carefully and safely. Something must have happened to her that night.'

'What are you saying, Lucy?' The voice had a familiar rasp. Janet was bringing her back to earth. 'What are you trying to imply?'

'I don't know myself. The police have examined her car, and

311

found nothing. I know that. But she was under threat. As I am.'

Blast. She'd done it again. Another indiscretion. But was this one so stupid? If she told the press about the letter, wouldn't it make it just that bit more difficult for someone to hurt her and get away with it?

There was silence in the room now. They were waiting for her to go on. Behind the back row she saw Dan, his face taut and unsmiling. The pause seemed to last a lifetime. Then she gave them what they were waiting for. 'When my house was blown up, I was lucky to escape alive. What you don't know is that I had received some threatening letters, and so had Suzannah, before she died.'

Another excited buzz of conversation that died quickly. Mike touched her arm. She must take care now. She nodded to him. 'I can't give you the exact details of the letters – they are with the police, of course. But they were completely deranged. Maybe from some mad stalker – I don't know. All I can tell you is that Suzannah received some too, before she died. And I believe there must be some connection between them, and her death. I just pray the police will track down whoever it is, and as soon as possible.'

They had their story now. There were a few more desultory questions about what she had lost in the fire, and whether she was considering modelling for *Playboy*, then Mike ended the conference.

He glanced at his watch. 'Tea,' he said, 'in my office. We can see what they're sending out on the tapes.' She agreed gratefully, and he took her into his quiet, pleasant office. The rolling news station was already carrying their report.

'Lucy Strong revealed today that she, and the late Suzannah Piper, had both received hate mail. She posed the question, was this why Suzannah died? And could this also be the vital clue to the bomb that destroyed her own home? A full report follows on the hour.' Lucy imagined the frantic activity in the newsrooms, as they found archive of her and Suzannah separately and together. It was time for her to leave. She drained her tea-cup, thanked Mike and went to find her car. Whether she had made a fatal mistake or not, only time would tell.

She glanced at her watch as she drove out of the car park. Camilla's invitation was for six. She would have to thread her way through the rush hour traffic heading West but she should just about arrive in time. She glanced out of the window. Headlights were reflected on the wet surface of the road, passers-by ran with umbrellas pulled down low over their heads for shelter. It was another bleak night, cold, windy, with a freezing drizzle. She thought longingly of Florida, Barbados, anywhere where December was warm and sultry, and cicadas sang in the trees. Anywhere at least ten thousand miles away from the chaos of her life.

She negotiated the traffic in West London, so deep in thought that the frustrating gridlocks were almost painless. After an hour and a half she was out in the countryside, heading down the long straight road to Whitbury. Soon she would reach the fatal bend in the road, where Suzannah's car had skidded out of control. She slowed as she neared it and then, to her horror, there was a sudden flash of light in the pitch darkness. She was almost blinded. Instinctively she turned the wheel to avoid it, then corrected the swerve as she felt her car begin to skid. She braked as steadily as she could without losing control on the greasy surface, and looked behind her at the corner. There was a sports car parked under a tree, and by its headlights she could see a man running back to it, a camera in his hand. Someone had been so determined to get today's picture of her, he had trekked out into the dark countryside. Who had tipped him off? She went back over her conversation with Mike, the press officer. She'd told him where she was heading that evening. Foolishly she hadn't warned him to keep it confidential. Perhaps he had used it to explain why he was setting up the press conference so fast, at the last moment. Perhaps one of his juniors had talked to a friend on a newsdesk, who had leaped at the opportunity.

She drove slowly on to Suzannah's house. The drive was lit, and as she reached the front door, there was a row of cars already there. Camilla let her in. Her fair hair was carefully combed and twisted up, away from her neck. She was wearing a plain black dress with tight long sleeves, expensive in its simplicity. She seemed suddenly grown up. She greeted Lucy briefly, Lucy hugged her, but the girl stood rigid. She was controlling herself, but this was going to be a difficult night for her.

Through the doorway Lucy could see a small crowd of faces she knew – Lesley and Mandy, Dan and Boris, Marion and Alex. As she walked towards them, Mandy looked at her and winked.

'Just get the boob jokes over quickly,' Lucy implored her. 'I want to try and enjoy this evening.'

Mandy relented. 'Suzannah would have loved the dress. She always said if you've got it, flaunt it every time.'

Lesley looked at her quizzically. 'Just please take me shopping next time,' she said, 'and I'll make sure you get a couple of shoulder straps sewn in.'

To escape their glee at her expense, Lucy walked over to the window where Alex and Marion were deep in conversation. They broke away from each other, self-consciously, as she joined them.

'What were you two saying?' she asked curiously.

Marion flushed, and said nothing. Alex met her eyes. 'We were reminiscing about the last time we were here.'

'When was that?' Lucy was surprised. Suzannah didn't make a habit of inviting researchers to Whitbury, even the strongest, most experienced researchers. 'Did she ask you to stay?'

'She didn't even ask us to have a glass of water. We had to bring down some last-minute research briefs she needed for the show the next day. We drove here late. She flayed us alive for forgetting to get hold of some information she said was crucial. Then she sent us on our way.'

No wonder Marion had looked embarrassed. All the same, Lucy decided to pursue the point, knowing it was risky.

314

'Suzannah was never like that when I worked with her. Tough, yes, and demanding, but she looked after her team. We were all very happy working for her.'

They looked at each other. Marion took her hand. 'Lucy, we don't want to upset you. We know how close you always were to Suzannah. And we accept she was brilliant at her work. That's frankly why we stayed on the team. Maybe she changed over the years, after you left the team. Perhaps as she got older, and she knew in spite of all the nips and tucks and Botox she was inevitably getting harder to light, she grew more insecure. She took it out of the cameramen. She took it out of the whole team. She could be a bully, Lucy. Not just to us, to everyone, from Dan down.'

And to her daughter. Lucy shook her head miserably. They were right. It wasn't at all what she wanted to hear tonight.

Camilla walked to the centre of the room and stood in front of the fireplace. As they sat down, Lucy looked around the room. There were only about a dozen guests. Camilla began to speak, with obvious effort.

'You were my mother's closest friends,' she said. 'I could, of course, have filled the house with people who claimed to be her friends, her colleagues, her fans. Filled a dozen houses in fact. But most of them, as Mum knew only too well, relied on her fame and her talent. They lived off it. If she'd lost her job, she would never have seen them again. She was never fooled by them. She knew the difference. You were her real friends. She could always come to you for help if she needed it. For all I know, she did. She wrote a letter before she died. In it she says she wants you to know how she felt about you. And now she is no longer here, she wanted each of you to have a memento of your friendship.

'Mother died far too young . . .' Her voice broke, but she paused, and steadied it. Then she went on, 'But for some reason she realized she hadn't much time. I used to tell her she was morbid. We used to argue about it. But she was right. She was

315

often, infuriatingly, right. She wrote this letter three weeks before she died, and in it she said something about each of you.'

Camilla had picked up a hand-written letter from a little walnut table. Lucy caught a glimpse of the flamboyant italic writing she knew as well as her own. Why had Suzannah been so fatalistic? Had the threatening letters given her intimations of mortality? Camilla began to read.

'"To Boris, my ex-husband and Camilla's father. You made me laugh, Boris, when otherwise I might have been angry or miserable. You gave me a job which became a way of life for me, and which consumed me like a forest fire. I don't know whether to be grateful to you for that, or not. Best of all, you gave me my beloved Camilla, and for that I can never repay you. I want you to have my Jaguar XJ6, because I know you envy me for owning it. I wish you many happy journeys in it."'

Camilla stopped reading, unable to carry on. Boris went to her and held her for a moment. There was silence in the room. Their minds were filled with the image of the car Suzannah loved and prized, as they had last seen it, a torn, mangled wreck. She had driven it to her death.

Camilla composed herself, and continued to read, her eyes on the text, determined not to break down again. '"Also, Boris, because you are as witty as Wilde, and as versatile, I want you to have my Oscar Wilde first editions. Enjoy them."' He looked across at the bookcase, with its copies of *The Happy Prince*, *De Profundis*, *The Picture of Dorian Gray*, and the plays. Then he caught Lucy's eye, and winked. Did that answer her question about his sexuality? That Suzannah had reconciled herself to Boris being 'as versatile' as Oscar Wilde?

As Camilla read on, Lucy watched her, astonished. The girl she had always thought of as a child had a new poise and fluency. It was as if losing her mother had catapulted her into adulthood, as if she had inherited from her mother the charisma, the capacity to hold a room that made Suzannah such a confident performer. What a paradox. Camilla had resented her mother's working world, but she had inherited her steely strength and her natural talent. Would she recognize that in herself? If so, how would she use it?

Lesley was standing at the front of the crowd, with tears in her eyes as she heard Suzannah's last message to her. Suzannah had left her some antique lace she had admired, and some precious Chinese silks. '"For twenty years, Lesley,"' Suzannah's letter said, '"your talent disguised my physical faults, so I got away with them, mostly. But even more important was the skill and kindness with which you disguised my emotional flaws, your support and friendship in my private life. You knew my secrets, nearly all of them, and you kept them to yourself. Thank you, Lesley."'

Lesley turned away, head down, and made her way to the back of the room where she could weep unseen.

Camilla doggedly read on. Mandy, Suzannah's agent, had been left a heavy, solid gold bracelet. '"Not because you are a tough negotiator, though of course you are. Not because you could sell a camel to an Eskimo, though you could do that effortlessly. But because your strength, and your energy, made me feel the battles were worthwhile. And because you know even more about me than Lesley does, and you forgive me everything. I hope."'

The room laughed, and Mandy raised her glass to Suzannah's memory. 'Yes, darling, everything. And I hope you do the same for me, when we meet again.'

'"Lucy,"' Camilla read, '"what an odd, interesting creature you were when we first met. And how you have changed."' Camilla paused for the laugh. '"You have gained so many skills, you have found a style that suits you perfectly, and you create programmes to be proud of. Congratulations. I want you to have my diamond and emerald brooch, because I bought it with the money I made from my first big series. Emeralds are said to be lucky, and they have always brought me luck. I want you to wear it whenever you feel happy, or need a little extra luck,

317

in the knowledge that wherever I am, I will be thinking of you. In addition, I want you to have any scripts or tapes or research documents you would like from my library. And if you are ever in any doubt about your future career, go for the best idea, made for the best motives, using the toughest journalism."'

Lucy was lost for a moment. It was as if her dearest friend were in the room again, talking directly to her. It was almost unbearable. But Camilla had moved on, to Dan, who had an expensively ornate French mirror, 'for future reflection,' to Alex and Marion, each of whom could choose their own keepsakes from her library. Lucy watched their faces. They had earned their gifts.

At last Camilla came to the final paragraph. '"Friends, let me leave you with a moment of pure pleasure. I have created this party because I want you to enjoy it. There is Bollinger on ice, there is caviar waiting in the kitchen for you. Stay as long as you like, and drink to our friendship. You are my favourite people. You made my life worth living."'

On cue, Suzannah's housekeeper came into the room with trays of champagne, and they took the glasses gratefully. Boris raised his. 'To Suzannah, wherever she is.'

'And whoever she was,' Lucy murmured silently to herself, and drank deeply.

Camilla said, 'Stay as long as you like,' and disappeared into the kitchen to bring out the caviar.

Lucy caught Mandy's eye, and saw that Mandy appeared to be downing her third champagne, judging by the glasses lined up beside her. Lucy went over to her, and whispered, 'I need to escape.'

'Good,' Mandy answered. 'So do I. Can I have a lift to London?'

'Of course.'

It wasn't what Lucy would have chosen, but there was no way to avoid it now. They went to the kitchen. Camilla was spooning caviar onto tiny rounds of fresh toast, as they kissed and thanked her.

'I'm sorry, but I can't stay,' Lucy whispered to her. 'I find all this heartbreaking. I need to be by myself.'

Camilla looked at her. Mandy was pouring herself another champagne, and balancing two rounds of caviar in the other hand. 'We both need to be by ourselves,' Mandy said loudly. 'That's why we're leaving together.'

Camilla raised her eyebrows, and mouthed at Lucy, 'Do you need help?'

Lucy shook her head. At least she was driving, and Mandy would probably fall asleep after an hour or so. They left the house, and Lucy turned her car in the sweep of drive. So much happiness in Suzannah's life was being packaged and wrapped up. She wanted her memories to stay fresh and vivid, but she feared they were blurring and disintegrating with every mile she drove away from Whitbury.

She glanced at Mandy. She sat slumped in the passenger seat, but as Lucy watched, Mandy seemed to revive. She took a tissue out of her Gucci handbag, and wiped her lips with it. 'Wonderful caviar,' she said with satisfaction. 'Suzannah certainly knew how to live, and how to die.' She settled back into her seat. 'It was fascinating,' she said, 'that party. To see who wasn't there.'

That at least was an interesting start to the conversation. Lucy decided to play along. 'Who do you mean? Who did you expect to be there?'

'Oh, nobody,' Mandy said. 'I knew Suzannah would never have paraded her love life, specially not in front of Camilla.'

'Naturally,' Lucy said. This was clearly half a dozen glasses of vintage champagne talking.

'All those sun-bronzed actors she liked to enliven her life with. None of them were about.' Mandy sounded disappointed.

What about Mandy's fabled discretion? Had it flown under the impact of tragedy and emotion? Or was it just the alcohol? Either way Lucy knew she should try to shut her up.

'But I was sorry not to see Jake,' Mandy ploughed on inexorably.

Jake who? Jake Carlton? Against her will Lucy was intrigued.

'Camilla surely wouldn't have invited Jake?' she asked Mandy.

'No, of course not. Suzannah was incredibly secretive about him. Nobody knew. Not even his own father. All the same, Suzannah could have found some way of mentioning him, some charitable bequest or something. That Chinese silk she left Lesley was worth a fortune.'

There was more than a tinge of envy there. Lucy tried not to show her avid curiosity. This might be the answer to the riddle. What had her friend been up to with Jake Carlton? And for how long? Lucy would never have guessed. Jake was far too young, too earnest, too married. But Mandy was the oracle, and the spirit of many glasses of Bollinger had inspired her.

'How long had they been seeing each other?' Lucy asked.

Mandy lay back in the front seat, her eyes closed. 'Oh, I don't know, dear. It must have been two years now, mustn't it? It was pretty intense.'

Was it indeed? So why had Suzannah never told Lucy about it? Had Lucy understood nothing about the woman she thought was her closest friend? Indignation rose in her. She controlled it.

'Who else knew, do you think?' she asked, keeping her voice light. 'Besides us?'

'Lesley, perhaps. Those little parties à deux in Suzannah's dressing room after the shows. She must have known about those. But I must say Suzannah was unusually discreet about Jake, for obvious reasons.'

'Quite.' Obvious reasons like the fact Jake was married, Lucy supposed. And that his father was producing Suzannah's programme. And that Jake himself was a teacher, and his school might well object. Especially since it seemed he and his pupils often came to the studio to watch the show, and they might conclude he was using the young people as a cover for his affair with the star presenter.

A memory jumped into Lucy's mind. The script she had found in Suzannah's library, the one that had been marked like a school essay – was that Jake's work? Had Suzannah kept it as a love-token, something to remember him by when they were apart? More and more interesting. But, if so, he must also have written the love letters she had kept locked safely in her drawer, so that she could read and reread them. The realization struck Lucy hard. Was Jake then the secret of Suzannah's smile when she had said her final goodbye to the camera?

Mandy was snoring now, as Lucy had predicted she would be, and the rest of the journey passed without more conversation. Lucy was deep in thought again. All the cards had been thrown up into the air, in a frenzied jumble, like the playing cards at the end of *Alice in Wonderland*. Was there a sequence in them? Or was it all chaos?

They reached Mandy's flat, in a smart block behind Holland Park. By now she was awake, complaining of a headache. 'It's not the Bolly,' she grumbled. 'I can drink gallons of the stuff without feeling it. I reckon it was the drive. I hate driving on an empty stomach.'

Not entirely empty, Lucy thought, but kept that to herself. Mandy turned back to the car, waving a diamond-laden hand, girded now with Suzannah's heavy gold bracelet. Then she walked steadily up to her front door, and found her key without too great a struggle. You had to admire her toughness.

Lucy drove north to Tom's house, digesting what she had been told. Tom was out, the house was in darkness, and as she unlocked the front door, Lucy found her mind wandering back to the intensity of their lovemaking. Was that what Suzannah had with Jake? Was that why their affair had lasted two years, only cut short by her death?

Lucy sat by herself in the study, and readjusted her memories yet again. Suzannah must have kept this relationship entirely secret – not a hint in the press, even her close friends had not suspected. Except perhaps Lesley. Lesley had hinted that there had been a glow about Suzannah those last weeks, that she had left very quickly after her last programme. Maybe Jake had been waiting for her that night. Maybe he knew something more about Suzannah's death.

Lucy urgently needed to talk to Jake now. She had to know everything he knew. She took out her battered, precious notebook, with every crucial contact number in it. Jake was there, school number and home. She dialled his home number. He answered quite quickly, and she heard the sound of children's voices in the background.

'Can I come and see you tomorrow, Jake? I have a problem, but I'd rather not talk about it over the phone.' It was a feeble reason, but he might be intrigued enough to accept it. He did.

'Sure, Lucy, I get home at four thirty.'

'May I come and see you then? Take a cup of tea off you?'

'Yes, that's fine. I'll expect you.'

It was as if he had been anticipating her call, as if he knew he had information she badly needed. She put down the phone and sat quietly in Tom's study. What was Jake, lover or enemy? Was it possible that he had written not just the love letters to Suzannah, but the hate letters as well? If that were so, when she went to visit him, would she be entering the lair of her own fiercest enemy?

She had no choice. Tomorrow she must try to discover the truth. Or perhaps a tiny fragment of the truth. Not for the first time Lucy wondered just how much of her dead friend's life she had ever understood.

CHAPTER FOURTEEN

Exhausted, she slept soon, and deeply. She woke with fumes still in her head, and a feeling of fragility. Last night's champagne was probably still flowing in her veins, though she'd been quite careful. Indeed, compared with Mandy she'd been puritanical. As her head cleared, she registered that through the wall she could hear Tom humming to himself as he walked around the kitchen. It was a comfortable sound. She wrapped her overcoat about her, but when she joined him, she saw the pile of morning papers next to him on the table. Her headache returned.

'Have you seen what's in them?' she asked nervously. 'Do you know what they say?'

He shook his head. 'What would they do without you?' he asked.

She shrugged, and began flicking over the pages. The pictures of her at the press conference were unflattering, caught in mid-speech, under headlines about 'Lucy's Secret Stalker' and 'Death Mail' and, to her indignation, 'Suzannah Murder Victim – Lucy Blames Police'. That was the last thing she needed now. She would have to rely so heavily on the police to help her make the next show. If these stories made them resent her, her job would be much more difficult.

She skip-read her way down the columns. By and large the stories were accurate, and the press were kindly. Most of them mentioned that she was planning the programme about Lord Parks, so the BriTV Press Office would be pleased. None of them referred back to Fred, so he would be relieved.

At the bottom of the pile she found a tabloid front page, with the picture taken when she was driving to Whitbury. Her face looked pale and intense, shot through the rain-drenched windscreen. She shut the papers with a sigh. Tom glanced at her, but seeing her deep in thought, asked no questions. She joined him in the routine they had created together, making coffee, warming up a fresh loaf in the oven, pulling French fruit yoghurts out of the fridge.

Lulled by the familiar chores, Lucy began working through a plan for her day ahead. She deliberately pushed to the very bottom of her mind all thought of her own danger. She was determined not to allow fear to disable her brain. Instead she had to build a ladder to the future, step by methodical step.

First she must speak to the police and reassure them that she didn't blame them for anything. The last thing she needed was to alienate them now. She had to make contact again with Max, if she could. She would meet Jake, and perhaps find the missing pieces in Suzannah's jigsaw. Then she had to work out a draft script with Dan for the Parks programme. And somehow, between all that, there was her own life to organize. She must find somewhere to live, she had to sort out her relationship with Fred. She glanced at Tom. Was he part of her life again, or not?

His face as he methodically read through the news stories gave very little away.

'What do you think of the papers?' Lucy asked.

He answered without looking up, still reading. 'I'm just trying to work it out. I don't think it's too bad. Apart from your implied criticism of the police, it may not do too much damage. There's just a chance it may jog someone's memory.' Maybe Jake's. If it was true that he was closest of all to Suzannah, perhaps Jake would have some clue about the author of those hate-filled letters, and her fatal last night.

Lucy allowed herself the small luxury of watching Tom while he read – his hands as he turned the pages, the curve at the corners of his mouth. At that moment he looked up, and they smiled at each other. It was good to be able to feel safe for a moment. But no matter how she tried to control it, she recognized the churning dread that was still there, in the pit of her stomach, the anxiety that never left her.

The newspaper stories reminded her of the truth she had tried so hard to block. Someone in the world outside this little house still wanted to kill her. Perhaps he was someone who wore the mask of a friend. Someone she had drunk champagne with yesterday. Someone she confided in, and thought she could trust. Or maybe he was a member of the paedophile ring. If so, they were rich and powerful enough to buy a contract killer and get rid of anyone who posed a threat. She had no illusions that Parks' death meant she was safe now. If anything, it put her in more danger. Now the others knew she was planning a programme about him. Perhaps that would rouse them to still greater desperation. But if it made them break cover to try to silence her, so much the better.

How much of this could she share with Tom? Only a little. The risk was that he might try to dissuade her from pursuing the trail that led to Suzannah's death. He might ask Lucy the questions she didn't want to hear. 'Why is this worth so much to you? Why put your own life at risk? See how Suzannah died, in the middle of her life, with so much to look forward to. Do you really want to go the same way?'

But she couldn't just switch her brain off. Instinctively she felt so close to the truth now. Her memory went back to the day before. The answer was there, somewhere. Try again. Work through what you know. See if anything reveals itself. She relived her drive to Suzannah's house, the dark road, the sudden flash of a photographer's camera, the swerve that almost skidded out of control as she tried to avoid him. She glanced back at the paparazzi picture. She looked grim and strained, driving on through the sleety rain. 'Lucy – is the stress beginning to tell?' the newspaper caption read, and it was a good question. Was it?

Suppose someone had been standing in the darkness on the same corner, the night Suzannah died? What if somebody – a photographer, or somebody else – had a camera with a powerful flash, and had suddenly taken Suzannah's picture, when she was least expecting it? Lucy had been slowing down at the bend, reliving tragic memories. But Suzannah knew the road so well, she might have been travelling at high speed, as she usually did. Suppose, in shock, she had twisted her wheel to avoid the glare, and the car had spun out of control – would that explain her accident? But why would a photographer have been waiting on that corner? Unless he had been tipped off about Suzannah's affair, and was hoping to trap her on the way to a rendezvous with Jake. It was, after all, the ideal place for a photographer to take up position, directly facing the driver.

It made a terrible sense. Lucy recalled suddenly the conspiracy theory of Princess Diana's death. Some people didn't believe that was simply an accident. They claimed that a photographer's flash gun could have momentarily blinded Diana's driver as he drove through the Paris tunnel at high speed. That, they said, would explain the mystery of the missing white Fiat Uno, whose paint was found on the bumper of Diana's car, but which has never been found.

Still deep in thought, Lucy showered, dressed in her sensible clothes, (that was another chore to add to her list, she must buy a few more jackets and shirts, all this black was so mournful), and drove to the studio. When she reached her office she found that her voice-mail was full. DI Johnson had left her a message saying that he was back at his desk and wanted to speak to her. She rang him first.

'I'm so sorry about the press,' she said apologetically. 'Of course I don't blame the police. I don't know where they got that from.'

'Don't worry, Miss Strong, we're used to being blamed. I got your message from Sergeant Ash. I would like to talk to you again. We've examined the photographs you gave us, and we have a little more information.'

'That's fine. I'll come down this morning if you like. I have an idea to put to you.' They arranged to meet at eleven.

Lucy went in to see Dan, and told him. He looked thoughtful.

'Be careful with the police,' he told her. 'Tread softly, Lucy. Don't try to steamroller them into it. They may dislike what they see as trial by television, specially now that Parks is dead.' That was true.

Dan got up from his desk, and stood with his back to the window. His eyes focused in mid-distance as he calculated the most effective way for her to negotiate with the police.

'If they're reluctant to let us use the pictures, why not give them the *Crimewatch* example?' he suggested. 'You could remind them how much information comes to the BBC after every one of those shows. It might work.'

'OK, Dan.' It was a good idea.

'In any case, give me a ring and let me know how it goes.'

'Of course.' Now she had to lie to him. She had no choice. She couldn't possibly admit she was going to meet Jake, and why. 'If the police give me the go-ahead,' she said, 'I think I'll work at the hotel on my lap-top this afternoon. I've got so much writing to do. I need to surf the Net to find out what there is there about Parks. And maybe Max will let me know how the boys react to the idea of being interviewed. But I'll be on my mobile if you need me.'

'Have you found somewhere comfortable to stay? Not that I want to pry.' Dan didn't sound suspicious, just interested.

'Yes. It's fine. Not specially comfortable, but it'll do. It's just an ordinary small place outside London.' How good she was at lying, once she'd started. It quite frightened her. 'I know it's ridiculous not to tell anyone where it is, but the police are adamant. They say once my address is known by one person, everyone will know, and they won't be able to guarantee my safety.'

Dan nodded. There was sense in that.

Lucy hurried on with her explanation, pushing a plank across the quicksand of lies. 'I think the police were shocked at the lack of security here, the fact that all our addresses get passed around. Personally I'm not bothered. I told them so. I know nobody on the team is a danger to me. It's just that the police have made a blanket rule, and they say I've got to abide by it.'

He seemed to accept that. Soon, please God, she would be able to force the murderer out into the open. And then she could share the truth with this man she liked, trusted and relied upon.

Dan walked with her to the door, and put his hands on her shoulders. He looked into her face and his eyes were kind. 'Lucy, for your own sake, tell the police everything you know,' he urged her. 'Don't try and carry this burden by yourself. Leave it to them. And please let me help, in any way I can.'

She looked gratefully back at him. He held her gaze. He seemed so strong and supportive that for a moment she felt like an insecure child.

He read her mind. 'You're doing brilliantly, Lucy,' he said. 'I had no idea you'd had one of those vile letters yourself. I don't know how you're holding yourself together, but you are. Just don't push yourself too far. Suzannah's dead now. We mustn't lose you. Let me help you.' The newspaper picture of her at the wheel of her car was on his desk. He glanced down at it. Clearly her taut, pale face captured in the flashlight had worried him.

She tried to reassure him. 'I know, Dan, I want to share every-thing with you. But at the moment I don't know any more than you do.' True enough about the danger she was in, the attempt on her life, the paedophile investigation. Not true about Suzannah's life. But then that wasn't Dan's concern at the moment. She took his hand in hers. 'If something comes out of my meeting with the police, of course I'll tell you straight away.'

Lucy drove to the police station, and sat down with the two officers in a small interview room. They were pleased to see her but they were tired. They looked as if they had been working through the night: their clothes were creased and their smiles were fleeting. Sergeant Ash gave her a cup of tea, which she drank greedily, and put a plate of chocolate biscuits in front of her, which she tried to ignore, but failed. DI Johnson brought her up to date.

There was no doubt that Parks' death was suicide. He'd left a note, and used the lethal carbon-monoxide fumes, ending his life comfortably in the car that had been such a status symbol for him. The police had searched his flat meticulously, but found no more pictures. They'd taken away his computer. Even if he had deleted any pornographic images, the computer experts in the paedophile squad should be able to find them, or traces of them.

Johnson showed her pictures the police had taken of Parks' body, with close-ups of the ring on his hand. 'As you said, Miss Strong, it's a one-off. He had it engraved when he was given his peerage. There should be no problem proving that the hand in your picture with the child is his. Now what we need to know is, who gave those pictures to you?'

'That's a problem for me,' she said, clinging as far as she could to fragments of the truth. 'As I told you, I met so many boys at the Thritham party, and I didn't know all their names. But I may be able to find out. Let me put another idea to you.'

She explained to them that she wanted to make the next programme a special report telling the truth about Lord Parks. It could serve both their purposes. She would try to contact some of the Thritham boys again, and interview them about Parks. And at the same time she would pick up any information they could give her about the child in the pictures. 'The best thing from your point of view,' she said, 'would be if we could show that boy's face on the screen. Obviously we must protect his identity, but he's got a scar by his ear.' She showed the policeman the mark, a white seam shaped like a V. 'We could show that in close-up. It must be a recent photograph. Someone might recognize him.'

Johnson looked pessimistic. 'They might. But we've had our experts analysing it, and they think the bedclothes look as if they might be French, or Belgian. In which case the kid might be French or Belgian too. They could have shipped a British kid out with them, of course. He's definitely been drugged, so anything's possible.'

329

Lucy shuddered. How much that child must have suffered, for the gratification of these monsters. Johnson made a phone call, then left the office. He came back to her carrying blown-up copies of the Parks polaroids. Magnified, they were even more horrific.

'I've put your idea to my bosses,' Johnson said, 'and I've been told you can use these pictures on your programme, as long as you protect the child's identity, and keep the picture decent, and as long as there is a serious public-interest, crime-prevention point.' To Lucy's relief, he put them carefully in an envelope, and handed them to her. She didn't want to look at them any longer than she had to. She put the envelope in her bag.

'Why not come to the show yourself?' Lucy said. 'Come and sit in our audience.'

Johnson looked alarmed. A television studio was a hostile environment. Policemen had lost their careers under those bright lights. Lucy rushed to reassure him.

'I promise I won't ambush you or ask you any awkward questions.'

'In that case I might take you up on it,' he said, tempted. It could well be worth it to him. If she succeeded in persuading any of the Thritham boys to take part, he would be able to meet and talk to them too.

Johnson and Ash continued questioning her for another hour, taking her over old ground, everything she could remember about the teachers in Wantage Grange School, in case one of them had a link with Parks, anything else the boys might have told her.

At last Johnson pushed his papers together, stood up, and said, 'That's it, for the moment, Miss Strong. Thank you for your help. The good news is that we've completed our examination of your house. We've got all the evidence we need now about the bomb. It was pretty simple.'

'What have you found out?' She couldn't bear to think about picking through the wreckage, the black, burned, sodden remains

330

of her life. So many precious things, photographs, sentimental trinkets, had been destroyed. She couldn't face thinking about how close she'd come herself to being blown to pieces in that house. But there were questions she knew she had to ask. 'Was my bomb connected to the one at Thritham? Do you know yet? Was the same person behind them both?'

Johnson hesitated before he answered. 'We can't be absolutely sure. At the moment, as I told you, we don't think so. It is still possible, though.'

Two killers then. They walked with her to her car. Instinctively she looked up and down the street before she left the shelter of the police station. Was she being cowardly and overdramatic? The road was empty. The Christmas decorations in the shop windows were cheerful. The world looked mundane, and ordinary, and safe.

She drove back to the studios, and went into her office. There were heaps of Christmas cards on her desk. Another chore she had to organize – she hadn't begun to think about buying cards and presents. She stood in the centre of the room and took the envelope out of her bag. Then she went next door, and put it on Dan's desk. She said nothing. He opened it, and when he saw the pictures he shuddered. He turned them face down on his desk. She understood his shock.

'I hate the idea of having these pictures here in my office,' he said. 'Sandra had better keep them under lock and key.' Lucy pushed them into the envelope, and handed them back to him, glad to be rid of them herself. It was as if a smear of corruption clung to the images, infecting everyone who touched them. They would have to be very careful how they used them on the show.

'I'll have lunch now,' she told Dan, 'and then I'll go back to my room and work there. I'll stay in touch.'

Lunch was a greasy, overcooked omelette. The canteen was notorious for producing uneatable food. There was a real skill there. Even the simplest sandwich had the texture of fleece, the bread had been so long in the freezer. She pushed the food around her plate, leaving half of it. Then she went to find her car.

She'd parked in her usual place, very close to the entrance of the car park. As she walked to it from the lift, she saw, parked on the other side of the barrier, a battered silver second-hand Toyota. It was badly parked, a metre or so away from the kerb. How selfish. It would be very awkward to swing round past him. She got into her car and drove up to the barrier. She stopped there, and searched in her bag for the swipe card to lift the barrier by the unmanned gate. Suddenly there was a huge explosive boom, a flash of light, and the Toyota exploded. Pieces of metal flew up into the air, clattering down onto the bonnet of her car. Her windscreen blanked, filled with a dense cobweb of tiny cracks that spread and merged with each other. Lucy cowered down as far as her seat belt would allow. There were shouts, people ran towards her. Her mind cleared, then filled again with horror. Another bomb. Someone had tried to kill her again.

The security man at reception reached her first, and dragged open her car door. 'Are you hurt, miss?'

As she sat, paralysed, she forced her numb mind to check her body for pain. No, there was none. She shook her head. A heavy pillar had absorbed most of the explosive shock, and protected her car. Her windscreen was destroyed, but the shards of glass had not blown inside, so she had not been cut. She was shaking, though. Her legs and hands were trembling, and though she tried to control them, she couldn't keep them steady. The commissionaire helped her get out of the car, and held her when she half-fell. She could already hear the blare of a fire engine forcing its way towards them through the traffic. Now the silver Toyota was a furnace, flames reaching as high as the naked branches of the saplings planted in the pavement. Had anyone been sitting in the burning car? She fought back through the smoke and fog in her mind, past the trauma of the explosion, and searched her mind for the memory. She thought the car had been empty.

She remembered to take her bag with her as she left her car, and walked slowly into the main building. The doors made of thick reinforced glass had cracked from floor to ceiling. Windows along the building had blown in. Fragments of the glass were littered over the pavement.

The security man took her to a small office behind reception, sat her on a sofa there, and put a glass of cold water in her hand. The white walls were decorated with the BriTV flaming sun symbol. It jazzed in front of her eyes, she closed them. She drank the water, while he switched on a kettle and produced a mug for her, a tea-bag, a carton of milk and a bag of sugar.

Lucy fumbled in her bag for her notebook, and her phone. Detective Inspector Johnson answered at once.

'There's been another bomb,' she told him.

'I know.' His voice was tight, official, businesslike. 'I've just heard. Where are you?'

'Still at the studios.'

'Stay there, Lucy.' He'd never called her that before. He must be shaken as well. 'I'll be with you in ten minutes.'

She tried to stand again, but the security man motioned her to stay where she was. 'Mr Jameson is on his way to see you, miss. And I wouldn't go outside, unless you want to appear on television. There's a couple of crews out there already.'

Of course. Drawn like moths to the flames again. She sat on the sofa, clutching the hot mug for comfort, grateful for his calm in the eye of the storm.

The security man was grumbling into his tea. 'I've told them a million times.' He turned to her, 'I've told them a million times, Miss Strong, they need more cameras round this building. They've got enough bleeding cameras out there now that it's too late. One more pointing at the car park, and we'd have had him, bang to rights.'

Lucy saw what he meant. The closed-circuit cameras had been installed so that they were pointed at reception, recording everyone who came and went there. Other cameras had been installed inside the car park, but none of them pointed at the entrance, where the Toyota had exploded. Whoever left the car there had found a blind spot, either by chance, or deliberately. There was still hope, though. Perhaps some witness, a passer-by maybe, had noticed the car being driven into position. No doubt the police would interview everyone.

Lucy cleared her throat and put down the half-empty mug of tea. 'You didn't see anyone hanging around this morning, someone who might have left the car there, did you?' she asked the security guard.

'I wish I had, Miss Strong. From my desk I can only see what the bleeding cameras show me, and the entrance to main reception. I've told them a million times it's not enough. Perhaps now they'll believe me.'

The door of the office burst open, under the impact of David Jameson's personality. He wore a bright yellow shirt, his jacket was over his arm. A big man, used to commanding a room, he was now propelled by the catastrophe on his doorstep. He strode across the room, and sat down next to Lucy.

'I can't believe we let this happen to you,' he said to her. 'Are you hurt? You must be terribly shocked. Do you need a doctor? We'll get you whatever you want, just say the word.'

His concern was oppressive. She did her best to smile at him, and moved an inch or two away. 'No, David. I'm fine. Lucky to be alive, of course. Somebody's certainly got it in for me.'

'I'll get the doctor to have a look at you, just to be on the safe side.'

'No, David, honestly. I've got a show to make. I was on my way home to write it.'

'Take it easy, Lucy. Take my driver. Frank will take you wherever you want to go. He was a police driver for years. He'll look after you. But let the police handle this one officially. Don't try to make one of your investigative shows about it. Now's not the time. This is far too dangerous. I'd much rather have you alive and well, and interviewing Madonna, than becoming a dead heroine. Go easy this Saturday. You'll have huge ratings

334

anyway. Everyone will turn on to see how you're coping.'

How typical that his mind had gone straight to his product. She was too tired to fight him. 'You're right, David. The police are on their way. I must speak to them, of course. But then I'll go home and rest. This is beginning to get to me.'

'I'm not surprised. Nobody will be surprised.' He got up, put on his jacket and then turned, slightly shamefacedly. 'Do you think you could just say a word to the BriTV crew? They're outside at the moment, all they need is a sentence.'

God, how could he suggest that, now, when she was still shaking? She looked down at her hands holding the mug of tea. 'David, I'm so sorry, I don't think I can string two words together.'

He sat down beside her again, instantly stricken with guilt. 'Don't worry, Lucy, they'll understand, of course.'

'Can you make a statement, David, instead of me?' That might buy them off. And it might please him too. 'Tell them I'm fine, but I can't talk to anyone till I've spoken to the police. Or say I've no idea who did this, but we're terribly lucky nobody was hurt.' She sucked in a deep breath, but it caught in her throat like a sob. 'Say anything, David. But please don't make me stand up in front of the cameras. I really don't think I can do it right now.'

He couldn't hide his disappointment. An exclusive interview with her at this moment, still shocked by the explosion, would have been the most glorious scoop. It would have sold all over the world. But he could see how frail she was.

He hugged her, and said, 'Don't worry, Lucy. It's just that everyone is so concerned about you, and the viewers would be deeply relieved to see you're all right. But I'll tell them. You stay here as long as you like.'

He bustled out, brushing down his hair with his hand and preening a little. He had once been a sports presenter, and the performer in him welcomed his moment in the limelight again. Lucy, watching obliquely through the office window, saw him standing on the pavement surrounded by cameras and micro-phones, his shoulders braced back, gesturing to underscore his words. He must be saying how shocked he was, they all were, by the attempt on her life, if that's what it was, and how grateful they were that she was unhurt. The questions continued, the crowd of reporters pressed closer, he was in his element. Thank God she wasn't being put through it.

The security man guarded the door to the office, only allowing the police to enter when they arrived – Johnson and Ash. Their familiar faces gave her confidence. She relaxed a little. Johnson saw that and smiled at her.

'You are in demand,' he said, sitting down next to her, and looking intently at her. 'Are you OK, Lucy?'

She nodded.

'Someone is really putting you through it. We'll supply police protection for you until we've sorted this mess out.'

She shook her head. 'I'll do whatever you say, Inspector Johnson, but I'd much rather not have a bodyguard. I'm not being stalked, I'm sure of that. This can only have happened because nobody knows where I'm living at the moment. So they had to try and hit me at the office.'

'But they knew exactly when you were leaving. That's what concerns us. Somebody timed this to coincide with you driving out of the car park.'

'Not necessarily.' She wanted desperately to convince him, and convince herself as well. She listened for any quiver in her own voice that might betray her. She was determined to show she could still be controlled and think clearly. Her voice stayed steady. Why did she mind so much? Maybe it was foolish or arrogant, but she needed to hold on to her independence. She had to prove that she was still in charge of her life. She loathed the idea of being followed everywhere by a strange policeman, who might resent her as much as she resented him.

'Whoever it is knew where the studios are, which isn't diffi-cult to find out. They're pretty well known and we show them in our titles, after all. So he knew I work here. All he had to do was park the Toyota and wait for me to drive out of the car park. He could have been watching for me to start driving out, and set it off. What sort of bomb was it? Did it have a timer on it?'

'Our boys are looking at that now. At first sight it doesn't appear to be very complicated, they tell me, but they haven't given me any details. Will you at least let one of our drivers take you home?'

She glanced out of the window. She could see Jameson's driver, Frank, a bulky, reassuring figure, waiting for her outside the back door of the studio. She knew him well, and liked him. Before Jameson had commandeered him, he had been on the general pool of studio drivers, and had often ferried her on film stories to and from location. When she was nervous or worried about a story, she had confided in him. He was an ex-policeman, burly, discreet, and fatherly. He spoke when she needed conversation, and stayed silent when he could see her mind was occupied. His hair was grey, his face was lined, he was an excellent, experienced driver. He was exactly what she needed at the moment.

She tried to explain to Johnson how she felt. 'Frank knows the score. He'll look after me. We know each other extremely well. If I feel like a bottle of brandy, he'll fetch me one. If I need to talk to someone, he'll let me. And at the moment that sort of friend is exactly what I need. Don't worry about me. I'm in good hands.'

He was unconvinced. 'Look at it from our point of view, Miss Strong . . . Lucy. We'll look such idiots if you come to any harm. I'd much rather have one of our boys looking after you.'

'I know that. I may be stupid – or selfish – but I'd love you to humour me just this once more. Please. I promise if anything happens again I'll take on a complete police protection squad – bullet-proof cars, the lot. I just don't think we're dealing with a very professional villain. He's tried to blow me up twice, or

337

three times maybe, and he's failed each time. This time he's failed so spectacularly he must lie low for a bit, surely.'

'It's a gamble, Lucy. I have to warn you, it's a gamble, and I'm not a gambler. Neither should you be. Not with your life.'

'I accept that. But I really believe I'm not at risk today. Whoever it is behind this must be licking his wounds, cursing me, plotting something else no doubt, but he's done his worst for the moment. Why not let Frank look after me, and drive me home, and I'll stay in touch with you all the time. You can certainly keep your tabs on me, no question.'

He argued with her, but in the end she won the day. Not because she convinced him that she was right, but because she was still so shaky, he could see she needed friends about her. So, reluctantly, he gave in.

'Have it your way then, Lucy. But I would like to have some idea, just briefly, who knew your plans for the day, where and when you were leaving the building.'

'Only the production team, really. We're putting together our programme about Parks, and I'm going to write it at home, everyone knew that.'

'Does anyone know where you're living, as far as you know?'

She shook her head.

'That's one good thing. Go home and have a rest. Try to put this out of your mind, as much as you can. We'll get him, who-ever he is. This could just have been opportunistic, as you say. He could simply have waited for you to leave, then he just took his chance.'

'Exactly. I can't believe any of my team is a phantom bomber.' She mustered up a smile as she tried to visualize it. They were all so outgoing, so noisy and boisterous. She couldn't imagine an Iago among them, consumed by jealousy or hatred, filled with motiveless malignity.

Frank came into the small, claustrophobic room to fetch her, his face filled with concern. Typically he said very little. He took her out through the back of the building to the car, a big, quiet

BMW with a huge surge of power in its engine. She huddled in the passenger seat as he threaded through the traffic towards the address she had given him of Tom's home. Suddenly she sat up. Her head had cleared. Her hands were no longer shaking. Why was she on the run?

'Frank,' she said, 'I'm going to change my mind. I had an appointment in Slough at four thirty. I want to keep it.'

His disapproval did not have to be put into words. It was apparent from his expressionless face, and his rigid back.

'I know what you're going to say,' she said. 'The police would be cross with me. But if you take me there, not a lot can go wrong.'

'I'm only thinking of you, Miss Strong.' Beneath the quiet, civil words, she could hear how angry he was. 'You need rest. Don't tear yourself to pieces. Go home. Have a quiet drink. No more hassle.'

She put her hand lightly on his arm. 'That's what I thought, Frank. And that's what the police told me to do. But I don't need rest. I couldn't sleep at the moment. I have to fill my mind with other things. Otherwise I'll just drive myself round the bend with worry.'

He didn't look at her, he was too angry. She was putting him in an impossible position. She tried to persuade him she knew what she was doing.

'Honestly, Frank, I know myself. Work helps me when I'm in this state. It's the only thing that does help. Please let me carry on as if I'm still in control of my own life.'

He could only obey. 'Whatever you say, miss.'

She took out her notebook and gave him Jake's address in Slough. He programmed his satellite navigation system to locate it. At least that eye in the sky would mean they were traceable, if the worst should happen.

As they drove, Lucy flipped down the visor in front of her, and looked at herself in the mirror. White face, dark-ringed eyes, pale lips. No wonder everyone was treating her as if she was on the verge of a breakdown. She pulled her make-up case out of her bag and painted a mask onto her face. A rosy flush on her cheekbones was dusted on by one brush, bronze gloss from another brightened her lips. That was better. Why burden the world with the way she really felt? Disguise the fear, and it would have less power to paralyse her. By the time they reached Slough and were threading their way through the quiet suburban streets, she was back in control again.

Jake's house was in a cul-de-sac, a narrow road lined with semi-detached houses, each with mock Tudor gables that must have seemed quaint and cosy when they were built in the 1930s. Now the stucco was dingy, and even the lit rooms behind their tightly drawn curtains, and the occasional candle or Christmas tree in the window failed to lift Lucy's spirits. It felt so tight, so prim. Perhaps in the spring when the twiggy almond trees were in bloom and children were riding tricycles on the pavements it would feel like a village, but on this chill December afternoon, it was inhospitable and dull. Orange glow from the streetlights revealed the lawns, neat as aprons, in front of each house, but as usual the numbers were illegible in the gloom. Frank drove at a walking pace, desperate to find a single house number, which might give them a clue. At last they discovered one on a garden gate, and by counting the neighbouring houses as they drove, they found Jake's home. At least it had a wreath of holly on the door. Lucy got out leaving Frank to wait for her at the kerbside, and rang the doorbell.

She heard children's voices, and then a woman in jeans and a sweatshirt opened the front door.

'Hello,' she said, her voice matter of fact rather than inviting. 'I know you, of course. You're Lucy Strong. I'm Elaine, Jake's wife. Come in.'

Lucy followed her through the narrow hall and into a kitchen at the back of the house. There was a smell of old soap powder, the noise of a washing machine constantly churning in the corner. Two blond children, one about six, the other perhaps three, were eating spaghetti on toast at the kitchen table, their mouths smeared enthusiastically with bright red tomato sauce. Elaine introduced them.

'This is Kate, this is Oliver. Say hello to Lucy.'

Neither of the children looked up, the spaghetti held their attention.

'Would you like a cup of tea?' Elaine asked her.

Lucy recognized the tiredness in her voice, and saw the lines around her eyes, symptoms of sleepless nights, hard-working days, too little fun. And yet as Elaine turned Lucy saw she had good bones. Her small, elegantly-shaped head was poised on a long neck, like a ballet dancer's. She must have been a pretty girl before the babies, and the broken nights, and the chores had taken over her life. Now her honey-blonde hair was tied back almost savagely to keep it out of the way, she wore no make-up, and her old blue sweatshirt had an orange smear down the front. Tomato and spaghetti again.

Lucy smiled at her, but Elaine didn't meet her eyes. Instead she called up the stairs, 'Jake, Lucy's here.' There was a muffled response, then Jake came clattering down, his arms piled high with papers which he forced into a briefcase propped by the banisters.

Lucy looked at him with new interest. This was not just a scruffy young teacher, this was Suzannah's lover. He had played a serious part in her life, but a deeply secret one. Lucy could see now why Suzannah had responded to him. His vulnerability was like a boy's. He had tousled dark blond hair, the eyelashes that fringed his blue eyes were dark, and he had an appealing puppy-like charm as he apologized to her.

'Sorry I wasn't down here to welcome you,' he said. 'I was miles away, marking a project about the Romans. All very bloodthirsty, full of gladiators and mad emperors.'

Elaine joined them at the foot of the stairs, two cups in her hands. 'I've made you both tea.' She led them into a sitting room at the front of the house, a small room with battered furniture, plain white walls, a fake coal fire flickering in the grate, and a

Christmas tree beside it, covered with multicoloured fairy lights.

'You can get a bit of peace and quiet here,' she said. 'Excuse me if I go back to the kids.' Squeals from the kitchen implied that tea had turned into a spaghetti fight.

Lucy laughed, and Jake said, 'Meal-times can be quite an event in this house. I'm sure Lucy won't mind missing it.'

Elaine turned and went out, but she left the door slightly ajar behind her. Whether from curiosity or suspicion, Lucy couldn't guess.

Jake looked at Lucy, waiting for her to begin. She cleared her throat. How should she broach this?

'You know, I think, Jake, that I was a very close friend of Suzannah's,' she said hesitantly. 'And you knew her quite well too, didn't you?'

His puppy-like openness changed instantly. His eyes narrowed with concentration as he tried to read her face, then he glanced towards the door.

'Suzannah? Is that what you wanted to talk to me about?'

'Yes, because we were so close. And I have serious questions about her death. So I wondered whether you have any theories about it.'

He dropped his voice. 'I can't possibly talk about her here. You should understand that. If you'd warned me that you wanted to come here to ask me about her, I would have said don't bother. There's nothing I want to tell you.' His voice was tight with fury now. His eyes were pale and bright.

'Then let's go somewhere else where we can talk. I'm not making judgements. I just need to know.' Lucy refused to be intimidated.

Suddenly a telephone began to ring in her briefcase, as shrill as the whine of a dentist's drill. It was the worst possible moment. Lucy thought about leaving it unanswered, then she realized she had to answer it.

Tom's voice was urgent and upset. 'Where are you Lucy? I've just heard there's been another bomb. Why didn't you ring me?'

'I'm sorry, Tom. I'm not really thinking straight. Of course I

342

should have rung. I just carried on working. It sort of kept me sane.'

'Well, I'm at home. I switched on the radio, and the first thing I heard was that a car-bomb had gone off at BriTV. They said you were safe, but I still would rather have heard about it from you.'

What could she say? He was right, of course.

'And I'm sorry, Lucy, but I've got more bad news for you.' What now? 'Your cover here's been blown, I'm afraid. A reporter from the *Daily Press* has tracked you down. He's camping outside the door now.'

'God.' That was bad news. Now she really had nowhere to hide. 'The police will be so furious with me, Tom. They insisted that nobody could know where I was.'

'Well, I should think it won't be long before a few more turn up. The world will want to talk to you. One of the neighbours must have seen you and tipped them off.' He was as irritated as she was, and frustrated not to be able to help her.

'Can't you tell them I'm not there, say you don't know where I am?'

'That's exactly what I did say. The reporter just said thanks, and settled down by the gate, obviously for the night. I can see him now. He doesn't look as if he has any intention of going away, whatever I say.'

Lucy swore to herself. How could she deal with all this? She would have to find somewhere else to stay tonight. But when, and where? The script for Saturday's show had to be written somehow this afternoon. It was going to be a difficult, dangerous script, she would need to show it to Dan in good time so that he could take it to the lawyers. Then when she'd done all that, where would she sleep? Should she find a hotel now, and leave Jake, abandon all the questions she had wanted to put to him? Things were piling up in her life and in her head. She was frightened that any moment now the load might become unmanageable.

'Thanks, Tom, for understanding,' she said to him. 'I'm so sorry I didn't tell you about the bomb. I'll have to find somewhere else to work, and spend the night. I've no idea where at the moment. Maybe I should find a hotel. I'll let you know what I decide to do.'

She put the phone back in her bag, and sighed. It was horrifying that her only sanctuary had been discovered. She felt naked, unprotected. She was completely vulnerable now.

Jake was watching her face. 'You've got problems?'

'Yes, you could say that. Pretty horrible problems. Someone keeps letting off bombs around me. I had somewhere safe to stay, but now the press have discovered that. I just don't know where to go now, or what to do.' Her eyes darted around the room, feeling the panic rising.

He tried to reassure her. 'Is there any way I can help? Anything I can do?' Seeing her so helpless, the danger that surrounded her blotted out the anger that had been surging through him.

'The most urgent thing is that I've got to find somewhere else to write this week's script,' she said. 'Your father will need to see it, and pass it to the lawyers. I can't go back to my own home – that's been wrecked. I don't want to go back to the studio, I don't feel safe there now, and I know the police would tell me to stay away. Now the reporters are staking out my friend's home, so that's no good either. I don't know what to do, where to go.' She was drifting. Life was out of control. It was a dangerous, unfamiliar feeling. She felt impatient with herself. There must be a way through this. She just had to shake herself up and think logically.

She sat with her head in her hands. Jake had never seen her like this. On screen she was in charge. He thought for a moment, then he took pity on her. 'You say you've got to show my father your script? What about going to his flat, then? I'm sure he won't mind. It's in Kensington. He lets me stay there when I have a late meeting in town. I've got the key. You could write your script there. Why don't I ring and ask him?'

She thought it through. That did sound like a possible solution. 'Thank you so much.'

Jake dialled Dan's direct line. He groaned with annoyance as the voice-mail answered, and began to speak slowly to the machine. 'Dad, it's Jake. Lucy wants to write her script at your place, if that's OK. I can let her in with my key. Ring me when you pick up this message.' He put the phone down.

'If I borrow your key, how can I get it back to you?' Lucy asked him.

'That's a point. One way would be for me to drive you up to London, let you into the flat, and leave you there.'

'That's daft. I've got a car waiting for me outside. Frank, the driver, would be happy to take me. You don't have to.'

'Well, he could drive up behind us and wait for you outside Dad's flat. That way you wouldn't be stuck.' Jake's eyes flickered. 'It would mean that we would have the chance to talk on the way up to London.'

So Jake had more to tell her about Suzannah after all.

Lucy went out to find Frank. He was parked at the kerb outside, sitting listening to his radio. 'Frank, if I drive up to London with Jake,' she said, 'can you follow us, and wait for me until I've finished the script? I'm going to work in Dan Carlton's flat. The press have found out where I'm living so I can't go back there.'

'That's fine, Miss Strong. I'll go wherever you want.'

Back in the house, she found Jake standing in the kitchen, talking to his wife. Elaine looked more strained than ever. She seemed almost unable to shake hands with Lucy as they said goodbye, and she never met Lucy's eyes. What was wrong with her? Lucy waved to the children. Most of the scarlet stains round their mouths had been wiped away now, and they were entranced by a cartoon video.

Lucy and Jake went to his car, and she climbed into the passenger's seat. The floor was littered with sweet papers, and old newspapers were piled on the backseat.

'I'm sorry about Elaine,' Jake said, reversing slowly out of the drive. His blue eyes were blank, and impossible to read. 'Elaine hates television people.'

'Why, because of Suzannah?' Might as well grasp the nettle.

'Yes.' His face in profile was tight and strained. 'Elaine never got over my friendship with Suzannah.'

'Friendship?'

'Well, what would you call it?' he asked.

An intense love affair, Mandy had called it. Lucy stayed silent, Jake answered his own question.

'I know what it felt like. It was like being run over, trampled into the ground. I was overwhelmed by her. At first it was love, I think. For both of us. Lust, too, of course. She had such energy. And I was impressed by the fame-thing, I admit. But I began to realize that although she liked going to bed with me, I didn't really impinge on her in any other way at all. I was her bit of fluff.' He laughed with self-disgust. 'It really got to me.'

'I thought men liked that. No commitment.' Her tone was light. But beneath it she felt a pang of guilt. Was that how Fred felt? Underrated? Patronized? That he had his uses in bed, but not much outside it?

'Odd, isn't it?' Jake was talking to himself now, his thin profile outlined against the dark window of the car. There were silver raindrops on the glass, the cold rain had started again. 'Women used to say they wanted to be respected. Now the roles are reversed. I'm complaining that Suzy only wanted me for my body. Stupid, that.' His mouth turned down with self-disgust.

'But your relationship lasted two years. It can't have been entirely meaningless to her,' Lucy said. She felt she had to reassure him. The contempt he was feeling for himself and Suzannah was pointless now, and destructive.

'But I put everything at stake for her – my wife, my kids, the lot. And she was just having fun with me. I was obsessed by her. I used to wait for her to ring me. My day didn't begin until I heard from her. I used to plead with her to let us spend more

346

time together. I know I talked in my sleep about her. That's how Elaine found out.'

'How did she react?'

'She was furious. And suicidal. She threatened me that she would kill herself. And kill the kids. I don't know how serious she was. I told Suzannah. She just said we'd have to be more careful. She told me to take some Mogadon to keep me quiet at night.'

No wonder Elaine had been so sullen. Perhaps she thought Lucy knew all this already. But Lucy needed to know more. She desperately wanted to understand what had happened the night Suzannah died.

'Jake,' she said, 'I've never been able to reconcile myself to Suzannah's death. She was just too competent, too much in control, to have that kind of accident on an empty road.'

She watched his fingers grip the steering wheel tightly. A muscle in his cheek spasmed, but he said nothing. She pursued him.

'Were you due to meet her that night? Where was she going?'

His voice was hard, now, sarcastic and bitter. 'Yes, I was going to meet her. I'd lied to Elaine, but I think she guessed I was on my way to Whitbury. Suzy had been planning one of her nights of passion – champagne, the lot. She rang and told me all the details. She loved all that. I'd liked it too, at the beginning. But each time I tried to talk to her about our life together, or I said maybe I should get a divorce, she'd laugh at me, or change the subject. Once she spelled it out to me. She told me that she could never marry a teacher, she would die of boredom trying to share my life. Could I imagine her at sportsday? she said.' His voice took on a sneering edge, as hers must have done. 'Or parents' evening? Could I really see her trying to show solidarity with her little hubby in front of the school? With her friends laughing at us both behind our backs?'

'At least that was honest of her. She made no promises to you.'

'It wasn't honest. It was humiliating. I meant nothing to her on any level except as convenient sex. I wanted to be with her all the time. I wanted to share everything with her. She wouldn't let me into her life at all. I wasn't nearly good enough. So that night I was going to put an end to it. She had almost destroyed me.'

There was so much passion in his voice. It was as if Lucy sitting next to him didn't exist. He was talking aloud to exorcise his hatred. That was all she could hear in his voice – bleak, sour hatred for himself, and for Suzannah. Lucy struggled in her mind. She desperately resisted his story, she longed not to believe him. This was not the easy, generous friend she had loved. But then she had never tried to possess Suzannah. There had been no jealousy in their relationship. Jake was describing an all-consuming passion. Suzannah must have seen his possessiveness, and rejected it. Their affair would have died that night if she had not been killed first.

That thought brought her up with a start. She glanced at Jake, driving steadily up the motorway. Only he had known exactly where Suzannah was heading that night, what time she had left the studios, and when she planned to arrive at Whitbury. In a way it had been convenient for Jake that Suzannah had died. Was it possible that Jake had made his own plans? That he had stood in the darkness beneath the trees, alone, waiting for her to reach the corner, and then with a simple camera flash, blinded her so that she had crashed her car? When his love had turned to hatred, did it run so deep, so corrosively in his soul? Covertly she looked at Jake, at his long thin hands on the wheel, at his nervous profile, as he sat biting his lower lip, staring fixedly out on to the road.

The silence between them was heavy. Now she felt it was threatening. Was she sitting next to Suzannah's killer, being driven through the winter rain? Her hands were cold. She felt her heart beating loudly. She folded her arms across her chest. This was absurd. She'd been shaken up so badly by the bombs, she'd begun to see murder everywhere. Jake was silent too. Only the steady headlights of Frank driving behind them comforted her. As long as he was there, surely she was safe.

Lights started to cluster along the roadside: London's sprawl had begun to surround them. Soon they were weaving their way through gathering traffic. Dan's flat was in a high, modern Kensington block.

Jake began to talk again – about his school, the children he taught there, but Lucy hardly answered. She hoped he might think she was exhausted, drained. Which was true. But the quickening in her breath was something else. She couldn't forget the way his boyishness had turned into a chill hatred. She didn't trust his charm any more. She'd seen beneath it the tricky, vulnerable man filled with resentment.

It was almost six. Still no word from Dan. They stood at the entrance to his flat, and Jake rang the doorbell. There was no reply.

'Dad must still be at work,' he said. 'We can go up and wait for him in the flat.'

Lucy saw Frank park by the kerb. She waved to him, then turned and followed Jake into the hallway. She realized that she didn't want to be alone with him in the flat. She told herself that was stupid. So many people knew she was with him. Jake hadn't attempted to cover his tracks at all. He'd left messages telling Dan where he was. Elaine knew where they both were. Frank was outside. She had no reason to worry.

They took the lift, a metal tube that quivered as it rose to the fifth floor. Jake let them into the flat, and switched on the lights. The rooms were light, bright and anonymous. In the sitting room there were papers spread on every sofa and chair. He went to a cupboard and pulled out two glasses, and a bottle of red wine.

Lucy walked restlessly round the room, then she sat down on the beige sofa. Her mind was crammed. There was so much work for her to do before tomorrow. She was deeply uneasy at

349

being alone with Jake. If her worst suspicions were true he was completely unbalanced. He'd been lacerated by his love affair with Suzannah. He could decide to take it out on her.

Somehow she had to get her script written, so that she could find refuge somewhere, be by herself again.

'Do you know where Dan's computer is?' she asked Jake.

'In his study.'

'Do you think he'd mind if I borrowed it and started writing?'

'I'm not sure, Lucy. He does all his private work there – his lectures and so on. He won't let me in there in case I rearrange things accidentally.'

'I won't touch anything, I promise. I just need a disk and a computer for an hour or two. I'm sure he'll be home in a moment, and then I can ask him. But I do need to get the script written.'

He wasn't keen, but he showed her to the study, along the corridor. She went in. The room was very dark. The curtains were drawn, and once again, there were papers strewn every-where. She looked for a lap-top. She couldn't see one. But a pinpoint of green light was on, from the monitor in a desk-top computer. Perhaps she could use that. Dan surely wouldn't mind. He'd be home any moment. She went over to the keyboard, and hit the space-bar. After a second or two, the screen came shock-ingly alive.

CHAPTER FIFTEEN

At first she couldn't work out what she was looking at. It was a jumble of words on the screen. 'BITCHBITCHBITCHBitch full of shit. Die, bitch.' What on earth was this?

She sat at the desk and scrolled down the page. Obscenity followed obscenity, each one violent and insane. Who could have done this? Not Dan, surely. She switched on a desk-lamp by the screen, and looked about her. The papers strewn everywhere were innocent enough – company memos, programme running orders. But next to the screen was a file bulging with newspaper cuttings. She opened it.

Someone had collected together the familiar pictures of Suzannah, cut out from magazines and newspapers over the last couple of years. Lucy gasped as she saw that each picture had been brutally defaced. Suzannah's face was scrawled over with ink each time it appeared, her eyes excised by a pencil, or perhaps a metal skewer. She had been blinded. With a shiver Lucy turned the pages, press cutting by press cutting, and gasped again as she reached pictures of her own face. She too had been crisscrossed with thick black ink. On some of them her limbs had been torn away. This was mad stuff, murderously psychotic. But who had done it? Could it have been Jake, the man who was waiting for her quietly outside, in the humdrum ordinariness of his father's sitting room?

She went back to the computer screen and read the jumble of words as she scrolled down. Jake's name was there, sure enough. 'FUCKLUCYDEAD. Kill kill kill bitch Lucy fucks Jake. Destroy devil. KILLBITCHTOO.'

Lucy sat back in the chair, winded. It was like a hefty kick in her stomach. She felt it as a physical pain, as the world she thought she knew collapsed about her. This was psychotic, crazy, and it must be Dan, the man she trusted and admired. All this time he had been harbouring this boiling hatred, first of Suzannah, then of her. Why? Because he felt powerless, over the programme and over his own body? Because Suzannah had taken his son, and possessed Jake, body and soul? Had Dan known about their affair? There must have been a deep flaw running through him, like a crack through a house, invisible on the surface, but growing and widening as it reached the foundations and the whole structure caved in. Did that make sense with what she knew of the man? There was so little she did know – just a bad marriage that had disintegrated long ago, no other scandal at all. Dan had seemed to be a quiet, tolerant man, with none of the tantrums or tempests that were so rife in the trade. Drugs, then? Always possible, but again, there were no signs or rumours. All she had was the evidence in front of her. And now it looked as if Dan had been intent on destroying her.

She breathed deeply, trying to exhale the horror that filled her, and looked around the office. There was a pile of new formatted disks on the desk. Automatically, she took one, slotted it into the computer, and started to transfer the file onto it. She needed her own record of this hideous outpouring. As the machine obeyed her instructions, she pulled three or four of the obscenely defaced cuttings out of the book, and slipped them into her bag. She looked carefully round the desk. What else was there to find? At first there seemed to be nothing unusual there, just the ordinary office tools: hole punchers, paperclips, fibre-tip pens, and – thicker than the pens themselves – laser pointers for Dan's lectures.

Her eyes focused on the laser pointers. There were three of them, covered with Chinese lettering. Why had Dan bought laser pens imported from China? They were easy enough to buy in Britain. She took one and put it into her bag.

The computer finished its work, she clicked the disk out of its slot and put it in the bottom of her handbag. Then, forcing herself to think clearly, step by step, she methodically switched off the computer. If Dan had shut it down himself, without his password she could never have read his vitriolic diatribe. So he must have left the machine on accidentally, never dreaming anyone else would see it. He was on his way back now. Please God he would not remember that he'd left the computer on – he mustn't suspect she had seen his secret file, or tampered with anything.

She switched off the light, put the file and the disks back exactly as she had found them, got up and went out to the sitting room to join Jake. He was reading a newspaper, and looked up at her as she came in and stood beside him. She pushed her hands into her jacket pockets to stop them shaking, and forced her voice into ordinary conversation.

'Hi, Jake, sorry to delay you, I've started planning the show, but before I begin writing, I need to make a phone call.'

'That's fine, Lucy. I'll put some coffee on.' He left the room discreetly and went into the kitchen. She pulled her mobile phone from her bag, and dialled the number for Whitbury. Her hands were clumsy with shock. Camilla answered at once.

'It's Lucy.' She was half whispering.

'My God, Lucy, how are you?' From the alarm in her voice, Camilla must have seen the news of the bomb already. 'Where are you? Are you OK?'

'Not really. That's why I'm ringing. I just wondered, may I come and stay with you? I don't know where else to go.'

'Of course. I'd be glad to have you. Come whenever you like.'

'Thank you so much.' The relief was profound. She couldn't be alone tonight. She had to find somewhere safe to digest this new horror.

As Lucy ended the conversation, she heard the front door click. She jumped, her whole body jangling with fear. Dan had let himself into the flat. She could hear him walking across the hallway towards her. Her heart started to pound, and she fought to control it. All the years she had spent in the studio, pretending to be completely calm when she knew a programme was falling off the air, when a late news story hadn't arrived or studio guest didn't turn up, at last that practice was paying off.

She made herself fiddle with the controls of the phone, as if she was looking for a number, clicking through the phone menu as Dan walked into the room. How could such a monster look so ordinary, a warm grey fleece zipped round him, his face relaxed and pleasant? Was this quiet man really concealing screams of anger in his mind? He saw her on the sofa, and stopped, shock in his eyes. His face lost colour as he stared at her.

'Lucy, what are you doing here? What's happened?'

'Dan, I'm so sorry. The press found out where I was staying. I had to move out. I didn't have anywhere else to go. Jake suggested I could come here. He let me in.'

'Jake? Why? Why were you with him?' Dan's voice cracked with suspicion.

Jake came in from the kitchen, and his father's eyes veered instantly to him.

'Hi, Dad. Lucy came to visit me this afternoon. I suggested she should come and write her script in your flat. We left a message on your phone asking if that was all right. Haven't you picked it up?'

'No, bugger the thing. I hate those phones. I switched it off. I was at a high-powered meeting Jameson arranged with the police. It lasted for hours. They're taking all these attacks on Lucy extremely seriously, quite rightly. We've had sniffer dogs in the office. They're going to put them all over the studio, the whole building, in fact. They're very nervous that this last bomb might have been an inside job, and Jameson won't let the show go ahead without every precaution being taken. I agree with him. Nobody wants to put your life at risk, or our lives for that matter.'

The bastard. Well, if he could wear a mask, so could she.

'I'm afraid I haven't got very far with planning the show.' To her amazement, Lucy's voice was easy and natural. Telling lies

354

was a valuable skill it seemed. 'I wondered if I could borrow a lap-top from you. So far I've just been making notes in long-hand.' Please God he wouldn't ask to see them.

'Sure, I'll find one for you. We can only put a rough outline of the show together this evening. We'll have to talk to the lawyers first thing tomorrow.' Good, talk of the script had distracted him.

Dan sat down on the sofa next to her. Her skin tingled with fear. Was she safe? Even though Jake was only a few metres from her across the room she was frightened of this man, this monster. The violence in him must be so near the surface, but if she hadn't seen the muck he'd spewed out on the computer screen, she could never have guessed. His voice sounded as calm and logical as it always had.

He was still talking about the programme, so she forced her-self to concentrate and listen to him. 'I'm sure we won't be able to transmit as much as we'd like to,' he said. 'The lawyers have already warned me we won't be able to implicate any of the other men in the ring without cast-iron proof. You know how rich Wilson is. Our lawyers practically need film of him in the act before they'll even contemplate naming him. It's sensitive stuff.'

Thank God, she'd taken his mind off her presence here in his flat. He mustn't find out that she had been into his office.

'What made you go and see Jake, then?' He had circled back, and although his voice was superficially light, there was a threat beneath it, like the ring of cold metal. Or maybe it was just that she could see now that the relaxed tolerance, the easy charm were a paper-thin disguise. It had been incredibly effective. But now she knew that beneath it there was poison, raw and dangerous.

Lucy didn't know how to answer his question. After a long moment of silence, Jake spoke.

'Lucy knows about Suzannah and me, Dad. She wanted to find out if I knew anything about the night Suzy died. Where she was going, whether I was meeting her, and so on.'

'What did you tell her?' The tone was still light. Dan was giving nothing away.

'There was very little to tell. I told her the truth. I said it had all gone bad between us. I said I was going to break it off, but I didn't get the opportunity.'

Lucy watched them carefully. If they both turned against her, she would be in grave danger. But for a moment she was almost forgotten – they were so intensely furious with each other. Jake's affair had angered Dan so deeply that he couldn't meet his son's eyes. The atmosphere between the two men was charged and heavy. This must have been a very old argument.

Lucy broke through their silence. 'I'm sorry, Dan. I would have told you I was going to visit Jake, only I wasn't sure you knew what was going on between him and Suzannah. I only just found out myself. She kept it very quiet.'

'Not quiet enough. Elaine found out. Jake nearly wrecked his whole life, his marriage, everything,' Dan said coldly. 'He's been a complete fool. He knows how I feel.'

Was that part of the reason why Dan had loathed Suzannah so much? Jake turned on his heel. 'I'm not going over this again, Dad. I'm leaving.' He walked quickly out of the door, and across the hallway. She was suddenly alone with Dan.

'I'll fetch my lap-top for you.' As he got up from the sofa his voice was warm, concerned to help her. She tried to smile gratefully at him. But would he have to go into his office to find the lap-top? Would he see that she had taken the laser pointer, or notice that one of his disks had gone? She felt paralysed as she watched him walk towards the door. But he didn't leave the room. Instead he went to the corner where a computer was stowed on a bookshelf, and brought it back to her. Looking down to hide her relief, she pulled her notebook out of her bag while he cabled up the lap-top, and by the time he came back to her side she had filled a page with notes.

'How would you like to begin?' Dan asked. He moved closer to her on the sofa. Her skin crawled. She longed to run, to put as much distance between them as she could. But she had no choice now. She had to lie, and be sweet and friendly, to keep him unsuspicious and contented. She began to type busily, copying her notes into the machine, then she sighed and stretched her legs. 'Will you forgive me, Dan, if I take your lap-top away with me and carry on planning the shape of the show by myself this evening? I feel exhausted now. It's been a horrible day. I think maybe I need a drink and a hot bath.'

'I could offer you both here.'

She made sure the wince she felt was invisible and put her hand on his arm. No one would ever know the courage that took her. 'You are kind, Dan. I do feel safe here with you. But I'm going home now.'

'Home?'

She couldn't possibly tell him where she was going. That would put Camilla in danger too. 'The police have found a place for me to stay. They've put me under their protection now.'

'Excellent.' He put his lap-top into its case, she put on her coat and slung the case over her shoulder. Dan walked her solicitously to the door, and then down in the lift, and out of the front door of the block. He walked out onto the pavement first, checking carefully to make sure nobody was watching or waiting for her. There he stopped and turned to her. Lucy forced herself to brush his cheek with her lips. As he held her, she realized that he could feel the panic rising in her. She tried to smile, and he put his arm tightly round her.

'Take it easy, sweetheart. Make yourself a big drink, have a foamy bath, relax. We need you bright-eyed and clear-headed for the show.'

She walked away from him to the kerb. Every inch of her spine could feel him watching her. Frank, parked a few cars down in the BMW, saw her, and flicked on his headlights. She ran towards him, and he opened the passenger door for her. She waved to Dan, who was still looking after her from the door of the apartment block, then she fell back against the leather seat next to Frank and pulled the seat belt tightly around her. Now, at last, she was safe.

'I'm going to Whitbury, Frank,' she told him.

'Right, Miss Strong.'

As they drove through the darkness and her fear subsided, she felt anger beginning to rise inside her. She welcomed it. Anger would help her, it would energize and focus her. Dan was the enemy. He was the one she had to vanquish. As the pieces of the jigsaw fell into place in her mind, her anger grew. He had known about Jake after all. Perhaps he had known that Suzannah was planning a night of passion with him. He had left the studio before her, and stood at the dark corner of the road, waiting for the car he knew so well to approach at speed towards him. Perhaps he had practised other nights, until he got the timing just right.

The minutes ticked by as she stared into the darkness. Suddenly she blinked and shivered. Frank was approaching that same bend now. She watched it go by, with its poignant little bunches of flowers, seeing Dan standing there in her mind's eye. What was he holding? A camera? Or had he run out into the road to distract Suzannah? How had he stage-managed her death so neatly that the police were sure it was an accident?

It was eleven before they reached Whitbury, and turned down the long drive. Camilla took one look at Lucy, and led her up the broad oak staircase to a chintz-filled room on the first floor. Lucy had last stayed there with Tom. She would have loved his arms around her tonight, but now she had only her consuming anger to keep her company. The bedroom was sweetened with the scent of hyacinths, from a large bowl at the foot of the bed. The bathroom was enticing. She had no luggage to unpack, she could just bathe and roll into bed. Camilla had laid out a black satin dressing gown, one of Suzannah's. The hot water round Lucy's body was as hypnotic as a lullaby. She lay in the big, soft bed, staring into the darkness. As her body relaxed into sleep, unanswered questions impaled her mind, like a forest of nails.

She woke with a gasp at half-past eight. Camilla was pulling aside the curtains, and through them Lucy could see that the garden was filled with silvery winter sunshine. The sky was palest rose pink, the light slanting across the frosty lawn and through the mist that clung to the branches of the trees. Camilla balanced a tray on the end of the bed, with two big cups of tea, and a plate of toast and marmalade.

'You were as pale as death last night,' she said to Lucy. 'I was worried about you. No wonder, with bombs going off all round you. What are the police doing?'

'Their best, I think.' Lucy took a gulp of hot tea. Now she was awake, the anger mounting inside her had hardened into cold fury. Suzannah deserved revenge. Lucy would make sure she got it. But that was something she couldn't share with Camilla. Not yet, at any rate. There were other mysteries that Camilla could help her with, though.

Lucy leaned back against the pillows. 'I had such happy times with your mother in this house,' she said. 'I still miss her so much.'

'Of course you do.' Camilla's eyes were soft as she remembered. 'We all do. She had faults. Everyone has faults. But she was unique.'

Lucy had to know the truth. 'Do you have happy memories of her, Camilla? I've been told you and your mum had real problems I knew nothing about. Do you think she was a bad mother?'

Camilla looked up sharply, resenting the question. Then she gave Lucy the benefit of the doubt. This was her mother's closest friend. 'Mum was driven. She was tough. You know that. But I can see now that in her way she wanted the best for me. It's just that her work always came first.' There was no resentment in her voice, or sourness. At least for the moment she seemed to have reached a place where she could accept her mother for what she was, for her strengths and her weaknesses.

'I had to come to terms with her job,' Camilla said, 'her fame, the hours she worked, all that. And I don't know that I blame her for it – not now, anyway. It was just the way she was made. A lot of men are made like that, and nobody blames them for it.'

Lucy watched the sun stretching across the carpet. In her memory she heard echoes of Suzannah's laughter in the corridor, full-throated, infectious. But behind it the tears of a child, Camilla's tears.

'Was she there to comfort you when you needed her?'

Camilla tugged at the sleeve of her dressing gown, covering the scars Lucy knew ran like twisted ropes across her wrists.

'Not always. I had some very unhappy times alone. But I survived, and in a way it's made me independent, made me think for myself. Made me determined not to repeat her mistakes.'

So she had forgiven her mother. Others were less forgiving. 'I was talking to Alex and Marion about her,' Lucy said. 'At the wake, they told me things I didn't want to hear.'

'Because?'

'Because they were unpleasant stories about Suzannah.'

Camilla said nothing, waiting.

Lucy hesitated. It was like bringing out a catalogue of disloyalties. But she persevered. 'They said one night they'd brought some work down here for her, and she'd sent them straight back without a word of praise, not even a cup of tea. I told them she was never like that with me.'

'There may have been reasons.'

'What reasons?'

'I guess that happened at a difficult time, a time when I had problems of my own. I think I remember that night.' Camilla tugged at her sleeve again. 'Dad and Mum had just found me cutting myself. That time it was serious. They were petrified. Dad was on the phone to the doctor. They were frightened I

360

might lose too much blood. That's when Alex and Marion arrived. I remember Mum frantically trying to get rid of them. She took them out into the hall and roared at them, so they wouldn't hang around and see me.'

Lucy looked at Camilla with dawning relief. That made sense. Suzannah could never have explained her loss of temper to Alex or Marion without betraying Camilla's confidence. That's why she had manufactured the scene. But there was more Lucy had to know. 'I've been talking to Jake Carlton as well.'

'Oh yes?' Now there was contempt in Camilla's voice. If Camilla had known of the affair, she definitely didn't approve of it.

'He's very angry with your mother, still. He says she despised him and used him.'

'He would.'

'Why do you say that?'

'Because he's such a wimp.'

That was a tough judgement. Like mother like daughter.

Camilla read Lucy's mind. 'Oh, I'm not saying Mum treated him well. She should never have gone to bed with Jake in the first place. She always told me you should fight your own weight, and she was way out of his class. But he's quite pretty, in an ink-stained sort of way. And he did follow her around, practically begging for it. So they had fun together for a couple of years.'

Camilla stood up, and walked to the dressing table. She sat facing Lucy, who lay propped up on the pillows, toast uneaten, absorbed by what she was hearing.

'But in the end it was clear that Jake had totally lost his wits over Mum, and she realized she had to stop him before too many people got hurt. It wasn't easy. She was fond of him, in her way. But the fun wasn't worth the damage. So she tried to let him down lightly, but he clung on and on. She tried being nice, she tried being nasty. On her last night I know she was going to get him down here so they could have a final night together. She was looking forward to it. Then the plan was that she'd explain why they had to stop seeing each other. But, of course, she never got here, so the chance never came.'

So that was why Suzannah had sneered at Jake's job, and told him she could never marry a boring teacher. Cruel to be kind, and it had almost worked.

When Camilla had gone, Lucy pushed back the bedclothes and stood up. That glint of happiness on Suzannah's face at the end of her last show must have been pleasure at the knowledge of the night ahead with Jake. Would she really have been tough enough to let him go the next morning? Could he have stopped seeing her? Who could say where the truth lay? Was there ever one truth? Death brings with it so many complications, so many different histories, such contrasting and contradictory memories, there was no point asking any more questions. The friend she knew, the friend whose memory she treasured, was the friend she would avenge.

She dressed quickly, and went down to find Camilla in the kitchen. 'May I work in your mother's study?' she asked.

'Of course. You won't be disturbed there.'

She went to the desk she remembered so well, still with the pens and paper perfectly arranged, the family photographs at either end. Camilla had left it untouched. Lucy got out Dan's laser pointer, its thick barrel covered with Chinese characters, and turned it in her hand. Why would Dan want something so obscure, so difficult to get hold of? She called up her favourite search engine, 'Google', on the internet, and punched in 'Laser pointer'. In minutes she had found what she needed. There was the answer, the facts she had been looking for were laid out clearly and precisely. She printed them out. Then she sat for half an hour, looking out of the window without seeing the terrace with its crumpled winter roses. The jigsaw was complete. Now she must work out how best to use it.

She would need a temporary home, just until the end of the week. Whitbury would be ideal, practically, and emotionally. When she asked, Camilla agreed without hesitation. She would still need Frank to drive her, for her own protection. David Jameson seemed pleased when she asked for him, and the police approved. The further she was from her home in London and her office in the BriTV studios, the better pleased they all were. Dan and the team could easily communicate with her at Whitbury by mobile and e-mail. If they were curious as to her whereabouts, they understood why she couldn't tell them. She told nobody where she was. Not Tom, not Fred. Nobody.

The days passed, strung tightly together, like the final week before a heavyweight boxing match. She was in training. So much was at stake, she must be absolutely ready for anything. This was a fight she had to win.

The team sent her their research on Parks as they uncovered it piece by piece. She sorted through the background cuttings they e-mailed her, and the pictures. In the evening she made phone calls to ensure that her friends would be in the studio on Saturday night to support her. Tom agreed to come. She rang Jake. Reluctantly, he too agreed. So did the policemen, Johnson and Ash. They wanted to be certain that the pictures they had released to her were going to be used in a proper context. Janet Lake accepted with alacrity, especially when Lucy promised her an exclusive story. Meanwhile, Lucy built her dossier, step by careful step.

On Friday she sat in the study at Whitbury and scripted the Parks programme. She looked at Suzannah's picture before she started to type – the smiling family photograph on the desk – and tried to draw some of her friend's strength from it.

'Come on, Suzannah, I really need you now.' She spoke the words out loud, almost like a prayer. If only Suzannah could help her strike the right note, without the hysteria of a witch-hunt, or the pomposity of a crusade.

She would begin by mourning the suicide of Lord Parks, a politician who had skilfully captured the public mood, and encapsulated the public prejudices. Gradually, as she wrote, she implied more doubt. Was this man as sincere as we all thought?

363

she asked. Were his own hands as clean as he liked to pretend? She stopped writing when she came to the most difficult moment in the script, the pictures of Parks with the child. They were the bombshell. How far would the lawyers allow her to tell what she knew?

Max had rung her on her mobile the previous day, but the news he brought was frustrating and disappointing. Each boy he had spoken to was adamant. None of them would agree to be interviewed, to support his story. And then on Friday Max came to his own decision. He rang her at midday. His voice was flat.

'Sorry, Lucy. I won't speak to you on camera. If the others won't talk, I can't.'

She had prepared herself for this, but still she tried to persuade him. 'We can disguise you, Max. We can blot out your face, and distort your voice. We'll protect you.'

'I know that. We all know that. I've said all that to the others. They still don't want to know.' He was suddenly decisive. 'I can't do it alone.'

'Could I persuade them?'

'Not a chance. They refuse to meet you again. They say they want nothing to do with your programme. They think if they come anywhere near you, Wilson will track them down, and silence them for good. They want to disappear completely so he'll never find them again. I can't say I blame them.' She heard the finality in his voice. There was no point arguing further.

'If that's your decision, Max, so be it.'

She nerved herself to ring Dan and told him. He groaned. 'That's that, then. If we don't get at least three boys to support each other's stories, the lawyers say we can't refer to the paedophile ring at all. They're adamant. Even if you had persuaded Max to talk to us on his own, if it got to court he'd be outnumbered and outgunned. We'd get sued to hell and back. We'd go down for millions. It can't be done.'

So the pictures were their only case, and Lord Parks their

only target. No other men could be named. She could never describe how they had passed the children between them. The viciousness and violence of their crime would go unpunished.

Lucy wrote on. She appealed for someone to come forward who might know the boy in the pictures. The graphic artists in the studio had magnified the close-ups of the bed and the bed-clothes. The viewers would not be able to see the child's frightened face, his glazed, drugged eyes. The camera would zoom in to see the scar beside his ear. To protect the boy, they would blot out the rest of the picture, so as not to show anything indecent, or explicit. But the viewers would certainly see the signet ring on Parks' hand, and understand its significance.

As Lucy wrote, day became evening. She e-mailed the pages of script to her office one by one as she wrote them. By six o'clock she had finished the script, and Dan sent her a message.

'Great stuff, Lucy. You've done it. The lawyers are happy. See you tomorrow. Have a good rest.'

She stood up, walked to the kitchen and made herself a cup of strong coffee. Then she went back to the study and started again. Now she could tell her own story. Now she would take the revenge she craved, for Suzannah and for herself. She could feel her friend reading it over her shoulder, urging her on. The words flew from her fingers onto the screen. Now and again she'd stand and look round Suzannnah's study, stretching her cramped mind and body. This was the challenge of her life. She would only have one chance.

It was past midnight before she finished the script, transferred it to disk, and turned off the machine. She walked to her room in a daze of tiredness. Camilla had long gone to bed. Lucy stood by her window and looked out on the dark garden. There were stars spangled over the clear, cold night sky. If Suzannah's soul was out there somewhere, Lucy hoped she approved.

CHAPTER SIXTEEN

Sooner than she could have believed, Lucy woke again. She switched on a light, turned to see the time on the clock by her bed, and felt a shiver of fear. Seven o'clock. Today was the day. Today it would all be resolved, one way or another. She dressed and packed, took Suzannah's briefcase from beside the desk, and pushed her files into it, with the disk, the folder of pictures and newspaper cuttings, and the laser pointer. Perhaps from tonight onwards she would be able to live normally again.

Frank was waiting by his car in the courtyard. Camilla hugged Lucy as she said goodbye, and drove to the studios. The countryside, bare trees drawn in charcoal, edged with silver frost, looked like a wintry bride's bouquet. She saw none of it. Her mind had concentrated down to the tiniest minutiae, like needle-point embroidery, checking and rechecking her plans for the day ahead. Frank drove her up to the studio entrance, where there were twice the usual number of security men waiting to check her in. They gave her a swipe card for her dressing room. She went straight to it, and pushed her briefcase to the back of the wardrobe there.

There was a gentle knock at the door. She opened it cautiously to find Lesley standing there, her arms full of flowers – crimson roses and lilies, their big white blooms streaked with pink and gold. Her voice was bright and matter of fact.

'These are for you, darling, to cheer you up. It's been a god-awful week for us all. This place is crawling with police and sniffer dogs. Let's hope they get the bastard soon, whoever he is. They've been all over this room already. I don't know what they're sniffing for, but I can smell them.' She took an air-freshener out of her bag, and sprayed it lavishly around the room. 'Have you seen tonight's dress?' she asked. 'Are you happy with it?'

'It's perfect.' The dress must be hanging in her wardrobe, but she hadn't given it a thought. Seeing that Lucy was absorbed, Lesley asked no further questions. She pushed the flowers into a vase in front of the mirror, hugged her and left.

There was still twenty minutes before rehearsals were due to begin. Lucy picked up the internal phone and dialled David Jameson's number. His PA put her through to him immediately.

'David, I need to speak to you. I'm in my dressing room. Could you find Shirley too?'

Five minutes later he strode into the room, with Shirley in his wake. Suddenly the small room seemed claustrophobically over-crowded. Lucy talked quietly to them, building her case. They were silent with disbelief. She showed them her evidence, the pictures, and the laser pointer. She explained what she wanted to do. When she finished, Jameson sat silent, brow furrowed, utterly shocked. He shook his head.

'David, I think Lucy should go with this,' Shirley said slowly. 'Suzannah would want her to.'

Jameson stood, and stretched like a dog shaking off pond water. 'I can't believe I've known this man so long, and yet all that time I knew nothing about him. It's a horrifying story, Lucy,' he said. 'My instinct is to go with it, as Shirley says. I've got to put it through our lawyers, though. Have you got a script? I can't let you say any of this without a legal check.'

She went to the wardrobe and pulled out the script she had spent all last night writing. He read it carefully, with Shirley leaning over his shoulder. He whistled to himself. Then he looked up at her. 'This is quite something. Are you sure you can carry it off?'

'I'm sure.'

Was she really? But she couldn't afford to question herself now, or to have doubts. The scaffolding of determination and anger holding her together would only last another few hours. Then she knew she was in danger of collapse.

Rehearsals started. As she walked into the studio, she saw Fred. It was like a shock of cold water, reminding her of another life. How could she have forgotten him so completely? He was standing by a camera and she saw his face brighten as she walked towards him. She kissed him on the cheek, but he pulled her towards him, and put his arms around her.

'How are you, Lucy? Why haven't you rung me? What's been going on?'

She extricated herself as gently as she could. She could feel his disappointment, but she had no time now to reassure him.

'I'm so sorry, Fred,' she said, knowing the apology would never bridge the gap between them. 'There's been too much going on. Let's talk later.'

'Fine.' His pride was hurt: he needed far more than that. But right now she had nothing more to give him. He retreated behind his camera. Dan came onto the studio floor and Lucy watched him steadily as he acted the role he was so used to. He was relaxed, smiling and in command. The disguise was perfect. No wonder she had never suspected the man beneath it.

He walked to the centre of the set.

'Let's have some quiet, now. This is going to be a difficult show tonight. Not our usual mix. But we all believe it must be said. So let's start rehearsing the script now, from the top.'

He went to his usual seat at the control desk at the side of the studio, where he could see the output of every camera and talk directly to the director in the gallery upstairs. Lucy straightened her shoulders and followed him. She forced brightness into her voice.

'Dan, as this is such a different show, do you think I could lose my big entrance? Would it be all right just to find me already in my seat at the top of the show? I think I'd be more comfortable.' Would he think that odd?

He thought about it. 'I know it's going to be a hard-hitting programme. The show business instinct in me always likes a dramatic start to the show, but maybe you're right. If that's the way you think it will work best, Lucy, I'm happy to go with that.'

She'd got away with it. He talked quietly into the microphone on his desk, explaining their decision to the team in the gallery. Michael, the director, began to reposition the cameras for this new opening.

Lucy went to her seat, and the Parks script she had wrestled with so long began to unroll across the screen. As Lucy read it aloud, Tina, the Autocue operator, followed with her usual precision. The pictures of Parks with the child came up on cue, producing a gasp of horror from the studio crew. They were well aware of the inflammatory material they were about to broadcast.

At lunch break, Lucy went over to Tina. 'Can you stay behind with me, for a moment, Tina? There are some changes I'd like to make.'

Dan called to her from his desk. 'Coming to the bar with us, Lucy?'

She made certain her voice was as light and casual as his. 'Yes, sure. I'll be with you in a minute. I just want to put a few more commas and full stops into the script. It's a very long read.'

'Fine, we'll see you there.'

Tina's Autocue machine was beside the scene dock, a cavernous storeroom, filled with a jumble of cages crammed with props, and stacks of chairs. Lucy took Tina to the back of the store, pulled out two chairs, and gestured to Tina to sit down next to her.

'I'm going to ask you, Tina, to keep this absolutely confidential.' She took a disk out of Suzannah's briefcase. 'Can you put this on Autocue for me? It's the revised script for tonight.'

Tina took it from her. Just then, two people came into the scene dock, but stopped by the door. Lucy peered round the stack of furniture to see who it was. She saw Fred with Nina, a new young floor assistant. Nina was red-haired, pretty and self-conscious, about twenty years old, with dusty jeans, and flushed cheeks. Fred pulled her towards him, his hand moving down from her waist. Nina giggled, and stayed in his embrace. He leaned forward to whisper in her ear. He was incorrigible.

Lucy decided she'd better interrupt now, before it became too embarrassing for everyone. She stood up, clear of the pile of chairs. Fred caught the movement behind the girl's shoulder, and his face froze when he realized who it was. Then he saw that Lucy was smiling. His arms dropped from Nina's body, and he whispered to her again. She nodded, and walked away. She hadn't seen Lucy.

Fred mouthed, 'Sorry, darling.'

Lucy shook her head, smiled again and mouthed back to him, 'No problem.' He turned awkwardly, and left.

She went back to Tina. The last twinge of guilt had left her. No point worrying about Fred. She didn't need him and, quite obviously, he didn't need her either.

Lucy ran to her dressing room to put Suzannah's briefcase safely away, then she joined the rest of the team in the bar. It was late for lunch, but she wasn't hungry and she easily turned down the offer of reheated pasta. If she was silent while the others chattered, nobody was surprised. They were used to it on programme day. When she had a heavy show ahead of her, as the day wore on her mind always focused on the script and interviews until they were imprinted on her brain.

After lunch they went back to the studio to rehearse the second half of the show. They had already prepackaged it. The team had put together a film biography of Lord Parks, inter-cut with headlines and interviews from the major cases of child abuse that hit the headlines during his career. He had been noisy and voluble each time it happened, castigating the police and his political opponents for their failure to protect children. It made ironic viewing now.

Lucy didn't stay in the studio to watch their film. She went back to her dressing room. Once she was made-up she told the team she needed time to be by herself, to collect her thoughts. Tactfully, they left her alone.

Her dresser, Sue, helped her put on the dress Lesley had designed for her, then she left. The black lace was simple, uncomplicated, and she turned back and forth in front of the mirror, registering how beautifully it was cut. She could relax now. She found a pair of elegant black court shoes in the wardrobe, and a plain silver necklace laid out in front of the mirror. She put them on. Then she reached into Suzannah's briefcase and took out the props she would need for the programme: the file of pictures, and the laser pointer. She sat quietly in her chair, practising the script over and over again in her head. She would not have the chance to rehearse it. Only when the show broadcast live would she, or anyone else, hear the words she had put together with so much passionate care.

There was knock on the dressing-room door, and she went to answer it. Dan was standing there. He looked concerned, and sympathetic.

'How are you feeling?' he asked. 'Are you OK?'

She tried to find words to answer him, but she failed. She held the door half closed, tightly against her body to prevent him seeing past her into the room, but he motioned to her to let him in. She couldn't find a way to refuse. Panic rose in her as he walked past her and into the room.

'Nice flowers,' he said. 'Who are they from?'

'Lesley,' she said, trying to steady her voice. 'She's such a friend.'

But his eyes had dropped to the laser pointer on the desk, with its giveaway Chinese lettering.

'Where on earth did you get that, Lucy?'

There was only one possible answer. Dan didn't need her to tell him. His face contorted. Suddenly he looked like a hungry dog snapping at its prey. She took a step back. The real man was looking at her now, the easy, affable mask torn from him. Instead there was a man who would not hesitate to attack her. He'd done it before. As he took a step towards her, behind him there came another knock on the open door. He stopped, and Lucy looked over Dan's shoulder.

371

'Thank you, Quentin.'

'The audience are almost in, now, Lucy.' Quentin, the floor manager, was standing on the threshold. He couldn't see Dan's face, and his tone was cheerful and businesslike. 'Do you want to come to the studio with me?'

She did. She quickly picked up the file and the laser pointer, and almost ran to join Quentin, brushing past Dan's shoulder. He turned as if to hit her, his hands were clenched.

'We'll talk later,' he said, his eyes red with fury. She didn't reply.

Quentin led her to the studio, and stood beside her in the wings. Together they watched the last of the audience arrive, her friends finding their reserved seats near the front. Tom was there, and he'd brought Camilla with him. The two policemen, Johnson and Ash, were sitting together in the front row, at one end, where the cameras could not see them. Max was out of sight of the lenses too, in the back row, looking pale and anxious. It was a risk for him to come to the studio, but he was determined not to miss the show.

As the last stragglers in the audience sat down, Quentin turned to her. 'Ready, Lucy?'

She nodded.

'Good luck,' he said automatically.

Today she would need all the luck she could get.

From the wings she watched Dan take up his position at his desk at the side of the set. She could see his face, but now it was completely expressionless. God, what control he had, like a strait-jacket binding and controlling his violence. The warm-up finished, and Quentin introduced her. 'Ladies and gentlemen, the star of the show, please welcome Lucy Strong.' Music played. She walked forward to speak to them.

'This is an important night for me, ladies and gentlemen, a very special show. I will need your help.' Her eyes moved over the faces of her friends. Janet had arrived late, and was sitting with her voluminous bag on her knee. There was a tape recorder in it, so that she wouldn't miss a word. Good.

Now there was a minute to go. Lucy walked to her chair in the centre of the set, and arranged her props carefully beside her on the desk. Quentin counted the seconds backwards from ten. She was alone now. No other guests would be there to support her tonight. As the film titles rolled, Tina hit her computer controls, and the script slid in front of the lens. Up in the gallery, David Jameson walked into the gallery and sat centrally behind Michael, the studio director. Michael looked round, astonished. This was new. The boss usually watched from his office, or his home. Shirley had come into the gallery with Jameson, and she sat down in the chair next to Michael. She laid a hand on his arm. 'Don't worry, love, just follow the action. Lucy's been working on a new script.'

Lucy glanced at Dan sitting at his desk. His face was tense and angry. But in the glare of the lights, surrounded by cameras, there was nothing he could do. Here, where Lucy was most exposed, she was safe, for the moment.

The titles ended. The audience applauded, then the sound dwindled as Lucy turned to the camera. They were live, on the air.

'Good evening,' she said. 'Thank you for joining us. Tonight we have a special show for you. We have a story to tell which may disturb you, but which we believe must be told. You will have heard of the death this week of Lord Parks, the former Home Secretary,' she went on. 'You may have seen him here, on this show, in this studio, when he talked to me about his life.' They played a clip from the show. Parks looked ebullient, and cheerful. As it ended, Lucy picked up that thought. 'Why should such a successful man want to take his own life? We think we may have the answer.'

She moved the story away from Parks, and on to another, different tragedy, one that the audience already knew about: the bomb that had killed so many boys at Thritham. Lucy explained the connection. 'A boy at that party gave me some pictures which may explain the riddle of Lord Parks' death,' she said.

373

The pictures filled the huge screen behind her as she described each one to the viewers.

'The first picture as you can see is simple enough, it's the late Lord Parks enjoying a drink.' The shot changed. 'But now look at the next one. We have blanked out most of it to protect the child, because it shows a boy of about twelve in the act of being abused. The police urgently need to find this child, and the men who did this to him. Perhaps you can help us track them down. Look now at the close-ups we have taken of the bed, and the bedclothes. Do you recognize them? If you do, the police would like to hear from you. You may be able to protect this child from more suffering.'

The picture changed again. 'But what about the man who is holding the boy down?' Lucy asked. The audience in the studio were completely silent, watching. 'This is a close-up of the man's hand. Look at that unusual ring. Now compare it with the close-up we've taken from the first picture of Lord Parks. It's the same ring. And here's another close-up from our own show, last week. Once again, Lord Parks was wearing the same ring. In fact it's a signet ring with his family crest. You can see it has a cherub on it. He designed it himself. Which means we can now identify the man abusing this boy. It was Parks himself.'

Now, at last, the audience stirred with comprehension, and shock.

But there was more. Lucy continued, 'Lord Parks knew we had these pictures. I met him earlier this week and told him so. I also revealed to him that we had given these pictures to the police. So, I believe that may well be the reason Lord Parks committed suicide the next day. He knew what was ahead of him. Disgrace and imprisonment, and justice for the children he hurt so badly.'

There was a collective sigh from the audience. This was almost too much for them to absorb. Lord Parks, that sturdy likeable character, the successful politician never off the screen or out of the headlines – could he really have been leading a double life? Was he responsible for such appalling crimes against children? While they struggled to accept what she had told them, Lucy carried on.

'The police would like the child in this picture to come forward, or anyone who knows him, or where he might be found. He desperately needs help. They believe more children may still be at risk. Lord Parks was not alone in this abuse. Someone else was there, taking these pictures. We need to find all the people involved in this crime if we are to protect other children.' That was as much as the lawyer would allow her to say. But perhaps it would be enough.

She took a deep breath. Tina hit a switch on the Autocue computer, and the new script unravelled before her eyes. She had never rehearsed it, but it must be word perfect. She owed that to Suzannah.

'Now I come to another report, and this time it's one that touches me personally.'

There was a babble of consternation in the gallery. Michael swung round in his chair. 'Where's she going now? Why isn't she linking into the Parks film package?' Shirley put her hand on his arm reassuringly. 'Stay with her, Michael. David and I have seen the new script. Just follow the words.'

Lucy was still talking steadily her fingernails pressed into her palms to help her stifle her own emotions. Above all, she must not break down. 'As you know, this programme was until very recently presented by Suzannah Piper. She was a dear friend of mine, and I know many of you felt the same. She was a consummate broadcaster, and she had friends all over the country. But one person hated her. He hated her with such venom that he killed her. Tonight I want to tell you how he did it.'

She glanced at Dan, sitting at his desk. His face had lost its impassivity: it was ugly now.

He spoke urgently into his microphone. 'Lucy's gone mad.

She's way off script. Tell Presentation to take us off the air, Michael. Now.'

But up in the control room, David Jameson shook his head. Shirley's voice was calm. 'Stay with it, Michael. Follow the action.'

Dan heard their voices overruling him in his earpiece, and he rose to his feet. But Quentin was next to him now, blocking his way, and the two policemen were walking towards him from their seats in the front row. He turned round in a panic, but the audience was behind him, the cameras were in front of him, there was nowhere to go. Now the policemen had reached him and were standing either side of him. Lucy watched him as he slowly sat down again, he had to listen to her. At last it could be told. It was time.

'Suzannah died driving home from the last show she ever presented. It was late at night. It was raining. She skidded on a corner, lost control of her car, and crashed into a tree. You will remember the stories in the papers at the time. Everyone thought it was a tragic accident.' Lucy picked up a newspaper front page from the desk. The camera zoomed in to the photograph of Suzannah's mangled car. It was clear that nobody could have lived through that crash.

'But why did she lose control?' Lucy asked. 'It was a journey she had made a thousand times. She knew every inch of the road. There was no other car involved. Some people speculated that she might have had a heart attack, but her post mortem revealed that she was in excellent health. So why did it happen?'

She dared not look at Jake, or Camilla, sitting in the middle of the audience. This would be an unbearable shock to both of them. Perhaps they wouldn't forgive her for it.

'Most people thought she must have fallen asleep at the wheel, maybe just for an instant. Long enough to make her wake suddenly and twist her steering wheel so that the car spun out of control and hit a tree. I too believed that must have been the answer. Until I found some letters. These were in Suzannah's desk.' She laid them out so that the camera could focus on them. 'And these were pushed through my door.' She put them next to the first, so that the audience could see them all, side by side. 'As you see, they are crude, and threatening. And all written by the same hand.'

The audience were utterly still. Janet Lake had found her tape recorder in her handbag, and was holding the microphone over her head. She mustn't miss a syllable.

Lucy leaned over and picked up her file. 'A couple of days ago, I made some more discoveries I want to share with you.' She pulled out the pictures and the print-out from Dan's computer, and put them carefully down on the desk next to her, angled so that the cameras could see them clearly. 'I was working at a computer in another office. I found an extraordinary piece of evidence there.'

Reading the obscene threats, seeing the brutalized pictures, the audience murmured in horror. Lucy let the cameras roam over them slowly. Then she went on. 'Who was responsible for all this violent filth, these threats against Suzannah? A mad stalker? A deeply disturbed viewer? No. Someone very much closer to home.'

'Who?' Michael barked out the question.

'Dan,' Shirley told him quietly.

'Three and Five, go to Dan,' he instructed, and instantly they were there. As the cameras found him, Dan's face was frozen in a new, savage mask, his mouth twisted with anger, his eyes fixed on Lucy. Still he did not move.

'I found all this in the office belonging to the executive producer of this show, Dan Carlton.' His face came up on all the screens in the studio. The audience murmured, and pointed to him sitting in front of them. Lucy went on.

'But how did he do it? How did he kill Suzannah? I discovered the answer in his office. Along with the threats and the pictures, on his desk I found this.' She picked up the laser pointer. A camera showed it in big close-up. 'This is a laser

377

used by lecturers when they want to point out a detail on a picture. The highly concentrated beam will pick it out. Vandals have caused accidents with these laser pointers in the past. You may have read about them.' She put cuttings on the desk near the pointer, where the camera could find them.

'Train drivers have been momentarily blinded with lasers like this, and bus drivers have too. It's so dangerous that there are regulations in this country limiting the power of the laser beam.' She turned the pointer, so that the Chinese characters showed. 'But this was not made in this country. This is imported from China, and its beam is twenty times more powerful than any pointers which are legally permitted here. Why did Dan need such a powerful beam? Not for a lecture. But as Suzannah drove home, when she reached the bend in the road, Dan must have been standing there, invisible in the darkness. When her car was almost upon him, he shone the laser at her windscreen. The beam is intensely powerful. It would have refracted on her windscreen, so that it didn't just blind her for that moment, it would have made the whole screen opaque. She swung the steering wheel to avoid the painful beam of light, then turned it again as she felt the car skid out of control, and she hit a tree with such violence that she was crushed. She died instantly. And Dan? What did you do then, Dan?'

He stared at her. Still he said nothing.

'Murder can be addictive, it seems. Suzannah was dead, but I was interviewed by the papers, and I said I thought she had been killed. So someone drove a car at me, straight at me, perhaps to kill me, maybe just to warn me to mind my own business. Was that you, Dan? Then the bosses decided I should present this programme in Suzannah's place.' She picked up the pages she had printed from Dan's computer. 'This rambling hymn of hatred I found in Dan's desk shows how much he loathed and resented me, as much as Suzannah.'

The cameras showed the reams of print, dotted and speckled with capital letters and underlining. Then they cut to Dan's face in close-up. Forced to listen to her, he couldn't avoid the truth any more. Lucy did not spare him.

'We had unmanned him, Suzannah and I. Professionally he was hand-cuffed to us, but he was too weak to control us. He came to hate us both. At first he thought the way to impose his power over us would be to frighten us. He wrote threatening letters to both of us. But threats alone didn't work. After he killed Suzannah, the mad diary he'd been secretly keeping shows how triumphant he was at getting away with it.

'But then I was quoted in the newspapers asking questions about her death. Not because I suspected him – I didn't. But because it just didn't make sense to me that she should die like that, for no reason. So he tried to kill me too. Conveniently for him, there had already been one petrol bomb, the one that caused that lethal fire in Thritham. So when more bombs were aimed at me, I thought someone connected to Wantage Grange School was trying to stop me discovering more.

'I was quite wrong. And because I never suspected how close to home they were – the petrol bomb that wrecked my house, and the car-bomb this week that I was extremely lucky to survive – both of them nearly hit their target. They were Dan's work, and you can see here how he rages that I was still alive and he had failed.'

Once again the camera panned over the words on the last page as Lucy found it. 'Fucking bitch Lucy lives not for long. DIEBITCHDIEBITCHDIE.'

Lucy shuddered with revulsion, and turned back to the camera. 'All this evidence will be handed straight to the police, who are here with us tonight.' The cameras widened their shot, to show Dan, standing now, between the two police officers. Lucy looked away from the camera, and spoke directly to the man she had trusted and relied on.

'Dan, I must say one last thing to you. You have taken from us someone we treasured. We won't forget Suzannah. None of us will ever forgive you.'

She had finished, and there was total silence. The audience sat in stunned distress, trying to absorb everything she'd told them. In front of them, the killer, his crimes revealed for the first time, walked off the set without a backward glance, the two policemen at his side. As he left, Michael cut to a wide shot of the studio, and slowly dimmed the lights. They faded to black, and Presentation took them off the air. Still Lucy sat in her seat, her body shaking with the trauma of delayed shock. She had been in so much danger so long – was she really safe now?

Jake, pale and deeply upset, walked from his seat across the set, following his father. How must he be feeling, knowing now that his father had killed the woman who had filled his life, whom he had longed to possess? How could he rebuild his family? Lucy felt desperately sorry for him; she watched him go, but he didn't glance back.

To her relief, she saw Camilla and Janet walking together up the stairway on the rostrum. They would provide strength for each other. They were already talking quietly together. Maybe Janet was angling for another exclusive interview? Lucy hoped not.

Where was Tom? She raked the studio with her eyes, looking along the rows of dark seats, in the shadowy wings, by the lit entrances. He wasn't there. He must have left before the programme ended. How typical. He'd escaped, avoiding the pressure when she needed him most.

She could see Max, standing at the very back of the rostrum, but he didn't meet her eyes. There was much unfinished business there. If she was ever to fulfil her promise and obtain justice for the boys, she must somehow persuade him to trust her again.

The audience were dispersing, talking together quietly. Lucy walked alone down the corridor to her dressing room, went inside and sat slumped in her chair. She never wanted to make another programme. She was exhausted, drained of all emotion.

There was a knock on the door, and when she went to open it, she found Lesley standing there.

The designer took one look at Lucy, and put her arms around her. 'I'll never know how you did that,' she said. 'I'm in shock myself. I still can't believe Dan's a murderer. There were rumours that his marriage had been violent, but he seemed so mild, such a nice man, never fussed or angry. It's always the quiet ones.'

She could see that Lucy had no energy to continue the conversation. 'Why don't you go straight home now, Lucy darling? I've packed everything for you, flowers and everything. They're waiting for you in the car. You've done enough for one day.'

'But where is home?' Lucy felt bewildered now, and helpless as the adrenalin which had energized her dissipated. 'I haven't got a home.'

'I think something's been arranged for you. Frank knows where to take you.'

It would be a relief to leave the studios. She didn't want to meet anyone. She had nothing else to say. She went to reception with Lesley, and looked for Frank. The big silver car was parked very close by, and he was standing by its open door, waiting for her to get in. As she bent down, she saw someone was already in the car. She drew back in alarm. Then she saw it was Tom.

Seeing how startled she was, he stretched out his hand to her.

'Jameson has offered you a suite at the Savoy tonight, courtesy of BriTV,' Tom explained. 'He thinks you ought to have a rest somewhere where nobody will find you. The Press Office will deal with all the questions tonight. Shirley suggested I might come with you, if you want me to.'

How dare Shirley jump to such conclusions. Lucy climbed into the back of the car beside Tom, her voice filled with indignation. 'I can't imagine why she would think I'd want anything like this.'

'Neither can I.'

As Frank eased the car out into the Saturday night traffic, Lucy turned to Tom. 'I thought you'd gone. I thought you'd decided to escape.'

'You're right. That would have been sensible. I don't need any more hassle in my life.'

'Is that all I mean to you? Hassle?' she said sharply.

'It's certainly part of the territory - hassle, and noise, and no time for the things that matter.'

Now he was going to scold her again. She was too tired for all this. But he was reaching into a pocket of his jacket, and pulling out a leather box.

'Look what I found in my study. You left it under your pillow.'

Suzannah's brooch.

Lucy opened the box, and saw the emeralds gleaming in the passing lights. They were supposed to be lucky. She looked at Tom, and then felt his arm circle her as he pulled her towards him. She didn't resist. It was good to be able to rest her head against him for a moment. She felt her body relax against him. What was she feeling now? It was a strange sensation, one that she wasn't used to. She felt safe. She looked up at Tom and he smiled down at her. There was so much to sift through and to question, but not now. He could see how utterly drained she was. There would be time.

'Well done tonight,' he said.

Patronizing bastard, talk about faint praise. 'I thought you didn't like trial by television, all that hassle and noise. You used not to like my work. You always said you hated my "Superwoman" act,' she said. Would that annoy him?

He laughed. 'I must be getting used to it,' he said. 'In fact, I wondered . . .' He stopped.

Was he nervous? Confident Tom, nervous? She couldn't believe it.

'Yes?' she prompted.

He cleared his throat. 'I wondered whether a homeless super-woman might need somewhere a bit more permanent to live.'

What was he suggesting? That she should move in with him? That they should start again? Surely not.

'I couldn't move in with you, Tom. Look what we did to each other last time. It would be a disaster.'

'Don't you think we've learned a bit since then?'

'What have you learned?' She tried to sound sterner than she felt.

'That we have to make time for each other. But if we do, I think we have something very special together. Love, and friendship, and respect. Not many people find all that in one relationship.'

It was true. And every time she'd needed him he had been there, protecting, without disabling her. With him she was stronger than she'd ever thought she could be. And her body was so comfortable in his arms, sex between them was so good, with him she felt complete and alive. But she was determined not to give way too easily. She pretended a grumpy reluctance.

'I can't stand another night in that narrow sofa-bed of yours.'

'I told you. There's a far more comfortable bed upstairs.'

Could it work this time? Could they live together again, without allowing the demands of their work to detonate and shatter their relationship? It hadn't worked before. But maybe they had changed, learned to value each other. What would Suzannah say? Be careful, but don't miss this chance?

'We'll have to work out some ground rules, Tom,' she said cautiously, but now there was a lilt of happiness in her voice.

He laughed. 'Good idea. Let's do that tonight at the Savoy. Unless you can think of a better way to use our energy.'

He bent his head to hers and kissed her. As he released her, she saw the back of Frank's neck was scarlet. Poor Frank, they were embarrassing him. She started to protest, but Tom kissed her again, and this time she didn't argue. She could almost hear Suzannah urging her not to carry on battling. She'd won the fight, she'd reached the place she'd been searching for. And it was a good place.

Tomorrow she must pick up the wreckage of her life. She must start to sort through the ruins of her house. She must seriously ask herself whether she wanted to continue with Suzannah's show. But all that was for tomorrow. For tonight, at least, Lucy realized that here, with Tom, she'd found her home.